42ND STREET

THE ORIGINAL NOVEL BY BRADFORD ROPES

Afterword by Scott Miller

Library of Congress Cataloging-in-Publication Data
Ropes, Bradford, 1905-1966
42nd street /Bradford Ropes.
p. cm.
ISBN: 9798734748114
1. Musicals—Fiction. 2. Broadway (New York, NY)—Fiction. 3. Forty-second Street (New York, NY)—Fiction. 4. Musicals. 5. New York (State)—New York—Broadway. 6. New York (State)—New York—Forty-second Street. I. Title.

Printed in the United States of America

Also by Bradford Ropes

Novels
42nd Street
Go Into Your Dance
Stage Mother

Screenplays
The Time of Their Lives
Why Girls Leave Home
Steppin' in Society
Swing in the Saddle
Good Lookin'!
Hands Across the Border
Man from Music Mountain
Ice Capades Revue
True to the Army
Glamour Boy
Angels with Broken Wings
Ridin' on a Rainbow
Melody Ranch
Hit Parade of 1941
Melody and Moonlight
Sing, Dance, Plenty Hot
Gaucho Serenade
Rancho Grande
Ladies in Distress
Meet the Boy Friend
The Hit Parade
Circus Girl
et al.

To Mary

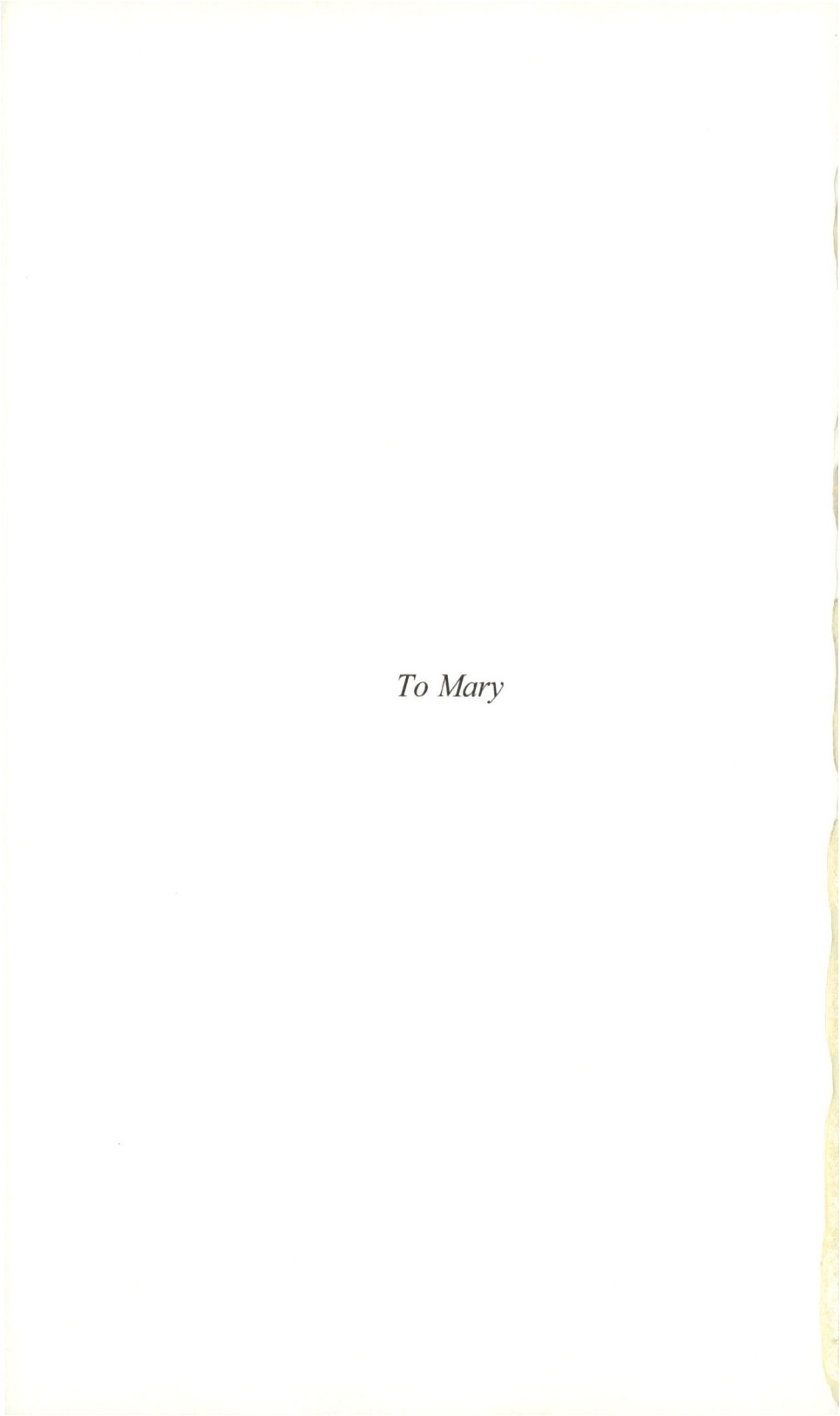

TABLE OF CONTENTS

Book I: Rehearsal 7

Book II: Opening 193

"Little Nifties: Inside *42nd Street*" 341

BOOK I

REHEARSAL

II

"Three good tunes and a kick in the pants for your wow blackout. Can ya make a hit show out of it?" Abe Green beamed expansively on the distinguished gentleman who occupied the seat of honor in his office.

Julian Marsh shrugged. "I've managed with less," he admitted, "but don't forget your dear public isn't the naive gathering of a few years back. The mere prestige of playing on Broadway won't mean much to the latter-day yokels who tread our pavements. We must convince them they'll receive their money's worth."

Si Friedman bent over the desk. "That's why we got you, feller. My God, Julian, we ain't sentimental guys, we're producers. We forgot all about bein' nice to our friends the minute the 'dear public' tightened up on the purse strings. Personally I like you, you're a swell egg, but you wouldn't get a dime outta me if I hadn't read your record for hits on the ledgers of our firm. Only two weeks in red ink, that's something."

"Sure—an' you like us, too," Abe Green pursued, "but you'd chisel us out of our last nickel without so much as a 'pardon me' if you thought it meant money in the bank to you. Here's the gag. We can get the coin all right, you know me when it comes to diggin' up the backers—we heard Conroy's tunes an' they'll get over, we think—but you're the baby with the class an' the ideas. Without you the show don't figure at all. We admit that cheerfully. So what are you gonna do about it?"

Julian Marsh got to his feet. He was tall, well tailored and bore himself like one who has been told he is a "natural aristocrat." Marsh was of English birth and this aided the illusion. There was no need for these petty cloak and suit prodigies to know that the Marsh family were plodding members of the British shopkeeper class.

"You know how these things are accomplished," he said. "Give me a free rein and I can promise you satisfaction. But I must have the final word. You two gentlemen are smart and ingenious, you have your own methods when it comes to securing the necessary finance—but your knowledge of showmanship is a trifle limited. That's why you're calling on me. Your speech on sentiment was admirable, Si. It's a minus quantity in our profession. I'm accepting your offer not because I have any flaming passion for you two boys but for the good and sufficient reason that I hope to make a little money. So do you or you wouldn't be wasting your time on a hot afternoon in June by flattering me, We've worked together before for the mutual good of all concerned. We can do it again."

"Fine, Julian. Sounds okay to me," Si declared. "We'll start right now. Abe, you get busy and round up more dough. This ain't gonna be a turkey. We'll panic 'em with more pearl curtains than they ever seen in their lives. I'll hop on the wire and send out some blah about the new magnificent revue which will be staged by the king of musical comedy producers, Mr. Julian Marsh. We'll phone Equity an' let 'em know there's to be a call for girls. Abe, round up all the agents an' see about principals. We got Dorothy Brock. We got John Phillips; we're givin' you a brand new comic who's slayin' 'em at the Palace this week—guy named Danny Moran. Put 'em all together—they spell 'Mother'!"

Julian March smiled. "You won't have to worry," he assured the two anxious gentlemen. "I think we can safely prophesy a good season."

The theatrical columns of the marring papers carried the first story of the new enterprise. The offices of Broadway's foremost agents were filled with applicants. In front of the Palace the "lay offs" wagered on the chances of success. Little girls soaked their silly heads in basins of peroxide and emerged in shining blonde glory. Threadbare suits were carefully pressed. Unshorn heads were submitted to the ministrations of the barber. Creaky tenors polished up their high notes. Shrill sopranos tortured the melody of Mr. Kilmer's immortal *Trees*. In three more days the first "call" for talent was scheduled. The agents moved with unwonted jauntiness. The ranks of Chorus Equity grew more hopeful. The music publishing firm which contracted for Russell Conroy's tunes was agog with speculation. Julian Marsh was going to produce the new Green and Freidman show. Julian Marsh, pampered idol of Forty-Second Street, was once more definitely in the running. On with the dance!

2

Jerry struck a rasping chord on the piano. "Hey, you kids, make it snappy!" he bawled. "One o'clock don't mean one-fifteen with this management."

The darkened recesses of the theatre came to life. From dressing rooms, from alleyways, from orchestra chairs in the auditorium they flocked, these chorus girls on the first day of their arduous five-week rehearsal.

Jerry Cole moved his hands over the keys as he surveyed them. To his blasé eye, they were just another bunch. Some malign fate turned them out by the thousands—pretty, ineffectual things in their flaring practice clothes who basked a brief moment in the spotlight of Broadway and then hurried onward to the oblivion of marriage. He recognized a familiar face—Lorraine Fleming from the chorus of *How's That?*, with her heart-shaped face and ever so blonde hair.

"Lorraine's been at the peroxide again," he decided.

Then Ann Lowell came lounging out of a dressing room.

"Jeez, that baby!" he muttered, for Ann was a notorious and dangerous gin hound.

Lorraine leaned her elbows on the curve of the piano. "H'lo, slave driver!" she chirped. "Got some nice hot lyrics for us?"

Jerry grinned. "Sure, kid. Still sing that lousy monotone o' yours?"

"Monotone, hell I took lessons. I'm a soprano, by God!" Lorraine squared her shoulders truculently. "An' don't go givin' the boss the idea I can't sing."

"Well," commented Ann Lowell, flinging her loose body into a nearby chair, "looks like old times, Jerry. How's the pocket flask?"

"Lissen, you," Jerry warned. "Better lay off that. You ain't workin' for the Shuberts now. This bunch means business."

"Aw, nuts!" snorted Ann. "Drop the tambourine, Evangeline Booth, and come down to earth." She swung one bare leg over the other, hunched far down in her seat and glared defiantly at Jerry.

Andy Lee, the dance director, pounded his cane on the floor.

"Awright! Awright! Come on, girls, we gotta lotta work ahead of us. Mr. Cole's gonna run through the lyrics for half an hour an' then I'll work with you."

"Big-hearted Andy," muttered Ann Lowell.

Andy Lee was feared by every chorus girl on Broadway. They told fearsome tales of girls in his ensembles who fell fainting from his routines. In appearance he was unimpressive—a little Jew of Ghetto extraction with vivid, restless eyes, and feet which were constantly beating out a sort of rhythmic tapping. Burlesque, vaudeville and musical comedy, these three had sired Andy Lee. Beginning obscurely as straight man to a red-nosed comic in *The Sporting Widows*, he had emerged through varying fortunes in the role of dance director. There were many who claimed Andy as the best hoofer on Broadway. Certainly the many movements of his feet were bewildering. He dressed meticulously in the fashion never seen above Fiftieth Street nor below Forty-Second Street.

"I'll bet he buys his clothes from Bill Robinson," Lorraine commented.

A semi-circle of chairs had been drawn up around the piano and these were filled by the "ladies of the ensemble." A chorus in full practice regalia offers an unforgettable sight; bathing suits molded tight to slim figures, rompers with starched frills, even an occasional outfit consisting of a boy's shirt and velvet trousers. Practice clothes are designed to give full freedom for body movements and they achieve their purpose. It must be admitted that the average male working through the rehearsal period is as insensible as a stone image to these revelations.

"And where are the boys?" Jerry demanded. His voice became a shade higher pitched as he asked this question and the final "s" trailed offensively into the air. Jerry was kidding. "Mac, call your men."

Harry MacElroy left his post at the piano and shouted, "Hey, you guys!"

Harry was assistant stage manager, and let that be catalogued as the world's most thankless job, combining as it does a penny's worth of mean authority with a pound of drudgery. The assistant stage manager must rival God as the all seeing eye. His the duty to see that every chorus member and every principal is in place at the appointed time, his the responsibility for all announcements concerning rehearsals; when props are needed the assistant stage manager must find them, when the boss wants a malted milk the assistant stage manager runs to the corner drug store, when a principal actor is absent the assistant stage manager reads his lines. As varied and unending as the labors of Hercules are the assistant stage manager's tasks. And when all is finished he must quietly resume his place in the rank and file and become to the eyes of the world just another chorus boy.

So it is not to be wondered at that Harry MacElroy's voice was strident with anger as he summoned the boys to lyric rehearsal. For five weeks, until *Pretty Lady* was presented to its public, he would continue to urge recalcitrant actors to their places, his voice would hold varying notes of blandishment, anger, scorn and efficiency.

"Hey, you guys," he repeated. "It's ten minutes after one." The "gentlemen of the ensemble" trouped in. They were slim eager-eyed youngsters for the most part, a bit abashed at the role for which Fate had cast them, but in the mind of each one was the resolve to "get out of this racket after another season." The chorus boy is much maligned. He is pointed out as the degenerate, effeminate male whom all normal boys should avoid. Each chorus finds two or three who maintain this doubtful standard, but the average chorus boy is a somewhat toughened youngster whose abilities do not quite measure up to his aspirations. In time he will rise from the mob to small bits, then to understudy, and, lo, the chorus boy is transformed, he has become a principal. But meanwhile he learns the value of self-obliteration. His haughty sisters have small use for the companionship of a chorus man, the boss regards him as a necessary evil, and so he is forced by an unfriendly world to become a solitary segment in the well-appointed structure of the modern musical comedy.

The boys hurried to their places and Jerry yelled, "Give 'em the lyrics, Mac."

With the celerity of a magician Mac produced printed slips of paper which were passed around.

Ann Lowell gave vent to a disgusted growl. "My God, what are these? Mother Goose rhymes?"

Jerry heard her. "Any time you can do better, sister, just wire Ziegfeld. He's dying to find new geniuses."

"I think these would go better in Swedish," Ann continued, unabashed.

"All right, you girls, quiet!" snarled Andy Lee.

"Wouldn't you know he'd put in his nickel's worth?" sneered Lorraine.

"Well, are you dames willing that I oblige on the Steinway?" shouted Jerry with elaborate sarcasm. "Or do I have to get permission from the Pope?"

No answer. There are times when it is not policy for a chorus girl to utter the wisecrack that is her birthright.

"Come on then, take the first one!" said Jerry.

I've got a rhythm—you've got a rhythm—
All God's chillun got a red hot rhythm—
Ticka Tack Toe—Ticka Tack Toe— Ticka Tack Toe.
Gotta go with 'em—gotta go with 'em—gotta go with 'em—
Ticka Tack Toe—Ticka Tack Toe— Ticka Tack Toe.
You'll find a movement that's most entrancing—
Something a Boston Cop just couldn't call dancing—
Ticka Tack Toe—Ticka Tack Toe— Ticka Tack Toe.

Heels were pounding time on the floor. One or two with a quick ear had begun to hum the melody under their breaths.

"The show's a flop," Ann Lowell declared impressively.

"That ditty sounds like Joe Leblang's *Love Call*."

"All right, girls, take it with me and for God's sake watch that 'E' flat on 'dancing'," cautioned Jerry.

It is wearisome business learning the many tunes which an optimistic composer has supplied. Some quietly disappear after the first hearing, others linger until dress rehearsal night, and often the hit song is not written until the show has been launched on its tryout week.

"I've got a rhythm, you've got a rhythm, all God's chillun got a red hot rhythm"—over and over again, searching out the snares of modern syncopation.

"Don't take too long," shouted Andy Lee. "I gotta work with 'em, you know."

"Try Lonely Little Love Nest," suggested Jerry.

"God, we got one of those?" muttered Ann, who was permanently disgruntled unless in close proximity to a gin high ball. Jerry struck up the syrupy strains of the inevitable love motif.

"Sounds like *Dardanella*," murmured Lorraine. For every theme song is reminiscent of a melody of former days.

Lonely little love nest—waiting there for you—
Storing up its sunshine—and its skies of blue.
Lonely little someone waiting for your call
Standing all alone—
You don't even phone—
Gee, where can you be?
Nights are dim and starless with your presence gone,
Poverty seems far less than me all forlorn,
Lonely little love nest, 'neath a shelt'ring tree
Can't you hear its Love Call—meant for you and me?

"And God bless mamma and papa," whispered Ann.

This particular song was destined to vanish from the present production and appear a season later as *Hot Cha Cha Mamma* by the simple expedient of changing the time. Jerry Cole could not foresee this, however, so he labored with the members of the chorus over its awful sentimentality.

"If they spring any more like this we might as well run out an' buy the tin cup an' pencils right now," prophesied Phyllis O'Neill.

At the left-hand corner of the stage Andy Lee's restless feet were twisting and turning in the most astounding evolutions. Teddy Wright, one of the more experienced chorus men, stole a look at him.

"Gonna be a tough season," he declared. "Andy's gonna have us hoppin' the buck like nobody's business."

There was an interruption at the stage entrance. After a rather spirited altercation with the door man, a theatrical agent appeared on the scene closely followed by a young lady sporting ringlets and a mother.

Andy glanced at the becurled young lady, noted her supple walk and groaned, "Jeez, another bender." For benders are those agile young ladies who touch their toes to their noses without so much as an extra breath. They are always accompanied by mothers. The virginity of an acrobatic dancer is unquestioned. As Ann Lowell remarked, "Most of 'em aren't out of a back bend long enough to lose it."

Mother and daughter lurked in the background, but the agent, like the fool of the ancient proverb, rushed to the corner of the stage where Andy Lee awaited him. Andy's pose suggested a caged lion.

"H'lo Andy," caroled the agent. He was a dapper gentleman boasting a mustache of the most splendid proportions ever seen in the Palace lobby. He and Andy possessed one secret in common—both were former hoofers. Andy, being a good one, had become a dance director; and Pete Dexter, being a bad one, had turned agent. Most agents are unsuccessful performers who take subtle revenge on managers by inflicting upon them all sorts of toe dancers, acrobats and prima donnas.

"Well, looks like you got a hit," said Pete Dexter, slouching beside Andy and surveying the little tableau of Jerry Cole and his singing choristers.

"Jerry, ask him up some night to frighten the children," whispered Ann Lowell.

Pete Dexter pushed the pearl-gray hat far back on his head and came to business. "I got a great bet for you, Andy," he said in the manner of a monarch who bestows favors on an humble subject.

Andy's shoulders hunched. "We're full up," he snapped.

Pete smiled. "Come here, Polly," he said, and Polly and her curls trotted obediently to the footlights. Mother followed at a safe distance.

Pete placed a fatherly arm about Polly's shoulder. "This is Mr. Lee, Polly," he explained with tender gravity.

The would-be addition to the cast achieved a bow and gulped, "How d'ye do." Andy nodded.

"I don't need no dancers, Pete," he repeated with gentle insistence.

Pete was not dismayed. "Jus' take a look at the kid's routine," he wheedled. "Hell, it don't cost you nothin'! You know me—I'm blasé—nothin' gives me much kick, an' I saw this kid stop the show so cold at the Jefferson that Will Mahoney couldn't go on. And me applaudin' my hands off like a ten-year-old punk."

"Yeah?" said Andy with a disconcerting lack of interest.

"Polly, dear, go put your clothes on," Pete ordered.

"Lissen, Pete, I got a rehearsal here," Andy protested.

"Twon't take three minutes," Dexter assured him. "And you'll be crabbin' for the rest of your life if you miss this chance."

Polly rejoined the Amazonian figure of her mother. "Where'll I change?" she piped. Pete looked to Andy Lee for a suggestion.

"Tell her to go in any room," Andy said. He was mentally running through the routine he had arranged for the *Ticka Tack Toe* number.

Polly and her mother disappeared. Pete pulled a cigarette case from his pocket, offered it to Andy, displayed his ornate lighter with due ostentation and then launched into the small talk with which agents while away awkward moments. Instantly the stage door man was at his heels.

"Can't smoke in here," he growled.

"Aw, Pop, have a heart," Pete begged.

"Orders," said Pop and marched away.

Pete tossed the offending cigarette into the footlight trough. "See you got Dorothy Brock in the show," he remarked. "That girl has her nerve. She won't come to no good. Why, do you know I called her up a month ago an' offered her the part an' she says she's not interested. An' the next thing I hear the James office has signed her for the part. That ain't playin' fair, you know. Not that I mind losin' the money—it's the psychology of the thing. God, who can ya trust, nowadays?"

He spread his hands in appeal to a remote justice. Andy muttered something unintelligible.

"An' I made that girl, too," Pete continued. "She didn't have nothin' but a back bend with a fan when I put her in *Happy Days*. Well—that's the breaks, I guess. Where the hell is that kid?"

Andy was beginning to wonder the same thing. The lyric rehearsal was on the verge of disbanding and Jerry Cole cast an inquiring eye in his direction.

"I can't wait all day, Pete," he whined. An agent holds some mesmeric power over the mightiest of Broadway's lords. Though time presses ever so fiercely they will spare a moment to look at some new protégé—all protests to the contrary.

Polly and her mother appeared from a downstage dressing room and Andy clapped his hands loudly.

"All right, girls," he called. "Move your chairs back to the wall an' take a minute's rest."

A buzz of conversation spread over the stage. In the maddening routine of rehearsal an audition is always a welcome relief.

"Let's get a load of Front Split Flora," said Ann Lowell, dragging her chair to the wall. "Mother looks like one of the Four Horsemen."

"Where's your music, Polly?" asked Pete Dexter.

Mother proffered an orchestration. Jerry Cole groaned.

"She probably chose some little thing from Debussy," he muttered. The average pianist for a musical show is not a quick reader and he dreads the moment when a fond parent will inflict on him a copy of the *Love Death* to be played as accompaniment to little Wilhelmina's toe dance.

Polly snatched the music and, in a spasm of girlishness, skipped over to the piano.

"With everything waving in the breeze," Lorraine commented inelegantly.

"What you got, kid?" Jerry inquired.

"Three and a half choruses of *Always*, eight bars introduction and the last sixteen bars fast for rolling splits," answered Polly in one breath.

"Do you dance this with a fan?" Andy Lee asked.

"No, she ain't got a fan," Mother broke into the conversation. "But she can use one—an' she does military buck an' Russian on her toes, too."

Mother subsided with startling suddenness and Jerry began to play. The tempo was not right. It never is. The dancer who finds her accompaniment correct at an audition remains unknown. Bad music provides the perfect alibi. If one fails in securing a coveted position, the pianist must shoulder the blame.

So now both Polly and her mother were humming loudly and tunelessly in an endeavor to whip Jerry to the proper speed.

"I think she'd better recite," commented Flo Perry.

The music was adjusted, Polly paid a frantic visit to the resin box, then signaled that she was ready. She danced remarkably.

"Like a zee-phyr," Pete Dexter explained confidentially to Andy. Her slim legs moved in poetic circles. She spun from one feat to another with disconcerting ease.

"Get them spotting walk-overs," breathed Pete ecstatically.

In the distance Mother could be heard beating time with her feet. When the accompaniment faltered she shouted an angry "Dum di dum *dum dum* di *dum dum*" to Jerry.

"Aw nuts," swore Jerry under his breath.

The awful moment of the rolling splits arrived. Mother was tense with fear. Andy Lee forgot his boredom and watched the proceedings attentively.

"I gotta spot in 'one' where we might use her," he said doubtfully.

"Lissen, the kid can dance on a dime," Pete Dexter promised him. "She's an artist. All the people I handle is artists."

On the floor Polly was turning like a human St. Catherine's wheel. This was the stunt known technically as "rolling splits" and it constitutes the aim of every dancer's existence, a sure fire finish. Jerry obediently accelerated the tempo. Polly continued to spin, Mother beat time and Pete Dexter sensed by the gleam in Andy Lee's eye that he had sold another performer.

Came the question of salary.

"The kid's all right," said Andy, opening the offensive.

"She'll be the talk of Broadway," Pete asserted,

"How much does she want?" Andy's chin went up aggressively.

"Well, I tell you, Andy, you know me—I always try to play fair. Now in vaudeville—"

Andy snorted. "This ain't vaudeville—this is production," he stated flatly.

"Sure—sure—I know, but you gotta pay for talent," Dexter objected, tugging at the vaselined tips of his mustache.

"Well, how much?" Andy insisted.

Dexter appeared to be considering. Polly, breathless and a bit grimy, retired to the sheltering wing of her mother who was watching the proceedings with gimlet eyes.

"We'll say one seventy-five," Dexter offered.

"We'll say one twenty-five," Andy Lee amended.

"Aw, lissen, Andy. You know I can't do that. Why, I got this kid under contract and I guarantee her more than that."

"One twenty-five, take it or leave it," said Andy.

"But, lissen, Andy. She's a great bet. Looks—class—everythin'," Pete expostulated in a final burst of desperation.

"I tell ya she ain't worth more than that to me," said Andy. "Jeez, Pete, you know show business. Ya don't get money like that for bein' a high kicker unless you're an Evelyn Law or a Hoffman girl."

Pete Dexter sighed. He had privately expected a maximum offer of one hundred dollars and a giddy feeling of relief surged through him.

"Well, I wouldn't do it for nobody but you, Andy," he wailed.

Lee strove to look sardonic. "Yeah—me an' Ziegfeld an' Dillingham an' the Shuberts," he corrected.

Pete Dexter was the picture of abject martyrdom.

"I'll go talk it over with her mother," he murmured.

"Okay, but don't bring that gorilla near me," Andy warned him. "She looks like the *Battle Hymn of the Republic*."

Pete Dexter went over to Polly and Mrs. Blair. Gone was the downcast expression. Mr. Dexter was positively beaming.

"Well, kids, it's all set," he glowed.

Polly expressed her appreciation with a slow back kick. Mother's face shone with all the radiance of a totem pole.

"How about money?" she demanded.

"The money's all right," Pete Dexter soothed her. "Better than I thought."

"Well, how much?"

"Now, lissen, Mother. Ya know ya can't ask the same price in production that you do in vaudeville. The market's over-crowded. Why, I know twenty agents want to get specialty dancers in this show—only I got entry. If Andy Lee wasn't a particular friend of mine you wouldn't get a look in."

Pete was every inch the benevolent *deus ex machina*.

"Don't try to stall me," cried Mrs. Blair. "I want to know how much Polly is goin' to get for this job."

"One hundred and twenty-five a week," snapped Dexter.

"A hundred and twenty-five," Mrs. Blair screeched. "Polly, go put your clothes on. You've been insulted."

"But, Ma," Polly protested.

"Leave me handle this. You go get your clothes. One hundred and twenty-five dollars! He's gotta lotta nerve and I've a good mind to tell him so."

Pete Dexter laid a restraining hand on her arm.

"No use raisin' a row," he said. "Lottsa girls'd be glad to get that much. You're livin' at home. You can be with your husband."

"The drunken bum," put in Mrs. Blair.

Dexter passed over the suggestion of domestic incompatibility. "You're playin' in a New York production, Polly can take her singing lessons and you only got eight shows a week." From Mr. Dexter one gained the impression that he had rubbed Aladdin's lamp and lo, Polly's path was heaped high with luxuries.

"An' outta that I gotta pay you ten per cent commission and I gotta join Equity," Mrs. Blair complained. "I'd sooner play for Fanchon and Marco."

Dexter's jaw clamped in a hard line. "Now get this," he threatened. "I can take Polly an' put her with the rest of the stars on Broadway or I can send her back to playin' cans for the rest of her life. I got influence in this town. These other guys, James, Brown, Lyons, they're just pikers, but I deliver the goods. Look at these other people—look at Dorothy Brock, she was like Polly when I got a hold of her, just a specialty dancer, and between you an' me her left leg kick was lousy, but I put her in the Winter Garden for a hundred a week an' she was glad to get it. Now Polly's got a kick that Brock in her best days never owned, she looks class and there's no reason why she won't be up in that four-figure column along with Brock in a few years if you'll lissen to reason."

He paused, seeing that the torrent of persuasion was battering down the woman's resistance. Mrs. Blair displayed signs of weakening.

"But we can't live on that," she objected. "Why, Polly's got singin' lessons, her buck, her horseback ridin' and her saxophone, and God knows she can't expect nothin' from her father."

Pete Dexter was quick to press his advantage. "One season on Broadway an' she can name her price anywhere," he vowed. "You gotta be known."

"Well, I'll take your advice, Mr. Dexter," Mother capitulated.

"I knew you would, I knew you would—an' believe me you won't regret it. Why, I got Polly's interest at heart—an' you know I got some of the biggest people in show business signed under me. Come over to the office sometime an' I'll show you their contracts."

"I hope we're not making a mistake," moaned Mrs. Blair.

"It's perfect, Mother, it's perfect. Now you stick around here an' watch the rehearsals an' I'll run over to the office an' get an Equity contract. Polly may have to dance for the Big Boss but don't worry, it's all set—whatever Andy Lee says—goes!"

Mrs. Blair retired to a settee at the rear of the stage. In front of her all was activity. Their brief recess ended, the chorus were falling into position under the shrewd eye of Andy Lee. "Come on, make it snappy now," he barked. "Little girls in front, boys in back, show girls in the rear. Y'see, the set is the garden of a Long Island home and you girls are on the verandah. Now, Mr. John Phillips comes down an' there's some dialogue which I'll give you later an' then into the number. All right, Jerry!"

Jerry played the chorus of *Ticka Tack Toe*. Andy Lee turned his back and sketched through a series of steps. There were apprehensive gasps. No doubt now that Andy Lee planned to outdo himself on this show, and that meant a laborious five weeks. The old timers shuddered, the new girls and boys looked on unknowing. They were to be the butt of Andy Lee's gibes in the awful month that followed.

"Oh, boy, here go those varicose veins," murmured Teddy Wright.

"Quiet!" snapped Andy. Teddy ducked out of sight behind a languid show girl.

Wearily, Jerry beat out the refrain of *Ticka Tack Toe*, time and time again. He was beginning to sicken of the tune already and there were five more weeks; Jerry began to cogitate on the comparatively happy life of a deep sea diver.

From one-thirty to five they were on their feet save for a short interlude of ten minutes. Already Andy Lee was running true to form. The routines were baffling. Many a girl retired weeping to a corner following the caustic comment of the dance director. It was said of Lee that he got results. On opening night he never failed to present a well-trained machine. There were feet that moved mechanically, fed by some unquenchable force which overcame the tasks imposed upon them. The thought of a season's work in a success spurred on these boys and girls. Past the limits of human endurance they went—day in, day out; dancing until blisters became festered sores, dancing until their very brains reeled and limbs responded automaton fashion to the shrill anger in Andy Lee's voice. Dancing from ten in the morning until midnight then taking their aching bodies to bed where the twitching of outraged muscles and ligaments made hideous the hours before dawn. Five weeks, like centuries, that must be laughed through somehow to achieve the Promised Land—a successful season.

The "numbers" that Andy Lee staged were always successful. He was lucky that way. And so the chorus grinned and practiced a new routine. In the stifling August heat such activities breed madness, yet the show must go on. They were not human beings with whom Andy Lee was dealing, but a well-ordered row of dancing shoes strangely vitalized, slow in comprehending at times through sheer fatigue, but dancing shoes that would be reduced to the mechanical perfection that marked all Andy Lee's work.

Lee's small eyes would gleam vindictively. His voice was the flick of a whip, wounding unbearably where no hurt was needed. Five weeks! Five weeks!

And even then the thing was not ended. After the opening night would come endless changes. Whole numbers over which they had labored for many days would be ruthlessly torn out, to be replaced by others even more difficult.

A chorus girl seldom sees the daylight when she is in rehearsal. From nine in the morning until after midnight she is pledged to her Great God Amusement—and Andy Lee was one of his mightiest apostles.

Someday the *Uncle Tom's Cabin* of the chorus girl will be written. Until then it is pleasant to picture a young, rather immoral young lady who finds her niche in some musical show and thus established sets out on a continual round of pleasure. For once, let a chorus foregather and strive to relieve with drinking the deadly fatigue induced by countless rehearsals, and the world bristles with indignation at what it terms a theatrical orgy.

And yet, what else offers itself? After a soul-racking day of tapping feet and swinging arms it is rather difficult to retire to a lonely bedroom and stare at unfriendly walls.

The human mind demands some other outlet.

So now the piano drummed, "I've got a rhythm—you've got a rhythm—all God's chillun got a red hot rhythm," over and over again. The craze for broken time dances had arrived and Andy Lee was a devotee of this complicated art.

"In ten more minutes I'll go right out in the alley and have kittens," Flo Perry groaned. "Give me the Living Curtain any day."

They kept on grimly because they must, for if Andy Lee were displeased he was privileged to dismiss any one of them and then the heart-breaking search for employment began all over again.

I've got a rhythm—you've got a rhythm—
All God's chillun got a red hot rhythm—
Ticka Tack Toe—Ticka Tack Toe—Ticka Tack Toe.

3

Peggy Sawyer surveyed her bruised toes ruefully. "Tenderfoot," she accused. Flo Perry smiled at her.

"Puppies on the bum?" she asked.

Peggy nodded. "This is pretty tough for the first day, isn't it?" she ventured.

Flo Perry made a vicious jab with her powder puff. "Yeah, but that lousy bum's a slave driver. I remember in *Paris Nights* we had a dance on a tree and eight girls used to faint regular every night."

Peggy's eyes opened wide in consternation. "I hope I'll be able to stand it," she murmured. "My—my heart isn't very good."

"Well, don't let the old buzzard get you; he always has to have some goat to pick on and he generally goes for the new girls," Flo Perry advised her.

They crawled wearily out of their practice clothes. In deference to a time-honored custom there was no rehearsal that first night.

"I'll bet that hurt Old Man Lee," Flo commented. "He'd keep us on our feet twenty-four hours if the Boss would let him."

"Is Mr. Julian Marsh really the Big Man?" asked Peggy.

"Sure—Marsh is the works around here, all right," Flo answered. "He always gets the damndest gang of rats to work with him. Seems like he goes looking behind old brooms an' things to find a lotta mugs so he'll appear to be Ye Perfect Gentleman by contrast. He's a wise baby, that Marsh."

"I liked him," said Peggy.

"Don't let the Oxford accent fool you, girlie. Marsh can be as big a bastard as the rest of 'em when he puts his mind to it."

Privately Peggy thought Flo's remarks were nonsense, but at this stage of the game it would be unwise to question the word of such a veteran of the ensemble.

"My clothes are wringing wet," she said, to change the subject. "Guess I'd better take them back to the hotel and wash them out."

"Yeah. Time to get out the old box of Lux again," Flo agreed. Then she asked curiously, "This your first show?"

"Yes, I'm a greenhorn from New England," Peggy admitted.

"Funny Lee picked you. He generally goes for the old timers," said Flo.

The circumstances of her selection remained vividly in Peggy's memory. First there had been the morning visit to Equity. Her friends assured her that was the quickest method of learning who was producing the show. At the Actors' Association she was informed that Julian Marsh was planning an audition for chorus girls the next morning. Julian Marsh engagements were much sought after because of his reputation as a shrewd and careful show man, so she determined to be on hand at the Forty-Fifth Street Theatre where the "call" was to take place.

An audition is always a memorable adventure. Peggy found the theatre with little difficulty and jammed her way past a score of girls lounging in the doorway. As usual there was a delay, for history reveals no audition which has begun at the appointed hour. The powers that be are so constituted that a prompt arrival is impossible.

From inside the theatre came a veritable Babel of voices. The Broadway chorus girl in her many-hued glory had turned out for this special occasion. There were ladies in ermine coats, carrying Pekinese dogs, whose manners were most excellent counterfeits of Park Avenue. Eyeing them with ill-concealed disgust, were the over-rouged, over-dressed Broadway chorus girls who knew a soft shoe dance from a waltz clog, but whose ideas of dress must have been gained in some bizarre and as yet undiscovered corner of the universe. There are many who claim it is an uncharted land not far from the Palace Theatre.

"Did you have a good summer at Deauville?" asked a soft voice at Peggy's shoulder.

"Yes, dear, but H. M. can be impossible at times," responded another voice. Her English accent would have incited an Oxford graduate to homicide.

These gorgeous, orchidaceous creatures were show girls. Their exquisitely formed bodies adorned advertisements for hosiery and lingerie. Their photographs were to be seen in lobbies, holding coyly to some leaf or mandolin as protection from the lascivious stares of mankind. One of the two ladies sported a cane and Peggy stifled a gasp at the monocle jammed tightly into her right eye. Surely this was the *dernier cri*. The show girls moved away with that swaying walk which comes after many evenings of parading down a flight of stairs as the Spirit of Love or the Spirit of Music.

Two derisive little choristers gaped after them.

"Get Minnie the Mountaineer," jeered one, indicating with her thumb milady who carried the cane. The dart shot home and quivered in the show girl's none too acute mind. She turned in regal anger.

"I'll give you a swift kick in the fanny, you little bitch," she yapped. For swans should never leave the lake and show girls must remain forever mute.

The rumblings of battle were dispersed by a disturbance in the auditorium of the theatre. Someone had entered through the front of the house and was walking down the aisle toward the orchestra pit. A tense hush fell over the gathering.

"There's Marsh," someone whispered.

"Andy Lee's with him," another added.

Peggy craned her neck to see the fabled Julian Marsh, sybarite among producers, by his own admission the elect of the gods. Like many others, Marsh had climbed the ladder from actor to manager. Possessed of an unerring instinct for business which he skillfully wedded to a sense of the artistic, Marsh was now at the height of his power. Illiterate Jewish theatre owners with no feeling for art except its echo at the box office sought Marsh because of his reputed smartness. It was Marsh who introduced soft lights and scrim drops into the revue, who molded ballets into the chaotic pattern of a musical show.

No one questioned the intellect of Julian Marsh. He played to perfection the bored man of the World who had turned to the stage as a child that seeks relief in some elaborate toy. He always managed an entrance surrounded by cohorts of secretaries and yes-men. His clothes were impeccable, his taste in cravats vivid but unerring. There was just the faintest trace of an Oxford accent in his speech.

Andy Lee, standing only shoulder-high to the great man, barked, "Quiet, please."

A secretary echoed this command. As though by common consent the great wedge of chorus girls occupying center stage moved to the rear, crowding against those who had captured the few available chairs and benches.

There is a sinister atmosphere in a darkened theatre. Shadows play eerily over the walls, thrown into bold relief by the solitary light which is planted center stage whenever the house is vacated. The men moving about in the first three rows of the orchestra were half-seen gods possessed of mighty powers. Theirs the right to withhold or dispense the much sought-after job. Permanent waves were pushed into place, bobbed hair straightened with a few deft passes of the comb, powder compacts held up to the uncertain light for a frantic moment and then shut with determined snaps.

Andy Lee, peering near-sightedly at the assemblage, deigned an occasional smile as he recognized some familiar face. Those who had worked for him before crowded to the footlights in the hope of being recognized.

For several minutes this state of affairs existed, while Julian Marsh and Andy Lee held conferences. These little heart-to-heart talks are part and parcel of an audition. What is decided remains a mystery, but for ten minutes producer and dance director talk heatedly, with frequent snarls of "Quiet! Quiet, ladies!" from a well groomed secretary.

"I'll get a ticket for parking my Rolls overtime," muttered one of the show girls, giving a vicious twist to one of the two silver foxes adorning her neck.

She was overheard. Show girls are always overheard.

"I hope to God they hold that special Bronx express they're runnin' for me," whispered one of the dancing girls with malicious intent.

The shaft fell on deaf ears. "And my chauffeur has to be at Wall Street by five-thirty," the glorified one continued.

"Just a good mattress for some tired business man," sneered the little chorus girl, and then a savage "Quiet!" from the secretary.

They waited there like restless inhabitants of some half world moving through dim shadows. In sheer desperation a young thing of no more than sixteen years fell to practicing a time step. The tender sensibilities of Julian Marsh were outraged.

"If there is any more of this unseemly noise I shall postpone the audition," he warned. The buck dance ceased with agonized celerity.

"They must be telling all they know," said Peggy's neighbor in a discreetly subdued voice.

"If they were just doin' that this conference would've been over long since," her friend replied.

Came signs of action. A table was produced from the dark realm of the property room and placed at the extreme right of the stage. The secretary stepped over the footlight trench, surveyed the crowd of applicants and shouted, "First group of girls form here," indicating with his pencil an imaginary line running parallel to the lights.

For all their eagerness the girls seemed abashed. Each hesitated to rush forward, fearing that such an attitude might indicate too desperate need of employment.

"Come along, girls," Andy Lee urged impatiently.

The monocled show girl and her friend stepped into the breach majestically. They were blue ribbon specimens and knew it.

A titter ran through the gathering as they caught sight of the glass jammed into the eye of the taller goddess, but show girls are oblivious to the laughter of the less glorious dancing girls. They took up their vantage point with an air of matchless boredom.

"Would you mind putting down that dog?" suggested Andy Lee mildly.

"Oh, I cawn't do that," protested the monocled one. "Fifi goes crazy the minute I leave her alone." And Fifi remained in the arms of her mistress.

"Any more show girls?" yelled the secretary.

Four more trooped over to the front of the stage. Trailed is perhaps the appropriate word. A show girl's walk is inimitable; compared with her, Mrs. Vanderbilt becomes a gawky parvenue.

When twelve ladies had presented themselves for inspection Andy Lee advanced to the very edge of the orchestra pit. He leaned his arms on the brass rail which separates musicians and audience and scrutinized the first batch with a keen eye. "First lady in green step forward," he ordered. A slender young woman, who modeled for some of the foremost shops on the Avenue in her spare time, marched one pace in front of her less fortunate sisters.

"The lady with the dog," suggested Julian Marsh.

This was the occasion for parley as Andy Lee always displayed antipathy toward the owners of Pekinese. His wife had devoted years of slavish devotion to one of the little beasts. But Marsh's word was law. Fifi and her mistress were enrolled for the edification of New York's musical comedy public.

From the first line three were chosen.

"Well, good-by, dear," drawled Fifi's owner to her girl friend. "No doubt I'll be seeing you at the Mayfair some Saturday."

"Will those young ladies whom I've selected please give their names and addresses to Mr. Squires," said Marsh. "And then pass quietly out of the theatre as we want to get through this with as little trouble as possible."

Mr. Squires was busy with pencil and paper.

"One Fifty-Six West Forty-Seventh Street," volunteered the Venus in green.

"Fifi and I are at Three Thirty-Three Park Avenue," said Miss Monocle with obvious relish.

"I'll bet her homework is tough," hissed one of the dancers.

Selecting girls is wearisome business. For two hours, row after row shuffled to the footlights to undergo the inspection of Julian Marsh and Lee. Back and forth, weeding out the undesirables, the axe of dismissal fell inexorably. From a multitude of three hundred, some sixty had to be chosen, and of these twenty would be dropped in little more than a week. The

Chorus Equity allowed a producer ten days' grace to find any unsuitability in the ranks of his chorus; after that no dismissal was permitted without the payment of two weeks' salary. One may work at fever heat to please an exacting overseer only to be told, "Sorry, there's no room for you," and the grind starts over again.

Peggy Sawyer held her own in the competition. A producer invariably recognizes a fresh recruit to Broadway. Only one year is necessary to add the hard veneer to that outward loveliness, and fortunate the man who can fill his ensemble with the unspoiled children clamoring at the gates of theatredom. The daughter of a minister of Paris, Maine, cannot but look different from the hard-boiled sisterhood of Times Square. The mills of Broadway's gods grind swiftly but as yet they had had little chance to reduce Peggy Sawyer to the common mold.

So now she was a full-fledged chorus girl. Even those blistered toes were a badge of success. She pulled on her stockings.

"Gonna eat downtown?" Flo Perry asked.

"I think so. I'm living over here on Forty-Third Street, the Hotel Windsor," Peggy answered. It was incredible how the simple act of putting on one's shoes hurt.

"You'll get used to that," said Flo, observing Peggy's struggle. "Wait till dress rehearsal."

"That tap dancing is terribly hard," Peggy complained.

"Well, you know what they say about the first fifty years. Only it's the first hundred in show business. Want to eat with Ann and me? I'm yearning to throw my body in front of a tenderloin steak."

"You're sure—" Peggy began.

"Now don't get delicate," interrupted Flo. "We're glad to have you."

"I'd love to. I'm meeting some friends of mine about eight o'clock but there's nothing do until then except to drop into a picture," Peggy admitted.

Ann Lowell drooped into the dressing room. "God, that guy's heartless," she complained. "Two days more of this and it's back to the ribbon counter for little Annie."

"Miss—Miss—well, *anyway*, she's coming to dinner with us," said Flo, abruptly terminating Ann's woeful litany.

"I'm Peggy Sawyer," Peggy explained.

"Well, I'm Flo and this is Ann, so let's take our tin hips to the British Tea Room."

"I've eaten there so much I'm beginning to look like the place," Ann whimpered.

"Oh, don't be like that. It's the nearest place, and I'm not dreaming of walking these I. Miller's any further than Forty-Eighth Street," Flo demurred.

"Okay. But you know the last time I ate there I woofed the cookies," said Ann.

"Well, lobster always makes you sick," Flo returned. "Come on then! Ready, Peggy?"

"Sure!" Peggy responded happily. "All right to leave my practice clothes here?"

"Nobody touches 'em, although after a couple of weeks' rehearsing they're apt to get up and walk away by themselves," said Ann with grim humor.

Outside the dressing room a swarm of girls were making the final preparations for departure. Diana Lorimer, the monocled owner of Fifi, was fretting.

"I don't understand what delayed the car!" She tapped a forty-dollar slipper on the floor in well bred impatience.

"Get her!" whispered Ann. "She certainly upsets one. What does she think she is-the Spirit of Equity?"

"Just pulling the Ritz," Flo explained, "She probably goes home on a bicycle."

"Isn't she the girl who lives on Park Avenue?" asked Peggy.

"Yes, dear, complete with her sugar daddy. She'll probably be marked 'X' in the diagram of a well known murder one of these days," Ann replied.

Peggy was shocked but contrived not to show it. One gets hardened to these things in time and the philosophical acceptance of Diana's methods by Flo and Ann taught Peggy many things. Diana with her Rolls Royce and her Park Avenue flat was an integral part of Broadway.

As Flo explained succinctly, "Just one of Broadway's whore-ified girls."

In a dark corner they came upon Polly Blair and her mother. The old harridan was laying down the law to her rebellious offspring.

"No, you can't eat now," she snapped. "Here's a swell chance to practice your nip-ups without payin' for a rehearsal hall, an' a dollar's a dollar these days."

"But, Ma, I'm so hungry," Polly blubbered.

"Hungry, my eye! Didn't you eat three plates o' beef stew this noon? That's plenty for any growin' girl. You'll be puttin' on weight if you're not careful and then who'll give ya a job?"

"I can't work in this light, Ma! Honest, I'll get up early tomorrow. I'm dead. Three hours in the studio this mornin', an' the audition—"

"Shut up before I smack you one. That's the gratitude I get for slavin' an' runnin' a lousy boarding house all these years. Don't you wanna be famous? Ain't you got no ambition? Here ya go landin' a class show an' you begin to bawl an' snivel like a two-year-old. I never seen the likes of it."

"If I get 'em good tonight can I go to a movie?" queried the girl dancer hopefully.

"We'll see how the money holds out," said her mother grudgingly. "Go on, now, get out there on that apron and let's see the nip-ups."

Polly walked to the middle of the stage with a lagging step.
"For God's sake, we ain't got all night. Get warmed up and then show me something," Mrs. Blair snarled. "Don't forget your resin, else you might slip an' break somethin'."

Polly raised her hands high above her head and bent backwards, her thin body describing a perfect loop. She remained in that position for a full minute, swaying back and forth, her mouth hanging open in sheer fatigue.

The three girls passed through the stage door into a canyon-like alleyway between two skyscrapers. "Stage mothers," said Ann. "God damn every one of 'em! That old bat'll have her pride an' joy in the grave in about five more years."

"And a little child shall feed them," said Flo.

"Pop" bade them a ceremonious good night, for the doorkeeper is always the chorus girls' friend. He runs their errands, makes their telephone calls and in dull moments reminisces about the dear days when he, too, trod the boards in New York City. And those *were* the days!

They wormed their way through the snarl of traffic and entered the British Tea Room. New York is the happy hunting ground for such establishments. At reasonable cost the tea room gratifies the actor's desire for Bohemian surroundings, good food, and an atmosphere at once congenial and yet subtly refined. For all performers are refined at dinner time (though one might make an exception in the case of female blues singers). It is only after the theatre, during the progress of some hotel party, that one glimpses the congenital vulgarity of many of Broadway's daughters. A chorus girl eats with the daintiness of a debutante, her hand holds the fork at just the proper angle; if, on occasion, her voice grows shrill she is hushed by more prudent companions. Only a sharp-eared listener could gather that these ladies with their well modulated voices and unimpeachable etiquette were chorus girls.

Upon entering the British Tea Room one is subjected to an open fire of curious glances. Actors instinctively recognize their kin and the sight of some well known face provides enough "dirt dishing" for an entire meal.

There were various coteries present when the three girls entered. At a table near the door an earnest group of young "Theatre Guilders" had gathered, their youthful faces puckered with the burden of carrying the weight of the theatrical world on their shoulders. These disdainful youngsters were apart from the motley; the fancy that they were torch bearers to a newer and better regime intrigued them, and so one heard murmurs of Eugene O'Neill and St John Ervine (with the "Sin Jen" precisely articulated) wafting from their nook.

Ann Lowell flashed them a look. "Christ and his Apostles got here first," she commented. The remark is not so irreverent as it sounds. On Broadway the Theatre Guild cult has assumed the role of a local Deity. At present they were joining hands to show how an intimate musical show should be produced, and admittedly they had succeeded beyond all expectations. In the year of Peggy's first venture on Broadway such names as Rodgers and Hart, Betty Starbuck, Romney Brent and Libby Holman were just commencing their ascension into the bright heaven of Broadway's luminaries.

Flo located a table near the wall which commanded a strategic view of the door. "Now nobody'll get in or out without my knowing it," she affirmed, settling herself as comfortably as possible on the inadequate chair. It is part of the tea room ritual to see that the guest is made uncomfortable. To achieve this end all sorts of furnishings are crowded into the dining room so that one is shoved into a far corner amidst a display of dubious antiques, and elbows and shins are scraped during the course of the dinner.

Over their "blue plate specials" the two more experienced girls sounded the depths of Peggy's knowledge and found them reasonably shallow.

"So this is your first offense?" said Flo.

"Except a home talent show in Portland, Maine," Peggy assented.

Ann shook her head dolefully. "It isn't worth it," she declared. "Why don't you go back to those beautiful cows and that thar mountain air?"

"Oh, we sweet young things have to descend on Broadway once in a while," Peggy protested. "Don't worry—I'll learn."

"Well, here's where I open the carpet sweeper and let out some dirt," Ann decided. "We've got to keep you a good girl until we play Atlantic City. After that, God knows what will happen once the buyers get to you."

"This head is tight on my two shoulders," Peggy assured them.

"Dearie, you need more than common sense," Flo explained. "With some of these guys, brains won't get you a thing."

"I think everybody exaggerates so," Peggy argued. "Why, from what you read in the papers I expected to find seduction waiting for me at every corner."

"Oh, good old Sex is still bouncing about," Ann agreed sagely. "The trick is to recognize it when you see it and holler, 'Take off that beard, I know you.' Oh, us girls have a tough time of it; pity the poor chorine with nothing between her and starvation except a flat on Park Avenue and a wealthy gentleman on Wall Street. The wages of sin are generally from $99.50 per week—and up."

"She's only kidding," Flo put in. "Some of those kids in the show are so pure they'd make a Methodist deacon blush with shame. You can go wrong in any line of work, but in show business they do grease the rails a little."

"I should think you'd be so dead after a day with Andy Lee that sin would be the last thing to enter your head," Peggy laughed.

"Oh, nothing ever happens during rehearsals; it's tryout week when you need your tin drawers. And look out for the baritones! A tenor isn't so bad, in fact he's apt to be a sister in disguise, but, oh boy, those baritones—hair on their chest and fever heat temperature."

"She's been in a Shubert operetta, she ought to know," Flo pointed out.

"No, on the level," Ann maintained. "For some reason or other a girl's resistance reaches a new low when she plays Atlantic City or Philadelphia. Boston isn't so bad because you can always feed the pigeons on the Common and avoid the facts of life. But those other two burgs. Why, I'd do almost anything to avoid a Sunday in Philly!"

"When to say 'no' and when not to is one of the world's trickiest decisions," Flo interjected. "Now, if Andy Lee asks you out to lunch just 'yes' him to death, but if he suggests supper say 'no,' girlie, say 'no'!"

"But can't a girl eat supper with a man without becoming immoral?" Peggy inquired.

"She probably can, but it isn't worth the trouble because no one will believe her. And one thing you've got to learn—whatever you do in show business, it's exaggerated a hundred times. If you have supper with a man you're his mistress; nobody in this game wants to believe good of his friends."

"So just watch your step and pal around with girl friends even when the orchids start showering," Flo advised.

"Sure," Ann seconded. "I always see the shadow of an abortion hanging over every corsage I pin to my swelling bosom."

The discussion hung like an evil cloud over the remainder of the dinner. The dark byways suggested to Peggy's mind by the words of Ann and Flo were terrifying and yet—inviting.

The Theatre Guild crowd was dispersing. Flo listened to their gay banter.

"They slay me!" she groused. "There they go, just rattling with culture and not one of 'em earns more than forty bucks a week."

"But they get a great kick out of it," Ann reminded her. "And if you laugh at show business you've got the whole racket licked. It's the only way."

"It's tough trying to laugh when you've got five bucks between yourself and the breadline," said Flo. "That's where those kids are lucky. They've got folks with dough."

The dinner ended, they divided the check three ways, left their tips and departed.

"Ramon Navarro's at the Capitol," said Flo. "I think I'll drag the body over there. Want to come along?"

"I'm meeting friends at the hotel," Peggy apologized.

"And a boy friend from way out in Ohio is dragging me to the Winter Garden," said Ann. "One of those kids you knew when—"

"Oh, well, myself's good enough company," Flo opined. "Skip the gutter!" She hurried off in the direction of Fiftieth Street.

"The grease paint's sure got Flo," Ann sighed, linking her arm with Peggy's. "I'll walk you to your hotel. The boy friend don't meet me for an hour yet."

They proceeded slowly through the early theatre crowds that were milling about Times Square. Although the sun was still slanting over the massive buildings many of the theatres shone with an extravagant electrical display.

"You know, Flo will spend her last dime to see some damn fool movie actor. Thank God, I've got sense enough to know there's something in the world besides the show game. Ya gotta look at it from all sides," Ann philosophized.

Peggy breathed deeply. "It is fascinating, though," she said. "I don't suppose there's another sight in the world like that." She indicated the glitter of electricity.

Ann remained unimpressed. "Yeah!" she assented. "It's flashy, an' the yokels love it. But to me it's just a lot of light."

On either side moved the motley of Times Square: gamblers, racketeers, sightseers and show folk. The cheapness of Broadway is stark and vivid. It clashes on the senses in a series of shocks. The women of Broadway are coarse and over painted, the men tough and avid-eyed. The clamor of traffic thunders between its rows of tall buildings, and even the sky above is painted yellow from the lights. The illumination is like hard sunlight, you can feel the heat from the signs as you pass along the street. A few blocks to the west reigns squalor; to the east stands the lofty splendor of Park Avenue; but the stream of Broadway runs undimmed, a thing apart. Into it pour poverty and wealth; they meet, converge in the mutual quest for pleasure, and then retire leaving Broadway to shriek in untiring raucousness.

A dull glow illumined the globe atop the Paramount Theatre, Times Square's newest landmark. The radiant hands of the dock pointed to seven forty-five. Broadway was awaking to its evening life. Crowds were disgorged from the subway kiosks at Forty-Second Street. They flowed over the pavement relentless as a tide. The theatre signs seemed to increase in frenzy. Broadway was a world gone mad with electrical display.

The two girls reached the corner of Forty-Third Street and paused.

"Won't you come up a minute?" Peggy invited.

Ann shook her head. "I'll get there early so the boy friend can treat me to a drink," she decided. "No use in letting him off too easy."

"Then I'll see you at rehearsal," said Peggy. "You've been swell, both of you. I don't know many people in New York."

"Are these friends from the home town you're meetin' tonight?" asked Ann curiously.

"Yes, two girls from the Pine Tree State who went Greenwich Village. I'm going home with them to get my weekly injection of culture."

"I s'pose that's okay if you like it. Personally I never went in for the big words much," said Ann. "Well, see you tomorrow."

"At ten o'clock," Peggy reminded her.

"God, yes; once more I start getting up in the middle of the night," Ann groaned.

They bade one another good-by and Peggy started toward the hotel. It was one of those institutions known as a "family hotel" and catered chiefly to out-of-town visitors of modest means.

Things were progressing nobly. Her first day at rehearsal and she had made two friends; everyone said the show would be a hit. Perhaps Broadway wasn't so impregnable after all.

When she entered the lobby her step was elastic, despite the rigorous day just passed.

4

Andy Lee took in the room at a glance. A disorder of finery was apparent everywhere. Discarded clothes billowed from the rocking chair, lingerie covered the bed. Under the chaise longue the red slippers which were Amy's particular pride lay on their sides as though brusquely kicked out of the way. From the shower in the room beyond came the sound of Amy's voice hymning the charms of *Charley, My Boy* in a tuneless monotone. Andy saw his Paris dressing gown crumpled on the closet floor as though someone had trampled upon it with thoughtless feet. In front of the window lay the evening paper in fine disarray, a breeze rustling through its pages with a sort of stiff whisper. Andy's thumbs hooked themselves in the straps of his belt and he stood, hat far back on his head, surveying the scene.

"Married life!" he soliloquized. "Give this little sucker a great big hand" He went through the pantomime of a left hook to the jaw.

Unwitting, Amy began to shrill:

Love when you love, then I'll be h-a-p-p-y.

"Any time," muttered Andy Lee grimly. The hissing of the shower ceased abruptly and he heard Amy curse as she stepped on the bath mat. No doubt the floor would be a puddle of soapy water by the time he got in there to shave and Amy's things would stretch over all the corners; dirty towels flung down anywhere; jars of powder and cold cream; a white comb with hairs still clinging to it—and, worst of all, the scent of Amy's body. No, he'd wait half an hour even though it meant being delayed at dinner. He stooped down to retrieve the paper.

"Hello, Honey," called his wife, opening the bathroom door. He looked up to see her advancing upon him, the sleek kimono drawn tightly about her figure. The swaying of her hips fascinated him; somehow Amy achieved a melody in movement. It was that very thing which had snared him, the feeling of rhythm in her body as she danced under his instruction. She had been lissome and graceful, and even now, when the fat crept about her hips and deepened the line under the exquisitely chiseled jaw, he realized the allure of her. Auburn hair fell about her forehead and she made a tossing gesture to shake it from before her eyes.

"H'lo, Amy," he grunted.

She was undaunted. In moments like this she could afford to be gracious for he was held firmly under rule of thumb by the evidence a sharp-eyed detective had picked up some three months before.

"How's the show?" she inquired. "You've been at it two days now."

He shrugged. "Like all the others," he answered. Then, "This room looks like a pigsty."

"Darling, I'm sorry," she cooed. "I didn't expect you home so early. And the weather's so awful I've spent an hour in the bath. See how lovely I am."

She opened her kimono with a deliberate gesture. He tried to avert his eyes but Amy's smile compelled him to look. When he finally wrenched away his gaze, he breathed like a man tormented.

"Still fighting me, Big Boy?" she taunted him.

He got up without answering and strode over to the bathroom. "Why the hell don't you pick up after you?" he shouted.

"Trying to start a battle, dear?" she asked. "It won't work, I feel too lazy. The room'll cool off in a few minutes and then you can go in and splash 'round to your heart's content. It must have been terrible working today."

"Never mind," he shot out. "It helps pay for a new car."

"What a sweetheart you are to think of that," she trilled. "Desiree and I were looking at some of the *sweetest* models this morning."

"Yeah? Well, don't go buying on credit until you see how the show's going," he admonished. "We don't want to be left high and dry."

Her eyes reproached him. "As though I'd spend my husband's hard-earned money like that," she cried. "Don't worry, dear. I've learned the lesson of economy and I'm going to be a true helpmate from now on."

"You're a slut," he shouted brutally and slammed the bathroom door.

For the fraction of a second her brow clouded and unpleasant words forced their way to her mouth. It took firmness to choke down a reversion to her gutter childhood. But one must remember that a lady does not act so crudely. She turned her back on the offender and contemplated the view.

The Lees' suite was on the thirtieth floor of the new Hotel Westminster and New York spread its summer panorama below her. Smoke twisted lazily from the factories far to the north and cast a pall of gray over the city blocks. On either side gleaming towers mounted far into the quivering heat. The late afternoon sun, slanting against a million windows, struck out squares of living fire. On the still air the sounds of river traffic were borne to her ears with unaccustomed sharpness. She distinguished the hoarse cry of the tugs and the sharper, more insistent note of the other craft. Directly beneath a variety of cars fought in the snarl of traffic; their horns blared angry protests and Amy thought of the passengers inside, perspiring and fretting, eager to be out of this too close proximity to the rest of humanity. The silk dressing gown clung to her with a gracious coolness. She rested her hand against the window frame and admired the graceful manner in which the lace fell away from her forearm, exposing the milky whiteness of her skin. It was a pretty conceit to think of herself as a goddess on Olympus, condescending to view from her watch tower the world below with its lesser mortals.

Poor Andy! What a struggle it must be for him to keep from embracing her! Her fingers traced the line of her chin a bit anxiously. No, that was no shadow; she must be more careful, that suggestion of sagging boded no good for the beautiful contour of her face. She considered the methods one might try for eliminating such a nuisance. Dieting was so distressing when there was such a plethora of good food in the New York restaurants. Horseback riding might do; it was smart and showed her to good advantage. That meant an expenditure for clothes, but Andy could be persuaded to agree to that. She wouldn't let him off too easily now that she held the lash of infidelity over his guilty head. God knew she might get tight some evening with Pat Denning and then Andy would have the laugh on her. There were unsteady moments when Pat seemed worth the risk. He was so tall and clean limbed, not a disgusting, hairy ape like Andy. But Pat was continually broke and she couldn't afford to pay his bills indefinitely. Andy had been known to grow wary. What would become of her pretty case once he learned that she was keeping a man? Keeping—such an ugly word!—and, really, she only bought him expensive presents; he paid his own rent. At least she thought he did. One never knew with a devil like Pat. It was foolish to be so blind as to think that she was the one woman in the world who recognized his charms. Pat was shrewd. Emotion entered but slightly into the game he had elected to play. The cost of keeping a gentle man to oneself was high.

She heard Andy snorting in the shower. A picture of his small, muscular form covered with lather nauseated her momentarily, but the vision faded and there was Pat, tall and slender in his bathing togs. She must pull a few wires to get him a job; one found a market for intelligent, personable would-be Englishmen quite easily these days.

Andy emerged from the bathroom to interrupt her reverie. There was nothing of the Galahad about Andy, his thin hair dripping with water, and his eyes reddened from the impact of the shower.

"More like a drowned rat," thought Amy.

Andy rummaged through the chest of drawers for his under-clothes. From time to time he encountered an article belonging to his wife and shoved it aside with a muttered imprecation.

"You're touchy as a bear with hives," remarked Amy, crossing the room.

He ignored her and continued his search.

"I've been good and laid out everything on the bed," she said. She pulled her lingerie from the counterpane on the bed and revealed a supply of fresh linen.

Andy growled his thanks and hastened to dress. And this time it was Amy who sought to turn away from the odious flesh of her husband.

"You're going out, dear?" she asked.

Andy nodded.

"We never eat dinner together now," Amy pouted, resting a hand on his sleeve.

Andy shook her off. "You've got me down," he answered. "Can't we leave it at that? God knows I'm sick of the sight of your face."

Amy flushed. "But darling, I did just what any woman would have done to preserve the sanctity of her home," she protested.

"What book did you get that out of?" he sneered.

"It's true," she reasserted with growing heat. "I forgave you. That's more than a good many wives would do. Why, I know lots of women that would have dragged you through the horrid mess of a divorce."

"Well, I know why you didn't; so snap out of it and don't act ga-ga with me. I know when I'm licked but I'll be god damned if I'm going to hang around and listen to your whining. And one of these days, lady, I'll get the proof that you framed that little deal on me." He shook an aggressive finger before Amy's nose.

She laughed shrilly. "So, you think you were framed, do you? Well, from what I saw you'll have a hell of a time proving it—and in the meantime you'll listen to me. Seducing a minor's a pretty stiff charge, you know, and you sure ruined that kid. If it weren't for me, you'd be sweating in the Tombs right now. So cut out all this wise talk about my face and treat me like a lady or I'll let the whole world see you with your pants down!"

She accented each word with a vicious slap of her slipper against the bed. Andy glared into her eyes.

"You're a bitch!" he yelled. She snatched the slipper from her foot and threw it in his face, leaving a livid welt.

"When you're dressed get out of this room," she shrieked. "An' don't forget I got the power to send you up the river for a nice long stretch, yuh louse!"

She departed in a whirl of draperies into the ornate parlor which they maintained for show.

Andy's hand shook so that it was difficult to dress. The nerve of that chorus trollop daring to talk like that to him! One of these days she'd be sorry; he'd trace every rumor against her to its source and when he had proved she was playing around he'd hit and hit hard. When she begged for mercy he'd laugh in her face. The bloodsucker! He pulled on his patent leather shoes, adjusted the uneven ends of his bow tie, and surveyed the effect in the glass. Here he was, as classy a guy as you found on Broadway, tied down to a hell cat like Amy. And all because he got drunk and went on a wild party with some fifteen-year-old kid. Then the next thing he remembered was the groggy aftermath when they found him in the girl's bed and she accused him of assault. Only on Amy's pleading did she agree to hush the matter and now that episode hung over his head like the sword of Damocles.

But something had been phoney. God knows he didn't fool with kids!

The mantle dock struck seven and he swore ferociously. Wasting all this time grousing about Amy when Lorraine awaited him. He parted his hair with painstaking care, adjusted the soft felt hat at a jaunty angle, and moved toward the apartment door.

Passing by the living room he heard Amy's feet pacing the carpet. The impulse to pucker up his mouth and blow a childish, vulgar sound through the half-open door assailed him and he yielded. The walking ceased and he closed the outer door of the apartment just as a dull thud told him that Amy's other slipper had struck the paneling.

"The happy married couple," he snorted.

But for a brief two hours all this would be behind him, for there was Lorraine to taunt him with her provocative half yielding. It was uncanny how the woman knew the right minute to withdraw, but he'd catch her napping one of these evenings. Lorraine was a show girl in the new piece and it required skillful work to keep the producers in ignorance of the fact that he was philandering with a member of the company. Once let that be known and his job wouldn't be worth much.

Thank God, Amy sensed that and made no move to interfere with this newest and most exciting affair. By the time the lift reached his floor he had regained the sensation of well being that warmed him during the greater part of the day. To hell with Amy! He'd keep on having his good time and if it cost him more because of Amy's gentle blackmail, why—the devil!—he could afford to pay.

The elevator dropped swiftly into the heat and confusion of early evening.

5

"Do we eat?" asked Harry Towne, fingering the few coins in his pocket in a sudden access of panic. Funds were growing low, and what remained must be spread over three or four more weeks; then perhaps the management would allow him to draw on his salary in advance. He got up from his chair by the window and went over to the bed. Terry Neill lay there, his mouth open, the suggestion of a snore issuing through his parted lips. "Hey, bozo!" Harry reiterated. "Do we eat?"

Terry sat bolt upright. "For God's sake let a guy rest will ya?" he grumbled. "What's up?"

"I feel the Crystal Room of the Automat calling me," said Harry.

"Yeah?" Terry stretched his arms so wide that the joints in his fingers cracked. "And what do we use for money?"

"Well, I got four bits with me, you got that quarter we found in the dressing room, so that oughta stake us to somethin'," Harry pointed out.

"I'm sick o' the Automat," Terry objected

"Well, suppose we crash the Ritz," Harry jeered with elaborate sarcasm.

"I wish Jack Meyer was in town," sighed Terry. "He'd lend me a few bucks. But, no, the goddam act has to go to Scranton and Wilkes-Barre this week."

"Maybe we shoulda stuck to vaudeville," Harry mused glumly.

"Nuts! You're in a production, ain't you?" Terry demanded.

"Yeah. A chorus boy with four bits. That's a wow! I should sing the *Star Spangled Banner* over that! And we coulda gone in that Dance Fancies act for eighty-five dollars per—" mourned Harry.

"Lissen, guy, you gotta sacrifice sometime; they'll let you play them cans till you're wore out and then they won't notice yuh. But get a season with the big guys an' you're all set. An' fifty a week comin' in steady ain't so bad. It's better than layin' off in Dubuque or Fort Wayne."

"It hurts my pride, though." Harry complained. "At least you are somethin' in vaudeville. Look at the hand we used to get for our military buck. I'm tellin' you, this chorus job is strictly from hunger."

"Sure, we went great the two weeks the act lasted," Terry assented. "But you can't show your notices to the landlady when she wants the rent."

"So I suppose we're rollin' in wealth now?" Harry Towne gibed.

"Awright, awright! We only been rehearsin' five days an' you start bellyachin'! Maybe they'll let us draw a little dough next week."

Terry tightened the knot of his orange tie, slipped on his coat, gave a hurried slick to the thick curly hair that fell over his forehead and said, "Allez oop."

They turned off the lights and stepped into the thick gloom of the corridor. This was a theatrical hotel and from all sides came the wailing of portable phonographs, the tuneless rhythm of ukuleles, loud voices raised in altercation as to the merit of some musical show, a chorus girl shrieking curses at the butter and egg man who had grown weary and refused to meet her that evening-the giddy atmosphere of Forty-Seventh Street.

"Get a load o' them hams," commented Harry.

"This clump's a madhouse," Terry said. "But the broad in 519 ain't so bad. Still, what the hell can ya get on two bits?"

The elevator arrived to interrupt the mournful train of his thoughts. The metal gate danged open.

"H'lo, George," Harry greeted the smiling operator. "H'lo, fellers," the negro returned. "Rehearsals begin?"

"Sure. Looks like a hit," Terry told him.

"Thass fine! Thass fine!" George was the recipient of confidences from the majority of guests in the Hotel Columbia. "Pretty good guy for a monkey chaser," said Terry as they pushed through the revolving door and descended the short flight of steps to the pavement. Harry nodded absent-mindedly.

"Got any butts?" he demanded presently.

Terry displayed a somewhat battered package of Luckies. "You'll take one o' these an' like it," he said.

Extracting a cigarette from the pack, Harry mutely implored his friend for a match. Terry obliged him with a light. "How's that for bein' a ham?" he said, indicating the stage door of the Palace Theatre with a nod of his head. Harry stared past him at the resplendent youth lurking in front of the gate which leads to the back stage of America's foremost vaudeville theatre.

"First time that guy ever got a break on the big time in his life an' now he's three sheetin' in front of the joint mornin', noon an' night. They even bring over his breakfast from Thompson's," scoffed Terry.

The hoofer under discussion intercepted their gaze and waved a breezy "Hello! How goes it, you guys?" he shouted.

"Oke," returned Terry. "Too bad you got such a lousy spat, but what the hell, they always walk out on closing acts."

"I should care!" jeered the more fortunate one. "At least I'm here an' a coupla production managers been after me already."

"Now if we'd stuck to vaudeville we mighta been there in a coupla months ourselves," said Harry. Terry's sarcastic laugh could be heard the length of Forty-Seventh Street.

"With the stinkin' turkey we were in?" he sneered. "Sometimes you kill me!"

"I seen plenty worse there," Harry defended himself staunchly. "An' if you hadn't been so damn high hat we'd've made Eddie Leonard's act an' that's comin' here next week while we're sweatin' our guts out for Andy Lee."

The two boys were plunged in gloom. The remembrance of the day's rehearsal and their own financial plight combined to sour the evening's outlook.

"D'y' suppose Jeff Mulcahy's got any dough?" Terry ventured.

They lingered on the corner of Forty-Seventh Street, under the lights of the Columbia Theatre, to discuss the probability of fattening the exchequer.

"Hell, I owe him ten bucks already," Harry growled. "It'll take half a season to pay debts, big boy."

"How about that fagot in the show? He's got a yen for you, maybe he'd come across," Terry suggested.

"Lissen! I ain't puttin' myself under obligation to no fag. He won't keep his hands offa me now. Someday, I'm gonna sock that guy!" Harry's shoulders squared with a sense of outraged virility.

"He ain't a bad egg, that Winslow, and them guys can't help themselves," Terry observed. "Why, I palled around with a nance for a whole season an' he never even tried to touch me."

"I s'pose that's what I get for havin' this truck driver physique," Harry regretted. The subject was definitely dropped.

The boys plunged into the Times Square traffic. Across the way the Automat gleamed its invitation. Lined up before its doors were the hangers-on of Broadway.

Harry recognized three at a glance. "Get the O'Malley brothers," he whispered to Terry. "I thought they was all set with a Pan route. Ya never can tell about these guys who talk big!"

The O'Malley brothers, three dark, sleek-haired youths who wore clothes of an extreme cut and sported patent leather shoes, greeted the arrivals.

"Hey, Terry; hear you're one o' the girls!"

"Harry, how does it seem to be with all them fairy nice boys?"

Harry swaggered. "Better than layin' off," he shot out. "An' when ya get goin' they's only eight shows a week!"

"An' Andy Lee promised us a specialty in the last act," Terry added.

"Specialty in your hat. They won't nobody lift a leg with Dorothy Brock in the show. She'll yell the theatre down," scoffed Pete O'Malley.

"Yeah?" snarled Harry. "Well, we stand in good, see? We gotta coupla good numbers an' Andy Lee likes 'em, so they'll prob'ly shoot one of 'em into the ballroom scene. What you boys doin'?" He stemmed the tide of questions and put one of his own.

"Oh, the office is fightin' about salary," Mike O'Malley replied airily. "They don't wanna give us our price so we're holdin' out."

"Oh, yeah?" Harry's voice was rife with disbelief.

"Didya see our notice at the Eighty-First Street in *Variety?*" asked Mike, with a motion toward an inner pocket.

"Sure, it was swell, swell!" Terry agreed, averting the peril of being forced to read the clipping from *Variety* that always lay within easy reach of Mike O'Malley's fingers.

"Ya gonna eat?" asked Eddie O'Malley.

Harry looked in at the shining expanse of restaurant with indifferent eyes. "We might as well," he said. "How about it, Terry?"

"Sure. Ain't you guys et yet?" questioned Terry.

The O'Malley brothers, it seemed, had not, so the five Broadway gentry plodded through the revolving doors into the surge of diners.

Some comedian wisely nicknamed the Automat the "Racket Club," for above the ceaseless clatter of dishes comes the nasal flow of show talk—half-caught sentences about "routes" and "lay offs" and "wows," though the word "wow" is more often heard on the second floor where a cafeteria is located. Here the more affluent show folk dine at ease, and the observant person learns the financial status of a friend by watching to see whether he eats on the first or second floor of the Automat.

Sundry voices called out to the O'Malleys as they entered and the five boys stopped often on their way to the food supply to exchange a flippant word or opinion, as to the merit of some performer, with a hoofer acquaintance who was already seated. There is an easy camaraderie about the Automat. For the moment pretense is down; though one may talk vaguely of big projects, one frankly admits by being present that money is none too abundant. But happy the hoofer who can produce definite proof of coming wealth.

"Gee, they's more lay off's every season," Terry remarked. "Guess the movies are doin' it. See that guy over there, he's Arthur Lorraine, swell legit performer. Why he got eight hundred and fifty smackers over the Orpheum. Boy, you sure gotta hang onto the kale when ya get it. He must be a pretty old guy by now."

Arthur Lorraine caught the boys' stare and returned it with a condescending nod. Caste must be observed, even in the Automat, and he had played leading roles with Robert Mantell in his time. At this moment, indeed, there might be a part for him in the new thing Al Woods was producing. Of course, it wouldn't be his sort of work; they weren't writing plays like that nowadays, but the Woods management was influential and one must ride with the tide.

Men milled about the section of the wall reserved for coffee, which costs only five cents and lingers on the stomach with gratifying warmth. An occasional sharp-tongued woman wedged her way through the slow-moving throng, ignoring the insinuating gibes of those about her, and gathered together her evening meal.

"How's this guy Lee to work for?" Eddie O'Malley asked. The boys found room at one of the white-topped, circular tables and deposited their supply of food, sweeping aside a litter of dirty coffee mugs and paper napkins.

"Okay," said Harry in answer to Eddie's question. "I guess he can get tough if he wants to."

"He sure was a swell hoofer in his day," Eddie enthused. "'Member them triple wings, Mike? God, what I'd give for a routine like that."

He attacked his plate of beans with enthusiasm. The table was silent save for the audible gulping of coffee.

Eddie O'Malley finally expressed the yearning of them all. "Wish the girl friend was in town," he mumbled. "I'm all set tonight."

"You're lucky, Harry," cried Mike. "How are the dames in your show?"

"Hell!" Eddie snorted. "They don't look at a chorus boy. I know. I was in the merry merry, myself, for a coupla months."

"So you guys are as hard up as the rest of us," Eddie sympathized. He stuffed the remaining portion of mashed potato into his mouth.

"They'll be plenty doin' once the show opens," Harry said. "When they get away from their heavy collegiate boy friends they'll be easy to handle. Right now we might just as well be a coupla A.K.'s for all we're gettin'."

"But that's almost five weeks," Terry groaned. "I wish to God that girls' band was in town. 'Member those hot mammas, Harry?"

"An' how!" Harry grinned. "But if y' can't even take a broad to a picture show she ain't gonna bother with you."

They accepted the wisdom of this statement, but there still remained the aching need for diversion. The conversation grew more furtive. Gone was the thought of visiting Jerry Mulcahy back stage. One urge dominated them, and this they were unable to realize.

"Jeez," Harry broke out. "I'm gonna find me some jane if I gotta hit the Drive for her."

"That's out," Terry objected. "The Navy's got first call on all them dames."

Harry crouched low over his mug of coffee. Instincts that the savage grind of job seeking and rehearsal had dulled were finding life and could not be denied. The others twitched uneasily in their chairs. It was unwise to let the talk drift to women for it spurred them to reckless thoughts.

Outside, the somnolent August night captured the city and covered the towers which shot far up into its protecting darkness. Broadway seemed a shade less frenzied as the theatre rush died down and only an occasional crowd from some nearby movie house loaned a temporary spurt to the becalmed traffic. There was always the grumble of the subway and the street cars clanging along their tracks, but the insane crush of humanity that chokes the canyons of Times Square between the hours of eight and nine was mercifully absent.

Harry got to his feet abruptly. "Well, we might as well get outta here," he said. "This joint stinks."

They scrambled to their feet and went outside where a line of youths loafed against the plate glass window, whistling at the unaccompanied women who passed. The boys joined those poverty stricken stags for a moment and surveyed the parade of ankles. Eddie O'Malley tossed his cigarette into the gutter where its dull glow shone for a second and then died out. He stretched his hands far above his head in simulation of a tremendous yawn. "Let's be movin', Mike," he suggested. "We can sit in on that game down at Joe's."

The three O'Malleys said good-by and went off to combat the awful boredom which had descended upon them. Harry and Terry stared at each other helplessly.

"We can't do that with two bits," said Terry.

Harry grew sullen with thwarted hopes. "Jeez, kid, we can't go back to the hotel an' hang around," he protested. "I'll go nuts. Feel like takin' a walk?"

"With these feet?" cried Terry. "Lissen, big feller, save 'em for tomorrow. Andy Lee's gonna be plenty tough."

Harry rammed his hands inside the pockets of his coat. "I got to do something," he repeated.

"Ya look like ya belong in the Bronx zoo," Terry remarked.

"God, Terry, seven weeks without a shot of booze, no cards, no women, just pluggin' to get in the chorus. I gotta do somethin'—this playin' 'round has got me screwy."

Terry caught something like a strangled sob. He put a hand on Harry's shoulder. "Maybe we can give somebody a ring," he suggested.

"We don't know nobody, ev'ry god damn one of 'em's workin', except us. Even the O'Malleys can play poker," Harry ground out.

Terry lost patience. "Aw, hell, sleep it off, big boy," he said. "Let the dames wait."

Harry jerked away. "An' another day like this tomorrer, an' after that four weeks more. God, we're human!" he wailed.

"Sure, we're human all right, but what ya gonna do about it?" asked the practical Terry.

Harry gave a hopeless shrug. "Let's hit for the Park," he suggested. "Maybe we'll find some bag slinger who feels like a hit o' charity work tonight."

They started off with lagging steps. Before ten block were passed all hope of adventure had deserted them. The few approachable ladies seemed peculiarly disdainful of their invitation to dally a while. At Fifty-Seventh Street they gave up.

"C'mon home," grumbled Harry. "It ain't no use. All ya get is a first class dirty look. Women are the nuts, at times, ain't they?"

Terry nodded vigorously.

6)

Julian Marsh watched the rising tide of darkness which slowly inked out the tiny ribbons of street below and left them in a well of black. From out the blue haze which hung about New York, evening advanced with the gentleness of summer time. In winter, the descent of darkness is swift and sure, like the quick curtain which terminates the second act of a melodrama, but in summer, the afternoon blends imperceptibly with deeper shadows and stars take their accustomed places in the sky.

To Marsh it seemed as though the yellow street lamps sent their rays reaching jealously toward these aloof stars, seeking to draw from them a millionth part of their unearthly splendor. The heat of the day was forgotten. A slight breeze stirred the shrubbery on the terrace. To the south the steel towers of lower Manhattan were shafts of blackness against the horizon, in the west the string of lights shone dully through a mist that obscured the Hudson. The sounds of traffic were muffled, the battalions of cars which raced over the pavement far below were no more than a procession of headlights, moving to the dimly heard accompaniment of motors. For the first time that day Julian Marsh knew peace.

These intervals of respite from the clash and hurry of rehearsal were destined to grow shorter and shorter as the play progressed. The Show is a jealous god. At any moment now the door leading to the terrace would be hurriedly thrust open and old Alice would summon him to the telephone for one of the wearisome disputes that dot the journey of a musical comedy to its ultimate fulfillment. Costumers would harass him with their plates, scenic designers would jabber endlessly about "drapes" and "scrims." The thousand and one units that made up the show found their way sooner or later to his door. In a sense he, too, was God, but not so mighty that the Show was not still supreme. "There is but one Show and Julian Marsh is His Prophet." The duties of a producer are manifold as the stars of heaven. He must be the nerve center of the show's being. One minute he is listening to the tirades of the men who have invested thousands of dollars in the confidence that he will return their money a few times over; directly after he must stem the flow of complaint from the humblest specialty dancer who feels that her number has not been allowed sufficient scope.

It had been a long journey, this, from the childhood spent in an English village to the pinnacle of fame which he had achieved in the past few years. There were memories of public school life in England; of Oxford; of theatricals first amateur and then professional. He liked to believe that the ascent had been splendid and inevitable, carrying forward with the sweep of Greek drama. He forgot the petty, disagreeable episodes—the cheating, the conniving, the faltering, the denial of friends, all the unpleasant landmarks along the way—and saw himself rising in majesty to the throne of the world's foremost producer. Privately he believed himself among the elect of theatredom. Though others might rival his achievements in a monetary sense he had always been musical comedy's perfect gentleman. His background was no mean street of the Ghetto. The spires of Oxford were deeply imbedded in his consciousness. The generations of sober British ancestors had left their mark. Meticulous of speech, conservative of dress, restrained in manner, he saw himself imparting dignity to a profession that was looked down upon by millions of laymen.

In those first years there had been many irritating incidents. He knew he was superior both in intellect and breeding to the rabble among whom he had cast his lot and it required a tremendous amount of repression to keep from hurling insults in the faces of these stupid, complacent bosses of the theatre. He hated their gutter instincts, their dreadful mangling of the English language; most of all their gross, pawing sensuality. To him they were peddlers with a god-given sense for the almighty dollar, Eventually he had triumphed over them, and now they bowed with deference when he entered their offices; they begged him to produce their shows, not because they liked him, but because the new beauty which he had brought to the stage was a potent aid to dying box office receipts.

The musical comedies of the pre-Marsh era had been cumbersome affairs. Few scenic artists dared to use their imagination. When the script called for a house, a solid enduring structure was built; if the setting happened to be an exterior the studios labored to reproduce nature through the medium of painted back drops, papier mâché trees, and foliage that grew in a weird and wonderful fashion. Marsh banished all these notions. For the practical houses, the crowded village squares, he substituted soft lights and filmy draperies and permitted only the most indispensable props to clutter his stage. He argued that visual beauty of this sort enchanted the eye of the observer far more than any painstaking attempt to copy the wonders of nature and crowd them behind the proscenium arch. If the scene be a garden, let the audience feel the enchantment of rose bushes and flower-bordered walks through the mediums of lights and curtains rather than by the use of artificial properties.

It had taken all Marsh's powers of persuasion to render this idea palatable to the managers. They wanted their shows to look expensive; the audience must be blinded and dazzled into admiration. Marsh preferred an elusive sense of richness. He won but only because the ring of money at the box office was the public's answer to his efforts. These Titans of the theatre were content to see their coffers swelling and hear the encomiums heaped upon their undeserving heads by a grateful press. Julian Marsh shuddered as an unkind premonition warned him of the weary campaign that lay before him in this new production. These men, Green and Friedman, were reluctant to open the purse strings, although they were seeking the best. With Julian Marsh at the helm all should go well, but one never knew.

His fixed determination to produce only the tasteful and beautiful had brought Julian Marsh many things. The somewhat competent young actor of a decade ago would scarcely have dared to dream of this apartment half way to the clouds, these hosts of subservient, boot-licking friends, this intoxicating sense of power that stole over him when he realized that the mind and will of every person engaged for the show was his to command. Ten years ago he had been called a good performer with visionary ideas. Now that the ideas were realities the quantities of well wishers who had "expected it all the time" were amazing. The visions had brought him money and respect, they had overridden the arrogance of his hated employers.

A musical comedy is a curious thing. It gathers its people from the four corners of the show world. In no other field of production does one encounter such a variety of temperaments.

Yet each of them must be shaped to one end, the success of the show. Dorothy Brock was a raging hell cat feared the length of Broadway, but at the behest of the show she became a shy, lisping ingénue. Andy Lee could indulge his lust with the many women who thronged about him since he had become a famous dance director, but once inside the theatre he shed all thought of these affairs and became the driving machine that turned out number after number to amaze and delight future audiences. The show was the great leveler. For the five long weeks of rehearsal, through the tryout period and well into the run of the engagement it dominated the lives of every person playing a part in it. Marsh, dispenser of favors, builder of costly box office successes, was slave to his own creation. Each waking thought must be for the show. Early morning might bring an hour's freedom from the grind, but as the weeks went by the show would possess him more and more completely, as it would possess the dancers, the singers, the musicians, the stage hands, the comedians, the authors and the managers. The play was the thing. About it revolved the lives of many people, their joys, their tragedies; but each moment of happiness was tempered with the reflection that the show must always be the main consideration, each tragedy lost some of its force because the show was dominant. A hundred individuals lived in almost perpetual association with each other knowing little of the outside life of the ones who were their boon companions within the walls of the theatre. A hundred souls, each with his own ambitions and ideals, molded to fit in the pattern which Julian Marsh conceived and which, when it was finished, would be presented to the public as the latest musical hit.

It was thrilling to be the hand which presided over the destinies of so many. In this, his seventh production, Marsh was still experiencing the giddy sensation of playing puppet master to scores of performers.

He delighted in striking fire from the temperament of those about him. In the heat of battle his own notions flamed high and presently a finely tempered scene was conceived. Each personality he sought to mold to his own liking. Though he was a lenient taskmaster who encouraged a certain amount of obstinacy from those he considered artists, he would brook no defiance in a show down. In the white heat of encounter he stormed and raved. This was excused on the ground of temperament, but it was more than that, it was the earnest endeavor to shape the ideas of another into his own mold. He never argued with players whom he regarded as his inferiors, they were favored with a cloak of icy indifference; but he was willing to wage war with a performer for whom he held high regard to the end that he might persuade another mind to his own way of thinking. From widely different natures he must extract by argument or flattery the best they were capable of giving. He was obliged to know the language of the Park Avenue leading lady and the Forty-Second Street hoofer. Outside the theatre he ignored the crass comedians and dancers who cluttered his show, but under the spell of rehearsal they were no more than chess men who must be carefully manipulated into their proper places on the board.

Though he loathed the artifices of the majority of women with whom he came in contact he was able to guide them past the dangerous shoals of too much ingenuousness with a sympathetic hand. Women disliked him intensely, for the most part, yet at rehearsal they listened with respect and obeyed his slightest suggestion. Toward men he was more lenient. Men he regarded as fundamentally honest performers whose egos might need a bit of restraining but who were otherwise straightforward types that did not require the careful coaching which he expended upon his feminine principals. He cared little for comedians but recognized their important place in the scheme of things and was content to give them their heads. If he drew the check rein a little tight on occasion, it was done with no malice. The psychology of comedians was foreign to him. If they acknowledged his genius he let them wallow in their own self satisfaction. That was the only requirement for an intelligent player under Marsh's supervision. He was permitted his own outlook so long as he admitted the fundamental superiority of Julian Marsh.

Marsh stepped over the casement of the long French window which led into the dining room and surveyed the cozy scene within. Old Alice had prepared everything to perfection, as usual. The silverware shone with a glow caught from the flickering candle rays. The lace which he had ferreted out of a dingy shop in Brussels lay the length of the old table that had been brought from his childhood home. About it had gathered generations of propertied English shopkeepers. He was the last of this line and with his death its echo would die out forever. In a tall silver vase roses stretched high in incredible beauty, their long green sterns tracing a graceful pattern against the half dark. The candlelight threw into relief sketches which lined the walls, of the scenes conceived by Marsh for past productions. In them all one found a delicate grace, the sure touch of a great artist. The appointments of the room were exquisite. The architect had caught the atmosphere of a high-vaulted room in some ancient castle. The ceiling, far above, was lost in shadow; in such a room it seemed fitting that a company of gracious ladies and gentlemen should gather. Broadway had its word for the effect which Julian Marsh strove to create. It was "class!"

The telephone in the study rang. Forestalling old Alice, Marsh crossed through the library into the smaller room beyond. Picking up the instrument he called, "Yes?"

"Mr. Friedman to see you, sir," said the switchboard operator.

"Damn," he swore. This was a strange fancy of Si's to seek him out at this hour. For a moment he feared trouble in the offing.

"Ask him to come up," he said, and replaced the apparatus on its hook. He hoped that Si would not be disposed to linger. There were far weightier matters demanding his attention than the woes of the Semitic gentleman who would be programmed as "Abe Green and Si Friedman present…"

He explained to Alice that dinner might be delayed and went to the door to await Friedman's entrance. Si was notorious for his spells of pessimism, and in the throes of gloom he was wont to unburden his soul to any listener, willing or unwilling. Marsh could hear the elevator car moving upward on its cables and braced himself for an ordeal.

The elevator door slid open and Si Friedman emerged. He was obviously in a state of turmoil. Grasping Julian by the arm, he hurried him into the apartment, leaving the elevator boy to gape after them in confused wonderment. The two men crossed the living room and stepped outside on the balcony. For a few seconds Friedman maintained a bitter silence. Marsh studied him curiously. The manager was short and squat with a nose curved scimitar-like and thick lips which were almost always holding tightly to a tremendous cigar.

"My God, My God," Si groaned, by way of beginning. He spoke with the slightest trace of accent, and ornamented his every speech with a set of hysterical gestures.

"Trouble?" asked Julian, seating himself on the stone parapet.

"That Brock. She's a bitch! You know she's a bitch, Julian!"
"Everyone knows it. Nevertheless she earns fifteen hundred a week and draws hundreds of worthy souls to the box office," Julian answered him. "What's the lady done now?"

"Done? Done? Lissen, that dame's poison. I wisht I'd never 've monkeyed around with her in the first place. But, no, Abe's gotta stick his hand in an' says she's a class draw at the box office; they like her over on Park Avenue an' she has a record for never appearing in a flop."

Friedman pulled furiously at the cigar. Crouched there in the dusk with puffs of smoke jetting from his mouth and nostrils he might well have been some beast of mythology. Even the sounds that issued from his throat bore little relation to speech, rather it was the snarling of an outraged monster.

"Your rages are superb," said Julian. "I think you missed your vocation, Si. What a blood and thunder star was lost to the world when you decided to become the producer of gilt-edged musical comedies!"

"Okay! Okay! Here's the sad story!" grunted Friedman. "I s'pose you know that Abe an' I only got a small piece of the show. Money was kinda tight when we came 'round to doing it, and what with the lousy season an' everything, we figured what the hell, why should we risk our cash when there's suckers to be had for the askin', glad to lay it on the line just for the kick of havin' somethin' to do with a Broadway production. You know Abe, he's good at that racket. For some reason or other they go for that little kike over on Sutton Place an' up in Westchester. God knows why, because his manners is strictly from hunger, but, anyhow they do, so Abe says just leave it to him, he'll find a couple of angels. I got myself talked into that, too, when, as God is my judge, I was all for corralling some nice cloak an' suiter an' have him put up the dough. Those guys from the Bronx and Thirty-Seventh Street think that a few thousands in a show is a free pass to get a feel from some of those good-looking dames they've been wanting to put their mitts on ever since they was kids. But, no, Abe's gotta have the Social Register. The Social Register don't mean one, two, three with me. So far as I'm concerned they're the mugs that come in late, messin' up all the love duets, tripping over their ermines and making enough noise to land the opera in cut rates by the second night. But, Big-hearted Si, I say go ahead, get me one of your gilded angels an' we can take him over for plenty."

Si paused for breath. Julian mentioned a drink but Friedman waved aside the suggestion. He was much too intent on finishing his tale. Alice came to the window, looked inquiringly at the two men and retired to the kitchen with a shrug of resignation. Dinner would be delayed a half hour at least. Si was off on one of his tantrums and she knew the man of old. She poured her grievances in the cook's disinterested ear.

Si launched forth on the second stanza. "So you know who Abe digs up? He heads straight for the top of the ladder an' comes back draggin' this Richard Endicott with him. I suppose you know all about the Endicotts?"

Julian Marsh nodded. "Very first family," he said. "Old aristocracy falling into the sere and yellow, and all that."

"Yeah, I guess so," said Friedman uncertainly. "Anyhow, this Endicott guy goes in for polo teams, bob sled races in Switzerland, an' cocktail parties with the crowned heads of Europe. All that hooey. But the bank roll would choke a horse—a whole string of horses, so that was the big idea, of course. I wondered how Abe got hold of this guy, because he didn't look like the kind that mixed his angeling with his dry martinis, but the cat popped outta the bag—he's nuts about our little Dorothy, the angel of light of musical comedy. Ain't *that* the pay off? Thinks she's the Broadway lily—an' of course you an' me know that dame's slept in more beds than George Washington ever did. So, because he loves Miss Dorothy with a pure passion he took a twenty-five percent piece of the show. Right then an' there we figured you'd get your jeweled curtains an' some more of the props you were yappin' for and we couldn't see our way clear to buying. So it was all set, Endicott agreed to buy in an' *Pretty Lady* was on the way. Abe and I figured we could chisel Endicott for more cash from time to time, because these things run into money an' by the time we get all the stuff you've been yellin' your head off for the past week, Endicott'll have to ante up plenty mazuma to keep the outfit running.

"But ya can't figure on Brock. She gets a big bang outta the mob Endicott pals around with, an' he's a nice little package to show off at the Mayfair ev'ry Saturday night; but when it comes to a little lovin' up, our Dot still goes for the guys with the fancy manners and not a dime in their pockets. She's common all right, the little tart! I bet she had every kid who owned a pair of trousers when she was with that child prodigy act years ago. So that's the fix we're in. Any moment now Endicott's gonna get wise to the fact that his virgin girl friend is keepin' some feller who's strictly on the bum and, zowie, no more cash and we start ridin' for the red ink."

He slumped into an abject huddle, the glow at the tip of his cigar died out. He was a picture to rend the heart of the coldest tabloid reporter extant.

"You mean he'll endanger his original investment just to spite Brock?" demanded Julian incredulously.

"Sure. What's dough to that guy? He could put out five companies of Pretty Lady without turning a hair."

"And where do I fit into the picture?" continued Marsh.

"You're not suggesting I take my shotgun in hand and fight for the honor of the production, I hope? I don't give a damn about Madame Brock and her sleazy affairs. Everything about the lady is cheap and tawdry. Naturally we can't afford to lose Endicott's good will, but what measures should be taken I'm sure I don't know."

"Well, they gotta be taken, all right, all right," moaned Friedman. "Mr. Richard Endicott has to think he's the white-headed boy with Brock until we've been runnin' at least three weeks. I tell ya, Julian, we ain't got enough dollars to float this thing without Endicott. We always slide into the red the first week on Broadway, ya can't help it with an overhead like ours, so we'll hafta hang onto the Endicott dough an' the way to do that is to make Brock behave herself."

"The only suggestion I have—is to take her to some veterinarian and have her spayed," murmured Julian.

"If only Brock had fine instincts that you could appeal to the way they do in books," mourned Friedman. "You know, *Camille* an' all that crap. But that gal's had her heart wired with Frigidaire. All she wants are these lousy goofers who can't pay their rent but who know their way around a bed without a blue print!"

"Who's the man?" asked Marsh.

"Nobody knows. It's strictly under cover. He don't run 'round with any of the musical comedy crowd, an' of course wild horses wouldn't drag his name outta Brock. She's got a strangle hold on this daddy all right. But jealous guys have a way of findin' things out an' any minute now Endicott's gonna hear about it. He'll be so sore he'll give birth right on the spot."

"McDermott's the man to see," Julian decided.

"Oh, oh, gonna get messed up with the beer boys?" cried Friedman. "Bad business. First thing you know we'll be shelling out to them for protection an' God knows what else."

"Mac's not a bad sort," argued Marsh. "And he could put the fear of God into the soul of Dorothy's gigolo. Scare him off and Dorothy will be forced back to the yearning arms of her millionaire playboy."

Friedman considered the proposition. The racketeers were just gaining foothold on territory that had been previously barred tight against their invasion. Where they had formerly entered through back doors in the role of bootlegger, front doors were being thrown wide open and they sauntered in as welcome guests. The surrender of America to Gangland was imminent. Marsh had encountered a number of these picturesque gentry at social affairs during recent months. They mingled none too easily with their more distinguished hosts. But though their shirt bosoms bulged in the wrong places and their table manners rather alarmed timid hostesses, they fitted well enough into the background of the cosmopolitan society which succeeded the post-war generation.

"Well, how do we do it?" Si questioned fearfully.

"We can't work miracles, Si," said Julian. "Personally, I have very little regard for this McDermott. He's a four flusher, a welcher and no doubt a coward at heart. But, in his florid way he does manage to keep in the good graces of our municipal underworld. Any night club operator must be able to do that. I'm not suggesting that Mr. McDermott run riot down the streets of our fair city, machine gun in hand, seeking out Brock's lover. It may be a tedious business, but we obviously can't afford to show our hand in the matter so we'd better leave this mysterious paramour to the mercy of McDermott's crowd."

"Well, we gotta act quick," vowed Friedman, understanding little of the address which Marsh was delivering. "But, my God, how do we make the proposal? I know lottsa those guys. I can talk their language all right, but I was never up against anything like this! They won't go haywire an' try to bump anybody off, will they?" He pulled out a very large handkerchief and mopped his brow.

"I hardly think so. These matters of intimidation are handled with a great deal of finesse nowadays. Remember, the play's the thing. What's a gangster or two compared to the success of *Pretty Lady*?"

Friedman shivered. "Julian, I don't like it, I don't like it at all. God knows I ain't got no helpful suggestion myself, but I'll go to bed ev'ry night dreaming about pineapples an' 'X Marks the Spot.' "

Marsh laughed. "McDermott's not nearly so deadly as you think. In fact the big shots among our gangsters regard him as a small timer, but he's sufficient for our needs. He won't act quickly, but when he starts moving I believe the Brock boy friend will be thoroughly scared."

Friedman got to his feet. He braced himself firmly against the stone railing of the terrace as though steadying himself for the decision.

"Okay, Julian, we'll see it through. Where d' we find McDermott?"

"He's running El Mirador, at present. It's the only swanky night resort to weather these midsummer evenings. I'm taking a party of friends there Thursday evening. Join us there and we'll have a talk with Mac."

"But that's day after tomorrow an' we gotta act snappy," Si fretted. "My God, Julian, anything can happen in two days. Here we are in the second week of rehearsin' the opera and you stall about somethin' as important as this. Suppose in the meantime Endicott gets wise?"

Julian led the way back to the living room. "Somehow I don't think he will," he assured Friedman. "We shouldn't be too hasty. We don't want to rush Mac into using anything stronger than words."

His last remark insured Friedman's acquiescence to the plan. "Okay, okay," he agreed. "I'll hop into my tux an' meet you there Thursday. What time do you figure on arrivin'?"

"I'll let you know at rehearsal tomorrow," said Marsh. "I'll have three or four people with me. Young Lawler, the Crosbys, perhaps Conroy will join us later." Conroy was the composer of the show's music.

Friedman's large nose wrinkled with distaste. "You drag that young punk Lawler everywhere," he complained. "Don't people's talk mean nothin' to you?"

Julian's face darkened. "I mind my own business," he snapped.

Friedman nodded. "I get it," he said. "Just the same he's pretty high hat, that Lawler. Better put a word to the wise in his ear."

"Billy's a gentleman," Julian Marsh stated loftily.

"Yeah! So was Whittemore, the candy kid," Si responded.

He saw that Marsh was disinclined to continue their talk further and started toward the door. Half way across the room the ringing of the telephone startled him. He saw Julian Marsh spring swiftly past him, as though with the sudden movement the producer cast ten years from his life and was young man once again. Marsh disappeared into the study with a muttered apology and Friedman stood his ground and waited.

Presently Julian returned. Some witchcraft seemed to have erased the tired lines about his face; in his eyes there was a look of radiant contentment. Friedman, who knew little of any emotion other than the greed for money, was strangely disquieted at the transformation. The sight of the other man's happiness reawakened sleeping memories which he was satisfied to leave to their slumber.

"You'll forgive me, old man," Julian said. "I've a guest for dinner. It's my first chance for a bit of relaxation. I'll meet you a few moments earlier at tomorrow's rehearsal and we can attend to the matter of Dorothy Brock."

He ushered Friedman to the door. Si took his dismissal with good grace and promised faithfully to keep his own counsel regarding the proposed encounter with McDermott. He stared into Julian's face as they parted. If ever love was written large on a man's countenance, Julian's was the betraying face. He pressed the buzzer which summoned the elevator and stood quietly beside Marsh, wondering at the fatuousness of this middle-aged genius. The door clanged open much sooner than he expected. Without lifting his eyes he started into the cage and collided with the young man who was emerging.

"Hello, Si," Billy Lawler greeted him familiarly.

"Hello, Billy," mumbled Friedman. "See you all tomorrow." He waved his hand in good-by. The elevator door slid into place slowly blotting out the picture of Julian Marsh standing there in the hallway, one arm about the shoulders of Billy Lawler.

7/

The detective was a grubby little man past forty who affected striped neckties and chewed gum constantly. Amy stared at him incredulously.

"Shades of Philo Vance," she murmured.

"Pardon," he said, unwrapping an oblong stick of gum with tender care.

"Nothing. So you got the goods on him, did you? You found out there was another dame. I mighta known you couldn't trust a guy as good-lookin' as he is."

"He don't look like no knockout to me," the detective observed.

"No? Well, lissen, Sherlock, did you ever hear of hidden charms?" demanded Amy, her eyes flashing.

"I get it. But ain't that what the scientists call, 'indulgin' your libido'? Bad business, Mrs. Lee, bad business. It'll drive a poor guy nuts!"

"Tell me what happened," Amy commanded.

'Well, after the rehearsal I sees this Brock gal gettin' into a cab. I t'ought right away—oh, oh, this is gonna run inter dough for Mrs. Lee but I remembered you told me to go the limit so I hopped inter the next yellow that came along an' started after her. Well, I guess she kinda hadda hunch that everything wasn't jake because by the time we reached Fifty-Third Street she hops out, quick as lightning, pays the driver, don't wait for her change and starts runnin' east. Of course I'm too old a guy to let anyone get away with a stunt like that, so I tails along. Sure enough she's headin' for a speakeasy and that's where lady luck was on my side. I knew the feller that ran this particular joint so I could get in without raisin' a row. I let her have ten minutes headway, then I strolls in calm as you please an' sits down at a table in the back. There she is talkin' very confidential to the Denning guy you think is so good-lookin'. They both seemed kinda startled when I come in, guilty conscience, I guess, but God knows I don't look like no bull, so pretty soon they was at ease and chattin' away a mile a minute. That dame's gone on Denning all right. She'd go out an' try to buy him the moon if he wanted it. Funny a hard-headed gal like her can get took in so easy."

"Lissen, you," hissed Amy. "I'm not paying you for your opinion of Pat Denning. He happens to be a gentleman, but you wouldn't know about that."

The detective grinned amiably. "I never tried doublin' for this Casanova guy," he laughed, "so you can't hurt my feelings. D'ye want to hear the rest of it or shall I take a seventh inning stretch while you tell me how much charm this Denning has and why he's such a knockout?"

"It'd be wasted on you," rejoined Amy. "Go ahead!"

"They stalled over their dinner quite a long time and drank a lotta wine. My God, hot as it was they could pour down that red ink. I just mingled with the spaghetti an' waited, hopin' hat they'd scram before I turned into a fried egg or somethm'. For a neat five-cent sample o' hell gimme a speakeasy on a hot night. She kissed him a coupla times an' he loved her up a little, with what you'd call technique, I suppose, an' then they got ready to leave. I gave my waiter the eye an' he rushed me the check so I was right beside 'em when they was payin' the bill. An', unless

I'm gettin' cockeyed in my old age, Brock slipped him the dough for it. Is it one of those things?"

"How should I know?" demanded Amy irritably.

"Dunno. Just thought you might. Anyhow, I heard her say, 'Now, sweet, we'll get the car and drive out to Stamford.' Sweet! My God, what a pet name! A guy must have a little pansy in his make-up to stand for anything like that!"

"Is that all, Mr. He-Man? Did you let them get away from you?" asked Amy, getting up from her chair and pacing the floor.

"Well, what the hell, Mrs. Lee. Stamford is Stamford! You ain't figurin' on all that dough just to keep your eye on a two timin' cheater, I hope? Why, that'd almost pay the bonus. Don't worry, they'll be back tomorrow."

"I knew he was gettin' away with murder," fumed Amy. "I knew it! An' won't I have plenty to say to Mr. Pat Denning the next time we meet!"

The detective edged toward the door. "Yuh can't tie up these pretty boys you know," he said. "They *will* do a little roamin' now an' then."

"I'll find a way to tie him up, all right," vowed Amy.

"Huh! The only kinda terms those guys understand is a blanket contract," guffawed the detective.

"Get out!" shrilled the enraged Mrs. Andrew Lee.

The road curved through a grove of maple trees to the foot of the hill. Before them stretched Long Island Sound. Overhead the sky was thick with clouds which veiled the stars and a damp wind blew across the water. Far off the lights of a steamer moved through the night. Though they were near the Boston Post Road, here, in the quiet of late evening, solitude enveloped them. Dorothy stirred restlessly.

"Pat, let's go on," she begged. "We shall be terribly late!"

He stared moodily ahead without replying. She shook his arm. "Pat!" she repeated. "I'm cold. The effect of that wine wore off long since. Put your arm around me and hold me close."

Pat obeyed but there was something impersonal in his touch. "What's the matter with you?" she insisted. "You've been like this ever since dinner."

"Like what?" he inquired absently.

"Oh—abstract—inattentive. It's most annoying!"

He patted her knee. "Sorry, darling. I've got the blues."

"Pat—I'm here."

He kissed her. "And that should be enough," he responded gallantly.

"But it isn't?" Dorothy prodded.

"Not quite. I'm unhappy as hell tonight."

"Then let's get away from here. I don't like it at all. Here we sit brooding like two of Mr. Chekhov's gloomiest mortals."

"Darling-" Pat began.

"Yes?" Something in the tone of his voice made her instantly apprehensive. She moved closer, pressing hard against his body.

"This is going to be good-by for a while at least."

She jerked away from him. "I don't understand."

"It's simple enough. The ways and means committee can devise no manner for appropriating funds. Behold your improvident lover!"

Dorothy laughed hysterically. "Pat, is that all?" she demanded.

"All, my darling? Isn't poverty enough?"

"Not nearly. So that's the reason for all this solemnity."

He nodded. "I've been on the well known uppers for three days now. Thanks to you I've managed nicely about meals and such details, but this morning brought a very nasty note from the rental agency."

"The beasts!" She was all sympathy for his plight. "I should have known that five hundred dollars couldn't last forever."

He shrugged. "Oh, well—I roused myself to action and lighted upon a deal that may prove profitable."

"What's that?" she inquired uneasily.

"Stock acting in Lexington, Kentucky. Cheerful prospect, isn't it?"

"Kentucky? Oh, Pat, you can't—you mustn't!"

"I'm afraid there's not much help for it. Rental agents and creditors can be pretty insistent, you know. I'm sorry to break it this way, darling, but you had to know. And, at the most, it will be only six months."

"Six months?" her eyes filled with tears. "But I'll die, Pat, I'll simply die. I can't imagine living without you."

"Nor I without you," he replied. "Shan't we be two sorry-looking ghosts?"

"I'm not going to permit it," she said firmly.

"Little Miss God!" he railed. "What can you do about it?"

She hesitated and bit her lip before answering. Pat eyed her covertly. Some notion had taken root in her mind. He prayed fervently that it might be the correct one. He turned away and indulged himself in a profound sigh.

"Pat—if money is the only consideration…"

"Then what, you angel?"

"I can help. I'd be *glad* to help!"

"Nonsense. As though I could accept charity from you!"

"It needn't be charity. We could call it a loan—a loan payable whenever you found it convenient."

"And does Madame Shylock have her pound of flesh?" he asked.

"Pat! This is for—for the sake of our love." She was every inch the self-sacrificing heroine of a first act finale.

"Sweet, you know I shouldn't dream of accepting," he protested.

"Not if I wanted it so very much?" she insisted.

"But I'll feel so damn humiliated. No, Dorothy, it's no go!"

Her voice was choked with sobs. "Pat, we've meant a lot to each other. Why should I fail you now? Believe me, sweetheart, I'd be the happiest girl in the world if I felt that my—my assistance could save you from taking this step."

He put his arms about her and their lips met. Suddenly she was crying.

"There, there, darling!" he soothed. "We'll talk it over later. Come along—dry those eyes and on to Stamford."

Dorothy brightened. "Then you're not going?" she whispered. "Oh, Pat, I've led you such a miserable chase. Dinners in cheap speakeasies where no one will find us—flights to Connecticut so that we might be alone without any fear of discovery. But, never mind, my darling, I'll find time to make it up to you."

He turned on the switch and pressed the starter. "As though you hadn't already done that a thousand fold," he smiled. "Are you ready, Miss Brock?"

"Quite!" She opened her purse and found a powder puff.

The car described a half turn and headed toward the Boston Post Road. A few hundred yards away they saw the motor cars that moved in slow procession along the highway. They were irresistibly drawn toward the lights which zigzagged past.

"I know you're going to love Stamford," Dorothy whispered.

"I can just see that early American soul of yours expanding in an atmosphere of hooked rugs and Washington pitchers."

"Splendid! I'm a new man, already!"

"And, darling, about the money. Will five hundred more carry you?"

"Well, I—to tell the truth—" Once more he eyed her shrewdly, wondering how great a sum he dared mention.

"We'll say six hundred then!"

"You're an angel." She strained forward until her mouth found his.

"Careful!" he warned. "These Connecticut cops are mean babies."

"What do we care?" She laughed recklessly. "We own the sun, moon and stars!"

He maneuvered the car into the slow parade on the Post Road.

"Silly, sensual little trollop!" he thought. "But not bad, at six hundred!"

8

The lounge of the N.V.A. Club was crowded. Danny Moran searched in vain for a familiar face. "Small time hams!" he muttered as two gentlemen in striped suits elbowed past, intent upon the familiar argument of salary. A song plugger from the Irving Berlin office called out a cheery "Hello." He had once served as a "plant" in Danny's vaudeville act. Those were the halcyon days of variety when the line between big time and small time was definitely marked. Now one plays three and four shows every day, and likes it. Danny thanked God for the astute agent who had rescued him from that morass and set him on his feet in production. All vaudeville performers were floundering now. The Albee regime was tottering to its disastrous close. The sycophants who had won long routes by spying on their fellow artists blanched when they imagined a future unprotected by the favor of Edward F. Albee. Danny saw one of them now, a bald-headed chap with a rasping voice and hawk-like nose who had played the finest houses in the country, not because of merit, but in return for certain information sent to the powers who sat in judgment in the Palace Theatre building.

Varied conversations floated through the air.

"So I waltzes up to G.P. and I sez, 'Now, get this—just because we took a cut at the Jefferson ain't sayin' we play for that money over the Simmons time. That was break-in dough an' the office agreed to it. I got a production cost to meet an' I can't take no more o' this stallin'. The Loew office wants the act an' as far as I'm concerned they can play it. Where the hell is your big time, now, anyway?' And the guy never opened his mouth. So we open at the Lincoln Square Thursday, all set pretty, an' Mr. Albee an' the booking office can kiss my—" The final vulgarism was blotted out by a shrill laugh from a buxom blonde lady of uncertain age who was being regaled With a dirty story by a sharp-featured Jewish comedian.

"That goes in the act," she caroled. "You're a panic, Lou. Say, what's this I hear about your signin' with the Shuberts?"

"Still a little uncertain, Maud," he responded importantly. "They want me but, hell, they don't pay no dough. I'm an artist an' I told em as much. When a guy can roll 'em in the aisles in Syracuse he's worth somethin'. An' everybody knows a revue without comedy, *stinks*! An' I want billing, too, but ya gotta talk tough to these guys or they'll walk right over ya. An' the Shubert contracts are a riot. Five years! *Sure*! But they'll like as not shove ya in the Rocky Mountain company of *Blossom Time* once the first season is over. I'm wise to 'em." The cigar moved forward and back in his mouth like a baton marking out the tempo of his words.

"Well, don't let 'em stick ya," advised Maud. "Do a Georgie Price an' make 'em pay. Hey, Danny!" The urbane Maud saw Moran and waved a genial "Hello." He sauntered in their direction, none too pleased that he must bandy words with that cheap comic, Lou Sharpe.

"All I gotta say about that guy," he once remarked, "is that it was a lucky day for him when Eddie Cantor was born."

"So ya got in a production at last?" Maud greeted him. Danny stiffened. "They been after me for years but I wasn't takin' any," he explained. "But with vaudeville in such lousy shape a guy's gotta do *something*. What the hell, it ain't a perfession now, it's a job." He nodded to Lou. "They tell me you been hangin' around the Shubert office."

"Sure," Lou assented, "After my two weeks at the Palace they was on to me like a pack of wolves. I couldn't go nowhere. Great date—that Palace—but, then, I forget, you played it once."

The shot went home. "They sure hold plenty of acts for a second week, now," mused Danny. "Talent's getting pretty scarce, I guess. All the big names are goin' into picture houses."

"Got good stuff in the show?" Maud interpolated.

"Fair! Fair! But they can't kid me. It wasn't Harry Keene wrote the book, it was Joe Miller. Boy, the cracks they give me, my part'll roll right over in the footlights an' die! But I'll fatten it up with some of the old sure fire gags an' paralyze the outfit. The music's good but they sure need a low comic."

"An' they got one," said Maud vigorously. "The best in the business. How's the gang to work with? High hat?"

"Aw, I don't bother much with 'em. Jealous, y'know. So god damn legitimate they think vaudeville is a new kind o' car. Wait till they hear my laughs."

"Ya gonna get good billing?" Lou demanded.

"We don't feature no names," Danny replied. "Just call it an all star cast."

"Too bad!" Lou commiserated. "I get big type right under the name o' the show with the Shuberts. An' next season the old moniker goes right on top, just like Jim Barton's!"

"How's the tunes?" the avid Maud inquired of Danny. "Ya got good numbers?"

"Yeah. Hot stuff. But no voices. I want 'em to give me a reprise of the hit song, endin' on that falsetto note that used to wow 'em in the act, but they're afraid to take the chance. An' God knows ya gotta be a lip-reader to get what the ingénue says."

"Who's she?" Maud pursued.

"Oh, some floozy named Brock. Gettin' kinda faded, if ya ask me."

"That belle!" shrilled Maud. "Why, my God, she's got callouses on her fingers from sewin' sweaters for the Rough Riders. I suppose ya got an Albertina Rasch ballet led by Florence Reed." The two comedians bellowed in deference to Maud's humor.

"Well, she'd have to get on a stepladder to kick higher than her head," Danny declared. "An' the taps in the buck routine sound like a nineteen-eleven Ford on a San Francisco hill! How these dames get away with it is more 'n I know!'

"They's somebody back of her," Maud avowed. "Some butter an' egg man put up plenty o' dough so she could waltz her fanny through that show, you can bet your last dollar."

Lou Sharpe moved away. "A coupla Feist men wanta run over a new number for me," he apologized. "I ain't got no peace now they hear I'm goin' with the Shuberts. Well, so long folks, and lottsa luck."

He disappeared in the throng. Maud glanced after his retreating form. "The line o' bunk that baby's been handing me," she exclaimed. "An' I knew him when he worked on the Gus Sun time for coffee an' cake."

Danny guffawed. "Prob'ly they need a good cheap funny man for the *Passing Show of 1912*," he gibed. "Well, how's tricks, Maud? Gettin' much these days?"

"The boy friend's been hittin' the bottle," said Maud. "An' that means no dates for a month. Then they tell us we got the Butterfield time, so I'm going back to my old job as the Belle of Lake Michigan. But, say, I'm tickled to death to hear about the show, Big Boy. I like to see a plugger like you get a break. Too bad they couldn't use Daisy." Daisy Moran was Danny's wife.

"Just between you an' me, Daisy's gotta lay off the feed bag," Danny confided. "She looks like one of Fink's Mules. But you know Daisy—no judgment! She was sore as hell when I come home with the contract an' was for movin' out an' leavin' me flat, but I pointed out that I earned as much alone as we got on the Big Time together once you take out excess an' sleepers, and besides there's no lay offs. So she's up at the joint sulking, with a bag o' caramels in one hand an' a picture of Buddy Rogers in the other."

"How's Madame Marsh to work for?" asked Maud.

"He's a pretty good guy, Maud; and, hell, these artistic fellers gotta be queer. That's why they're artistic, I guess!"

"I hear he's puttin' his boy friend in the show."

"Billy Lawler? Yeah. Ritzy kid, too. Thinks he runs the show. I'd just as leave tell him he can't boss me just because he's Julian Marsh's mistress."

"Well, kid, keep your knees together, an' any time you an' Daisy feel lonesome, drop 'round to the Hotel Columbia. Dave'll be glad to see you an' we can tear a herring or I'll throw a salad together." Maud waved a flippant good-by and went to join the McGinnis Sisters, harmony singers, who always thrilled her with their rendition of *Swanee River Moon*.

Danny Moran was experiencing the thrill which comes to a self-made man who has achieved his goal. Many bitter years lay behind: week after week in the dreary, smoke-grimed towns of the middle west where frozen-faced audiences stared up at the rostrum as he cut the crazy capers which eventually won for him the soubriquet, "King of the Nut Comics."

"There ain't a dump this side o' hell that hasn't played Moran and Moran," Danny was wont to say.

Danny and Daisy were picturesque figures in the crazy quilt pattern of vaudeville. Products of the most wretched street in Brooklyn, stepping from a precocious childhood into the toughening atmosphere of back stage, they were at once the hardest and most lovable couple to be encountered on the Keith circuit.

Daisy's grammatical flights were world famed. It was she who inquired of a stranger at a restaurant where they dined after the show, "Would you mind passing me the sugar, if I'm not too inquisitive?" And it was Danny who glibly explained to his associates that he knew a certain picture was good because he'd seen it run off in the "rejection" room.

One effusive critic in South Bend referred to Danny as the "grease paint vagabond." His kind-heartedness was proverbial; his practical joking universally feared.

They still chuckle over the story of Danny and the lady billed as the Chinese Nightingale. This occurred in the days when Danny had hauled himself into the class of featured performers. In the neighborhood houses the names of "Moran and Moran" headlined the bills, wherefore he and Daisy were startled on arriving at the Riverside Theatre for orchestra rehearsal one fateful morning to discover the name of the "Chinese Nightingale" above theirs on the marquee. War clouds gathered. The management was adamant; the Nightingale was a novelty act and the office wanted to build her up properly.

"I'll say she's a novelty," growled Danny. "When she gets through they pass 'round slips to the audience for them to guess what she's tryin' to do, an' the one who comes the nearest gets an autographed photo of Albee."

No effort on the part of Moran and Moran succeeded in dislodging the Nightingale's name from electric lights.

"If she's so good then we walk out," Danny decided.

The management was agreeable, for Danny had been drinking and at such times the quality of his turn was dubious. Danny and Daisy descended the stairs, each carrying a bundle of soiled clothes. In her dressing room the Nightingale warbled in a voice which belied her name. Danny tapped on the door and the Nightingale answered his summons. Then Danny proffered the bundle of laundry.

"Have this back by Thursday," he said with a triumphant smile, and Moran and Moran passed through the portals of the Riverside Theatre for the last time.

Then there was the incident of the stately prima donna who topped the bill in some midwestern town. Danny's account of that episode belongs among the most cherished anecdotes of theatredom.

"I 'member one time me an' Daisy was playin' over the Orpheum, in the days when it was a real circuit, an' we got this Madame Duclos on the bill. The Madame was a coloratura soprano, which meant she could bellow like a stuck pig and the audience loved it, at least part of 'em. Well, the Madame was a big shot, even though she looked like she rated the title, so in their quaint jolly way they headlined her all over the circuit, and there couldn't nobody speak to her or she'd drop dead from the shock of havin' to talk to vulgar troupers. At every performance they stretched a carpet from her dressin' room to the stage and Her Majesty dragged her three hundred and ninety pounds over this to her eagerly waitin' public. Then she'd start bellowin' *Lo, Hear the Gentle Lark*, and we'd run the water in the dressing room or recite *The Charge of the Light Brigade*—anything to shut out the noise.

"Well, the first day Daisy didn't get the gag about the carpet. She thought a pipe had busted an' the floor was wet, or somethin' like that, so we was on right after the Madame an' down bounces Daisy, walkin' square on the carpet. Well, the Madame hit the chandelier. None was to walk on her damn carpet but Madame, by God, an' she looked at Daisy so hard through her trick lorgnette that Daisy says, 'I'm a tall, thin blonde, Madame, jus' to save you the trouble.' Madame gives a belch of indignation an' runs into her room.

"Daisy didn't say nothin', but come time for the next show, we was almost on an' the stage manager was raisin' hell wonderin' what had become of Daisy. She was dressin' at the head o' the stairs and I hollered to her to make it snappy because the Madame was on her fifth encore and might get through any hour. Well, Daisy opens the door, lookin' like Queen Marie after she'd taken a dose of salts; an' quiet as you please, just as the Madame is puttin' in an appearance; she slings a roll of toilet paper down the stairs, waits till it finishes unrollin' way down by the entrance in one, an' comes sailin' down the stairs, walkin' on her carpet, an' makes an entrance—givin' the Madame the horse laugh on the way."

They were like that, Danny Moran and his wife.

Fifteen years of trouping had resulted in the offer of a contract in the Julian Marsh production. The vaudeville world is feverish and crowded with color. Daisy sighed that they would miss it all—the sleeper jumps—the bedlam of a company car en route to the coast, with its ukulele soloists, its men playing poker in shirt sleeves, and its quota of acrobats with their worldly wise offspring. No more orchestra rehearsals on those drab Mondays when they stumbled in half dead from a racking night spent in an upper berth; n more quarrels with refractory stage hands who refused to help in setting up the props; no more heated arguments over the spot on the bill.

"Hell, woman, you'll be a lady of leisure," Danny pointed out.

"An' who wants to be parked in this god-forsaken dump all evening?" Daisy demanded with asperity. "I tell ya this much, Danny, if you don't put a resin box in the front hall, I'll go nuts."

"Aw, you can run around with Sue Wilson and the O'Brien sisters. They're layin' off till their Pan route starts in October," Danny argued.

"Now who wants to spend ev'ry evenin' dishin' dirt with a lot o' gabby women. You just leave me stay in a speakeasy an' drink beer, that's the only way I'll be satisfied," said Daisy with finality.

"An' grow fat as a house," her husband jeered. But Daisy compromised and afternoons when Danny was engaged in rehearsal found her seated at the window poring over the cumbersome scrap book in which she had pasted every newspaper notice of the act since the beginning of their alliance, twenty years ago.

One finds a simpler, more straightforward honesty among the people in vaudeville than in any other branch of the profession. The neurotics of the show world avoid it, looking down the length of their noses at the humble folk of the two and three a day. There is true comradeship in this branch of the profession, and its petty quarrels lack the virulence of the frays in which the legitimate artists participate. Vaudevillians are the plodding humdrum folk of their calling. Life for them is a simple matter of routine: arriving in a town, rehearsing the orchestra, playing the required number of shows, and then a period of relaxation—time for a game of cards or a visit to some neighboring speakeasy. Life stretches before them as a series of weeks and split weeks with a bungalow on Long Island, free from mortgage, as the Alpha and Omega of existence. They know the value of thrift and each season finds the tidy bank account swelling. From time to time their circle of friends grows, an easy-going band of performers who murder the King's English, talk shop from morning to night, and who are cheerfully ignorant of the fact that such men as Mencken, Freud, Kant and Pater exist. Eugene O'Neill they know because *Variety* tells them that his plays are invariably box office winners. Now and then a comedian is cast out from vaudeville upon the Broadway shore, like a fish out of water; for the first week he gasps in the unfamiliar surroundings and then, with the adaptability possessed by all show people, he falls in with the newer mode of things.

But the unsung legions go on. About their performance is an inescapable mediocrity. They lack sparkle and chic. Presumably their turns will never reach the Palace. But they plod along, unenvious of their more lustrous confreres, content that the Long Island bungalow stands to welcome them at the end of an arduous trip over the Interstate Circuit.

So it might have been with Danny and Daisy Moran. "Ham actors" they were stigmatized. "You can't see the Palace lobby for the small timers hanging around it."

To which Danny's response would be, "Just give me big billing an' the next-to-closing spot an' they know where they can stick their damn Theatre Guild."

The sharp clash of personalities in this musical show bewildered Danny. He rallied at the call to arms when some "bit" of his was in danger of being slighted, but the miasma of hatred and petty jealousy which lay over the production he could not fathom. It was an atmosphere of constant vituperation, coals of fire heaped on the head of some luckless individual the minute he or she had passed from earshot. There was the smoldering dislike of Dorothy Brock for the second leading lady; the amused contempt with which Harvey Mason, the second comedian, regarded the less polished Danny; the friction between Julian Marsh and Andy Lee; the bickering of the chorus girls.

Yes, musical comedy was a bed of roses, thorny side up. Still, there was recompense in hearing the compliments of less favored friends who dropped into the club house depressed and wilted from a day of three and four performances in the neighboring vaudeville houses. Two of these acquaintances were approaching now, the Rafferty brothers, harmony singers and comics. Mutual greetings ensued.

"Well, well, Danny, and how's Equity's newest darling?" Pat beamed and offered cigarettes.

"Oh, he ain't so bad," he confided. "Course ya can't run the whole works like you do in vaudeville, but what the hell, the dough's good, the show looks like it'll panic 'em and in these days it's a swell feeling to be set for the season."

The Rafferty brothers agreed. They were having their troubles.

Manny Rafferty launched out on their tale of woe. "Well, we get over to Jersey City with the new layout an' the first thing one o' them hard-boiled stage managers tells us he can't give us all the lines we want for to hang our stuff. Boy, we got more props than the Barnum an' Bailey circus; drops, clothes an' I don't know what the hell else. So I sez, 'Lissen mister,' I sez, 'them drops gets a line apiece or we don't open today.' That kinda got him, see, 'cause we're the headline act an' he's gotta take care of us, union or no union. So he says come ahead, he'll see what he can do. Well—we hangs the stuff, with that bunch o' gorillas growling like someone had fed 'em raw meat and Joe goes to rehearse the orchestra. They must've picked 'em up at a novelty contest, Danny; ya never seen such mugs. Didn't know soft shoe tempo from fast buck, an' the waltz for the sister team—Jeez it sounded like *Yankee Doodle* played by George Bernard Shaw on the xylophone! So Joe, he says real sarcastic like, 'ya would play a flash act in vaudeville,' an' I comes back real wisecrackin', 'It's what the office is pinin' for, big boy, class an' color.'

"Then our comp'ny arrives with a coupla mothers we didn't know existed, because it seems the sister team ain't sisters an' each one's got an old lady. Well, they start raisin' hell about dressing rooms, like they always do; you know the line, 'My daughter's an artist an' she ain't dressing up three flights of stairs for the best act in vaudeville,' which they goes at great length to hint we *ain't*. Joe hits the ceilin' an' says, 'Lissen, them two harmony howlers is just a lotta hooey as far as I'm concerned, an' from what I heard o' their singin' they oughtta be dressin' in the animal room; we only stuck 'em in the act because the office wanted girls.' Well, one ma takes a sock at him with the suitcase, an' we have to put her out of the joint. First the girls said they'd quit cold, but we talked plenty V.M.P.A. and they come down to earth an' climbed into their trick costumes. Boy, I seen funny dressin' in my time, but if you'd shown me a blue print o' them gowns I'd've give up guessing what it was. Then to make matters worse they got midgets on the bill an' every time ya went on stage a midget hopped out of the water cooler or the telephone. No kiddin', they got in your hair. We go on Number Five, see, swell spot an' all that, but it don't mean nothin' 'cause they'd walk out on the Virgin Mary singin' *St. Louis Blues*. Everything goes wrong; they pulled up the wrong drops, the orchestra started playin' the sisters' waltz out for that wow essence we held over from the old act, an' they blackout just when one of the sister team is makin' a strip change. So she hollers out, 'Where the hell's them lights, I'm up to my fanny in midgets,' like the nice refined girl that she is. Y'see the midgets followed us, an' they was all in the entrance in one, real unprofessional like, watchin' us flop. So when we come to take bows the ushers musta handed around ether, the audience just looked up as much as to say, 'What a hell of a way to earn a livin'.' So Joe an' me are through with class acts, the drops go back to Cain's and we dig out the big shoes an' go back to low comedy in one. They ain't no money in the flash racket."

Danny agreed with them that the flash idea was "cold." More than that, in a spasm of generosity he gave them a couple of sure fire gags for the new act, "guaranteed to lay 'em in the aisles." A gratifying sense of well being filled him. They looked up to Danny Moran now; Danny was a legit comic, and as such subject to the envy and awe of his vaudeville contemporaries.

"I'm lookin' at the world through rose-colored glasses," Danny hummed, jamming a tremendous cigar into the corner of his mouth. Now for some coffee and waffles at the St Regis and then home to Daisy. He hoped to God laying off didn't make her too fat because they might have to do the old act once the show closed and Daisy sure had a nifty figure when she kept in trim.

Still humming he passed through the portals of the National Vaudeville Artists' Club into the clamor of Forty-Sixth Street.

9

El Mirador, atop the roof of one of New York's swankier hostelries, was the sole night club to brave the scorching blasts of midsummer. The cool breeze that eddies continually about the summits of Manhattan skyscrapers made dining bearable, and fortified by an excellent cuisine and a superb tango band this new rendezvous was the smart place for the stay-at-homes during July and August. The smart crowd liked the various innovations, such as the sliding roof which was opened on fair nights permitting a view of the stars, and the glass dance floor with colored lights beneath it which threw a magic glow about the dancers as they swayed to the rhythm of the band. Despite the heat many couples were formally dressed and they were waltzing sedately to the strains of the latest Continental hit when Julian Marsh entered with his party. The head waiter welcomed him with much bowing and scraping and called sharply to a servile Greek who ushered the group to their ringside table. McDermott caught sight of them and left the table in the rear of the room where he was sitting with Polly Blair and her mother and went over to join them.

As soon as he was out of earshot, Mrs. Blair's fingers pinched the arm of her daughter in an agonizing grip. Polly emitted a low whimper and was promptly shushed by her fond parent.

"Now ya gotta be nice to Mr. McDermott," explained Mrs. Blair. "He's the big boss around this joint an' he owns plenty of night clubs. With the lousy salary you're pullin' down in the show ya gotta double in club work in order to make both ends meet. God knows I slave myself to a shadow for that drunken bum of a father of yours an' it still ain't enough, so you gotta do your bit."

"Yes, Ma," said Polly obediently.

"McDermott's nuts about kids so if you watch your step we oughtta collect plenty for this date," Mrs. Blair rambled on. "I knew he went for you the minute I set eyes on him. Those big, paunchy guys like to get their hands on somethin' young. We'll just play along with him an' you trust your mother to get a lot out of him an' still make him keep his distance. I didn't play ten years with the Golden Crook Girls for nothin'."

"He tried to kiss me tonight," Polly whined.

"Let him, a kiss don't do no harm, an' he won't try any funny business for a long time yet. You're still a minor," Mrs. Blair reassured her.

"But he's so sloppy," Polly complained. "I don't like to kiss the old bastard." Polly's Elizabethan English was the result of close companionship with her mother. Mrs. Blair could grow quite expansive when the situation demanded it. She was not too careful about her daughter's vocabulary, indeed many of Polly's slips seemed quite right and proper to her mother.

"Ssh, someone'll hear you," hissed Mrs. Blair. "All these waiters is stool pigeons for the boss. Ya gotta watch your step."

"Do I go on tonight without pay?" Polly demanded.

"Yeah. It's kinda like an audition," said her mother. "I couldn't help it. I screamed the place down in Dexter's office this afternoon but it didn't do no good. They don't buy nobody without a tryout these days. Why, even Cortez and Marie had to do an audition and they was with Ziegfeld for *three years*."

"I guess we're all set though," said Polly more confidently. "If Mr. McDermott likes me he'll do the hiring, won't he?"

"Sure. All you gotta do is limber up, see that the orchestra keeps a good tempo, and watch McDermott that he don't get too free an' easy with his hands."

Meanwhile, Walter McDermott was playing the genial host to Julian Marsh and his friends. Oblivious alike to the bored contempt of Billy Lawler and the freezing unresponsiveness of the Crosbys, he wedged his chair in between Marsh and Mrs. Crosby and launched into a glib recital of the woes of a night club manager. Billy Lawler toyed impatiently with his glass. Crosby turned a fixed stare on the dancers. Julian alone heeded the long and complicated tale with which McDermott was regaling them. He had no liking for the sleek well fed gentleman at his side, but policy dictated a friendly mien. Walter McDermott could be a generous host or a treacherous foe as the mood suited him. An unimportant figure in the newly risen force of gangland, he managed to retain the respect of the numerous public enemies by dint of much conniving and wire pulling. He knew the shady secrets of local magistrates, the unmentioned vices of men high in public office, and wielded the bludgeon of exposure most effectively. His keen sense of scandal, extraordinarily developed through years of association with the disreputable lights of the bar and politics, was now serving him in good stead. Without this knowledge of the wrongdoing of the various public employees he would have met short shrift with the new gangster regime, but they found him convenient as a go-between who knew the exact moment to swing the tide in their favor. He was hated by some, feared by a few and trusted by no one, but he was always a serviceable ally. Although he possessed little actual power, with much contriving and plotting he managed to attain his end. He was just the sort of figure needed for the messy business Julian had in mind. McDermott's course was often devious, and he could promise no swift solution to the problem in hand, but eventually he would achieve his purpose.

McDermott finished his story with a triumphant gesture, failing to notice the inattention of Marsh's guests. When the flow of words had ceased Julian found time to catch the racketeer's eye and signal the desire for a private conversation. He indicated the men's room with a slight nod of his head and received a knowing wink from Walt.

The festivities were interrupted by the advent of Si Friedman, quite melancholy in his dinner jacket. He bade a perfunctory good evening to McDermott, whom he feared, and squeezed into the remaining space left for him at the table. When the Crosbys rose to dance Billy signified that he was content to watch the activity on the floor, and so Marsh and McDermott repaired to the men's room. Walt made a gesture of dismissal to the wash room attendant who promptly fled with a muttered, "Yes sir, yes sir, yes, Mr. McDermott," leaving them alone among the white tiles and mirrors.

"What's up?" queried McDermott by way of opening the conference.

"Walt, I'm going to ask a little favor," said Julian. "I presume you'd be interested in helping our show to succeed."

McDermott lit a cigarette and said nothing. His eyes narrowed a trifle but otherwise his demeanor was unchanged. Walt had sat in on too many poker parties not to know the danger of too mobile a countenance.

"We're in danger of going on the rocks and you wouldn't like that, would you, Walt?" Julian continued persuasively.

"Christ, no, I've got a piece of it myself!" Julian's eyebrows lifted. "Indeed? How much?"

"Ten per cent. Abe talked me into it. What the hell, it's something new. If you go floppo I ain't too much in the hole," said McDermott.

"Then I think this proposition will appeal to you even more strongly. We're going to have trouble with Brock."

"Oh, oh! Pushover Annie! Why do you get dames like her?"

"The dear public, Walt. You should know all about them, yourself."

"Sure. I know my dear public all right. Funny how they go for somebody like Brock. She an' her *You an' Me and a Cup of Tea*. The song shoulda been *The Navy an' Me and a Quart of Scotch*."

"Well, our darling Dorothy has worked up one of those interesting triangle situations for herself. It seems that one of the Endicott clan has designs on her chastity and feels so strongly in the matter that he has been persuaded to take a twenty-five per cent interest in the production."

Walt whistled. "The Endicott kid?" he said. "He's up here most every night with a Sutton Place crowd. Brock's in the money this time, all right. What's she been doing? Trying to bitch it all up?"

"Yes. Dorothy can't withstand the lure of her gigolos. She has a new kept man on the string and not even the Endicott millions can budge her from that particular bed."

"That's the pay off," declared Walt indignantly. "An' my cash tied up in her trick opera, too. She could stand a good clip on the jaw, that one."

"It wouldn't help," Julian hastened to assure him. "There's a far better way. We must reach Dorothy through her boy friend."

McDermott nodded grimly. "Sort of throw a little scare into the boy?" he said comprehendingly.

"Exactly. The difficulty is to locate the boy."

"That won't be hard. Brock don't cover her tracks. I'll have all the dope I need pretty soon." McDermott threw his cigarette to the floor and crushed it. "Let's scram, Your friends'll think there's something between us."

Two guests entered the room. They greeted McDermott who gave each one a friendly clasp of the hand, and then he departed, followed by Julian Marsh.

The tango band was playing an insinuating melody and couples were stalking languidly about the floor in what they fondly believed to be a correct version of the Argentine dance. McDermott seized Julian's arm and gesticulated with his forefinger.

"See the guy dancing with the girl in the white outfit? She's the dame with the swell sun tan."

Julian nodded.

"Well, that's Endicott. Nice-looking guy, isn't he?"

Julian caught a hurried glimpse of a tall, well set up young man who wore his clothes nicely and danced with a pleasing authority. His partner wore her hair back of her ears, sported her sun tan proudly, and conducted herself in the manner of one of society's daughters doing her bit of slumming.

"Rather fine-looking chap," Marsh observed. "It's strange he should be messed up with anyone so thoroughly common as Brock."

"Don't kid yourself, boy," Walt derided him. "Mr. Endicott has the manners down pat, but you want to get a load of him after three drinks. Baby, does that language sizzle! Brock prob'ly taught him a couple of good ones, at that!"

They rejoined the Crosbys and young Lawler and shortly after Walt made his excuses and withdrew. Mrs. Blair saw him heading in the direction of their table and nudged Polly. Polly's tired face brightened, she assumed a smile of shy coquetry and beamed upon Walt with the look of innocent childhood.

"Better get into your things, kid," said McDermott. "It's time for the show. Just take things easy and don't get scared. They're high hat folks but they won't bite you. An' if they're too stiff to applaud for your tricks, don't let it get you. It's tough making 'em give in, but a Park Avenue crowd is always like that."

"Oh, Polly'll be all right," her mother stated. "She's a good trouper for a kid. Run in an' put on your waltz dress, honey. I'll come right in an' stretch your back for you in a few minutes."

Polly trotted away accompanied by the smiles of her mother. When she had vanished Mrs. Blair turned on McDermott. "I wouldn't do this for many people," she said. "My daughter's recognized as the best acrobatic dancer in show business, you know. Just ask any agent along Broadway. She took it kinda hard, you askin' her to go on like this without any pay, but I explained that you only had her interest at heart an' you wouldn't let her down. I seen you talkin' to Mr. Marsh. It's funny he should be here tonight. You know, we're going in his show."

Mrs. Blair said "we" in the manner of most stage mothers, who assume the duties and responsibilities of their offspring to such an extent that they really feel themselves one being rather than parent and child.

"Sure, I know. Nice fellow to work for, too," said McDermott.

"I noticed you were real chummy. He's a real gentleman, Mr. Marsh is, a real gentleman. I'm proud to have my daughter work for him."

The tango was ended and the couples drifted back to their tables. Walt pointed out some of the notables to Mrs. Blair.

"That's Richard Endicott. You know, the old Endicott family. They tell me he goes for your leading lady, Dorothy Brock," Walt confided. 1'

Mrs. Blair's lips compressed in a thin line. "Huh!" she said. "I suppose I'm talkin' out of turn, but I must say he'll have the devil's own time with that lady."

"Why, I never heard much about Brock," said Walt artlessly. "The usual hooey they spread about any star, of course, but I guess she's as straight as anybody else in this racket."

Mrs. Blair assumed a pose of mystery. "Maybe so, maybe not," she declared. "I live over in the West Forties, you see."

"Well, so what?" demanded the keenly interested McDermott.

"Nothin'—only there's an apartment house across the way that's kinda funny if you ask me. Not that I'd talk, but I've seen Miss Brock comin' out of there a coupla times—an' it ain't from a visit with some girl friend."

"Yeah? Well, whaddya know. Feel like a drink, Mrs. Blair?"

"We-e-ll, I don't mind if I do."

10

At three in the afternoon New York sweltered under a blanket of intolerable heat. Living fire seemed to eddy through the canyoned streets sending its blast into the farthest corners. Overhead, languorous clouds moved along the edges of skyscrapers as though rendered indolent by the heat which shriveled heaven and earth. Inside the Forty-Fifth Street Theatre the damp coolness of early morning had vanished, and although sheltered from the blasting sun the company assembled there wilted under the breathlessness which hung heavily about their heads. Four or five principals had crowded into the narrow areaway giving onto the stage door and it was to the accompaniment of newspapers used in lieu of fans that much speculation as to the future of the show was bandied back and forth. From the stage came the monotonous clatter of buck dancing, punctuated by savage cursing from Andy Lee, and from the orchestra pit Jerry Cole droned out his interminable accompaniment to *Ticka Tack Toe* over and over again. Andy Lee had set his pace and it behooved all weaklings to keep step. The thought of his wrath loomed like a threatening spectre, and many an aching limb was goaded into new activity by the fear of a stinging reprimand.

Rehearsal is a deadly grind enlivened at times by sundry incidents, such as the episode of Helen Fitzgerald. Helen strolled into the Forty-Fifth Street Theatre during one of Andy Lee's outbursts and was assailed in vigorous terms by that young man.

"And what do you want?" he demanded. All eyes stared.

Miss Fitzgerald was unruffled. "Oh, Mr. Lee," she gushed, "I tried so hard to get here before, but you know what these vacations are and I simply *had* to stay another week. I'm afraid I'm awfully late, but I *do* want to get in your show."

The weary choristers had thrown themselves prostrate on the floor, thankful for this interval.

"Well, can ya dance?" Andy Lee growled.

"Oh, yes, Mr. Lee," gurgled Miss Fitzgerald. "I'm a specialty ' dancer."

"Well, we only got chorus jobs, so you're outta luck," snapped Andy.

"Of course, I'd consider that," Helen Fitzgerald assured him magnanimously.

"That's nice of you!" said Andy with broad sarcasm. "Have you got a routine?"

"I'll just run through a few steps," Helen suggested. "Then you can judge for yourself. May I have some music, please?"'

Jerry's fingers automatically sought the keyboard. They would continue to do that for two more weeks, running over and over the same chords until it seemed that the keys were worn thin from the pounding of his fingers.

Helen cocked an attentive ear to catch the tempo. Then, a cherubic smile wreathing her face, she began to dance. The routine contained one figure, a step technically known as "Off to Buffalo." It is held in derision by all good hoofers as the simplest step in the dancing category. Along the apron of the stage went Miss Fitzgerald performing her "Off to Buffalo" with all the majesty of a Pavlova. Andy Lee ground his teeth in disgust.

"Lissen, girlie," he yelled. "That's lousy! That'll never get you anywhere."

"It'll get me out of here," rejoined the imperturbable Miss Fitzgerald, and continued her "Off to Buffalo" across the stage and out the door into oblivion.

In revenge for this slight to his person Andy Lee kept the chorus on their feet for a solid two hours. Blistered toes were treated to a quick alcohol rub and then the sufferers dashed back into line, fearful of incurring Lee's wrath. In the oppressive heat two young ladies were overcome and an ambulance was summoned to take them home. Needless to say there was no reimbursement for those torturesome days they had put in. At the whim of the producer any chorus girl may be worked until she drops in her tracks. The philosopher of show business opines that "it's just the breaks." You may survive and then there lies ahead a season of idleness save for the eight weekly performances stipulated in all contracts.

Peggy Sawyer found herself near to tears. Somehow the knack of the "time step" escaped her. It was exasperating to be able to count out the proper rhythm in her mind and yet fail so dismally when she essayed the step with the other girls. At the end of two hours when Andy Lee's voice had grown hoarse from the continuous stream of abuse with which he browbeat the chorus, a halt was called and Peggy stumbled toward the stage door, numb with fatigue.

For two days Terry Neill had watched Peggy. She was good-looking and she was an unknown quantity. The majority of the girls he ignored, but Peggy aroused his curiosity. She might be worth cultivating. He had witnessed her frenzied struggles and as the crowd milled toward the alleyway he shoved his way through until he found himself at Peggy's side.

"Lissen, sister," he said, seizing her hand, "I think I c'n set you right about that time step if you ain't too tired."

"Oh, if you would!" gasped Peggy gratefully. "I'm worried to death and I see Andy Lee giving me dirty looks."

"He can't help the dirty look, he was born that way," Terry jeered. "Come on—let's get back of the piano and I'll hold a demonstration."

Peggy made a hurried excuse to Ann and Flo and followed Terry. They found Jerry Cole about to take his leave.

"My God, you kids are gluttons for punishment," he groaned. "Why don't you park your dogs for a coupla minutes? The old bastard's gonna start in hot an' heavy as soon as he gets his second wind."

"Mr.—Mr.—" Peggy sought to recall Terry's name. "This boy's going to help me with the time step. You see, tap dancing is all Greek to me!"

"Go to it, folks," said Jerry. "An' may God bless you!"

He picked up his hat and strolled toward the stage door where Julian Marsh was waiting to confer with him. Billy Lawler stood at the producer's left, impatiently tapping his foot. He had no wish to converse with Jerry, whom he regarded as an upstart and a vulgarian, as well as the instigator of the rumors which had been started about Marsh and himself.

"Get a load of those two kids," chuckled Jerry, coming up to them. "Ambition personified. Breaking their necks to get a lousy buck break because they think maybe they'll be stars some day. What a racket!"

Billy, forced to recognize Cole's presence, nodded slightly and murmured, "Might as well give them credit for the idea, at any rate." He turned to stare at Peggy and her perspiring instructor. It was the first time he had considered her as a separate entity. Heretofore she had been one of a conglomerate mass of be-rompered dancers. Now he saw an attractive youngster who bore herself with a certain distinction that the average chorus lady woefully lacked. Having no desire to be present at the conversation between Marsh and Jerry, he sauntered across stage to the spot where Terry was laboriously expounding the mysteries of the time step.

"It's a tough dance, all right," he smiled. "You deserve a great big hand for all that energy."

Peggy and Terry glanced up, startled. Terry colored with annoyance. He had never before addressed the unpopular juvenile and he was hard put to frame a civil reply. Fortunately, Peggy stepped into the breach.

"'I'm so stupid," she mourned. "Every one of the girls can dance rings around me. Perhaps I'd better retire gracefully to the plain sewing and stitching that's supposed to be part of a nice girl's life."

Billy Lawler shook his head. "Not with those dimples," he contradicted. "They're strictly a front row proposition. Broadway would be losing a lot if it failed to see that smile."

It was Peggy's turn to flush. Her confusion was very prettily managed and both Terry and Billy were equally entranced. At that moment Julian Marsh shouted to Lawler and indicated his impatience.

"Right with you," called Billy. Then he grasped Peggy's arm. "Lots of luck," he said. "I'll be cheering for that time step."

He waved a friendly good-by and rejoined Marsh. The two quitted the theatre arm in arm, oblivious to the scrutiny of the two chorus members.

"That was awfully sweet of Mr. Lawler," sighed Peggy.

"Huh!" scoffed Terry. "That—" he checked himself.

"I suppose you believe all those tiresome rumors," said Peggy. "I don't. Anyway, what business is it of ours?"

"None, except that that guy's mean. He's got Marsh right where he wants him and the feller that don't talk pretty to if Mr. Lawler 'll find himself out of the show so quick he'll think he was never in it."

"Oh, that's silly," remarked Peggy. "Let's get back to our time step."

"Right!" said Terry. "Watch me."

His shoes tapped out the rhythm of the time step. Peggy shook her head hopelessly. "You'll have to do it slower," she declared. "I simply can't follow."

"Okay, babe. *Watch!*" Terry commanded. "Da da *dum* da da *dum* dum, da da *dum* da da *dum* dum. One two *three*, one two three four. Come on. Gimme your hand. Da da *dum* da da dum dum! No, no, kid, on your left. See, like this: Da da *dum* da da dum dum, one two *three*, one two three four. Come on, count it out with me. Watch that left foot. That's it, you're gettin' it. Steady now, and for God's sake watch that left *foot*."

Andy Lee stepped from the stage box on to the apron. "All right, everyone," he called. "It's two-ten now. Get your lunch and be back by three o'clock sharp. And anyone that don't want to stay with this management just report at five minutes after three."

With subdued shouts of thanksgiving the company made a rush for their various dressing rooms. During rehearsal period the chorus are permitted to change their clothes in the quarters which are assigned to the leading players once the show has opened. From all sides came the gay laughter of a crowd released from imprisonment.

Terry looked up inquiringly. "Guess we better eat," he suggested. "Lee's gonna be the rest of the afternoon on this new buck number an' you'll need plenty on your stomach. How— how about goin' with me for a bite?" He broached the subject diffidently, in a flash of inspiration.

Peggy understood. "I'd love to," she answered. "But, of course, it would have to be Dutch."

He made a movement of refusal. "Otherwise I'll have to run along with the girls," Peggy ended firmly. "I know how it is during rehearsal time. We need every red cent we can lay hands on."

Terry smiled. "I guess you're right," he admitted. "Only I hate to ask a dame—girl—out to eat an' then let her pay for her own."

"Everybody does it in show business," Peggy counseled. "I'll get out of these clothes and be with you in a jiffy."

"Don't hurry," Terry called after her. "I know a joint just 'round the corner where they have swell blue plate specials."

Peggy waved assent and ran into the dressing room. She found Ann and Flo grouped menacingly about her portion of the make-up shelf.

"Are you eating with us?" Flo demanded.

Peggy flung aside a shoe. "As a matter of fact, I've made a date, girls," she confessed.

"I knew it," mourned Ann.

"With that wisecrackin' hoofer?" Flo persisted.

"I—I don't know his name," Peggy admitted. "He's the tall, good-looking boy with brown hair. He's an awfully good dancer."

"That's the one," said Ann grimly. "Now, lissen, while the Mother Superior opens up. Those guys aren't any good—they're only out for as much as they can get, an' they haven't a nickel in the world."

"I'll bet he's makin' you pay for your share," snorted Ann.

Peggy giggled. "Well, I told him I wouldn't go unless I paid," she explained. "I thought show people always went Dutch."

"Get her," Flo moaned tragically. "Sure, we do; but we wouldn't be caught dead with one of those cheap hams. Believe me, girlie, hoofers are no good. They get so used to making every waitress they meet that once you're with 'em ten minutes they got hand trouble."

"If he gets fresh, sock him one for me," advised Ann. "An' don't make any more dates with him because Flo and I know some nice Columbia boys that'll be back in town next week. You don't want to be trailing around with a flat tire like that when there's real class to be had. Why, these boys got a Packard car."

"Much chance we'll have to use it working for Lee," Flo supplemented. "Come on, Ann, I hear the buckwheat cakes serenading. Let little Peggy have her fling."

"Shut him up the minute he starts telling you how he stopped the show at the Jefferson," Flo warned. "They always do—and it's always the Jefferson."

"And don't walk past the Palace Theatre with him," supplemented Ann, "or you'll think it's old home week. He'll want all the lay offs to know he's made a chorus girl."

"He seems like a nice harmless boy," Peggy declared. "And it was very nice of him to show me the time step. I've been scared to death that Lee would yell at me."

"He'll want to show you more than a time step," said Flo significantly. "But if he suggests a party just tell him you're N.V.A.—Never Very Anxious."

"Hey, dumbbell," called Ann. "Stop gabbing and set your mind on food. We haven't got all day. His Majesty Lee awaits without."

"Without common sense or decency," added Flo. The two girls stalked from the room.

Peggy dashed some cold water over her face, pulled the slip-on dress over shoulders and wriggled until it lay in becoming lines about her body. Then she adjusted her hat at an attractive angle, added a speck more powder to her nose and was ready for the first rendezvous with Terry. He stood at the stage door waiting. The sun loaned a blinding sheen to his hair, and the purple stripe in his Style-Fit suit sent its wild cry of defiance into the summer air. Peggy gasped apprehensively. Terry was the Eighth Avenue sheik to perfection. From underneath the voluminous cuffs of his trousers peered patent leather shoes with cloth saddles.

"I hope I didn't keep you waiting long," she murmured. "Oh, it always takes a dame a long time," he said genially.

"How about it? All set?"

"Yes. We're not going far, are we? I'm nearly dead." She indicated her feet.

"Naw. Just over on Eighth Avenue. It's a nice little dump. We'll see the gang there."

Peggy had a presentiment of Ann's derisive laughter when the splendor of Terry Neill met her eyes, but she straightened her shoulders and merely said, "That'll be fine."

Terry fell into step. "This your first show?" he inquired. "Yes," she replied.

"You're not a New York girl, are you?" he persisted. "No. I come from New England."

"I thought so," Terry ejaculated. "I can spot that damn 'A' every time."

"Do you think New Englanders talk funny?" she demanded.

"A little. They sound like they was tryin' to be high hat, but I guess it's just their way. You know, 'aunt' for 'ant' and 'dahnse' for 'dance'—like a limey."

"But we're brought up that way," Peggy insisted. "I've always talked like that—with a broad 'a'."

"I bet New York seemed funny after them little jerk water towns up north," said Terry.

"Oh, we have cities in New England. New York isn't the only place in the world, you know."

"Ain't it?" said Terry in a tone of disbelief. "Well, it sure is in this racket, anyway. You gotta hang 'round New York if you wantta get a break in show business. Me an' my partner found that out. We tried all the cans around Chicago, booked all that western vaudeville time, but, hell, that don't get you no place, an' they always want you to work for coffee an' cake, so we come east and got in the merry merry."

"Oh, I didn't know you'd done specialty dancing," cried Peggy.

"Well, I don't flash much o' my stuff 'round the theatre," Terry explained. "Too many birds willin' to cop it. Boy, you work years gettin' a good routine an' then everybody uses it. Look at Bill Robinson. He done more to help the staircase business than all the house building booms combined."

They swung into the devastated area of Eighth Avenue. That No Man's Land lay fuming under the afternoon sun, its up-flung trenches alive with the workmen who were laboring on the new subway. Their feet sounded hollowly on the temporary wooden plank that served as a sidewalk.

"Ya heard the gag about the reason they was digging up Eighth Avenue? Because Albee's son lost his ball," said Terry, striving to add a note of levity to the conversation.

Peggy smiled vaguely. She was unfamiliar with Mr. Albee's reputation, having confined her attentions to the legitimate end of the show game. Ahead of them they discerned other members of the company plodding toward the small restaurant further down the Avenue.

"I do hope they'll keep me after the tryout weeks," said Peggy a bit worriedly.

"Don't worry, kid; with your looks an' personality they'll be giving you 'bits' before the show opens," consoled Terry. "An' I know-I seen Marsh watching you."

"I don't think Andy Lee likes me," argued Peggy. "His routines are *so* hard."

"Lissen; what Marsh says, *goes*. An' if he likes you, you'll be on that set if they have to wheel' you in. Andy Lee has plenty o' guys kidded, but not me. Why, that bozo was a vaudeville hoofer just like me—only he happened to get a lucky break."

They reached Ye Eate Shoppe, a small cubby hole wedged in between two second-hand clothes shops. Inside a vociferous mob was shouting for service. Peggy and Terry made an effective entrance. The gathering stared up at them and a conspiracy of nudges ran through the room. Peggy affected not to see this and they crowded into a space which was optimistically called "Table for Two."

"Now, lissen," Terry whispered. "You gimme the check an' we won't settle this till we get outside. I'll pay the cashier for both. You know, saves *your* feelin's; makes a girl look cheap to be seen payin' her own check."

Peggy nodded understandingly and they corralled the perspiring waitress. She was inclined toward short answers, as the sudden descent of theatrical hordes had done nothing to improve her temper.

"Well, sister," said Terry genially, "what've we got?"

She flashed him a withering glance. "Did ya ever try reading?" she snapped and poked a grease-stained menu in front of his nose.

"Nice lady-like little girl," Terry observed. "Just the thing to wrap up an' take home to that old-fashioned mother of yours."

"Yeah!'Well, if you were chasin' around waitin' on a bunch o' wise guys maybe you'd look pretty snappy wrapped up *yourself*," the lady assured him. "We ain't got pork, we ain't got roast beef, this is the last order of beef stew, whaddya want?" The sentences hurtled forth with machine gun rapidity. Terry blinked and cast a wary eye on the menu.

"I'll try corned beef hash," said Peggy weakly. The waitress nodded her consent.

"Gimme frankforts and beans," Terry commanded. "An' we ain't got a lot o' time, either."

The Amazon glared at him. "Say you, we didn't send out no engraved invitations askin' you to come here," she bawled. "We got feelings, too, so take it easy. Ya'll get your beans when they're good n' ready," and with that she flounced off.

"I told you this was a swell joint," grinned Terry. "She's so used to waitin' on Queen Marie that actors give her indigestion. They're such unimportant people."

"Huh!" came a distant voice. "Actors! Look out, or Equity'll be suin' you for libel!"

Terry disdained to answer the retort. "You know it's nice to meet a sweet girl like you for a change," he said earnestly. "I knew you was regular the minute I saw you."

"That clean mountain air look about me?" Peggy suggested.

"Don't try to kid me, sister, 'cause I wrote all the answers," Terry adjured her. "I mean what I say, you're like a breath of spring air after some of these dames."

"If you're going to compliment me like this I'll simply have to know your name."

"God damn, might know I'd forget it! I'm Terry Neill, used to be Towne and Neill, or Neill and Towne, I should say."

"I'm Peggy Sawyer." They bowed gravely to one another. Then Peggy asked, "Did you like vaudeville? Some friends of mine wanted me to go in an act but I preferred the chorus."

"Well, Peggy, you're better off," said Terry. "No you're set for the season, you can take buck lessons an' vocal lessons; matter of fact I'll be glad to learn ya plenty 'bout tap dancin' 'cause me an' Harry had some real swell routines. Ya gotta keep pluggin' in show business nowadays. The old stuff don't go. Why, look at the kids in the chorus, clever as the devil. Five years ago' any one of 'em could've been featured in the best musical show on Broadway and gotten away with it. Now they hoof in the merry merry. An' why? Because the competition is too much; all these guys like Chester Hale an' Allan K. Foster an' Russell Markert come along an' they expect a whole chorus to do what one specialty dancer done in the old days. An' so ya gotta keep practicin' an' learnin' new stuff—an' you gotta get class, too, because dancin' don't,; mean nothin' if you ain't got the showmanship to sell it. Look at the kid we got in our show;

prob'ly a lousy hundred a week is all she gets an' she can bend like a pretzel, while there's girls like Evelyn Law can't do half the stuff, but they pull down five hundred an' more 'cause they got the class. They can go out there, wear clothes, an' look like a million dollars."

The waitress interrupted this flow of divine wisdom. "Here's your beans," she snapped, and set the plate on the table. Terry saw immense frankfurters swimming in a tide of molasses, and from either side the beans swarming as though to annihilate the sausage by sheer force of numbers. Terry was not assailed by any delicate promptings. He attacked the food with fork, knife and spoon. Peggy watched him, amused, and faintly disgusted. In New England, nicety of table manners was inborn. When Terry finished his plate was a morass of thickish brown syrup which he promptly mopped up with a piece of bread. And yet there was something likeable about the boy sitting opposite her, an honesty that even the hardening years of pavement life could not entirely bury. Under different circumstances he might have been a splendid chap; the ingredients were there, friendliness, charm, good looks and a pleasure in helping other people. She decided that Terry wouldn't be such bad company after all, Flo and Ann to the contrary. Of course his manners were boorish and his taste in clothes pathetic, but these were surface faults and once remedied she felt that Terry would present a most admirable front. He was smiling at her now. She flushed slightly, as she realized how absorbed she had been.

"Givin' me the double O, are ya, kid?" he jeered. "Well, I guess I'm one o' those rough diamonds they talk about, but b'lieve me, I can be okay with reg'lar folks."

"You've been awfully nice to me," said Peggy warmly.

"Aw, that ain't half," he replied with a grandiloquent gesture. "When we come back from the outta town break-in I'm goin' to drag ya 'round to some real classy joints."

"By that time you'll be rushing some other girl," she taunted, with the time-honored instinct to flirt with this too willing male. He leapt to the bait. "Any time, sister, any time," he scoffed. "I don't mess around wit' ev'rybody, you know. I'm particular. Why, I could be goin' with a real vaudeville *headliner* now if I wanted, but, hell, I can't put up with these girls who gotta be babied ev'ry minute. I like 'em hard to get; you know, real women—like—like—well, like you."

"Anything else?" piped the waitress, eyeing him balefully.

"We'd better hurry," said Peggy in a flutter of anxiety. "Most everyone's gone and I've got to have my practice clothes on in twenty minutes. There isn't time for dessert."

"Leave me finish this cup o' coffee an' I'll be right with you," Terry agreed. "Give us our checks, will ya, sister?"

The waitress flung down the bits of pasteboard.

"An' I hope all your children are theme song writers," cried Terry. He gulped down the remaining portion of coffee und swaggered to the cashier's desk. Peggy was close at his heels, consulting the watch on her wrist.

"Now take it easy," he reminded Peggy. "You can settle this with me later." He put the money down on the counter, received his change, and, complete with toothpick, escorted Peggy from the restaurant.

11

The brief intermission for lunch was hailed gratefully by the hard working principals of Pretty Lady. They as well as the chorus had labored unflaggingly through the heat of the morning and a temporary respite was more than welcome. Andy Lee, who had been watching the progress of the book rehearsal after permitting the chorus to leave, hastened back stage once more and found himself face to face with Lorraine Fleming. She had obviously been lying in wait, eager to snare him.

Her hands fluttered reproachfully. "Hello, big boy," she whispered. "I thought you'd forgotten me." She laid her head against his shoulder.

Andy cast a swiftly apprehensive glance into the dark well of the auditorium. "Take it easy, babe," he entreated. "The wife said she might stop by this noon. We gotta cancel that luncheon date."

"Oh, and I didn't bring a cent downtown with me," pouted Lorraine.

"Well, for God's sake take this," Andy urged, shoving a five dollar bill into her receptive palm.

"And I simply must stop for that coat at Sak's. They said they wouldn't hold it another day."

"How much is it?" groaned Andy, counting the sheaf of money in his wallet.

"Eighty-five dollars, Andy. It's a real bargain," Lorraine's voice dripped honey.

"Take this hundred and beat it. I haven't got time to talk with you now," said Andy. "And, Lorraine, cut out gabbing to the girls, will you? I tell ya we gotta be careful."

Lorraine's eyes opened wide in protest. "Why, Andy, I haven't said a word," she protested. "It must be one of those sluts in the dressing room. They looked over my shoulder when I was copying down your phone number in my note book. They haven't any sense of honor."

"You know if Amy gets wise there'll be hell to pay," Andy cautioned her.

"Don't worry. I'm used to handling wives," Lorraine promised him. Well, thanks for the money, old darling. It's just a loan, you know. I'll pay it back as soon as we're on salary."

"Well, I won't hold my breath till I get it," said Andy.

Lorraine stiffened. "I hope you don't think that I'm the kind of a girl who takes money from men without paying it back," she snapped. "I've always prided myself on never allowing a debt to stand."

"Baby, just be good to me, and I'll be the one who owes money," whispered Andy.

She patted his hand. "Sweet boy," she cooed.

From the back of the theatre a musical voice trilled, "Oh, there you are, Andy, darling. I can't see a *thing* in this darkness."

Lorraine slithered away and Andy scanned the darkened reaches of the auditorium.

"Hello, Amy," he called. "Wait out front. I'll be right with you." He picked up his hat from the stage manager's table in the wings and hastened through the small door which led from back stage, past the boxes to the theatre.

Amy looked charming; even her spouse unwillingly granted that. She was attired in cool flowing green that set off beautifully the red in her hair. Sometimes he apostrophized himself as a fool for yielding to the blandishments of other women when the law bound him to one so attractive as Amy. It was the curse of a fickle nature, and the material cost was high.

Amy bestowed a wifely kiss on Andy's cheek. "I couldn't find you anywhere," she confessed. "And then I saw Lorraine Fleming so I *knew* you must be there."

Andy winced. "I was just explaining an entrance to Lorraine," he said.   :j'

"I should think she'd need a good exit," Amy commented.

"She's sort of dumb about picking up her cues," Andy continued, ignoring the last thrust.

"Yes, I noticed that," rejoined Amy. "You gave her the 'go' signal about five minutes before she had sense enough to beat it. What was it you handed her?"

"Oh, just the address of a hat shop," answered Andy guilelessly. "She liked the hat you were wearing last week when we met her on the avenue and I told her I'd find out the name of the place."

"You must have looked in that crystal of yours, sweetheart, murmured Amy, "for I'm sure I never told you where bought it."

They crossed the deserted lobby and entered Forty-Fifth Street. Automatically their feet turned toward the Forty-Sixth Street Chop House, where the more important members of the *Pretty Lady* company were gathered for luncheon. Here were congregated the juveniles, prima donnas, ingénues, specialty dancers of the vast machine—and, especially, the comedians. There is a pretty legend concerning these last-named gentry—far from being the boisterous creatures of their stage environment one finds them morose beings whose lives have been blighted; the inevitable Pagliacci motif. It is touching, this legend, and the publicity manager of any production forces it down the throat of the gullible press at least once during the existence of the show. As a matter of fact, no one is more unrelentingly humorous than the Broadway comedian, particularly the younger of the species. Mellower artists may be content to rest on their laurels, but the youthful comic is in a perpetual lather, saying or doing that which will bring shrieks of merriment from his little circle. Remove the comedian from behind the footlights and the only obvious change is a more bawdy trend in the stories he tells. But the wisecracks go on, maddeningly, eternally. Many a thespian of no particular literary aptitude has been discovered perusing *Gray's Elegy* after a session with one of these Forty-Second Street pantaloons. And in the Forty-Sixth Street Chop House the loud and strident voices of the funny men drowned all the lesser chatter.

Amy paused a moment at the door before entering. She had been considering her husband's voluble excuses and felt called upon to deliver a subtle warning. "I'm so glad it wasn't money you gave Lorraine, dear," she smiled, "because I'll need lots this afternoon. Madame Frances is in a dither about that new evening dress and I've simply got to pay her."

Andy experienced a chill of warning. "More gowns?" he cried. "Hell, Amy, you had two last week that set me back five hundred bucks. I'm not the U.S. mint, you know."

"A girl has to do something for amusement when she's left alone all the time," sulked Amy. "And when you consider how much I know you're getting off very cheap."

Andy lost his temper. "I'll be damned if I'll stand for this blackmail," he shouted.

"Ssh!" cautioned Amy. "People'll hear you. There's not much you can do about it. People are so nasty about the Mann act. And, anyhow, you can't expect to run a harem without paying a luxury tax."

They turned into the Chop House and all controversy ceased. Familiar voices greeted them from all sides and they were once more the ideal couple. The tables were filled, but Amy's keen eye caught sight of two vacancies at the one occupied by Dorothy Brock and John Phillips.

"Let's go sit with Dorothy," she suggested. Andy mistrusted her Giaconda smile but suffered himself to be led in that direction.

Phillips rose to his feet. "We thought we'd sit here if you didn't mind," gushed Amy. Phillips protested extravagantly that it was a most desirable arrangement. Dorothy merely looked cool and rather triumphant. Andy, who sensed the antagonism between the two ladies, was at a loss to account for Dorothy's all-conquering air. From the way Amy's eyes narrowed he knew that she was raging inwardly.

"Try the chicken," Dorothy suggested when they had settled themselves. "It's gorgeous. That's a lovely dress, Amy; it goes so well with your red hair. It's funny, darling, I never realized it was quite that shade."

"Oh, yes," responded Amy. "Don't you remember that time you had yours dyed taffy color and wanted me to go with you and I said that this shade of auburn would do me quite nicely?"

"I suppose the sun *does* touch it up a bit," Dorothy admitted "But, anyhow, the vacation's done you loads of good. I've never seen her looking so young before, Andy."

"Young," Amy mourned. "Do you realize that ten whole months have passed since the last time we went out together, Dot? That was at your birthday party, you know; the time someone stuck thirty-two candles on the cake, just for a joke, of course."

The arrival of the waiter brought a cessation of hostilities. Amy decided to try the chicken. "Although it might give you ptomaine poisoning," said Dorothy.

"No, dear, no such luck; my digestion's cast iron," Amy comforted her. John Phillips began to look acutely uncomfortable. Andy chose to disregard the little tiff entirely.

"How do you like the show so far?" asked Amy. "Andy says you have a fine part."

"Oh, it's good enough," returned Dorothy. "Of course it will be better once I can get my own personality into it. You don't know how lucky you were to marry a rich man, dear. The things they expect you to do to be a star nowadays! It takes real genius."

"Yes, you certainly have to give everything," Amy agreed.

"Isn't it terrible? That's why I say you folks who began years ago were fortunate, because you made your reputation before they started demanding so much from their stars."

"Oh, darling, you don't know the half of it," said Dorothy. "You went to married life clean from the chorus without experiencing any of the heartaches we artists go through. But at that you were wise. Any woman who realizes her limitations will always get ahead."

"Don't you think we'd better get back early and run over the duet, Dorothy?" interposed John Phillips. "The harmony in the last half of the chorus is pretty ragged."

"Two more weeks for that, angel," said Dorothy. "And Mr. Lee will keep us hours too long as it is. You're the most conscientious slave driver I've ever met, Andy."

"The thought of millinery bills is in front of my eyes," said Andy spitefully.

"Amy, don't tell me you're *extravagant!*" cried Dorothy. "And here's your poor husband struggling to bring home the bacon."

"No, dear, not exactly," Amy corrected. "My money just goes into the P.O.N.W. fund—Protection of Neglected Wives. You see Andy comes home nights so seldom that I nearly shot him once thinking he was a burglar. And things like that are apt to make a girl a widow so that she's got to have a little laid by."

"You never know who will get shot nowadays," parried Dorothy. "I heard last evening that a certain married lady may get pushed into oblivion any moment if she doesn't stop trying to run around with another lady's boy friend."

"Really!" said Amy. "How melodramatic! But then you know how married ladies are these days, dear, always capable and able to take care of themselves. I'd place my bets on the married ones any time."

The two ladies were becoming unwise. Both John Phillips and Andy felt the introduction of a personal note into discussion. Imminent revelations were averted by the timely advent of the chicken. In the breathing spell both Andy and Dorothy recognized the wisdom of silence, now that mutual threats had been exchanged. The talk turned to the music, the show and flowed along harmlessly enough. Only Andy was strangely distant. Dorothy's words renewed his perplexity at Amy's unexplained absences. Somehow he hadn't given her credit for the nerve to undertake a clandestine romance but the sharp clash of words just passed could have meant nothing else. Not jealousy, but a feeling of relief smote Andy's breast. To get something on the chaste and circumspect Amy had been the dream of his life during the last few months. It meant a considerable lessening of the bonds which chafed him. He could not shake off the yoke entirely, for the damnable facts surrounding the case of the young girl were too sickening, but if Amy were confronted with unmistakable proofs of her own guilt their roles might be reversed.

Andy finished his meal in high spirits. Amy watched him with some misgiving. In the spiteful exchange of wit with Dorothy she had failed to consider Andy's sharp ears. For the gratification of her own dislike she had endangered her little affair with Pat. Andy's smirk boded no good. She cursed herself for a consummate ass and jabbed viciously at the remaining portion of chicken on her plate.

"A meal sure does a fellow good," glowed Andy. "Hurry up with that demitasse, hon. I feel good-natured this afternoon. How about treating my little girl friend to a coupla tickets for the *Follies* matinee? You haven't seen the show yet. You can take Desiree along."

Amy fumed but saw that the wiser course lay in acquiescence. And Andy meant to pay for the dresses so she needn't trouble herself on that score. Dorothy opened her jeweled powder compact and applied new lipstick. John Phillips, still harassed, picked up the checks, and they departed in a barrage of sweet good-bys. In the confusion, poor Phillips was saddled with the entire bill.

Amy faced her husband. "Andy, you're so sweet not to fuss about those dresses—I really need them," she cooed.

"I guess I can afford to be generous," he replied. "Looks like a good time ahead."

"You mean for the show?" she questioned with deliberate obtuseness.

"For the show, and other things," he replied. "It's funny how women will ruin a perfectly good graft just to score a point on someone they don't like."

"But, sweet, when a woman holds the whip hand she can afford to be reckless," Amy indicated.

"Well, one poison stops another so I guess one adultery... well, honors are even."

Amy rose. "Do get those seats," she begged. "I'm dying to see the *Follies!*"

12

At two o'clock on the same afternoon an unforeseen event occurred in the life of Pat Denning. He lay stretched on the divan in his living room, perusing the theatrical column of the *World* with little interest, when the telephone bell rang. Yawning, he got to his feet and went. over to the instrument. A worried and unmistakably Semitic voice asked for Mr. Pat Denning. On being reassured that this was the gentleman in person, the caller revealed himself as Conway Clarges (né Moe Blatt), theatrical representative. From time to time Mr. Clarges-Blatt had proffered Pat engagements which were a financial prop in those lean weeks between affairs. At the moment Pat was not interested, for the combined support of Amy Lee and Dorothy Brock made his lot comfortable enough; but one should have an eye to the future and so Pat agreed to present himself at Mr. Clarges' offices within the hour.

He dressed with meticulous care, squandered twenty-five cents on a carnation for his buttonhole, and presented a radiant figure when, forty-five minutes later, he opened the door to Conway Clarges' outer office. It is one of the rules of show business to appear expensively clad no matter what one's financial standing is. Only the most independent performers can afford to look dowdy. For the rest, producers demand sartorial perfection of the actors they employ. One may deny oneself diversion, but a modish wardrobe is *de rigueur*.

Pat lounged up to the wooden railing behind which a very blonde young lady sat intent upon her typing.

"Mr. Clarges?" he inquired.

The divinity glanced up with that haughty abstraction which is reserved by stenographers for all job hunters. "Who's calling?" she demanded.

"Tell him Mr. Denning's here. Your office called me at my home just about a half hour ago."

The lady thawed perceptibly. "Oh, yes, Mr. Denning. Sit down, won't you? Mr. Clarges is in conference just now but he wants to see you. He won't be more than ten minutes."

She indicated a chair and followed his tall figure with a glance of unconcealed admiration. In this respect she had the better of her sister Frieda, she reflected. Frieda was employed by a vaudeville agency and had to put up with a succession of ham actors whose loud clothes and unspeakable manners offended Frieda's delicate sensibilities. "And one thing, the men that come in here have class," exulted Miss Elsie Levey.

Pat seated himself and studied the other occupants of Mr. Clarges' office. He caught the suggestion of a smile on one face, looked closer, and recognized Geoffrey Waring, dressing room companion of an ill-fated dramatic production which had been launched two seasons ago. Waring crossed to Pat's side and the two men shook hands.

"Anything new?" Pat inquired.

Waring shook his head. "Same old story. They'll be charging me rent in this office. It looks like a tough season."

"It's the movies," said Pat, presenting the actor's familiar alibi.

"I made a test for Famous Players the other day," Waring observed. "Hope to God it comes out well because I'm sick of this racket. I prefer shame in Hollywood to artistic starvation in the fast and furious Forties. Cigarette?"

No smoking here, please," Miss Levey interrupted crisply.

Waring retired his case. "Did Clarges send for you about this new Morgan production?" he questioned.

I don't know," Pat replied. "I just got a call to come down here. What's the new piece? One-set melodrama, I suppose. That's about Morgan's speed."

As a matter of fact he's going in for bigger and better things," said Waring.

Oh, a circus!" suggested Pat ironically.

Nope. High class British drawing room drama. And at least two settings are mentioned in the bond."

"Good God! He must have something on Cain's warehouse!" cried Pat. "But how in the name of heaven did he choke down all that British repartee?"

"Some 'yes' man told him the story in one syllable words, explained Waring.

"Have they got anybody for it so far?" Pat inquired.

"Yes. Lionel Blake and Daisy Heming. And Bob Scarborough's directing."

Pat whistled. "Morgan must be shuffling the horses," he vowed. "Why, that's a combination to turn old Belasco green with envy."

"I hear there's plenty of smart talk. Some good old melodrama gone Lonsdale. Morgan wouldn't touch a thing unless it had one murder."

"I wonder where he got the money," murmured Pat.

"Don't know; but Equity says it's okay. I stopped in there on my way down. Little precaution I always take with these fly-by-night outfits."

"Did he settle up those checks for his last flop?" asked Pat.

"Every penny. They gave me a bright fatherly smile at Equity and said, 'Go to it,' " Waring declared.

"Sounds good," Pat admitted. "And I've been laying off a hell of a long time."

"How do you do it?" Waring demanded. "You look as well dressed as an Aarons and Freedley chorus boy." "Technique, my boy, technique," Pat assured him grandly.

"How are all your women?"

"Well, the wife is raising hell because I can't dig up any alimony, but I'm officially bankrupt so there's nothing she can do about it. Meanwhile I got in with a Village gang and have two or three minor affairs on the fire at the present moment."

"The Village? God deliver me from those washouts," grimaced Pat.

"Oh, this is quite on the level. You won't find a starched-collar lady among them and every girl there thinks a bunch of violets is the nicest present for a boy to bring his girl friend. These aren't sophisticates, young feller, they're naturalists."

"Meaning—?" Pat prompted.

"Home town folks—corn fed idealists. Nice people want to express themselves."

"It sounds different. How about inviting me down there?"

"With your Park Avenue urbanity? Not a chance, Pat. I want an unchallenged field."

"You know I never mix business with pleasure. And at the moment I have two propositions that are keeping pretty close tabs on me," Pat told him. "I'd relish a little bucolic diversion. Say when."

"Come on down with me tonight then. And bring your own. We're all poor and haven't the price of a quart between us so all contributions are most gratefully received."

"I'll bring two quarts as initiation fee," Pat promised. "Good enough. We can rustle up the tumblers and I'll cadge cracked ice and ginger ale out of the Italian woman on the corner. But be prepared for the truth about things. You know, 'Life is real, life is earnest,' and all that."

"I understand. Art with a capital 'F'. Don't worry, I shan't crack a smile," Pat assured him. "I may even indulge in philosophy myself. I've been told there are the makings of a good soap box patriot in me."

"One girl plays marvelously. Strictly modern stuff, of course. She'll try to convince you Mr. Gershwin copped his *Rhapsody* from Debussy's *Cathedral under the Sea*, but once that's off her chest you're in for a real treat."

"Good music, good liquor—your little proposition is developing," said Pat.

"You'll be entertained. And no wisecracks, mind you. There are a couple of young kids who haven't been brought out yet and far be it from me to tell them what's wrong. They just think they're artistic and different. So leave 'em alone. They'll learn soon enough."

Miss Levey called, "Mr. Denning, won't you go inside, please?"

"I'll meet you here in ten minutes," said Pat. "Don't go 'way, because we'll slip over to my place and murder a couple of cocktails. There's fire water just fresh and bubbling from some old darling's private yacht."

Waring nodded assent.

Pat passed through the gate and entered Clarges' office. He found the jovial East Sider expansive in welcome. "Vell, vell, Pat!" Mr. Clarges exulted. "T'enk God, I found you. Look at dis—swellest part ever—and money!" His eyes sought the ceiling in rapture.

When Mr. Clarges' exuberance had diminished somewhat Pat glanced over the script of the new play and found it vastly to his liking. He appreciated Clarges' subtle compliment in showing him the piece. An agent extended that courtesy only to his most valued players.

Pat pursed his lips and mentioned a staggering salary. Mr. Clarges glared protest. Pat graciously listened to compromise and eventually the matter rested at one hundred and fifty dollars a week. "An' only t'ree weeks of rehearsal," beamed Mr. Clarges. "Dis is soft! Dis is soft!"

Pat emerged from Clarges' sanctuary well satisfied. Now he could view the temperamental rantings of his two lady loves as inconsequential. If either proved too tyrannical he would bid a complacent adieu and retire to the dignity of his self-earned income.

Outside Waring still cooled his heels. "Any luck?" he enquired.

"All set," said Pat. "And there's a nice bit for you. Lots of luck." He gave Geoffrey a friendly pat on the shoulder.

Mr. Waring was favored of the gods that afternoon, so half an hour later the two men left the Titus Building and ventured into the afternoon tide of Broadway.

"I'm three blocks from here," said Pat. "Let's hike over and take up that option on the cocktails."

Waring was agreeable and the two men set out at a brisk pace. Their progress was halted innumerable times by curious acquaintances who wanted to know what the hell their smiling demeanor meant. When it was explained that both Pat and Geoffrey had secured engagements these acquaintances were properly awed and hastened away to share their envy with other friends while Pat and Geoffrey continued their triumphal stroll.

They arrived at Pat's apartment a quarter of an hour later, climbed the three flights of stairs which were a constant source of embarrassment to Mr. Denning and flung themselves into the nearest easy chairs to cool off.

"I can't afford a man," Pat apologized, "so we'll do the honors ourselves. That's the hell of being poor."

Waring cast an envious eye about the apartment. "Poor? You and Peggy Joyce," he sneered. "No kidding, Pat, you're the marvel of the century. And the greatest wonder is how that old S.A. holds out indefinitely. The Heavenly Father put the stuff in you all right."

"And how Adam's rib is taking it out," Pat moaned. "In three more seasons I'm retiring to Persia and taking up the old family job of Grand Eunuch."

"I suppose you're still favoring the C.O.D. method?", asked Waring, with a nod toward the lavish furnishings. "No checkee—no shirtee—"

Pat nodded. He had been mixing drinks and now presented n glass to Waring. "Try this, old man," he said. "It's an old Spanish recipe."

Waring sipped the drink appreciatively and smacked his lips. "Nectar!" he cried ecstatically.

Pat nodded. "That's how I got it!" he replied. "Necked her plenty and ye good old vintage was forthcoming."

Waring noted the complete absence of photographs in the apartment and commented on the fact. "All under lock and key," Pat explained. "I file 'em away and when it's time for an appointment the right picture comes out—not before." Waring was impressed at his friend's shrewdness.

"You know, this old dame was a sport," Pat continued. "Liquor like that set her back plenty! Have another?"

Waring's glass was proffered with alacrity.

In fifteen minutes they agreed they were charming fellows, deserving of the finest gifts which life bestows. The gin diminished alarmingly. Pat waxed enthusiastic on the subject of his newest amours, but stubbornly refused to reveal their names though submitted to an artful inquisition by his friend. He was a canny person who had learned the value of secrecy through long and bitter years of servitude to women. So engrossed were they in this little discussion they failed to hear the energetic peal of the doorbell. It shrilled again and again, cutting knife-like through the beautiful oblivion which they had built about themselves. Shrewish and nagging the ringing continued until Pat shouted in exasperation, "What the hell is that?"

"Sounds like a bell," said Waring helpfully.

"Course it's a bell-front door bell, but damn it, why's anybody wanna ring it now?"

"Perhaps they want to get in," Waring suggested.

"Bright boy!" cheered Pat. "Per'aps they want to get in—per'aps they want to get in," he mimicked Waring's voice. "The question is—shall we or shall we not let them in. How 'bout it?"

"It's your house," said Waring, disavowing all responsibility.

They pondered a moment. "Who is it?" Waring asked.

"My dear, dear chap, I'm not Princess Wahletka; I cannot prognosticate without inquiring, and to inquire would reveal my presence hereabouts. Hereabouts!" he repeated, charmed at the sound of the word.

"It might be a fire, an' they're firemen!" said Waring.

"Nope. We'd smell smoke. Mos' likely it's women."

"You damned old egotist," cried Waring.

"Course it's women. Who else would call? One of my big moments is doing a little checking up."

Someone pounded on the panel of the door in front them. "Ssh," hissed Pat, raising an unsteady finger to lips. "The enemy are upon us."

"Let me in!" screeched a woman's voice. "I know you're home, Pat Denning. If you don't, I'll kick the door down."

Pat was thoroughly alarmed. "You'll excuse me, old man, won't you? I'll have to settle this right away. Can't you go take a shower or something?"

"I think I'd better leave through the back way," Waring declared, picking up his hat. "She might start flourishing guns."

"Nonsense, nonsense, nonsense! My women don't own such weapons. Be a good chap and see me through."

"Right! But, my God, these women scare me!"

"Tell that hussy to stop talking bass!" screamed the invisible lady rattling the door knob. "She'll tear something she can't sew. Nobody's fooling me!"

Pat shoved the frightened Geoffrey inside the bathroom and turned the key on the outside. Then he hastily tidied the living room, lit a cigarette, assumed what he fervently prayed was an air of nonchalance and stumbled to the door which was being subjected to a shower of blows by his indignant caller. He opened the door with an abrupt jerk and was nearly bowled over as Amy rushed in, screaming at the top of her lungs.

"What in God's name got into you?" he shouted angrily. "Don't take that tone to me, you big bully. Just because I caught you in the act, you're trying to scare me."

"Amy, I swear—" He put his arms about her.

She gave him an energetic shove. "My God, what a breath. You're cockeyed. And it smells like rotten liquor, too. I suppose *she* gave it to you."

"Amy—I give you my word there's no lady in this apartment," said Pat, clutching at her sleeve.

"Stop it! Save that story for the Uncle Wiggly hour. I know what I know. That trollop's hiding in the bathroom right now."

"Darling, she isn't a trollop in there!" objected Pat. "She's a he."

"Don't lie to me," said Amy in tragic scorn. "I suppose she's struggling into her step-ins right now. Well, this is the show down. Is it me or that creature in there?" She faced Pat defiantly.

Pat fumed. "You're an undignified and disgrace— disgraceful little baggage," he reproached her. "I tell you this apartment is untainted by femin—femin—by female presence."

Amy scurried across the room and assailed the bathroom door. "Come out, you rat," she challenged. "Come out and I'll make a character actress outta ya."

"Won't you please try next door?" pleaded Waring from the bath. "The lady in here is very low and mus' have abs'lute quiet.

Amy staggered in amazement. "It's a man," she cried. "A man!"

Pat swelled confidently. "Just as I said, m'dear," he triumphed. "A *man*!"

"What's a man doing locked in the bathroom?" Amy demanded.

"It's the one spot where a man has a *right* to expect privacy," Pat maintained.

Amy wavered. "Well—" she began. "I—"

But by now Pat Denning was aroused. Many words which he had been saving for just such a scene welled in his throat. At that moment Amy was the most hated person on earth

"You're an evil, malicious female!" he barked, picking up a book from the table and pounding it against a chair to emphasize his words. "You're a lady wolf in cheap clothing. Go 'way. Don't bother me. I'm through! G'wan back to your husban'. And don't bring your homework to the Pat Denning Finishing School for Young Ladies because, s'far as I'm concerned, you're graduated."

A sudden notion struck him. As Amy stiffened with rage and prepared to stamp her way out of his life he shouted,' "Furthermore, here's a graduation present from me to you with much love." He flung the book at her back and stamped into the bedroom.

Sobbing, Amy bent down to pick up the volume. Then she ran down the stairs and out of the house. Once outside, she glanced at the book and discarded it with a vindictive snort. It was entitled *Old Greek Lays*.

13

When a few moments had passed pat began to repent the spectacular interlude. It had been very fine standing up there telling Amy to go to the devil, but that meant a little more scrimping and hoarding, the sort of thing he abominated. And it left his yearning for luxury to the tender mercies of Dorothy Brock who stammered indecencies in his ear with all the shyness of a dewy-eyed virgin. Amy, at least, was forthright; she had her passion and put it away from her. While indulging she became the savage animal, but with surfeit all the hardness of twenty-three New York summers returned to her. Not so with Dorothy. She contrived to lend the flavor of seduction to each yielding so that she was able to blush in pretty confusion and give to Pat the irritating impression of having violated a maiden.

"It takes a certain kind of genius to face the ultimate moment with a look of frozen wonderment when you've been at it ten years," Pat mused. "Oh, well; dear God make the new play a success so that I can lose those Seventh Commandment Bloo-hoo-hoos." His voice rose in an eerie wail.

Waring entered from the bath refreshed and a bit more coherent now that he had been allowed to soak under the shower.

His glance was still a bit bleary, however, and was plainly in terror of the return of Amy, smiting out vengeance.

"I say," he gulped. "Now I know what they mean when they talk about the wages of sin. What pleasant little bird of passage you attract to your nest, Sir Lancelot."

"Shut up. I've got to bathe and shave if I'm going to your damned party," snarled Pat. "You'll find fruit and soda biscuits on the table if you're hungry."

"Hungry? Good God!" cried Waring with a snort of disgust. "I think I shall take my wreath of daisies and shepherd crook and hie me back to the flock."

"You'll jolly well stay here," Pat commanded him. "Now that you've crocked up my arrangement with the light of fading years at least have the decency to see me through this party tonight."

"You don't suppose her husband would be inspired to pay a social call, do you?" Waring quavered. "Because if there's any possibility of that I shall take the well known wings of the morning."

"Her husband is probably engaged in pursuits of his own," said Pat. "So there's nothing to do but eat soda biscuits and pray that I don't cut my chin. You don't want to introduce a hacked and bloody man as the comrade of your drinking sprees."

"Can't you wear a beard and say you're in training for Morris Gest?" said Waring.

"A beard doesn't give me an aesthetic look. I look merely poverty stricken, which is too damn near the truth of matter to be comforting."

"Some girls like beards," Waring intoned.

"You're still tight," yelled Pat. "Go munch soda crackers and amuse yourself by spitting out apple seeds." He turned the nickel handle of the shower and a needle-like spray fell hissing into the bathtub. "God, that sounds good." He stripped off his clothes, left them in a tumbled heap on the floor and stepped into the tub. "This'll make a new man out of me."

"Three cheers for the new man," cheered Waring feebly. "Nice to meet strange people." He regarded the soda crackers with aversion, likewise the fruit. There remained nothing but the array of glasses on the sideboard. The faint shimmer of the glass held him in a vise. He saw such cool and lovely depths in which one could lose oneself. He investigated the bottle, examined the cocktail shaker, and ended by mixing himself another drink. This was weak-willed and he castigated himself firmly, in fact so firmly that he felt sorry for himself and had to take a second drink to cheer up.

Pat stepped out of his bath and found Waring still lingering among the cocktails. The stinging water had cleared his head and he delivered to his dejected companion a ringing lecture on the evils of drink. Waring vowed never again to look upon the wine while it was red.

"And get in there and brush up," Pat finished. "You look like a refugee—or a Communist—or an actor—or something poisonous. You'll find a variety of combs and brushes on the shelf, also aspirin. I'll fix some black coffee because I see that black coffee will play the role of ministering angel tonight."

Waring fairly blubbered his thanks and tumbled into the bathroom from which he returned polished and gleaming. Pat eyed him with approval. "You're good-looking, you know," he asserted. "It's too bad you haven't the stamina for my racket. We'd make a great team."

With the memory of Amy Lee still vivid, Waring shuddered. "No thanks, Pat, I'll follow that still small voice conscience," he answered. "It's better than the wild yell of vice that went surging around here this afternoon."

Pat swallowed his coffee. "That was an exception," he explained. "If I hadn't been drunk the lady would still love me.

But, to hell with her! It does a man good to be his own boss once in a while."

"Do you think we'll get out before the other one turns up?" asked Waring fearfully.

"My second flame will not flare up this evening," said Pat. "Thank God for that, because I've got an uncontrollable yen to stroll through green fields and pick strawberries with a girl whose lips are cool as the dew and whose eyes shine into mine with the light of complete innocence."

"Another good subtitle writer gone wrong," moaned Waring. "You won't find the green fields or the strawberries in the Village, but there's just oodles and oodles of innocence.",

"On to the oodles, then," cried Pat happily. "How much liquor do we want?"

"Oh, enough to make the back yard palatable," Waring hazarded.

"Roughly three quarts," Pat decided. "Where's the Scotch?"

They left the apartment with bulging hip pockets an summoned a cab. Waring gave the driver an address near' Sheridan Square and they rolled toward Fifth Avenue through. a jam of theatre-bound vehicles.

"Your public and mine," Pat philosophized. "Damn the lousy little souls! It's because they won't appreciate my art that I am forced to turn into such shameful byways to earn a living."

"Just the same, it will seem good to be looking out into their faces again," Waring breathed. "I'm damned sick of the pictures that hang on the walls in the agents' offices."

"Be independent like me," Pat advised. "I let 'em come after me. An agent hates to give employment to anyone who needs it. That goes against his grain. But cultivate an air of indifference and he's on your neck in no time."

The taxi shot under the Sixth Avenue El. Crowds moved along the pavement, their drabness accentuated by the yellow blear of light which came streaking from shop windows. Warm sickly odors embraced the air and the heat of the day still lingered over the city blocks. Cheapness, blatancy and glare melting into a gaudy kaleidoscope—that was Sixth Avenue. Overhead the elevated trains hurtled past, stabbing the night with ominous thunder. Children cried, taxi drivers cursed, shop owners hawked their wares, throngs gathered before the soft drink emporiums, leaning elbows on the sticky counters while they bellowed at the harassed clerks who strove to wait on them. The taxi sped along the gloomy stretch of the avenue, past the caldron of Thirty-Fourth Street and into the shabby neighborhood south of the Macy-Gimbel line.

"I wish he'd taken Fifth Avenue," grumbled Pat. "This damn street is so depressing. Look at 'em, Jeff—the motley—the backbone of ye great American People grubbing among their reeking alleyways. Of such is the Kingdom of Heaven."

They lurched through the twisting labyrinth of Greenwich Village. From out the grime and squalor peered an occasional doorway of great beauty, relic of the aristocracy which once had walked about these streets. Their destination was a gloomy-appearing structure squeezed in between two warehouses which pressed hard on either side. Under their shadow the house seemed to be fighting for existence, gasping though throttled by the bulk of its neighbors.

"Well, here we are," said Waring superfluously.

Pat looked about with misgivings. "Thank God we brought that extra quart," he muttered.

"It's not bad inside," Waring apologized. "The kids have fixed things up rather nicely."

They paid the driver and mounted the ancient staircase to the front door. From far above the lights shone down into the stair well, lighting their path. The air was heavy with the smell of recently cooked meals.

"It's an Alpine climb so you'd better start yodeling to up your courage," Waring advised.

Pat groaned but set out following Geoffrey's lead. "Maida's an amazing youngster," Waring confided. "Believe it or not she harks back to a ducking in the best Baptist manner, to say nothing of numerous maiden aunts whose cold exteriors must certainly have cloaked a multitude of sins."

"God, what a stink!" Pat groaned. "Wops, I suppose."

"Don't be finicky, old son. What would the Village be without smells? Incidentally, Tony, on the next floor, brews a swell shot of hooch. Reasonable, too. If I weren't in such gilt-edged company I'd stop in for a few moments on my way up. But not with private stock such as yours to be had."

"Jeff, is this what virtue does for a guy?" asked Pat plaintively, pausing on the third landing to catch his breath.

They resumed the ascent, passed the fourth landing, impenetrable gloom still loomed above. From behind closed doors issued the wailing of children or shrill morsels of conversation mounting in truly Latin crescendo.

"You'll be surprised to find how easily goodness rests on their shoulders," said Jeff. "Honestly, they make fair play and ambition sound like the real stuff. Here we are!"

He paused before a door which fronted the flight of stairs. Pat heard overtones of conversation and piano playing.

"Now I'm in for it," he thought. Jeff rapped loudly with his knuckles. There was no appreciable lessening of the din, but presently the door opened and a girl of perhaps twenty-three stood facing them. She was utterly commonplace; her clothes, her hair, even her good looks were damned by a certain lack of distinction that is achieved by so many wholesome people. She gave Jeff a welcoming grin, stretched her hand in greeting to Pat and invited them both to enter. Pat found himself in a narrow box-like partition that was probably known as the front hall. The piano player's music became distinguishable; she was playing the waltz motif of *Three Shades of Blue*.

"Quite a gang," said Waring. "You'd better render thanks unto little Caesar here. I've brought beaucoup firewater."

The girl, Maida, patted his cheek. "Angel!"

"Not me," Jeff protested. They walked into the over-crowded, smoke-enshrouded living room. "Hey, everyone," Jeff shouted. "Come meet the Good Provider."

The merrymakers forsook their pursuits of the moment to crowd about Pat and Waring. When explanations were achieved and introductions passed around Pat was hailed as a jolly sport and assigned the next dance with Millicent, a pretty blonde who, Maida explained, was "the Edna St Vincent Millay of our humble group." Most assuredly there was poetry in Millicent's feet; she trod the floor with moonbeam lightness and, dancing with her, Pat discovered that the chafing confines of the room were nonexistent, they were immortals blazing a pathway to the stars.

"You're new," said Millicent. "I saw you come in Geoffrey Waring and guessed that Jeff had cornered more heavy sugar. Don't you like the sensation of feeding the multitude?"

"That good old 'more blessed to give than to receive' sensation," laughed Pat. "I had no idea you were like this. I pictured a glum-looking group, with scrawny necks and weird vocabularies, sitting in the candlelight while some pale young man read poetry."

"We're too intelligent for that," contradicted Millicent. "Of course, you'll find a few tremendous minds peering over number thirteen collars but, thank goodness, they don't let their wisdom interfere with their good time, so we manage to keep pretty gay—for paupers."

"I'm in that genial state myself," Pat stated.

"Not really!" she marveled. "But there are dollar signs oozing out all over you."

"Merely conceit," Pat informed her. "The church mice and I are brothers under the skin."

"I can tell by the way you talk you're an actor," Millicent averred. "Have I ever seen you?"

"Not unless you attend first nights. My engagements rarely last longer than that."

"You must have one of Jeff's qualifications, a nose for smelling out flops," said Millicent.

"You've hit it. That's why I just keep two paces ahead of gaunt starvation. In days of affluence I clothe myself regally so the old monster's breath won't be too chill on my person. However, this is a time for joy. Jeff and I will soon be working."

"Splendid!" cried Millicent. "And that's the end of our dance, darn it, but we'll exchange toasts over the rims of our glasses, won't we?"

"And dance together many, many more fox trots," he promised.

New acquaintances surged about them. Millicent was herded into a far corner and Pat found himself confronted by Maida and another young lady whom he had not previously encountered.

"Mr. Denning, I want you to meet another member of your abominable profession," said Maida. "This is Peggy Sawyer." Pat liked the eyes and the gentility of Peggy. "Let's sit down," he suggested when Maida left them. "It may be my imagination, but you've got that rehearsal look under your eyes."

"Flatterer!" she chided him. "Most men tell me I'm quite lovely. Of course, they're all liars and you are absolutely correct. I've been on my feet all day."

They searched for chairs. "It's pretty beastly," he sympathized. "Are you in musical comedy?"

"Yes. Just chorus." She smiled wryly. "My first experience on the stage."

"Don't tell me there were bathing suits and prize winning cups back of your fatal step," cried Pat.

"Not even a popularity contest," Peggy declared. "Just the will to succeed. You've read about that, haven't you?"

"In some book, I believe. Well, I ought to congratulate you but I can't. It's a rotten existence."

"All you wise old people say that," Peggy complained. "Now I'm just a raw down-easter and I like the excitement."

"I wouldn't leave it for the world," Pat swore. "But it can be pretty devastating."

"Still, you'd take it in preference to dull and honorable marriage in Paris, Maine, wouldn't you?" she pressed him. "With a bucolic husband and the prospect of red-cheeked babies?"

"The red-cheeked babies sound delightful," he said. "But I admit that the bucolic husband is a drawback. And Paris, Maine, doesn't exactly lure me. Is there really such a place?"

"Why, of course. A thriving metropolis of good, honest-to-God Yankees."

"Well, well. We do live and learn, don't we? Still, who am I to assume the mantle of omnipotence? Have you ever heard of Tunis, Ohio?"

"Never," she confessed. "That's my home," he smiled.

"But you've become a New Yorker," Peggy pointed out. "A suave well-fed man of the world."

Pat made a fearful grimace. "I suppose you picture me as Michael Arlen sort of person who meets ladies in green hats, spills epigrams with that bored air which marks the perfect clubman, and who will reach a deserved end by running an Hispano Suiza off a cliff or drinking the poison concealed in a Borgia ring."

"You fit the portrait admirably. And now do utter some epigrams."

"My dear, the Hispano Suiza and the epigrams are non-extant. I struggle for a living like Geoffrey Waring; earn a few dollars every now and then; squander them on Sulka ties and

Dobbs' hats and then haunt the agents' offices for another engagement."

"Then you must be hiding your light under a bushel," Peggy affirmed. "You have the English gentleman quality that all Americans worship. There's a hint of feudal castles in the background. I can't find anything of Tunis, Ohio, in your well-kept self."

"I fought for years to destroy the likeness," he confessed. "Even a pseudo-Englishman has a better chance in the Land of the Free and the Home of the Brave. When I become more definitely Oxford I shan't be in need of a job, I promise you. The only thing casting directors fear is a real American. Broaden your A's and you are hired on the spot."

"But Maida tells me you and Mr. Waring have an engagement now?"

"Oh, yes, we are both going sensationally drawing-room. Something was bound to turn up. I've been idle so long that I was beginning to speak of my career in the past tense."

"I should like a real play," mused Peggy. "In the chorus you are part of a machine, except for the fact that instead of coils and wires you possess joints and muscles which ache when you exert them too much. No matter how high your standard you're still only a cog in the works; there's no chance to be a definite personality; you must kick in time, bend in time, exit in time. I'll get fed up with that in quick order, I imagine."

"No good complaining. We have to take what's offered here in New York. If you drop out there are a thousand others eager to replace you. That's why there's no security. You keep pounding madly on your treadmill so some lesser person won't pass you; you're worn out maintaining the pace, and when all is said and done you haven't advanced an inch."

"But you've had fun trying," said Peggy. "Made lots of interesting friends, filled your eyes to the brim with color, and when you get old you can readjust the plate of false teeth and dream about the days when you struggled to keep step with the millions."

The floor space was cleared and Maida once more raised a silencing hand. "Gertrude is going to play," she announced.

The group settled back in their chairs and applauded. small, dark-eyed Jewess got to her feet and walked over to the piano.

"What's it going to be?" she demanded.

There were scattered shouts for Scriabin, Debussy, Godowsky and Gershwin. One sentimentalist called for Thais, but the others hissed scornfully, whereupon he left the room, offended and sought solace among the collection of bottles. Gertrude sat down and presently a strange jargon of notes began to weave their tortured spell. Frenzied chords followed one other, seeking out the core of all discontent and transmuting it into the flashing fingers of the pianist. Chords quivering with pain, conceived in labor, echoed into oblivion like cry of protest. No melody, no form, just savagery ground out by white hands. Gertrude's face wore an enigmatic smile, though her playing answered some aching need.

"I'll be damned if she doesn't like the stuff," thought Pat. The sound drained him of resistance; he became a part of nightmare pattern. Then abruptly Gertrude ended. Slowly the room resumed its normal proportions. You could hear a gentle hiss, like a sigh of release.

She swung into the sadness of a folk song. Pat thought of windswept fields and the grain swelling like a yellow tide while for above clouds raced against their eternal background and the sun burned steadfastly. Then came a fragment of old Polish tune pregnant with sorrow and death; a momentary lightening when the mood changed to a sprightly theme, then once more, somberness. For more than a half hour pianist remained seated. At last, like a paean of modernity beauty of Gershwin's *Rhapsody* crashed through the room and then the concert was over. They applauded wildly and demanded more, but Gertrude explained that her hands were numb. Pat could well believe it; the wonder was that such power could dwell in the slight frame of the little Jewess. At his side Peggy remained motionless.

"God, to be able to play like that," Pat muttered. "What the hell is this drawing room comedy? Why should I be pleased with myself? What have I done—ever? Isn't it damnable how good music stirs up a sense of futility, Miss Sawyer? It's really very bad for the ego."

The feeling of emptiness which so often ensues from unwise drinking laid hold upon Pat. Here he was, Pat Denning, twenty-eight years old, bound for perdition in a reckless sort of way, without even the excuse of grandeur to motivate his going. The way was cluttered with countless intrigues, parties that lasted until dawn, sessions of talk with similarly placed friends; and while he busied himself achieving nothing men wrote music that reverberated through the centuries. The desire to build something worthwhile which stirs most of us at odd moments began to rise in Pat Denning's breast. It may have been Gertrude's music or perhaps the friendship of the girl beside him; difficult to say what spurs us on to the idea of great endeavor. Before long the inspiration sputters to unwept death, but for one short hour we are wrapped in the glory of the clouds. Pat visioned a scornful parting with Dorothy Brock; flinging her many presents to the ground and walking away, destitute, but with a new feeling of cleanness enfolding him. That was the worth-while way; the span of life was short and he must hasten before the shadow of declining years fell upon him.

"Let's have a drink," he suggested. The plan met instantaneous approval and they crowded into the kitchen.

Maida waved them all back. "Jeff and Mr. Denning come help mix things," she called. "The rest of you clear out. I can't have you bobbing about." They waited apathetically drinks were forthcoming.

Millicent and Peggy got into conversation.

"He's nice, isn't he?" Millicent probed.

"Awfully glib, though, like all legitimate actors," Peggy joined, avoiding the blonde young lady's snare.

"That's the nature of the beast. They always see a well-turned out butler and hordes of Dukes and Duchesses in the background. It's that drawing-room training."

"I can't believe that he'd be sincere for more than ten minutes at a stretch," said Peggy. "I'm sure the strain would prove too much."

"Don't you believe it!" cried Millicent. "Even actors can be decent. You have to allow for a measure of conceit and a tolerable lot of affectation, but dig deep under and these drawing-room dummies are surprisingly human."

"At least the quality of his liquor is unquestioned," Peggy compromised. "For once, you can really believe the labels."

Maida emerged from the kitchen bearing a tray full to over flowing with good things. Pat followed close at her heels. Waring hovered about, wearing the rubicund smile of one who has found a god and shared his discovery with friends. Rapturous exclamations greeted their arrival.

"Give me that lovely apricot-colored doo-hickey," called one of the girls.

"Bourbon! Shades of my ancestral chateau!' shouted another.

"*Et voila la veuve Clicquot*," chanted Waring. "Heave to, my hearties—heave to but not up!"

Hilarity prevailed. Pat found his way back to the seat beside Peggy. "The hail fellow well met," she mocked. "How does it feel to be the dispenser of good cheer?"

"Excellent!" he responded. "I was rather low until this heaven-sent deliverance arrived. But, I say, do let me fill your glass."

"Better not," warned Peggy. "The good folk of Paris, Maine, aren't educated to such rare liquor. It's apt to go to my head."

Millicent joined them. "You know you've excited controversy," she interrupted. "Greater distinction hath no man than that."

"Controversy? I? My dear, I'm such a simple person; you'll find no complicating inhibitions. You see me as I am, personable, care free and extremely poor."

"Peggy doubts your sincerity."

"Good God! That was unkind corning from you, Miss Sawyer!"

"Millicent shouldn't have mentioned it," Peggy deprecated. I'm sorry."

"But now that the subject's been raised, let's argue," Pat suggested, pulling Millicent into the vacant chair beside him.

"I'd rather not. You're a false friend, Millicent." Peggy glowered, attempting to withdraw. Pat restrained her.

"Sorry, darling," said Millicent, "but Mr. Denning doesn't mind, really. It flatters him to think we care a hang whether he's sincere or not. Now look at poor Jeff Waring. Nobody troubles to sound the depths of his soul; we take him at face value. But you're intriguing, Pat Denning. You've aroused feminine curiosity, and that is a real tribute."

"You know, Miss Sawyer, you're right—after a fashion," confessed Pat. "I've been drifting in the mazes of pretense for so long I shouldn't know a real, honest-to-God sincere thought if it jumped up and bit me."

"There you are, Peggy. You win, after all," said Millicent.

Peggy looked acutely uncomfortable. "You've overstated my case, Millicent," she defended herself. "I'm a bit distrustful of gentlemen whose replies to any question are a little too apt for human comfort, that's all."

"In other words, you like an epigram in its proper place— behind the footlights?" asked Pat.

"Yes. A stage setting gives a certain truthfulness to wit that is lacking when the same remark is made in every day surroundings."

"In other words my conversation is a little too precious."

"Oh, not that. Rather the talk of a man on his mettle cause he hopes to get a good notice in the Times tomorrow morning."

"I am chastened. Henceforth I shall talk about the weather and the latest styles."

"Please don't; I should loathe that. And we always have a sneaking liking for the very thing of which we disapprove," Peggy reminded him.

"But I want you to approve," he said. "I want that approbation most terribly."

Millicent departed with that fifth-wheel-of-a-carriage look and they were left to their discussion.

"I really do want her to like me," Pat was thinking. "It would mean a lot to have this girl care."

"Perhaps you'll allow me to devote some time to proving my innate fineness," he said aloud. "It won't be dull and I'd be having a grand time."

Peggy shook her head. She was far from averse to flirtation with this young man and yet—Pat Denning would be dangerous to any woman, no matter how level headed.

"At least one luncheon," Pat begged.

She surrendered. "Very well."

"Sometime this week?" he pursued. "Tomorrow?"

Peggy smiled. "Very well, tomorrow," she agreed.

"Fine. I shall be properly humble, a throwback to my Tunis, Ohio, days."

They were conscious of a sudden quiet which had taken possession of the room. Gertrude was once more seated at the piano. They settled back to listen. Pat took in his surroundings; a starved-looking room hung with bad water colors which he guessed were the work of Maida. The grimness of the light fixtures had been masked by painted shades, the inspiration of some artist with fantastic inclinations. But here, futility was not depressing, for underneath the gaiety lay a spark of hope. If one did not succeed today there was always a tomorrow bright with promise. That thought was most comforting to Pat.

"This is swell," he said to himself. "I like their racket. With someone like Peggy beside me I'd go for all this in a big way." And the music of Gertrude imaged the longings that lay in his own heart.

14

At ten o'clock they shuffled to their places, the boys and girls of the *Pretty Lady* chorus.

"Get the suitcases under Andy Lee's eyes," whispered Ann Lowell. "Bet he's been having a row with the ball and chain."

"Snap into it! Snap into it!" yelled Lee, his small eyes glittering venomously.

"Ouch! Somebody throw him a hunk o' raw meat," Flo suggested. "Jeez, my dogs are killing me. One more day of this and it's back to the laundry for me."

Peggy ran out of the dressing room hooking her practice costume. "Late again, Miss Sawyer," bellowed Andy Lee. "You new girls haven't no sense of responsibility."

Harry MacElroy darted about like an agitated hen. Already he was becoming convinced that the title of assistant stage' manager was an empty honor.

A show girl stalked into view, a Pekinese dog trailing her heels. "Well, Queen Marie, an' where have you been?" snapped Lee.

"I simply had to have my hair waved," the beauteous one explained, "Come, Dolores, mamma's gotta dress and dance in a lousy rehearsal."

"Any time! Just take it easy!" called Andy Lee sarcastically. "MacElroy, are they all here?" he demanded.

"All except three of the show girls," said Harry.

"Show girls! I'll be god damned if I use show girls again. All they gotta do is walk downstairs in time to music and you'd think we was puttin' 'em out by makin' 'em rehearse at all. Lissen, MacElroy, tell those ladies we're not runnin' a finishing school so they'd better drop their tea cups an' come on down," Lee fumed.

"Hey, Jerry, try that *Manhattan Madness* number, will you? Now, lissen, folks; this has gotta be snappy stuff, so on your toes ev'rybody, and put a little life in it. You've seen the Harlem dinges—well, go to it—*wiggle*!"

Jerry was beating out the tom-tom rhythm of a new number. "Watch me," Andy Lee commanded. Hat pushed far over his eyes, he simulated the slow writhing dance of the Harlem negro. The middle part of his body gyrated with effortless ease, first one foot shuffling back, then the other. His audience was entranced. In the turmoil of rehearsal they had lost sight of the fact that Andy Lee was probably the greatest dancer the Ghetto had produced. For the first time was revealed to them the boy who danced because a melody in his soul taught him that means of expression; danced from the unsavory East Side streets to the stages of vaudeville houses which were in their hey-day a decade ago; danced before crowds which stretched over the three thousand miles of vaudeville circuits; danced until the art became his God and, like a bountiful God, it was now repaying him.

Peggy, gazing at him, thought that here was artistry no less thrilling than Gertrude s music. It was an outpouring of joy which found its medium in Gertrude's fingers and in Andy Lee's feet. The slouch, the gaucherie of the Negro were reproduced to perfection. Each gesture of body and arms was one of a series of details which made the dance a masterpiece. Andy was improvising now; all thought of the business of the day vanished, he surrendered to the lure of Jerry's music. When he stopped they wanted to applaud, but because he immediately resumed the part of taskmaster they resisted the impulse. For a fleeting moment Andy Lee had allowed them a glimpse of his heart and now, furious at this weakness, he railed at them the more bitterly.

"Now, try a little of *that*, you folks!" he cried. "Try an' get some feeling into your work. Look as though you liked to dance; take a lesson from me! I know my business, that's why I'm up on this stage now, tryin' to put a little style into you punks."

Their efforts seemed quite futile and he stormed across the apron, cursing them for a gang of arrant fools. They took his invectives stolidly, because a chorus member is not allowed self respect. The temperament of his superiors demands outlet. In private he may damn them to perdition, but during rehearsal the chorus worker stands dumbly by, waiting for the curses to end. Two hours without surcease they tumbled through the intricate routine, rather like animals goaded to the last measure of endurance. And this was only the third week.

All life was concentrated in the endeavor to master that step. The world resolved itself about the tapping of Andy Lee's feet. To the more experienced the ordeal was not so terrifying but newcomers, like Peggy, grew sick with dread even after three weeks, each time their clumsiness drew the fire of Andy Lee's gaze.

In the, foyer of the theatre the principals were rehearsing, familiarizing themselves with lines that would be abruptly torn out after the first night. This would continue for a few days more, and then chorus and principals alike would share the stage. The first three weeks are hectic, for it often happens that the presence of a principal is required in two places at the same time; when he fails to make an appearance the dance director and the book director alternate in sessions of rage.

Dorothy Brock was summoned by MacElroy to rehearse the *Manhattan Madness* number. She could not leave the book rehearsal as Mr. Hart needed her. Andy Lee wanted to know whether he or Mr. Hart was the more important. Mr. Hart retorted with equal heat that the dancing end was merely mechanical, all attention should be focused on the lines because it had been proved over and over again that a musical show stood or fell on its comedy merit. Mr. Lee sent back word that a faststepping chorus had been the salvation of many an entertainment and that from what he had seen of Mr. Hart's work the stronger the dancing the better, for all concerned. Mr. Hart vowed he would not countenance the sneers of an incompetent hoofer. Mr. Lee informed him that instead of wasting his time criticizing the dance direction he would be better employed tightening his first act because at the present moment it was about as funny as *Desire Under the Elms*. In between skirmishes the chorus essayed *Manhattan Madness*. The principals continued their game of battledore and shuttlecock, dashing out to devote a few minutes to Andy Lee and then hurrying back to the lobby where the quest for laughs was going on. Mr. Hart was having the devil's own time with Danny Moran and Harvey Mason. Both complained that the division of fun-making opportunities was unfair, both glared when the other was assigned a particularly juicy line. The situation was not improved with the advent of Julian Marsh, bearing the news that the *I Gotta Rhythm* number was to be dropped altogether in favor of a new tune.

Jeez," Andy Lee complained. "Here I spend my good hours teachin' these dumb clucks a swell routine an' then the number's thrown out. I'm through—I wouldn't mess around with an outfit like this. The show'll prob'ly flop anyway."

r. Marsh's secretary exerted his influence; oil was spread upon the troubled waters and the chorus went over to the piano to learn the lyric of a new song entitled *Nobody Else*.

Terry Neill slipped into the chair beside Peggy. "Hello, kid," he whispered. "How's the time step?"

"Coming along fine, thanks," she answered. "You're a good teacher, Terry."

"Hell, that's all right. Ya gonna eat with me this noon?"

"Oh, Terry, I can't. I've made a date."

"Oh, I see!" he grumbled. "Well, how 'bout dinner tonight?"

"All right, Terry; although Ann and Flo are coming along. I can't leave them again."

"God, can't we go alone? Them dames don't like me."

"Yes they do, Terry. Now don't be silly. We'll all Dutch."

"We will like hell. I'm payin' for this!"

"Terry—did the well known rich uncle drop dead?"

"Never mind that. I got money. Can't you stall them girls?"

"I'll try, but Ann might be offended. And she's been awfully nice to me."

"Tell her you gotta see folks from home. We won't run into 'em."

"All right, cut out the gabbin'—cut out the gabbin'—" shouted Jerry Cole, banging his fist on the piano. "Take your lyrics an' try to get the tune. Jeez, this show business is sure one madhouse. C'mon!"

In a far corner Julian Marsh argued with the costume designer; on the stage Andy Lee fought with the company manager; in the lobby Mr. Hart battled with the principals, and around the piano the chorus shrilled lyrics time and time again until they became a meaningless tangle of words. Jerry perspired and swore; Harry MacElroy growled at the shirkers among the boys and girls who refused to sing; at the stage door Pop was repelling further applicants for jobs. Otherwise, peace lay over the *Pretty Lady* production. This state of affairs would mount in frenzied crescendo until the opening night.

In the auditorium two or three mothers watched the proceedings. Their tongues were barbed. Polly Blair's mother turned to Mrs. Wallace, whose daughter was the feminine half of the team of Walters and Wallace.

"B'lieve me," said Mrs. Blair, "they can fuss an' they can fume, but when all's said an' done it'll take the specialty dancers to stop the show. That adagio your kids do is beautiful, Mrs. Wallace, real beautiful. An' while I hate to talk about my own daughter, Polly ain't never failed to stop a show with them spotting tinsicas o' hers."

"I think you're right," said Mrs. Wallace. She came from California, paradise of all adagio dancers, and prided herself on being a lady. Privately she thought Mrs. Blair a bit vulgar, but there was no one else to talk to and the prospect of untold hours alone in her hotel room was so formidable that she acquired the habit of dropping into the theatre for a bit of a chat. "Of course, my little girl, Mona, had a terrible time making a dancer out of her partner, but they do real well, if I do say it myself. He used to be a wrestler, you know. Never took a lesson in his life, but Mona's smart as a whip. Everybody tells me her name'll be up in lights some day."

"Right along with my Polly," agreed Mrs. Blair, forcing an amiable smile, although all the while she was of the secret opinion that someone concerned with the Walters and Wallace combination must know "where the body was buried."

A little to the right sat Daisy Moran and one of the McNeill sisters. On stage Danny Moran was "faking" the comedy dance which was to top off the new *Nobody Else* number. Daisy watched him with admiring eyes. "B'lieve me," she said, "they can talk all they wantta but it's comedy puts the show across. Ya can get singers an' dancers for a nickel a bunch, but where are your good comics? God, I was sick when Danny told me the price they signed him for. He's worth twice that. Two good belly laughs is worth ten troupes o' ballet girls."

"Ain't it the truth?" sympathized Glory MacNeill.

In a box were Susy Phillips, wife of John Phillips, and sister and boon companion, Nellie.

"I wish you could hear John sing that gorgeous number," Mrs. Phillips enthused. "Course Brock's terrible, you never know when she's goin' off key, but John sure sings it lovely. After all, ya can have comedy and dancin', but without a good singer the show's lost. Look at plays like *The Student Prince* and *Blossom Time*."

In the front row Marsh and the costumer continued the row. "You've got to spend money for clothes, Mr. Marsh. No matter how good the music is, or the comedy, or the dancing, if your company doesn't look chic it's just too bad. The public will laugh it off the boards."

"My dear man," Marsh retorted, "the way I stage a show, the costumes, the music *or* the people don't count. It's the artistry that goes to make for success. That's why Green and Friedman are paying me my salary!"

And on stage Jerry Cole reiterated, "Now you gotta get this because if the music flops ya might as well send out engraved invitations to Joe Leblang."

In their ornate office Green and Friedman were berating one another. The cost was prohibitive. Brock was through, she'd had her day and no one but a "dumbkopf" would engage her as leading lady. And Marsh! Too autocratic—why, he even ordered them to stay away from the theatre, talking to the bosses like they were hired help. And, furthermore, Lee wouldn't have the dances finished in two weeks. The Philadelphia opening might be ragged—if only they'd engaged Louis Seymour in the first place!

A little world imbued with restlessness; most of the talk was the harmless sputtering of nerve-wracked minds. Out of chaos would come the desired effort; producer, dance director, authors and costumer at last in complete accord. But the heart aches before this was achieved! The many separate egos, each drunk with the thought that upon him alone depended the success of the undertaking. Not one soul connected with this enterprise but felt himself the superior of his associates from the lowliest chorus boy to Julian Marsh, himself.

Meantime—hammer, hammer, hammer! On your toes, boys and girls, we've got to have speed and action. Look alive! No matter if you have done the thing a thousand times, once more; and this time *smile*, use the old personality! Come on, girls! A little style; you're not working for Tiller. You can afford to act human. Watch that break, little girl on the end—hey, you, on the right, don't move like a cigar store Indian; loosen up, swing your arms! Jerry, take that last chorus over again. All right, girls, back to your places. Come on, the letter formation—no, no, *no!* Jesus Christ, what's wrong with you dumbbells! Like *this!* One, two, three, four, five, six, seven, eight! Hey, you on the end, wait, *wait!* Oh, my God, go on, get out and sit down in the corner and watch the rest of them. Hey, are you dancers or cripples? What the hell do I care if your feet hurt? How about mine? Don't I stand on my feet all day? Come on, one, two, three, four, turn— turn, *turn*, god damn you. All right, Jerry, cut it! Now, lissen, we're going to get this figure if it takes all night. On your feet everybody; no stalling—take your original places and we'll go through the dance. Come on—one, two, three, four—five!

15

In the days which followed Pat Denning and Terry waged war. From the moment of their first dinner together when Peggy Sawyer told Terry of the charming young actor with whom she'd lunched, Terry sensed a rival. He reckoned shrewdly that, while he had the advantage of seeing Peggy constantly and assisting her through the fearful strain of rehearsal, he lacked the glamour and polish of the better educated Denning. Peggy was grateful; she defended Terry against the aspersions of Ann and Flo; yet the part of her which he could not reach lay defenseless before Pat's courtship. Pat could converse, Terry merely talked. Pat saw the world as a shining tapestry peopled with gay folk who moved through an atmosphere of make believe. Terry's world was the matter of fact domain of city streets and show business—especially the latter. Get Terry off the subject of the "profession" and he floundered like a fish out of water. Baseball he knew; but one didn't discuss baseball with girls like Peggy, so he must perforce talk shop. To Peggy, after weary hours spent in the confines of the Forty-Fifth Street Theatre, it was a relief to hear of things likes books and paintings. Terry was hopelessly ignorant of those subjects. Reading held no charm for him and his knowledge of art was restricted to the comics section. Yet in

Terry she found a depth and sympathy which Pat lacked. Pat rattled on amusingly about any number of topics; he could laugh or be serious at will. But Peggy recognized all that as surface froth.

At lunch with Terry the conversation ran: "Well, Peggy, whaddya think o' the new number? Lee may be a tough guy hut he sure has ideas. Did ya notice that variation he got on the old 'Off to Buffalo'? Boy, that tickled me pink. Just goes to show, a hoofer's gotta have brains just like anybody else only they don't nobody give him credit. Why, that's gonna be the prettiest little number in the show. Watch it panic 'em the opening night. You know, ya get lots o' wise folks out front on the openin'. All the lay offs, an' the critics, an' agents; God, ev'rybody! That's the time to sock it over. If ya stop the show the openin' night you're made. Look at Harriet Hoctor. They yelled their heads off at her an' now she's with Ziegfeld. Course Marsh is clever, an' he sure knows class, but those numbers are gonna do the trick. I give Lee credit. Ev'rybody hates his guts but he delivers."

"Yes, Terry."

"Ya know, Brock's lousy. Honest to God, I hate to pan anybody, but she oughtta do a nip-up and fade outta the picture. Didya ever hear anything like that duet with Phillips? The Cherry sisters in their best days never sang like that."

"Yes, Terry." A fork was brandished somewhat wildly by the young orator.

"Name, that's what counts, nowadays. Don't matter how hum you are as long as ya got the reputation. Why, Brock's all set for moth balls an' they're puttin' her out there to play a sixteen-year-old flapper."

"Yes, Terry."

"Now, if I was runnin' this show I'd get a girl—well the Marilyn Miller type. Y'know—class, looks, personality. An' Brock's got two left feet when she dances. Didja get the way she points her heels when she kicks? Looks like Flat Foot Annie!

And, God, Peggy, the taps! To get away with you'd have to be Hope Hampton."

"Yes, Terry."

"An' that finale's all wrong. Dancin' on the stairs! Jerry Wayburn did that fifteen years ago. Honest to God, how some o' these guys get to be producers! An' then they got the nerve to charge five bucks a throw. An' Moran's gags—he musta copped 'em from the Aesop's Fables. That one about 'No, she's an officer's mess'! Every comic on the street has pulled that one. An' puttin' a love duet at the end of the show. They walk out sure—ya gotta hand 'em laughs, laughs an' *more* laughs. But can ya tell those guys anything? Naw—they know—they're the big guys—they wrote show business! Only they ain't so wise. Didn't Ziegfeld put on *Betsy* an' the Shuberts *The Merry World*? 'Course I'm not sayin' it ain't a great show; the music's a little weak, but they can stick in a couple tunes an' they'll get by. Gee, honey, you ain't said a word."

"Yes, Terry."

With Pat, this would be the course of conversation.

"Well, lady, wish this were cover for two at the Grand Hotel in Capri. Then we'd finish our sweet and climb the to get a view of the Bay. Anacapri, Peggy—the most perfect spot in the world."

Pat had never visited Capri but he had read Norman Douglas.

"Yes, Pat," said Peggy obediently.

"You know, dear, some day when I'm through grubbing my way through tawdry drawing room sets that saw the light of day in the first production of *Mrs. Bumpstead Leigh*, I'm going to take the millions and millions of dollars earned from Mr. Morgan and hie me to the Mediterranean, where I shall probably die from the strain of listening for 'Fifteen minutes, please.' I was born to be favored of the gods, Peggy; all the things I can't have mean so much. I want to grow old in some villa near

Cannes, drinking side car cocktails with Scott Fitzgerald. I want to play baccarat at the Casino with the Dolly sisters. But the problem is, what to use for money?"

"Yes, Pat."

"Can't you see the two of us honking around Paris in one of those absurd little taxis; following the sunset beyond the Etoile and on into the Bois? And dining out there under the trees with wealthy and decadent young people? Or strolling in the grounds of Villa d'Este on Lake Como? We should have been Rockefellers, Peggy—not chorus girl and rather bad juvenile lead respectively."

"Yes, Pat."

"Anyhow, I'm going to cherish the dream of clothing you in fine silks and laces and sitting you in the Grand Écarté for all the world to see. Someday we'll move into the world of the Ritz bar, you and I, and stagger from cocktail to cocktail in a sort of rainbow haze... And now I suppose you'd like to eat?"

"Yes, Pat."

"From Capri to blue plate specials. Oh, well, c'est la vie, as I always say in my very best Roumanian. They do have good lamb chops here. How about it?"

"Yes, Pat."

"And in the dim distant future if we're very good children there might be the Taj Mahal. I don't know why I want to see that particularly unless it's because it shines so in photographs. I've picked out a merry little hell of wishing, haven't I?"

"Yes, Pat."

"But just watch your boy friend. Some of these days he'll capture a spinster of fifty with a Kansas accent and an oil well, and then see him burn up that royal road to romance, provided said spinster can be put back in the grab bag, or, as a last resort, treated to a nice prussic acid cocktail."

"Yes, Pat."

"Well, here come your lamb chops. Sop them up like a good child, and then Pat'll walk back to the theatre with you. By the way, we start rehearsals tomorrow."

"That's fine, Pat."

"The outlook isn't so bad for a legitimate show. The leads are awfully good and I've quite a hankering for my own part. So, here's wishing us Plenty."

It was impossible to resist Pat's banter. His high spirits were irrepressible; poverty and failure, alike, could not daunt him. She visioned Pat as the ideal playmate; a Richard Halliburton sort of person with whom one might live under endless skies of blue and give the lie to all rumors of tragedy and discontent which filled the world.

To Terry, life was bounded on the north by Fiftieth Street, and on the south by Forty-Second Street. Straight through the core of his being ran Forty-Seventh Street—and nearest to his heart lay the lobby of the Palace Theatre. Travelling with Terry would be a route, with Pat a shining adventure. But once the adventure palled, Pat's substance dissolved to shadow while Terry remained the solid, tangible companion. Impossible to think of married life with Terry; bad grammar—bad liquor—bad ideals. And Pat? Good grammar—good liquor—and no ideals. Dreams, to be sure, but dreams have an evanescent quality and one wearies of sharing their transports.

"I'll probably marry some downright Yankee farmer and retire to give birth to countless boy scouts whose moral fiber will be so tough that there will be little chance for imagination to break through," thought Peggy.

"You might as well laugh yourself to perdition," Pat summed it up. "No sense marking out the way in neat little packets labeled Orpheum Circuit, Interstate Route and Lay Off season. We'll all reach the same hell eventually so let's be gay about it."

Neither Pat nor Terry was the virginal young man whom Peggy, in her most proper moments, conceived as ideal mate. Their sins were certainly of scarlet hue and she did not deceive herself that her love would wash either of them white as snow. On the contrary, both might wander off in search of further Elysian Fields once the humdrum of familiarity threatened the union. Yet both were undeniably attractive, and each held a certain fascination for her that she found difficult to resist. One was so greatly the complement of the other. It was a unique situation.

Each young man was spurred on by the knowledge of his rival's existence. No names were mentioned, for to both the occupation of the other was an object of scorn. Motivated by delicacy and more than a little caution Pat refused to put in an appearance at the theatre. One never knew when Dorothy Brock or Amy Lee might descend upon the tête-à-tête. He saw Peggy to the door and then took to his heels with a speed that achieved dignity only by virtue of his air of self assurance. If Terry witnessed the arrival of the two, he held his peace and refused to discuss this new found menace with Peggy.

Dorothy continued to visit Pat. He bore these interludes with stoicism because they provided pocket money to entertain Peggy. His straitened circumstances allowed small leeway for extravagance, and many times the lavish presents of Dorothy found their way to the pawnshop to procure real money for dinner. Pat's sophistry inured him to any qualm he might have undergone for such double dealing. When one acquires Dorothy's years one cannot demand unremitting devotion. So it was that the elaborate cigarette case vanished from the apartment, its absence glibly alibied by Pat should Dorothy press the point.

Fortunately these séances were rare, for the grind of rehearsal hampered Dorothy, and now that Pat was no longer a free agent, but subject to rehearsal himself, she found little chance for trysting.

If the unpleasantness of his dilemma troubled Pat, denied himself too great mental stress. The time for et was past. The world owed one a living and to some the w and means are abundantly provided. When one's viewpoint is unmoral the straight and narrow path widens appreciably so that one may walk at ease. Cynicism is an excellent guise for weakness.

Pat considered marriage. The idea tantalized him. He dreaded old age, and the thought of loneliness appalled him. With dubious prospects he could not afford to take a wife and surely life held forth no indication that his lot would be bettered. "Senility in an atmosphere of plush and gilt, that's the ticket," he once said. But plush and gilt were costly. To Pat, bank balances were unknown, although several ladies had donated a checking account in a burst of ardor.

"Therefore the dot must be considerable," he mused.

Peggy fitted in with none of these theories. She was gracious and lovely, but impoverished. Pat had little faith in the "love in a cottage" idea. And since he lacked business instinct, he must look to his spouse for the financial support. He often toyed with the idea of playing the stock market, but the obstacles were lack of funds and a woeful conception of business. And even cynicism balked at the prospect of an income for two wrung from the pursuit of ladies like Dorothy.

"Thank heaven, I've not sunk that low," breathed Pat in his best Dion Boucicault manner. The problem was unanswerable. He could not marry Peggy and yet he desired it above all else.

Pat saw that harlotry had its limitations. He lived in constant dread of exposure, not by reason of its effect on his social standing—that was secure against such a trifling shock—but because of Peggy's reaction. Pat cherished the ideal of mutual respect; on such rockbound principles was marital happiness established. He felt no shame but he dreaded Peggy's scorn. All this was very trying to a man when he was in rehearsal. Moral problems are always irksome and to be confounded at a time like this was damnable.

"Damn! I wish I'd never met the girl," he cursed.

He discussed the matter with Waring. "Jeff, what sort of magnificent gesture do I make? Shall I be a gentleman of the camellias and send Peggy packing to a virtuous and simple-minded consort? Because I love her—hellishly—I guess that's the proper word for it. But a girl doesn't want a male whore on her hands; she's bound to suffer a fracture of the ideal complex. And without said prostitution where does little Patrick earn his daily bread?

"Take yourself, Jeff. You're reasonably moral. You get tight and you philander in a nice Baptist manner, but the flesh pots can't claim you for their own. Now in me you see one totally damned. I don't know which punishment will overtake me first, death or impotence. In the event of the first the worst I have to fear is hell fire; if it's the second I shall grace the workhouse or the stage door of some Broadway theatre. And think of it, Geoffrey, my friend, love can come even to sing like me. I do love the wench—and on the surface I'll make a splendid husband. But I can't earn my keep and that's 'cause I refuse to slave; and the primrose path rather goes to seed when there's a wife in the offing. How manage a rendezvous when the flower of my heart is in the kitchen cooking spinach? We both know we're destined to go on, year in, year out, fighting for an occasional part, letting seven weeks of work represent our season, borrowing from friends, scrimping, starving, growing old, because we lack the genius to escape mediocrity. We'll never be good actors, you and me, we're presentable clothing store dummies with a flair for dialogue. In thirty years they'll relegate us to the part of the family retainers and Southern judges. I haven't the glimmer of a talent for writing, my features photograph badly so there's no hope of Hollywood, and I want to take a wife. Oh, Geoffrey, Geoffrey, loud laughter from the ballroom! The ghosts of all the happy shipping clerks in the world rise up to taunt me. They have their wives, their Fords, the little nests at the very mention of which Tin Pan Alley goes completely ga-ga. No, Jeff, I must marry a lady of means and—unlike happy-ending story books—the princess of my heart is enrobed in gold. She'll wed some damned hoofer or insurance salesman or filling station clerk and have splendid babies. Cue for music, professor. Make it *Broken Hearted*, very legato."

"I suggest a monastery, old timer," said Jeff Waring.

"Don't be an ass. I'd look frightful with my head shaved."

"Can't you grow very Barrie-esque and embrace the clear and simple life?"

"I haven't enough funds to be whimsical. I defy you to point out any whimsy in a Ninth Avenue tenement—which address would be the limit of my resources."

"Then, my precious youngster, you've got to be big and brave and say good-by to the girl."

"The trouble is that I shouldn't survive, if I didn't say good-by. I can't abide the threadbare carpets and the darned socks. Might as well lay it to temperament, but I'd go mad in those surroundings. I'd have to use infidelity as an outlet—and then the whole game would be ruined. Jeff, I've come to the conclusion that I'm low down and rotten."

"I guess you are, Big Boy. Let's have a drink on it."

Terry Neill and Harry Towne likewise held conference.

"So you wanna get married?" sneered Harry. "Jeez, I shouldn't've let you outta the baby buggy."

"Cut it, will ya, Harry? Can't you see I'm serious? God, I feel like hell, an' you go rubbin' it in. I know I'm a sap—but what can I do? I'm nuts about the kid. Don't suppose she'd take me tied onto a five year contract with Dillingham, but, hell, a guy can't help fallin' in love, can he?"

"No—but he can fall out. Why don't ya lay the dame an' get it over with?"

"She ain't that kind—besides I don't like her that way."

"Aw, come out of it! You, the answer to the Chambermaid's Prayer. You're the first hoofer I ever met that wasn't out for all he could get."

"Can it, will ya, Harry? Jeez, a guy can't have decent t'oughts without one o' you bums razzin' him. I gotta have a wife an' family some day, ain't I?"

"I don't see why."

"Well, ev'ry guy's gotta. Y'know, the world needs children-an' all that."

"Sure I know. But why marry?"

"What the hell good are a lot o' bastards? Anyhow, it's the proper thing to do. Didn't you ever go to church even when you was a kid?"

"Don't make me laff—I gotta cracked lip. The nearest you ever got to a church is the Roxy Theatre. Why, if you were to go to confession the confession box would fall right over."

"Okay-okay-but now I wanna settle down. I gotta mission in life."

"You copped that outta the lyrics—now don't try them ten dollar words on me because all that's wrong with you is too much sunburn."

"Don't you think she's a swell-lookin' kid?"

"Who? Peggy? Sure. She's all right. Little meaty about the parts, but that'll wear off when she's danced more."

"An' what a lady, Harry. I'm scared goofy when I eat with her."

"Well, when in doubt *don't* use your knife. Thassall I gotta say."

"I think she likes me. She sure plays 'round with me a lot."

"Plays 'round, is *righ*t. Baby, how you waste time is nobody's business."

"I s'pose you made the whole chorus by now?"

"Not yet, but gimme time. No marryin' for me—there ain't no novelty in it.".

"Well, I'm gonna ask her. There ain't no harm in that."

"Take it easy, kid. On fifty a week you think you're gonna get by?"

"Well, she's got her pay comin' in regular, an' we won't have no kids, for a while."

"Sure—but how about layin' off? You'll get by easy this year, but how about the next, an' the one after that? You ain't got no dough laid by."

"I'm startin' in right now."

"Well, go to it; but don't forget, you ain't Jolson or Harland Dixon. An' it takes plenty money to live in New York. There's about twenty weeks each year when ya won't get salaries, which is okay unless you're sick—but then what?"

"Jeez, Harry. Me an' Peggy is both healthy."

"Yeah? Well, I say a guy oughtn't ta marry in show business till he's pullin' down two hundred smackers per because he don't get it steady an' he winds up at the end of the year averagin' about fifty per week."

"We could get along. I'd live anywhere with Peggy."

"An' how about her? An' if she's such a lady how does a tough guy like you rate with her, anyhow? Ya may get by now, but that ole sex appeal can't hold out forever an' then how's that vocabulary o' yours gonna stand the gaff? She'll meet plenty o' snappy guys, all the janes in show business do if they're lookers, an' when she compares them with you, you're jus' gonna be outta luck."

"Sure—I know. She's got a guy like that playin' her now."

"There y' are! If you're hookin' up with a kid like Peggy, try a coupla months at night school. Because at present you ain't got a thing in common except each other."

Hunched over their malted milks during the noon recess Ann and Flo took Peggy to task.

"Say, what's the idea of dropping us for that funny-looking hoofer?"

"He isn't funny looking, Ann. He's an awfully nice boy. I don't see why you won't come along to eat with us. We'd love to have you."

"Sorry, but I'm not mixing with the breed. Now, listen here, Mary Miles Minter, you're not going to get ga-ga and fall for a chorus boy, are you?"

"Can't I eat with him a few times without being accused of falling in love?"

"You can *not*. Not with an actor. They don't take you to lunch just for the pleasure of watching you eat."

"We talk nothing but shop. Terry *can't* talk about anything else, I'm convinced."

Well, just hand him a bunch of lilies and sing Tosti's *Good-Bye*."

"I can't hurt his feelings, Ann. Think how he's me."

"Sweetheart—some of the kids are all right to play around with, but the minute you start going steady with them it's just too bad. You crab your chances with real fellers an' what do you get for it? Corned beef hash at Childs. Why, I bet while you were smiling at your boy friend over a coffee cup in the St Regis, Flo and I were dancing with our college kids on the St Regis roof. And between the two St. Regises there are two avenues—so you better get wise to yourself and pick the right one."

"College kids are stupid. They carry flasks and want to neck."

"Let 'em. They won't give you hydrophobia. An' they all use Listerine."

"It isn't that. I'm fed up with gay collegians. I like to talk seriously."

"Well, what a great help that hoofer must be! Now you're good looking and you can dance. The boys at Columbia get a kick out of trotting around with chorus girls so why park your fanny in Childs when it'll rest so comfortably on a night club chair?"

"An' if you're thinking of falling in love," added Flo, "for God's sake pick out a guy who's seen a fingerbowl some place besides the movies."

"You act as though you thought I'd marry Terry."

"Stranger things have happened, little one. But take the advice of Hard-Hearted Hannah—when the rent comes due all the triple taps in the world won't save you."

"The idea is this," Ann continued. "Unless a girl's pretty clever she's stuck in the chorus till they wheel her out. At that, girls get a better break than boys, because there's more call for women principals and if a manager is sympathetic you can twist him 'round your little finger. But even so you'll find a thousand kids for every part, so most of us hang on in the merry merry and like it. We know we've got to resign some day, but it's fun, the work isn't so tough once you get through rehearsing, and you can spend most of your time in New York. If your folks live here you can even save a little money. But a girl's got to marry and there's no point getting into the chorus unless you've got your eyes open for some nice kid who comes rolling along oozing dough. It's easy enough to laugh off money, but what can you do without it? Actors never have any. Show people and sailors are always broke. Suppose you go temporarily insane and marry a per- former. Well, the first season he's got a good job, so you live on Park Avenue, buy a car and think the world's your little tin horn. Then what? If he's got enough cash he puts on a show; it flops, and you're sunk. If he's only saved a little the next season's sure to be tough and the dough goes anyway. If he gets wealthy on the stock market he decided a love nest with some *Follies* cutie would be just too snappy for words, and so there goes the money for mink coats on the back of a show girl. And if he stays home he's temperamental and cranky. He's got to think about his art and if you don't do things just so he raises hell. So no matter how you look at it, any girl who marries an actor is a fool.

"Now take college boys. Their dads generally have lots of money, they're decent kids except for too much boozing, and when they get fat and middle-aged they'll be a credit to the community. You can settle back an' have children because you know the old income arrives regularly every week. You're. in a swell family and it's all hunky dory. To marry an actor, you've got to be nuts on the romantic idea and even then you'll find he's all wet. Every actor carries his own little set of footlights around with him and he's always performing for somebody's benefit. Generally his wife has to be the audience and help put over the laughs when things aren't going so good. If you marry a legit, you get Shakespeare with the grapefruit; marry an opera singer and it's *Pagliacci* in the bathtub; and marry a dancer and you get a time step and break every time there's a pause in the conversation.

"He's bound to be conceited because ego was invented for actors. They've got to be stuck-up; if they don't think they're great nobody else will. And it's just as tough for the husband. He may be the jealous type, and every minute you're away from him he pictures you carrying on with some other guy. You can't always be in the same show together, so while you're parked in Chicago he's fretting away his young life in Boston. Then one or the other goes off the handle, gets caught, and there's another divorce suit. Grab your husband, get out of show business and you'll be happy. So I guess that kinda washes up you and your two grease paint Romeos."

"Ann knows," Flo explained. "She married the tenor in a male quartet."

"Sure—he was so sold on the idea of four-part harmony he thought he could keep two other girls happy besides his wife. But little Ann wasn't singing contralto to the best soprano on the Main Stem so I got my kiddie car and went home to mamma."

"I'm so sorry, Ann," said Peggy. "I didn't know you'd been disappointed in love."

"Disappointed, the devil. It was the best thing could happen to me. From now on I spend my lonely hours with gentlemen who do *not* wear red-rimmed collars."

"We're going out with those kids tonight, so come along," Flo urged. "Nobody's dressing up; just a little jaunt to El Mirador. The show's good and the boys don't mind how much you eat. Come on. Get your mind off this damn opera."

Peggy considered. "I told Terry I'd go to the midnight show at the Strand," she said.

Ann shrugged hopelessly. "There y'are," she argued. "Midnight pictures at the Strand! What kind of a future for a girl is that? Now there's one nice-looking boy named Standish you'll adore."

So Peggy agreed to accompany them. She saw Terry watching her from across the stage and experienced a sudden pang. But the girls were right. She needed noise and color to relieve the whirring days in the machine. Terry must understand. He couldn't afford to take her to those places, but he mustn't be jealous if she went with other boys.

And Pat! She'd love an evening at El Mirador with Pat, but that, too, was out of the question. Surely something was lacking in her make-up. She consistently picked boy friends whose financial status was so humble.

Harry Towne saw the two girls pleading with Peggy. He nudged Terry. "Betcha two grand them dames are givin' you the works, baby," he crowed. "They. ain't lettin' little Peggy step out with a chorus boy. She's swell bait for college kids and them broads know it. You better ask the dame up to your room to hear your radio, and then let nature take its course, because that's the only way *you'll* get a break!"

16

The head waiter eyed the incoming party with disfavor. College boys and chorus girls were a dangerous combination. The youngsters liked to get tight and show off, and the girls egged them on. He had little hope of relegating them to a corner table; those youngsters wanted a ringside location or nothing. One of the boys greeted him affably, with that touch of condescension which collegiate youth reserves for anyone who is engaged in menial work.

"H'lo, Louis. Got our reservation?" demanded Warren Standish.

"Good evening, Mr. Standish. Have you a reservation? I didn't see it on the books."

"Sure. Mark Ames called up about ten o'clock, didn't you, Mark?"

"Uh huh," answered the boy thus appealed to. "I didn't talk to Louis, though. Whoever it was promised me faithfully he'd have a ringside table."

"I think we're booked up, Mr. Standish," Louis regretted. "Perhaps I can fix you up, though. I always do my best for you, Mr. Standish."

"Don't I know, Louis, don't I know! And I certainly appreciate the fact. So just this once more won't hurt. The girls are from Marsh's new show so we want to treat 'em right. How about that ringside table now, feller?"

Louis snapped his fingers and a waiter hurried over. "Take Mr. Standish and his party to Number Forty-two," Louis commanded.

"Yes sir," said the waiter. "Good evening, Mr. Standish. Pretty hot night, isn't it?" The party walked down the narrow lane between the tables and settled themselves at the places indicated by the waiter.

From her vantage point Mrs. Blair watched the proceedings. She nudged Polly, who was straining her eyes to finish a story in *True Confessions* magazine before time for her performance.

"Get those chorus girls!" muttered Mrs. Blair contemptuously. "Not one bit of talent and they come to show off in a joint like this while we have to sweat blood to make both ends meet. Well, they better make the most of it because they can't last long."

Polly nodded without looking up from her story. Her mother tweaked her arm viciously. "You pay attention to me when I'm talking to you, young lady, an' put that magazine away. I guess I'm entitled to a little respect after the years I've slaved and slaved so's you could have a decent bringin' up."

"I was payin' attention, Ma," Polly whimpered. "This story's gettin' real exciting. The artist is just goin' to seduce the girl."

"Fine stuff for a young girl to be readin'," Mrs. Blair sniffed. "What'll Mr. McDermott say if he finds you fillin' your mind with such truck?"

"Aw, nuts to Mr. McDermott. He's always got hot pants," said the delightful child. "I wish he'd lay off me for a change."

"Shut up! Mr. McDermott's been very nice to both of us. Him an' me are real pals. Now, for God's sake, pull yourself together. He's comin' over to the table right now. Act like you was glad to see him or I'll beat hell outta ya."

Walt descended upon them, beaming. "Well, well, well, ladies!" he horded. "I swear to God, Mother, you're getting younger ev'ry day. Better watch your step, Polly, or your ma'll be cuttin' in on your boy friends." He gave Polly's bare knee a gentle slap. Polly favored him with a ghastly smile.

"Nice crowd tonight," said Mrs. Blair conversationally. "You sure pull them in here at the club. I was readin' in the *New Yorker* that this is the swellest hangout in town. Polly, look, there's Norma Shearer. Oh, an' Irene Rich. I hope you make 'em get up an' make a speech, Mr. McDermott. I love to hear them movie stars talk."

Peggy was dancing with the Standish chap. He was holding her so tightly that she had difficulty in breathing. His feet executed all sorts of maneuvers; he kept humming the melody the band was playing, his hand stealing further and further down her back.

"Get Standish!" Ann commented to her partner. "He thinks ev'ry girl is a pushover for him. You college guys kill me."

"Aw, don't mind us. We're just out for the hell of it," Mark soothed her.

Peggy resented Warren Standish's attitude. He seemed to hold her in contempt, and although he was willing enough to embrace her and attempt a few kisses, she knew he mentally catalogued her as a cheap little gold digger who could be had for a price and then discarded the moment someone more attractive came along. She made her conversation as formal as possible, ignoring the many innuendoes with which he sprinkled his talk. If this was the life for which Ann and Flo were such rooters she was disappointed. These university Sir Oracles were not to her liking. She preferred the glittering insincerity of Pat or the well meant blundering of Terry to this irritating combination of superiority and sensuality. When the number was over they retired to their table, flasks were opened and the hilarity increased.

The lights overhead were dimmed and the floor show began. They applauded the procession of torch singers, masters of ceremony, and dancers, imbibing the contents of the many flasks all the while. Peggy rigorously limited herself to one drink. She was chary of the gleam in Warren Standish's eye; it warned her of approaching trouble. Restraint was forgotten and their shouts and boisterous laughter soon made them the most unpopular group in the room. Peggy was miserable. She lowered her head in order not to see the disgusted glances leveled at their table and prayed that the ordeal might soon be over.

Standish bent down and whispered something undistinguishable in her ear. Though she failed to make out the words his meaning was unmistakable as he accompanied the remark with a stealthy move of his hand.

"He's tight! Don't pay any attention!" implored Flo.

But the one drink had given Peggy sufficient courage to defy the pleadings of her friends. She faced Warren Standish, thoroughly outraged. "You cheap half-baked kid," she stormed. "What makes you think I'd consider any proposition you could make, for one minute? College boys! Your mothers ought to spank every last one of you. Is a flask of bad Scotch and an order of chicken à la king supposed to be my fee? Do you want even your affairs with women at bargain prices? You make me *sick. Good-night!*"

She sprang to her feet, upsetting the glass at her elbow and fairly ran to the shelter of the ladies' retiring room. Her burst of derisive laughter echoed in her ears and she flung herself down on the divan, burying her face in her hands while the matron hovered anxiously above her, equipped with smelling salts and a glass of water.

"Well, the dirty little chiseller!" ground out Standish. "Why the hell bring a washout to a gay party like this? If some of your good judgment, Ann, it *stinks!*"

"Who's a chiseller?" Ann menaced him. "Why, I'd like to crown that funny-looking mug of yours with the Standish coat of arms you're always yelping about. You lousy punk with your cut whiskey and your bedroom manners. On the make for everything that earns a living. And you've prob'ly got a lotta goddam tarts in your own family!"

Standish raised his hand to slap Ann, but was forcibly held back by the more level-headed Mark.

"Come on, let's get out of this," he begged. "If this row ever gets out we'll catch holy Ned from the dear home folks, Ann, pipe down. You're cockeyed! You know Warren's a good kid only that funny Sawyer kid riled him. Sure she's a chiseller. You all are, an' more power to you. I got the car parked outside, let's get out before Louis throws us out."

"I won't go a step with that bum!" Ann wailed, pointing an uncertain finger at Standish.

"Now, now, be a nice child!" Mark was alarmed as the prospect for an amusing evening dwindled. "Warren'll cool off—an' we can leave the kid here. She'll be all right."

The three boys staggered to their feet and unceremoniously bundled their companions out of the room.

"Sorry, Louis," Mark apologized on the way out.

"You better be," blazed the head waiter. "Some night you fresh guys are gonna be beat up."

"Who'll do that?" shouted Standish truculently.

"Aw, Warren, snap out of it," pleaded Mark. "We don't want to make the can tonight. God, you can ruin any party!"

Standish was chastened by the last remark and allowed himself to be led to the elevator. Flo and Ann, swaying on their feet, made a half-hearted protest at this cavalier desertion of

Peggy, but they were soon wheedled into an amiable frame of mind. After all, Peggy was out of kindergarten.

Unaware of their departure, Peggy was repairing the damage her little emotional spree had wrought. Her eyes were swollen with weeping, and the tip of her nose had shaded to a most unbecoming pink. Someone had spilled a drink down the front of her dress, and there was a cigarette burn on her skirt. She eyed her reflection in the glass ruefully and took a vow that tonight was her final rendezvous with college boys. Freshened and slightly calmed she felt in her purse for money with which to tip the matron and discovered, to her chagrin, that she was entirely without funds. Not so much as a dime could be found in the tiny bag. The situation was ludicrous and more than a little embarrassing. She would be forced to borrow cab fare from Ann or Flo in the presence of the detested college boys!

"Excuse me a minute," she mumbled and hastened out of the room in quest of her two friends. An empty table greeted her eye. The full force of her plight dawned upon her.

"Damn Ann and Flo," she swore.

She re-entered the ladies' room and sought a solution to the dilemma. There was no possibility of locating Ann and Flo, but by some remote chance she might reach Pat Denning by telephone. It was a gamble at best, for Pat spent very few hours in his apartment while the hot spell was at its peak. Still there remained only an ignominious confession to the man who would probably handle her without gloves as the perpetrator of a most annoying scene.

"I—I wonder if you could loan me a nickel," she said hesitatingly to the matron. "I want to make a phone call without disturbing any of the members of my party and I have no change in my purse."

The matron accepted this carefully worded explanation at its face value, and, digging into an enormous black pocketbook fished up a handful of change. She held out the coin. Peggy selected a nickel, murmured her thanks and fled to the foyer of the club where the public telephones were to be found. Fortunately she remembered the number and called "Bryant 4537" into the mouthpiece. There was a series of buzzes and finally the click of a receiver being removed from the hook. She almost sobbed so thankful was she that Pat happened to be at home.

"Hello. Pat?" she called.

"Yes. Who's this?"

"Peggy Sawyer. I know it's beastly of me to get you out at this hour, but I'm in a dreadful predicament."

"Not really. What's our little New Englander gone an done?"

"Taken the advice of her worldly wise sisters and stepped out with college boys. Oh, Pat, it was awful!"

"Where on earth are you?"

"At El Mirador. It's very chic and I'm very miserable. Won't you please come and rescue me? I haven't a cent to my name and one can't borrow cab fare from a stony-faced head waiter. Oh, Pat, isn't it a crime?"

Not too bad. You might have been put on the spot and found yourself faced with a long hike home. Sure—I'll be hero of the occasion."

"Thanks loads. I'll go back to the ladies' room and wait there. Our party was rather noisy so I'm not exactly a member in good standing. I'll be in there making myself scarce when you arrive. Have them send a page boy to call me. You're a darling to do this for a little simpleton like me."

"You know I'd come to the ends of the earth, darling. Just take your heaving bosom back to the matron and I'll arrive pronto. Shall I wear that blue tie you like so much?"

"You can appear in a bathrobe if you like."

"Miss Sawyer! What can you think of me?"

"I think you're swell. Bye. And do hurry! And Pat, give the page boy a quarter. I'll have to tip the matron."

"Right-o. And, listen, dear lady. I'll hold the cab because it's a tough job locating fifteen and five cabs in the neighborhood of El Mirador. So be ready to dash like mad. You know how those meters get going. Bye."

Peggy left the oven-like interior of the telephone booth and for the third time retraced her steps. The matron looked up in a disinterested manner at her entrance. She was wondering when the tip would be forthcoming. Peggy believed her appearance was less distrait, and sank onto the lounge to collect her thoughts. Ann and Flo would be furious, no doubt; she had let her sponsors down badly. But she found it impossible to convince herself that the two girls really liked this sort of thing. Surely life held more for them than a succession of parties with callow, empty-headed school boys. An hour's ride in a Rolls Royce did little to atone for the drinking and leering conversation that followed. Peggy was ready to subscribe to the philosophy of the gay nineties torch singer who warbled that "rags is royal raiment when worn virtue's sake."

A knock at the door distracted her thoughts. The matron got up and answered the summons. She returned to inform Peggy that Mr. Denning was waiting. Peggy saw her pocket the tip the page-boy had brought as she fled from her sanctuary and hurried to meet Pat.

"Pat, you're the most unbelievable darling."

"Why, angel, you look like the surrender at Yorktown."

"I feel much worse. Let's get out of here."

"Right! On the way down how about a speck more power on that nose. It's sort of a beacon for weary travelers right now."

"Oh, dear! I thought I was my dazzling self once more. Where is that elevator?" She jabbed hysterically at the button marked "Down."

At that juncture there came an interruption. Walt McDermott and the voluble Mrs. Blair sauntered through the trance to the dining room, little Polly trailing disconsolately, in the rear.

"My God! Get Mother," whispered Pat. Mrs. Blair was afoam with chiffon and tulle, giving somewhat the effect of an exploding milk bottle. A large picture hat flopped about her face, serving as a welcome mask to the multitudinous wrinkles which veined her cheeks.

Peggy giggled nervously and the sound attracted Blair's attention. She looked up incuriously and then quite suddenly her expression altered to one of mixed amazement and disbelief.

"Y'see that feller over there near the elevator?" she mustered, stabbing at the air with her forefinger. Walt, who had given little heed to her talk, nodded.

"Well, that's the guy—that's him. You know, the one Dorothy Brock used to be callin' on all the time when he lived across the way from me on Forty-Sixth Street."

McDermott was galvanized into action. "You're sure of that, Mother?" he demanded. "You'd know the guy anywhere?"

"I certainly would. That's him, all right!"

Walt snapped his fingers. The page boy hurried over to him.

"Get Scotty in here, right away, kid," he said. The boy scurried into the main room of the club.

The globe over the elevator door glowed red. There was no time to be lost. "We've gotta stall here a minute," said Walt. "I gotta special reason for doin' it—you help me out an' ev'rything will be peaches for you an' Polly from now on."

Mrs. Blair nodded vigorously. "Then what time will we have rehearsal tomorrow?" she said loudly to Walt.

"Oh, I don't know. How's four o'clock?"

Peggy and Pat were inside the lift awaiting their departure with ill-concealed impatience, Through the curtained doorway Walt saw the gangster, Scotty, hurrying toward him.

"Or will that be too early?" he stalled. "Well-" Mrs. Blair temporized.

Scotty barged into the foyer and went up to McDermott. "Yeah, boss?" he asked.

McDermott glanced swiftly at Peggy and Denning, saw that they were unaware of his scrutiny and gave instructions to his henchman in a subdued voice.

"I want you to follow the guy that's takin' the little chorus moll home. He's the feller we been lookin' for in this Brock mix-up. Find out where he lives an' then phone me from a drug store or someplace handy. Nothin' rough, y'know, take it easy till we know where we're at."

"Okay," said Scotty.

Mrs. Blair and Polly stepped into the lift with Scotty at the heels. Peggy breathed a sigh of relief.

"It's about time," she commented, bestowing an unfriendly stare upon Mrs. Blair. Mrs. Blair did not deign to notice her.

As he turned to face the metal gate of the elevator Scotty gave Walt McDermott an understanding wink. Then the door closed and the car shot down to the street level.

17/

Danny Moran stared down into the grimy courtyard. From across the way came the shouting of drunk revelers. Through the opened window he saw a room full of besotted performers, high balls in hand, going through the paces of the usual evening brawl.

"Lousy small timers!" he branded them.

Daisy looked up from her novel. "I think the MacNeill sisters are over there lost in the excitement. How 'bout you an' me draggin' the bodies over an' rescuin' 'em? Glory swore to God she meant to get cockeyed an' pass out tonight and you know that gal when she makes up her mind."

"Huh! Leave that old battle axe take care of herself," muttered Danny. "She can hold the fort against the navy an' marines. Jesus, I wish that mob would pipe down. Lot o' drunken bums."

Daisy stared at him more closely. "Seems to me you're kinda gettin' up on your tin ear these days," she remarked. "Always crabbin' 'bout small timers an' hams! Y'know, the Theatre Guild ain't sent no ambassador over here to our joint to request the honor of your services next season."

"Can the wisecrackin', will ya?" shouted Danny irritably. "God, here I come home from a tough day at the theatre an' I got to lissen to the wife beefin' at me far into the night. It's killin' me!"

"Well, it's a cinch you won't die of good nature," rejoined Daisy. "I think a good shot o' gin 'd kinda calm *you* down, s'matter o' fact!"

"I ain't drinkin' with a bunch like that. No brains! No class! No distinction! They'll be strictly Loew time to the end o' their days."

"Well, baby, seems to me I remember a few seasons when you hurled your pink an' white body 'round that circuit," was Daisy's comment.

"Okay. Rub it in! Anyhow, I progressed. God, Daisy, I sure rate with the gang at the theatre. They think I'm aces."

"Yeah? Well, watch that head or you'll have t' be wearin' the Grand Central Station for a hat."

"I get it. Just because I got the brains to realize I ain't used my full possibilities you folks with your small time minds start razzin' me. I sh'ld think you'd wanna stick by me, insteada yelpin' your head off."

"Who's yelping? My God, you're actin' crummy tonight. Y' better go in an' sleep it off."

"Sleep it off, hell. I'm goin' out for a walk. Maybe I'll see some real people if I can get far enough from the Palace."

He started toward the door. "Get a load of who's tryin' to pull the Ritz," jeered Daisy. "Y'better watch your step. You've propped up the wall outside the Bond Buildin' so long the whole place'll cave in if you decide to quit supportin' it."

"Says you," retorted Danny ineffectually, escaping to the comparative safety of the hotel corridor.

"Give my regards to Lady Plushbottom," screamed Daisy after him. He ran through the hot corridor toward the elevator.

Dorothy Brock favored Endicott with an ecstatic hug. "A star sapphire! How did you know?" she gurgled.

"I'm psychic. Read it in the stars. Evangeline Adams always consults me in her important cases."

"Dick, it's silly just to say 'thanks.' You're so darned sweet. Look at the boy, blushing through that perfectly swell Southampton tan."

"There are lots of sapphires where that one came from, a peck of diamonds, handfuls of rubies. Lord, kissing you is like doing your bit of kicking the gong around."

"Does this beauty stand for anything in particular?"

"I wish you'd call it an engagement ring," Endicott plead "Dick! What a grand way to propose!"

"Come on, sweet. Join the clan. We're snobbish as hell but we Endicott men have a weakness for ladies like you."

"Darling! Not till all this rehearsing is over and done with!"

"Better say 'yes.' Else there'll be no feather curtain on opening night!"

"What'll you do, Mr. Endicott? Burn it?"

"Burn it, hell. I'm buying the damn thing."

"Buying it?"

"Sure. Didn't you know? Technically I'm your boss. No 'yes,' no feather curtain. Now what answer are we giving?"

"*Dick.*" She kissed him once more.

For the second time that night the bedroom door slammed. Amy hammered at the panels until her knuckles bled, but there was no reply.

"I know you were with that bitch last night! I know you were! It's gonna cost you your job, that's what it's gonna cost you. I won't have any trick chorus girl makin' a fool outta me. An' you have the nerve to accuse me of cheatin'. Being married to you is the most humiliating, exasperating, degrading experience a girl could have. I'll fix you, though! I'll fix you.

You'll be sorry you tried to pull a fast one on me. When I get through with you Lorraine Fleming wouldn't look at you if you was God and the Marx Brothers rolled together." Andy Lee rolled to his left side, snoring lustily.

Pat didn't like the looks of the strangers who accosted him near the door of his house. They were nicely dressed and obviously had no intention of panhandling, but the determined manner in which they blocked his path made him uneasy.

"Can you tell us where a party name of Denning lives?" the shorter of the two asked, shoving his face uncomfortably close to Pat's nose.

"Why, of course, I—" caution prompted him not to finish the sentence.

"Go on," said the larger man. "You—what?"

"Nothing! I don't know many people in the neighborhood."

"The idea is this. This Denning's kind of a wise guy and he's playin' 'round with a dame who don't want him. We thought we might tip him off what a lousy jolt he'd get if he didn't let the dame be."

"Who the hell are you?" demanded Pat. "I'm on my way!"

"Oh, no, Mr. Denning. Whatcha think 'bout what we said?"

"I'd say it was none of your god damn business."

"Oh, yeah! Well, how's this for a sample?" A heavy fist crashed into his face. He dropped to the sidewalk. One of the two men ground his heel into Pat's unprotected forehead. Then the two vanished into the gloom of the night.

And while these events were taking place, *Pretty Lady* was being shaped into acceptable form. Nothing must stand in the way of the show. Success or failure waited and there was no man who could say which it would be. But beyond the petty squabblings of the Morans and the Lees, the cunning avarice of

Billy Lawler, the madness of Dorothy Brock, the hopes and fears of a hundred others, the Show strode toward its fulfillment.

BOOK II

OPENING

II

The sweltering dog days of august relinquished their hold. Winds from the Atlantic swept through the sun- scorched streets. Life, which had lain torpid beneath the shriveling heat, stirred again. At the Forty-Fifth Street Theatre the pace of rehearsal was geared to a higher pitch. From nine in the morning until long after midnight the *Pretty Lady* company went through their strenuous routine. To produce a musical comedy in five weeks is a heart-rending task. In five more days the company would entrain for Philadelphia where the opening was scheduled for the following Tuesday. Everything looked ragged, producers and cast alike were disheartened. Only the trite saying, "A bad rehearsal makes a good performance," buoyed them. They fought doggedly on against the disappointments of a mediocre score and a book that, but for the inventiveness of Danny Moran and Harvey Mason, would have plunged any intelligent audience into the depths of despondency.

Chaos reigned. Green and Friedman quarreled with Marsh, Si bewailed the heavy cost of production; the very sight of the shimmering stuffs which would be fashioned into the curtains required by Julian Marsh appalled him. With Philadelphia in the offing a ragged confused piece dragged its way across the Forty-Fifth Street stage night after night. Impossible to lay a finger on what was wrong—the first night audience must tell them that. It seemed inevitable that that the bits and numbers chosen by the cast for success should fall flat at the opening. Time and time again the truth of this phenomenon has been proven. Naturally the chorus reflected the disgust of the others. In some uncanny manner the most guarded secrets find their way into chorus dressing rooms. Some chorus girl always knows the closing date of a show before anyone else. If, after the opening night, you want to know who will receive his two weeks' notice, ask the chorus. They have had it, confidentially, that this or that will occur and it generally does.

So, as is often the case when a management is floundering the chorus were drilled and re-drilled. An unoccupied stage during the last week of rehearsal looks bad to any chance visitor; he might circulate the report along Broadway that the management has a flop on their hands and it is difficult to fight these reports once they gain headway. Sometime the sheer manual and mental labor calamity is avoided—as in case of George White's *Manhattan Mary*, which caused direst predictions when opening in Atlantic City and return to New York to give them the lie.

Life was consecrated to the effort of seeking relief from aching feet. Andy Lee had outdone himself and it was fore ordained that the chorus would be acclaimed on the opening night—if they survived. The dancing standard is raised each season, and newer and more difficult steps must be found. The average chorus girl has to combine tap dancing, ballet dancing, acrobatic dancing and singing with the paramount qualification of good looks. She may come from Sioux Falls with high hopes, bearing in her hand the diploma from Reade's School of the Dance, only to find that a thousand others can equal or excel her efforts. If her appearance is pleasing she joins the ranks of the chorus; if not she returns to Sioux Falls. But they all fight on in the hope that someday someone will recognize that still small spark of talent and present the sought after opportunity.

Peggy spent these last few days in town alternating between the costumers and the theatre. Each night after rehearsal had ended, a list of the names of girls whose clothes must be fitted was read off, together with the hour of their appointments. At eight-thirty Peggy stood before the glass at the La Belle Studios while a perspiring seamstress tucked and pinned—at nine-thirty she dashed into the dressing-room at the Forty-Fifth Street Theatre, threw aside her street clothes, donned her practice rompers and presented herself for the long siege of dancing under Andy Lee's supervision.

Dance routines over which weary days had been spent were ruthlessly torn out because they overshadowed the work of Dorothy Brock. A duet between the second juvenile leads, two up-and-coming youngsters, was eliminated on Dorothy Brock's request.

"Why don't they cut out the whole show an' just bill it Miss Dorothy Brock in an evening of Songs, Sayings and Imitations," growled Danny Moran. "The imitations being that of a dancer. It wouldn't be very good but they might laugh."

Little Polly's high-kicking routine was removed because Dorothy Brock wished to bolster the *Lady, What of Love* number. Polly's mother, screaming imprecations, was forcibly ejected from the theatre.

"Wait till you get a load of Brock's snappy little waist-high kicks," murmured Ann Lowell.

"After she gets through that dance she'd better take Lindbergh out for a bow," added Flo.

Green and Friedman were content; Dorothy Brock was their featured player and all talent must be molded to fit with her performance.

Jimmy Allen, eccentric dancer, was informed that his dance must go unless he cared to teach Dorothy the routine and perform it with her. Rather than decline and run the danger of two weeks' notice after the premiere, Jimmy assented.

Discontent smoldered dangerously near the surface. Through it all Dorothy Brock retained her blithe and ingénueish disposition. She had faced countless situations like this and the grumbling of a few supporting players left her undeterred. She meant to be the shining light of *Pretty Lady* no matter how great the pressure was brought to bear. The combined weight of her prestige and Richard Endicott's financial interest forced all lesser considerations to the waived

"Lissen to her singin' that reprise," hissed Flo, "She's had enough blue notes to find the Lost Chord by now. An' I hope you noticed the wrinkles under the chin. She'd better not stand still or the ivy's liable to climb right up her."

"That dance with Phillips looks like the chariot race from *Ben Hur*," commented Ann Lowell scathingly. "You could put on a tall hat an' walk under that split Brock does for the finish. I suggest they get the show girls to form a tableau under the split an' call it the Rainbow of Love. Something's gotta be done to save the number."

"An' wait till you get a load of her clothes," said Flo."I thought the maternity gowns they wished on us were bad enough, but I'd give ten bucks to know what that fur on her evening cloak was when it was walking around. An' *God*, those picture hats! That belle trying to get away with picture hats an' curls! Why, she heard Lincoln free the slaves!"

"Her boy friend's the heavy sugar for the outfit," Lorraine Fleming informed them. This information had been pried from Andy Lee during one of many drinking bouts. "He's on the stock exchange, you know—big polo player, golf wizard, one o' them big putter an' brag men. He used to sit in the front row ev'ry night to hear her sing *You an' Me and a Cup of Tea* in the last show, but it wasn't till he connected with General Motors that she tumbled like a ton o' bricks. He's invested securities in her name, gave her that swell sapphire she keeps flashing—and that belle's all set for life. An' the joke of it is I hear she's keeping some ham actor that doesn't own a pair o' pants to his name."

"Look at that dance! Are you screaming? Get those pins in the air, Annie. Dancers may come and dancers may go, but there'll never be another like our Dot," jeered Flo and added devoutly, "Thank God."

"An' her kicking about the *Flying High* number. I hope you're well! Said the number was too strenuous for her to sing right after all that hoofing. She could be *all* out o' breath an' start singing and the audience would never know the difference."

But lack of popularity failed to impair Dorothy's high spirits. She knew her Broadway. No grumbling actors paid her salary. Let them curse. Her name in lights over the theatre was ample recompense for any hatred her tactics might arouse. Every chorus girl vowed then and there that once she rose from the ranks and found herself a featured player she would show a little sympathy to the other players. All embryo performers suffer from this altruistic complex. Luckily for their careers a more hard-boiled philosophy is formulated ere many months have passed and the erstwhile Good Samaritan, once she has gained a foothold, learns to guard her position jealously.

At six o'clock 'the company was dismissed for dinner. Pat had mentioned an engagement for the evening, an excuse that Peggy was willing to accept, as the battered condition of his face made him a somewhat conspicuous companion. So Flo, Ann and Peggy went to a nearby Chinese restaurant and consumed portions of chop suey. The conversation was loud and caustic. They were three chorus girls "on the pan."

"Well, Brock's got everything except the mortgage by now," Flo commented.

"Don't it give you a pain?" said Ann. "Here we got real artists in the show and that dizzy belle grabs everything in sight. She'd better wear a Benda mask in the last act; the audience is going to get sick of the sight of her face."

"That's what it means to have influence," Flo growled. "B'lieve me, the guy who cracked about the wages of sin being death didn't know his New York. Y' see, all she has to do is start a rumpus that they're not giving her enough to do and the boy friend tightens up on the purse strings. And how Green and Friedman need that money!"

Peggy was quiet. For the first time the fascination and the tragedy of this existence broke upon her with full force. Here were over one hundred souls concentrating all thought and energy upon a musical play which, when brought before the public eye, might be totally lacking in popular appeal and all the labor of many weeks would go for naught. Among the chorus girls they were speculating already what to do if the piece failed. Money was scarce and the season for productions was past. If *Pretty Lady* closed, they would be left high and dry until word of a new show was noised about and the maddening round would begin again. There is no gamble alluring as show business. Millions of dollars are swept away; reputations flame high and then die to ashes in a season or two, and still performers strain forward. The glamour of the footlights is irresistible and even those to whom steady failure has brought discouragement find themselves lingering on the fringe—hoping against hope that at this late day luck may turn.

2

Pat Denning lighted a cigarette and stretched his lean frame in a prolonged yawn. Sitting there in his apartment with the silk dressing gown which had been Dorothy's latest gift draped about him, he felt content. In retrospect he saw his life as a dalliance along purple paths which led to unfruitful valleys. But now a new impulse had laid hold on him. The soft linens of the sinner were to be exchanged for the monk's coarse raiment. Instead of fine liquor more humble refreshment would grace his dinner table. The day of atonement had arrived.

The cause of this ecstasy of the spirit was not far to seek. It spread tentative wings soon after his recovery from the blow delivered by gangland's representative that felled him and for a few days threatened to mar his pleasing features permanently. It soared high into the heavens of good intention when Peggy Sawyer shyly admitted her affection for him. Now was the time for a good man to come to the aid of his better self. He, like Paul of old, had seen the light and was willing to forsake the sins of the world. He had little faith in his power to hold Peggy once the true facts were known, so it behooved him to sever those ties which bound him to the chariot wheels of Dorothy Brock.

Unseen forces were at work; the termination of his affair with the musical comedy actress was necessary to the peace of mind of several individuals. Very well, then, he was not one to question the power of these adversaries, he would abdicate most cheerfully and leave the shadows of illicit love for the bright sunlight of Peggy's companionship. He fingered his jaw tenderly. The fist of his assailant had left its mark; the wonder was that his nose retained its shapely contour and that the fine line of his chin had not been battered into shapeless pulp. A vivid Italian sunset effect still graced the region directly beneath his eyes. He remedied this as well as possible by the application of healing ointment and dark powder. More, he was careful to be seen only in subdued lights, seated where the left half of his face was but dimly visible. Fortunately the interior of the theatre where he was rehearsing was dark and he managed to linger within until the majority of the players had departed. Peggy and Geoffrey alone were aware of his plight, and the former had been easily pacified with a stock alibi. Geoffrey wisely enough asked no questions. He was sure that the battering ram which had connected with his friend's face was manned by those forces of darkness from whom Pat drained his living.

His new play bore the earmarks of a hit. This was a stroke of good fortune for Pat. A kind destiny was granting financial independence for a short space of time, and by dint of much economy he might continue his courtship unaided by the monetary assistance of la Brock. But the parting must come. He poured himself a third drink which served to bolster his waning resolution. He wondered if Dorothy would play the hell cat. Hitherto she had been pettish or yielding, as the mood prompted, but now, faced with this ultimatum, she might fly into a tantrum and create a scene that was certain to cause him to be ousted from the apartment. Then caution reminded him that the robe he wore came from Dorothy and that this moment of renunciation might be delivered in an atmosphere of greater sincerity were he to choose garments of his own purchase. He rummaged through numerous closets and brought to light a suit of subdued blue which seemed somber enough for the occasion. One does not bury an old love in the finery of happier days and the problem of selecting the proper cravat presented itself. To locate a suitable necktie required persistent search; Pat was a young man who could, and did, wear loud colors with impunity. The necktie, dark gray in shade, was lifted from among its entangled fellows. Then he considered the problem of liquor. Suppose Dorothy were to wax dramatic and want to drink a toast to the dear departed days. He thought this unlikely, but the vagaries of womankind are many. Perhaps a chaste decanter of wine would not mar the pathos of the interview. Dorothy might faint and require a stimulant. He checked over a list of his acquaintances who had abandoned mistresses in the hope that one of them might give him pointers on the handling of such a contretemps, but he reflected that all these gentlemen had supported their amours, while with him the situation was unhappily reversed.

It must be unique in the annals of sin, the gigolo turning in fine scorn upon his protector. He wished Dorothy would hurry. Those damnable rehearsals were apt to delay her for hours nowadays. One never knew when the whim of a bull-headed director would chain the cast to the theatre for many unnecessary hours.

He began to pace the floor and wished he dared risk another nip, but that might prove fatal. One does not bid a hiccoughing farewell to one's demimondaine existence; it is better to go forward with the clean light of sacrifice in one's eyes. He wished that he might be granted some manner of a sign, even as Paul, but nothing disturbed his meditation save the screeching of a neighbor's radio. It was past six and he engaged a table for dinner at seven. It was shameful to hurry through this ordeal. He must allow his proud and sinful self to be humbled under the wrath of Dorothy, for the path to renunciation is hard. Damn the woman, anyhow! If she fails to appear within the next quarter of an hour he would leave a note. No, that wasn't the proper move; letters were damnable things, ghosts that loomed alarmingly when one believed them long dead.

But where was Dorothy? He ran through the speech he prepared, pausing appreciatively over several savory morsels. If only his tongue did not play him false when the crucial point arrived. From somewhere came the pealing of a bell. He sprang to the buzzer, every nerve alert. To his horror, he saw an ill-concealed tremor take possession of his hands. One longing glance was flung at the decanter but he found strength to resist.

Dorothy was coming up the stairs. His heart grew cold within him. Tales of women who avenged themselves for fancied slights assailed him. He remembered Dido, roasting on the funeral pyre whose embrace she chose when the arms of Aeneas were denied her. Surely Dorothy would attempt no spectacular heroics. Above all things she wanted to live. He heard her footstep upon the landing. For an agonized second he considered retreat; an abject surrender to the unholy power of Dorothy.

But no, Peggy had shown him the braver way. A left hook to the jaw had aided this resignation of the spirit, but it was Peggy who was leading him toward the light. He must think of Peggy. Her happiness was at stake. The separation should come tonight.

He felt quite ill when he heard Dorothy's knock, but braced himself and called, "Yes; darling, I'll be there in a moment."

Darling! Words of endearment fell so easily from his lips. She would expect to be cajoled and kissed. He flung open the door with what he hoped was a stern uncompromising glare in his eyes. Actually he looked a little dazed. Dorothy thought he had been drinking and began to reproach him. An air of restraint shadowed their meeting. Dorothy walked inside, sank into her chair and fidgeted, Pat tarried near the door, summoning from far corners the courage which her entrance seemed to have dissipated. Ridiculous to comment on the small gossip of the day. There were graver issues to be met.

"I thought you'd never get here," he began. "Lee kept us overtime. I'm terribly sorry, Pat."

"It doesn't matter. You look rather tired."

"I am. Rehearsals are hellish. Can't I have a drink?"

"There's wine. Shall I pour it for you?"

"Wine, Pat? Can't you scrimmage up a whiskey and soda?"

"Dorothy—Dorothy—there isn't time for that—"

"Time? But, my dear, we've got hours. I want to talk to you."

"And I want to talk with you, Dorothy."

"Indeed? Who's the creditor now? Finchley or Dobbs?"

"It isn't that exactly, Dorothy—"

"I'm glad to hear it. You're an extravagant whim for a lady, Pat."

"I've always tried to give value received."

"I'm not complaining. But Pat—I—it's difficult for me to say this—" She fingered her handkerchief uneasily.

"Then don't try, Dorothy. I think I understand," he soothed her. "You must hear me."

"Pat, I can't let you keep on talking under a false impression."

"My dear, I'm not. Won't you listen?"

"The lady's privilege, Pat? And I will take some wine. It looks very inviting."

He filled a glass and handed it to her. He saw that she was trembling and guessed that once again an uncontrollable longing for his kisses had seized her. The heart of a woman is a bottomless well from which she can draw unnumbered bucketfuls of emotion. After man is exhausted and satiety has laid hold upon him woman can still summon the forces of love to her side in undiminished strength. He prayed that Dorothy would free him without tears. He would appeal to her pride. Vanity has checked hysteria far more effectively than all the logic in the world. He began to rearrange his speech, only half listening to the words which stumbled from Dorothy's throat.

"Pat, you know how tremendously happy our little—friendship has made me. You're a dear and I could heartily endorse your—well—merits. But, dear boy, this thing must end sometime and I thought the break should come now. I m going out of town in a few days. We shan't be able to see one another for three weeks and in that time the wound may heal. For I can't go on, Pat. It wouldn't be honorable. There is a man you may know, Pat; a fine upstanding Wall Street businessman who has been very kind. Naturally he makes certain demands of me which I can't decently refuse. And it would be shameful to deceive him any longer. For a time I was satisfied because I knew you needed me and I've always felt tenderly toward you. But today Richard found certain letters and asked me questions. Things came to light that I preferred to keep hidden, We had a stormy time of it and he told me that I must part with you. Of course I hate the idea, Pat, darling; don't suffer so—please, my dear! You're breaking my heart! But Richard is so good to me. He has an interest in our show and I can't turn him down, You understand, don't you, Pat?"

Pat's mouth twisted into a bitter smile. "I understand, Dorothy," he said meaningly. "I think I've understood all along. From the first moment I allowed you to give me money I knew this time would come. You were not content with taking my pride and my self respect, you must rob me of the love I consider my due. Of course, I can't stop you. I don't pretend to be a millionaire—my financial status will always be the same. But I did give you one sincere thing—my love—and you've rejected it. I wish you all the luck in the world, my dear, but I can't help feeling that little happiness can be granted to the woman who betrays her lover. You took so greedily the little I had to offer and now in return you strike with the cruelest weapon known to your kind. What have I done to deserve this? Why should another man hold you in his arms?"

There were tears in Dorothy's eyes. A strangled sob escaped her and for a moment she was wordless under the sting of Pat's accusation. Then she smiled up at him. "Pat, I deserve your hatred, I know. But we women are weak and we have to consider ourselves." She twisted the star sapphire abstractedly. Pat's keen eye noted the newness and expensiveness of this latest bauble.

"With you there would be no future," Dorothy continued. "Just going on in the same fashion until we tired of one another and dislike would smother all our nobler instincts."

"You think I could ever dislike you?" cried her heartbroken swain. "Oh, my dear, how you misjudge me!"

"But, Pat, you are strong and able to bear these things. I'm not worthy of the affection you want to give me. Richard is gross, materialistic. I shall miss your sensitiveness, my dear, but I cannot feel that I should sacrifice myself utterly. Still—if you wish—"

Pat's eyes softened. "I've been too harsh," he whispered. "What a selfish brute I was to seek to hold your love when I could give you absolutely nothing in return."

"I think you're the sweetest man I've ever known, Pat."

"No. I'm a rotter—I'm a cad, but according to my lights, I have loved you. Please believe that!"

"Then we can say good-by without bitterness?"

"Without bitterness, sweetheart. I really meant what I said about wishing you good luck. And permit me to add that I consider this Richard of yours a very fortunate young man."

'Pat, I can't find words to thank you."

"May he make you very happy, Dorothy. I could not have done that."

She held out her hand. "Good-by, Pat," she said tremulously.

He grasped it and raised it to his lips. "Good-by, carissima, and for the love you gave me, many thanks."

She fumbled in her purse, and produced a check which she thrust into his palm. He let the bit of paper fall to the ground as though its very touch seared his fingers.

"I can't accept that," he said with dignity. "You mustn't mar the good-by with such a gift. Please take your check back." At the same time he made out the word "thousand" written in Dorothy's flourishing penmanship. He bent closer to distinguish what number preceded the thousand.

Dorothy shook her head. "It's little enough, Pat. I wanted to buy you something very beautiful but there wasn't time. I've made the check out to bearer for obvious reasons. Please, Pat, I want you to have it."

"I shall burn every penny—or every bill, rather," he cried passionately.

She blew him a kiss. "I hope not, Pat, for it comes to you with much love. Good-by, my dear." The door closed, shutting off his view.

The irony of what had come to pass failed to amuse him. He was still shaken by the pseudo anguish he had worked up for Dorothy's benefit. But now that she was gone his more practical self intervened. He stooped to pick up the check. Then he dressed for dinner.

At seven o'clock Pat, seated across the table from Peggy, reached over to squeeze her hand. Her lack of resistance was encouraging. He looked into her eyes, still careful to keep the damaged part of his face hidden in the shadow.

"So you're leaving me, young lady. And what does the desolate gentleman do?"

"Bear up with sundry stimulants and go about the business of life," she replied promptly. "After all, Philadelphia isn't the end of the earth."

"How little feeling you grant me," he sighed.

"I can't agree that you've been dealt a death blow," she retorted.

"But you know that I'm going to miss you frightfully."

"Certainly. That's only right and proper. But, we're sure to meet again."

"In thunder, lightning, or in rain?" he questioned.

She patted his arm. "The man *is* desperate when he's reduced to quoting Shakespeare," she said.

"Hang it all, Peggy, don't I get one encouraging glance?"

"Pat, you wouldn't do such an old-fashioned thing as propose marriage?"

"My darling, I haven't the capacity for such daring. Only an adventurer would broach that subject if his financial affairs were like mine."

"I'm disappointed. I'd hoped to hear the love-in-a-cottage theme."

"Don't make fun of me, Peggy. I'm being serious."

"And so am I. Look at my consommé. It's growing cold."

"The devil take your consommé. I'll order some fresh. Peggy, do you love me?"

"Perhaps. Not enough to take you seriously at any rate."

"Then you won't say 'yes' and make a good man of me?"

"You're not abject, Pat. There's too much of the arrogant male about you."

"Damn it, I can't go on my knees."

"Pat, darling, concentrate on food. You have an ailing look. I refuse to be hurried into matrimony. What about this career that I've wished upon myself?"

"Peggy, I'll allow you all the freedom in the world as long as our addresses coincide. You'll find me the blue ribbon winner among easy-going husbands."

"That's just it, Pat; everything about you is so easy-going. Especially your cash."

"Peggy, you're a mercenary trollop. Those candid gray eyes have deceived me!"

"Pat, I'm nothing of the sort. I simply wish to save you a racking sense of responsibility. If I were disabled you'd feel bound to support me. And suppose you were quite incapable of the burden? Then wouldn't my husband damn me to perdition?"

"I'd do no such thing. Please don't have those sordid ideas. Peggy. I'll manage well enough. This new play's going to be a winner."

"It can't run forever. And then what would Mr. and Mrs. Cassius do about their lean and hungry look?"

"We'll take tin cups and go blind together. At least we'll have each other."

"No, Patrick, baby. I shall stick to my life of shame for a while longer."

"Am I to consider myself dismissed?" he demanded.

"No, just temporarily suppressed. I imagine you'll burst forth again in no time."

"You're right about that. I intend to wed you, woman."

"Let's talk about our respective shows. We're on much commoner ground occupied that way."

"Very well. Eat your consommé and shut up. I think I shall remain a bachelor."

"Do! I can picture you sitting silver-haired and alone before a pine fire."

"The way you worry me there won't be any silver hairs. I shall sit alone, all right, but the flames will make flickering shadows on my bald dome."

"Then I'll be the meager little spinster who drops in occasionally to give you a scalp treatment. We'll set our bridgework firmly in our mouths and chat about old times!"

"You won't be living then," he vowed. "Some exasperated young man will have shot you."

"Oh, Pat, how lovely to go out that way, with one's picture on the front page of the *Graphic* for an obituary notice. Can I count on your salt tears being shed over my grave?"

"You can count on nothing. I shall say it served you jolly well right."

"Beast! Is Chateaubriand steak really as good as you say, Patrick?"

"Yes, damn you. And I hope it gives you ptomaine!"

3

Let's check them over once more, for good luck! Stockings—shoes—underwear—hats—rubbers— Peggy supposed it was foolish to cart all this stuff along but Lord knows what kind of weather to expect in Philadelphia; and, anyhow, she couldn't burden Maida with too many things. All these books—they certainly took up a lot of room, she'd no idea the way things collected. Nothing in the top drawer, second drawer, third drawer, oh, damn it!—her new blue dress, well, that must be crammed in the suitcase, she just couldn't open that trunk again. Nine o'clock! Where in the world was Pat? He knew she wanted to be at the station by nine-thirty at the latest. Let's see now. Anything else? Good Lord, yes, all her toilet articles! Stupid idiot! Dumbbell! There wasn't a square inch of space left—she'd have to stick the tooth brush and the bottle of perfume in the pocket of her coat. That would look pretty—marching through the station, pockets all bulged out with tooth paste and 4711 toilet water! Where was Pat? She had half a mind to go on without him. It was most inconsiderate to keep her waiting like this. Too bad she'd refused Terry's services. He at least respected her desire for ample time. But careless, scatter-brained

Pat—God love him! Never would she let this happen to her again. Ten after nine. Oh, damn you, Pat, damn you!

The telephone rang and she hastened to answer. Mr. Denning is downstairs—well, it's about time, ask him to come up, thank you. Click! Now to get all these bags together. Wasn't packing a mess? One more hasty inspection bringing to light a pair of discarded slippers that might come in handy on rainy days. A knock on the door. Pat? Yes! Good! I shan't be a minute.

He really was good-looking in his gray summer-weight clothes and panama hat. Thank heaven for tall men! She gave him a perfunctory kiss and pointed to the luggage. He grimaced wryly but picked up the suitcase, the handbag and the portable typewriter without a word of complaint and motioned her toward the door.

"You're awfully late. I was so worried!"

"Late? Nonsense! You've got hours! I'd never dream of leaving before a quarter to ten," he scoffed. "You New England women!"

"At least we're reliable," she answered sharply.

The elevator was crowded but they wormed their way inside and waited in constrained silence until the ground floor was reached. Instantly they were faced with an onslaught of bell boys. Baggage, sir! Carry your bags, mister? Taxi, mister? Yes, sir, I'll take them!

"Go 'way," Pat laughed. "This is my picnic."

The boys retired, discomfited, and she and Pat sped to the side entrance of the hotel. The taxi starter caught sight of them and rushed forward. Pat surrendered the luggage and stowed Peggy inside the first cab. Pennsylvania Station! And, driver, hurry please—the lady is nervous! Off with a grinding of brakes and a lurch that threw her into Pat's waiting arms. On for half a block and then a wait for traffic. She w tremendously excited. The clock on the Paramount tower pointed to nine twenty-five. Taxis swarmed over the street, each playing the well known

Manhattan game called beating the lights. The red glow changed to green and they started again.

"I suppose it's useless to suggest that you write Pat said.

"Not at all. I'm a very good correspondent."

"What hotel are you going to?"

"I don't know yet. I'm leaving that to Flo."

"You and your chorus girl friends."

"Well! Oh, Pat, tell him to hurry. It's half-past nine."

Another red light, as effective as the shining sword that barred the two sinners from Eden. Cabs on either side of them. Pedestrians hurrying along the sidewalk. The sun beating down on the roofs of tall buildings.

"I wish I could drive all the way by car, like Dorothy Brock."

"Cheer up, sweet child. Perhaps, some of these days—!"

"Pat, are we going to be rich—ever? Ouch!"

Another bump that tumbled her into Pat's embrace. This time he kissed her. She looked up half resentfully, decided she liked the feeling of his lips against her mouth and subsided in abject femininity.

"You're the most ridiculous person. Here we are five blocks from the station, you've twenty minutes at least and you're trembling like a deer—or is it doe?"

"I'm trembling at the thrill of your kiss," she jeered.

"You aren't the first to do so," he reminded her.

The taxi swung down the enclosed slope that led to the station. Soon porters were shrilling in their ears, dragging them from the interior of the cab, snatching the luggage before there was time to protest. Pat tipped the chauffeur generously, seized Peggy's arm and guided her through the maze of travelers to the barrier before which the majority of the company were assembled.

It was a scene of uproarious confusion. Tearful mothers clung to their dancing daughters and warned them by all that was sacred and holy to ignore the voice of temptation if it went whispering through the narrow streets of Philadelphia. Glamorous show girls, sprouting orchids and silver fox furs, bade languid good-by to the college students and brokers who were keeping them. Musicians trudged through the gate to the lower level where the train awaited them, their instruments tucked firmly under their arms. Peggy caught sight of Terry clowning boisterously with Harry Towne and another chorus boy. Flo was running along the concourse to the newsstand in belated quest of a magazine. Ann was calling shrilly after her. The company manager stood at the gate, perspiring copiously as he checked each member of the company who passed him and went down the steps to the train. There was an air of hysterical excitement. They were one and all almost frantic with expectation. Pat signaled the porter to wait and pulled Peggy closer.

"I won't go any farther, darling," he said. "From this. point on you are at the mercy of the musical comedy world. May God have pity on you!"

"Oh, Pat, it's so exciting!" she gasped.

"Isn't it? Promise me one thing, sweet. Promise me the same nice child will return from Philadelphia. No quick changes to a hard-boiled chorine."

"No quick changes, Pat!"

"Oh, hello," said Flo, coming up to them.

"Hello, you," Pat greeted her. "Take good care of the infant!"

"Don't worry. She'll be parked in a twin bed right next to her old Aunt Jessie, here. No roaming about for about for this youngster."

"Stout feller!" Pat thanked her. "Oh, Peggy, here's a little something." He produced a novel with a bright yellow jacket.

"Bad reading for good little girls," he explained.

Terry was approaching them. Somehow she didn't want Terry and Pat to meet. She grasped Pat's hand. "Good darling. Wash behind your ears and don't forget to change your undies!"

He bent down and kissed her. Flo obligingly looked away. From out the corner of her eye she could see Terry's flush of displeasure.

"Good-by, angel. Remember what the good little girls do."

"Don't worry—if she hasn't got one, I have!" Flo assured him, pushing Peggy before her toward the barrier. Peggy turned to wave a last good-by, then she and Flo ran down the steps to the train platform. Pat tipped the porter and bade him follow the girls, then turned on his heel and walked away.

A number of the principals were promenading along the stone walk beside the coaches. Peggy, her eyes on the jacket of the book Pat had given her, stumbled and found herself gazing into Billy Lawler's face.

"Whoa, there, child," he called gaily. "Too much traffic for light reading!"

"Oh, hello," she said. "I'm in such a daze."

"May you always be in one," he responded. "It's most becoming."

"Huh!" snorted Flo when they were out of earshot. "That one!"

The day coach which had been reserved for the chorus was already crowded. The two girls deposited themselves in the nearest available seat. Behind them a portable victrola ground out the latest fox trot hit while from ahead came the twanging of a ukulele. Chorus boys, stripped of their outdoor garments, raced up and down the aisles, badgering the girls, shouting to one another, making wild holiday of the trip. Someone produced a flask of gin. There were noisy shouts and demands for a nip. Peggy snuggled far down in the plush seat and let contentment sweep over her. This was the first step. The victrola played on and on, the ukulele shrilled in nasal protest, the chorus boys rioted through the car. Presently a voice called, "All aboard." They were on the way. Dress rehearsal tomorrow night—and then! She closed her eyes and surrendered to the overwhelming happiness that possessed her.

4

Dress rehearsal night! The long vacant theatre quickened to the stir of new activity within its walls. In the orchestra pit the leader waved his baton. He had stripped to his shirt and wore no collar, for the heat from the stage was unbearable. Beads of sweat stood out on his forehead and trickled onto his neck. The thirty musicians focused their eyes on the score for the thousandth time. It was now past eight and they had been playing steadily since three o'clock with an interval of thirty minutes for supper. Julius, the leader, was hoarse and croaked his orders in a rasping whisper that hurt the throats of all who listened to him. His eyes were glassy with weariness and pain battered against the walls of his head.

"We'll take that just once more, boys. It's pretty tricky. Remember, four in a bar and a hold over on that 'E' in the final measure. Right!"

The baton described an arc in the air, the woodwinds found life, the horns struck up their strident clamor. On the stage a tangle of silken drop curtains and the battens on which they were hung met the eye. Various properties used in the different scenes were piled together in what seemed to be a hopeless disarray.

Occasionally a forlorn individual wearing a dressing gown, face partially smeared with make-up, would wander to the footlights to inquire how long before the rehearsal started. The company had been summoned at seven-thirty and, as is customary with all dress rehearsals, things bade fair to get into movement by midnight. The strictest orders had been given out that all members of the cast, principals and chorus alike, must be made up and dressed by eight o'clock at the very latest.

They were all in their dressing rooms now, opening long-disused cans of powder, applying grease paint to their cheeks, searching through their make-up boxes for eye liners, lip rouge, rabbit-foot brushes and boxes of dry rouge. In the back of the theatre Julian Marsh, Green and Friedman and the company manager went over the running order of the show. Because of the elastic nature of the musical comedy it is possible to switch a number from one act to another, or to insert a new interlude at a moment's notice. Nothing is more subject to change without notice than the running order of a musical show during the formative weeks of its existence.

There were the usual slip-ups. Curtains and costumes had failed to arrive; one scene proved to be so ponderous that twenty minutes would be required to set it; the chorus wardrobe was complicated by so many hooks that the wardrobe mistress swore they'd never be able to make their changes. All this is part and parcel of an opening. Since time immemorial, costumers, scenic designers and artists, meeting on common ground for the first time, find that the efforts of each hinder rather than help the other.

In the chorus room bedlam reigned supreme. They were installed in quarters directly underneath the stage; thirty girls, each with her little portion of make-up shelf which must remain inviolate. And there were those who, like the virgins of old, had arrived without many necessities. Borrowing was frequent, and the acrid comment caused thereby more frequent. Overhead sounded the ceaseless tread of the stage hands hauling scenery into place. There came shouts of, "Watch that line!—You ain't clear yet!—Hey, take it easy! You're gonna get tangled!—My God, will a coupla you eggs get some sense?"

Through the din they distinguished the tapping of some buck dancer. "I would get in a show with hoofers," Flo groaned. "Give 'em two square feet of space an' they'll go into their time step and break. They've found the secret of perpetual motion all right." She shook her fist at the unseen dancer.

When the girls were made up they went into a curtained section of the cellar where the wardrobe mistress had unpacked the costumes and laid them out in the order indicated by the running schedule. Harry MacElroy, nearly bursting with anxiety, ran by shouting, "Only ten minutes more, girls! Only ten minutes more!" He would continue to do that for another hour and a half.

Those ladies who were ready for the opening chorus went upstairs pursued by shrill warnings by Mrs. Packard not to sit down and rumple the dresses. No one ever obeys this order and no wardrobe lady can hope for a season free from constant panic lest the dresses in her charge be torn or dirtied.

They were constructing the flight of stairs for the first act finale. A few of the girls dodged through the entrance to the boxes into the front of the house and sat down to watch the proceedings. Sweating men bustled about, armed with hammers and saws. And still the unknown buck dancer, like Poe's *Raven*, continued his tapping.

In the orchestra pit Julius was exhorting his men to new endeavors. In back, the conference of the managers seemed was momentarily becalmed.

Flo sighed. "We're in for the night all right," she moaned.

Slowly the rest of the chorus filed into the auditorium and seated themselves. Julian Marsh, roused by the slamming of many seats, came charging down the aisle.

"Girls! Girls!" he yelled, "No one's allowed in front of the house tonight. If you're all dressed go back to your dressing rooms and wait till you're called."

They trouped back sullenly. The dressing rooms were stuffy and overcrowded and the constant glare of lights hurt their eyes. In the auditorium there was darkness and a breath of air. They would be on their feet for seven or eight hours and wanted to conserve as much energy as possible. No one has yet devised a systematic manner of running a dress rehearsal. It seems to consist of a minimum of actual work and a maximum of standing about waiting for something to happen. Too often the dress rehearsal is the parade ground for the vaunting egos of the moguls in charge. So much authority has to be asserted that there is little time for the show. The principals stalk to and fro in front of their rooms exchanging curt nods and frequent questions as to what is happening. Dress rehearsal is far more strain than the premiere which follows it.

The theatre was a seething caldron of nerves pitched to the breaking point. Even Dorothy Brock was imbued with the general restlessness and sought to quiet her rasping nerves by tuning in the radio installed in her room. Its squawking lent a nightmare touch to the reigning confusion. Doors were slammed in an abortive attempt to shut out this new menace. Miss Brock disregarded the mutters of anger. As featured player she was immune to criticism. John Phillips knocked at her door with an urgent request that they run over the new harmony arrangement for their duet. With a sigh she turned the dials, muffled the blare of the jazz band and instructed her maid to admit the tenor.

One hour crawled by; the stage hands continued to perspire; the managers were still seeking to evade that impasse in the running order; Julius swore at a clumsy bass viol player; and the tap dancer exerted his energy in devising new breaks.

"If they ever hang that guy he'll do a time step on the end of a rope," said Flo. The shower of taps rained pitilessly down.

"There were thuds and imprecations. Still the company waited. Principals began to look like prowling beasts. They stalked to the footlights, and with hands held before their faces, to shield them from the glare of the lights, peered into the front of the theatre. Most faces were grotesque masks of white where powder had been applied to keep the grease paint from losing its freshness.

Finally at ten-thirty came the tocsin. Once more Harry MacElroy was stirred to frantic life. He sped along the corridors bellowing, "Overture—everybody—overture!"

They came crowding to the stage with sighs of relief. "Everybody on stage," shouted the stage manager, and the company ranged themselves along the apron.

Julian Marsh stood in the aisle, near the cornet player. Behind him were grouped Green and Friedman and Forrest, the company manager. Company managers arrange transportation, give out passes when business is slack and carry the woes of their employers on their shoulders. They are worried looking men who must be fated to die in their early fifties.

"Everybody's attention!" called Marsh impressively. "Now we are going to run straight through the show tonight without stopping, because we want to see how long it runs. So everyone stand by, please, and give as much assistance as possible. There's a lot to be done—we're handling a top-heavy production—and it requires the cooperation of each and every one of you to get this show in shape for tomorrow night. Please be ready for your cues—stay back stage and don't come to the front of the house—and, above all, keep quiet. No talking or singing—don't speak above a whisper! Thank you. Overture, Julius!"

The most ironic statement ever made in the history of the theatre is the one in which the promise is made to run through the dress rehearsal performance without interruption. If in any musical comedy they were allowed to finish the opening chorus without a storm of protest, the entire company would be prostrate in amazement. Consequently no one is able to gauge the length of the piece until after opening night.

"Everything set?" Julian Marsh demanded of the stage manager.

"Well, Mr. Marsh, I think we'll be all right, but it's a tough job for the boys to handle. We're gonna need lottsa stalling in one."

"That's why we've engaged our comedians," said Marsh. "Very well then, if that's the only difficulty let's start at once."

The overture thundered forth. There is nothing quite like the thrill of hearing the songs, which for weeks have been pounded on a tinny piano, suddenly finding new beauty in the orchestrations which the composers have devised. Tunes so hackneyed by repetition that the very mention of their names brings forth groans, surprisingly become singable. The company listens with cocked ears and approving smiles. Somehow a full orchestra lends an encouraging note to the undertaking. From it the performers take new heart. Weariness is forgotten—they only know that the very numbers which tried their patience sound enchanting and toe tickling.

The asbestos curtain was quickly lowered and then raised. The curtain of blue silk which masked the opening set was lowered into place. The chorus assembled in their given places. The rehearsal commenced at ten-thirty. At midnight they were still wrangling over the exit made by the girls after the opening chorus. When the dispute was amicably disposed of Julian Marsh received a sudden inspiration to try a new lighting scheme. So they posed for another hour amidst a tumult of such cryptic orders as:

"Kill your reds and dim down your blues!"
"All right, floods! And watch the bunches!"
"Now bring your reds up slowly! Right! That's better!"
"All set then! Full up! Opening chorus again, everybody!"

The first act crawled on at a snail's pace. At two o'clock in the morning, after sundry delays, they reached the finale of the first act. A temporary recess was granted and the information given out that coffee and sandwiches were to be found in the lobby.

This is a time-honored custom of dress rehearsal night. At about two-thirty in the morning a company whose gleaming finery belies the red-rimmed, sleep-heavy eyes, hurries into the theatre lobby where coffee is poured from huge containers and sandwiches of ham and cheese handed to every member. Let it go on record as the sole instance of generosity from a management. Some day some enterprising person is going to remark that there is no reason why actors should be fed for nothing and regular prices will be asked for this early morning meal But until then it is the unhappy lot of a management to be forced to revive the drooping spirits of its players with sandwiches and coffee, gratis, The interval lasts half an hour and then the matter of rehearsal is resumed.

Complications arose. Comedians were rushed into the breach and instructed to deliver ad lib comedy if the stage crew should fail to set the next scene in time. Behind the curtains were tears and anguish because costume changes were impossible in the prescribed space of time. The dresses for the aerobatic dance number were long trailing affairs which made any terpsichorean feats perilous. Green and Friedman stormed and raved. Julian Marsh shouted invectives. There were individual and collective tantrums. Temperamental principals sought fountain pens with which to write out their two weeks' notice, then and there. For the thirtieth time the wardrobe mistress threatened to leave.

The majority of the company bore these incidents with stoic calm. After all, such frenzies come under the heading of necessary evils. They were beyond fatigue, now, and number after number was executed with machine-like precision. Occasionally a leg faltered or a tired arm refused to swing at the correct angle, but the fear of sharp reprimand exalted them far above the complaints of the flesh. At three-thirty the chorus performed the whirlwind maneuvers of the recently restored *Manhattan Madness* episode in flawless style. Even Andy Lee was moved to compliment.

Peggy Sawyer sank onto the bench which was used as a prop in the rose garden scene, and began to cry softly. It seemed as though a thousand demons were hammering at her temples and forcing her very eyes from their sockets. Terry Neill, practicing an intricate wing nearby, saw her and hastened to her side.

"It sure is tough, kid," he sympathized. "But they gotta let us go in three more hours."

"Three hours! Oh, Terry, I don't think I can stand it. These shoes are altogether too small and now my feet are a mass of blisters."

"Sure, I know—I know!" he soothed, "But all the kids are like that—nearly dead. It can't last forever. You better change into your rose dress. They ain't stallin' as much as they was and the show 'll move quicker'n you think."

She smiled gratefully. "You're a dear to bother about me, Terry," she said.

"I'd like to be bothered about you the rest of my life," he assured her earnestly.

She was moved to feeble banter. "Terry,-- love making in the midst of this uproar?"

"Damn it, Peggy, you've gotta give a guy a break one o' these days. Why not pick on me?"

"The way I feel now there won't be anything left of me to say 'yes'. Oh, Terry, why didn't I choose some nice quiet profession like ditch digging?"

"I dunno. I'm glad you picked the chorus. Make it snappy now. This scene is almost over."

She threw him a kiss and ran down the stairs to the basement. He sighed. These pangs of unrequited love could only be vented in a buck dance. He resumed his hoofing. Turmoil in the dressing rooms—turmoil on stage where the "lines" supporting curtains had fouled, and setting the scene was temporarily at a standstill. This meant another three quarters of an hour wasted. The girls freshened their make-ups and went upstairs. Here they lurked among a confusion of coiled ropes and discarded properties, awaiting their next entrance.

Mrs. Blair cornered Andy Lee just as he ducked out of sight behind the shadow of the proscenium arch.

"What spot you putting Polly's dance?" she demanded.

"We've got to figure that out, Mother. Don't get yourself in an uproar. Everything's gonna be okay."

"Okay, hell. That Brock woman had one o' Polly's specialties cut out an' now she's tryin' to queer the waltz with the fan."

"Now, Mother—"

"Don't 'now, Mother' me. I get the idea, all right. Well, so help me God, I'll fix that dame if it's the last thing I ever do."

Andy Lee shrugged and went his way. Rampaging mothers were no novelty to him. Mrs. Blair ran to the dressing room, bristling with rage.

A stage hand informed Danny Moran that his wife was waiting at the stage door. Danny snorted impatiently and left the set to find what mission had rooted Daisy out of bed at such an hour.

He found her leaning wearily against the brick wall of the alley. At his approach she brightened and put out her hands to welcome him.

"H'llo, baby. My God, ain't you done yet?"

"No, we got a lot more. What's the big idea?"

"Big idea of what, hon?"

"Disturbin' me like this. I gotta get back to the rehearsal. You don't seem to realize we gotta opening scheduled for tomorrow night."

"Sure, I know. Don't get your bowels in an uproar. If I'd known you was gonna turn on me like this I'd a' stayed in bed. I s'pose this is the thanks I get for worryin' about you."

"Aw, drop it, Daisy. I'm too damn tired to argue with you. I'll be seein' you sometime this mornin'."

"All right, hon," she said hopelessly and turned away.

He was ashamed of himself but made no move to remedy his blundering. Daisy made him feel a bit sheepish, of late, hanging around him the way she did. He wished she'd get the idea of a little "class" under her hat.

At four o'clock came the tragedy. The rose scene was over and Danny Moran was reading a scene of comic patter with Lionel Crane, an old man past seventy, who played the role of a deputy sheriff. Danny gave the old gentleman a resounding whack on the back and started into the house which was erected at the rear of the stage. Suddenly, with a choking cry Crane stumbled forward. A convulsive shudder twisted his gaunt body—he pitched headlong to the floor and lay still.

The spectators were petrified. Then various men, more alert to the dire necessity of action than others, shouted orders. The stage manager rushed forward and knelt at Crane's side. The chorus crowded in the wings. The musicians laid down their instruments and peered over the footlights. Two or three girls began to cry hysterically until they were hissed into silence.

"What's wrong?" demanded Marsh, horrified.

"I think Mr. Crane's dead," said the stage manager.

Someone screamed. There were agitated whisperings from all corners. The managers were stunned.

"We've got to call a doctor," said Andy Lee. "Props!"

A grimy giant shoved his way to the front of the stage. "I can call Doc Levering," he volunteered. "He's the house physician. It'll take him a half hour to get here."

"You're sure he's gone?" Friedman demanded of the stage manager. His features were rigid with fright.

"Yes sir. Felt his pulse. There's not a flutter. I know a little about these things. Been through the war. Musta been the old heart that gave way, is how I dope it out."

"Yeah," seconded Andy Lee, "he was a pretty old guy."

The body lay prone, giving a macabre note to the gay scene of the rose garden. Green was frantic.

"If he dies here they gotta call the coroner. We won't be able to open tomorrow night. He's gotta be taken away. Oh, my God, my God!"

"He was a Catholic! Why don't they call a priest for him?" shrieked a chorus girl. "You can't just leave him layin' there."

"Sure, they gotta treat him decent," assented another. There was a moment's diversion when Ann Lowell fainted. Willing hands carried her to the dressing room while the assistant stage manager went searching for restoratives. They were found in astounding quantity in the dressing room of one of the principals.

No one knew what to do. On the stage was a dead man—a member of their cast who had departed with appalling swiftness. Someone said that a Catholic church was nearby and the priest's home was next door to it. Si Friedman offered to rout him out and left the theatre.

Minutes dragged by. The awful immobility of Crane's body began to unnerve them. An agonizing quiet descended over the entire theatre. From time to time someone would tip toe across the stage, eyes averted from the shrouded form stretched there like an ugly blight on all that was living and beautiful. There were mumbled prayers. The sight of the dead man moved some of them to repentance. Others turned away and went in quest of a "shot" to soothe their jangling nerves.

Friedman returned with the priest. The Catholics in the company greeted the reverend father with cries of relief and crossed themselves fervently. Father Reilly mounted to the stage and assured himself. that the man was dead. At this juncture the doctor came upon the scene and made his examination which was purely perfunctory as the little spark that might have flickered a short while was stilled forever. Old Man Crane belonged to the forces of eternity.

The heat from the footlights made them perspire. Overhead the floodlights beat down. Marsh requested that the company assemble on stage. They surged forward in the anachronistic finery of the rose scene. Little girls wore wide-brimmed picture hats and dresses whose stiff folds were covered with flowered patterns. Chorus boys awkwardly clutched their silver-colored top hats and tried to step lightly so that the metal cleats nailed to their dancing shoes would make as little. noise as possible. Show girls moved in yards of billowing chiffon and ballet girls in short starched skirts resembling rose petals. Danny Moran appeared in the absurd plus fours that were sure to be greeted with unrestrained hilarity at any performance. All hovered over the prostrate figure of a man seventy who had answered his last cue. The priest lifted hands in prayer. They fell to their knees, some crying softly, others dry eyed but frightened.

Green and Friedman removed their hats. Julian Marsh collapsed into one of the turned down seats. The voice of the priest rose in Power as he commended the soul of this poor player to Almighty God the Father. An electrician dimmed the glare of lights until the harshness was banished and a softer glow pervaded the theatre. At one side stood the doctor, grave and worried. It was his task to clog the swift moving wheels of justice by giving a certificate which swore that Crane died in the ambulance. If it were known that the death occurred on the stage an inquest would be demanded and the opening night would have to be postponed. In such a crisis, deception seemed the wisest course. The doctor knew his show world. Its members were not calloused, but they had learned a thousand times over that phrase, "The Show Must Go On." Marsh began to speculate as to Crane's successor. The thought came mechanically, welling above the sorrow which had risen in his heart. A man has duties;

an investment of one hundred thousand dollars cannot wait upon the passing of one human being.

The services were ended. Slowly, in a dazed fashion, they retired to the wings. Two stage hands covered the body and carried it through the door into the alleyway. An ambulance had been summoned and the white-coated interns relieved the two men of their burden. The priest bade Mr. Friedman good night and quitted the place. The doctor assured Abe Green that he could hush the matter successfully. None of the city officials would know that Lionel Crane had died in the theatre. It was a risky procedure, but with such vast sums of money involved one must be prepared to take chances. He was promised an ample fee and left, after a few parting words of instruction. The rehearsal continued.

Now new problems encompassed them. A successor to the part which Crane had so suddenly vacated must be found. Regardless of the distrait feeling which troubled the entire company, the second act must be readied before they left the theatre.

It was an incident in a life filled to overflowing with the bizarre. They went on, not through an indecent haste to make up for lost time, but rather because the very rehearsing provided an outlet for pent up nerves. Lines were fumbled, lyrics forgotten, dancing routines lost all semblance of unison. Julian Marsh got to his feet.

"Ladies and gentlemen," he begged, "we have all passed through a terrible experience. No one grieves for that poor man more than I do. But we must leave the dead to Providence. They are beyond our jurisdiction forever. It is only by carrying on this good work that we can hope to show how deeply we feel our loss. Mr. Crane was a gentleman and a trouper. He wanted this play to succeed. Heart and soul he was for the production. Don't fail him now. It is a fitting tribute to a great man that we can bear up under calamity and finish the work which he had hoped to see completed.

Thus appealed to they forgot all despair. Old Crane might be watching them even now, urging them to go ahead. They had lost a well loved friend and in death he must not be betrayed. Their efforts should stand as a monument to him.

At eight o'clock a group of tired performers entered Childs restaurant for breakfast. They had been rehearsing continuously through the night save for the episode of Crane's passing. Now they were dismissed until noontime for three hours of sleep if aching limbs permitted; and then once again they would go to their dressing rooms, put on grease paint and hurry through the second act. Tonight was opening.

5)

Opening night in Philadelphia! Abe green chewed savagely on an unlighted cigar. He stood against the wall at the rear of the house and watched the audience assembling. There were many familiar faces, for Philadelphia is only two hours distant from New York and theatrical people make the journey when some particularly important premiere is announced. It gives one a sense of importance to return to Broadway and impart the knowledge that such and such a piece is destined for success or failure, as the case may be. Abe nodded to one or two agents who had placed people with the show, talked with the star of his last season's production who was "resting" at the present moment, chatted with an influential millionaire of the city, and kept an anxious eye on the quantities of unfilled seats.

The box office reported a fairly good advance sale, but Philadelphia buys cautiously nowadays. For too many years it has submitted to the indignity of being known as a "dog town." Producers doubtful of the merit of their plays rent a house in Philadelphia and proceed to offer half-readied shows to the theatrical public of that town. A succession of mediocre presentations has left Philadelphia distinctly hostile to new enterprises and only the magnet of a cast plentifully studded with "names" can coax dollars away from the thrifty burghers of that metropolis. Now the good town folk wait until the morning following the premiere, when their favorite critic will tell them whether the latest attempt is worth seeing or whether it is but another flash in the pan. The wisest among them delay until the closing day of the engagement, for by that time everything is in readiness for the New York opening. Hence a first night out of Manhattan attracts a heterogeneous collection of New Yorkers and local first nighters who feel that their presence is a social requirement rather than a mental relaxation.

There was a profusion of white shirt fronts and décolleté gowns this evening. These Philadelphia matrons were not above displaying an heirloom to the vulgar gaze of the motley. The orchestra were filing to their places. That tension which hangs over such events seemed rampant. A speculative mood laid hold upon the audience. Advance reports had seeped out despite all the care exercised by the management. Green and Friedman were doubtful about this opus. Dorothy Brock was slipping—they might have to replace her before a New York run was attempted. The music wasn't up to the composer's standard—in a few days numbers from industrious Tin Pan Alley tunesmiths would be interpolated. Green listened to the hum of conversation with a sickly grin. An iron hand had laid hold on his stomach and was rending the muscles without mercy.

A patter of applause greeted the entrance of Julius into the pit. He was an established hand at the game—his baton had controlled the scores of countless operettas. Since the days of *The Merry Widow* the name of Julius was one to conjure with. There followed an agonizing pause while the orchestra awaited the signal from the stage manager. Green visioned all sorts of mishaps. The crew were still unfamiliar with their work. The props were unwieldy and more men were needed. There had been mutterings from union officials. The stage manager was on the verge of collapse.

Green recalled the frightful calamity of the preceding year when an offstage gun, firing a salute on what represented the deck of a battleship, caused the entire setting to collapse and fall like the temple of the Philistines about the players' heads. That was another shot heard round the world. The story was a byword along Broadway, for who does not experience a thrill of satisfaction when a theatrical magnate bites the dust? Years of yeoman service will not serve to blot out the memory of Ziegfeld's *Smiles* or Carroll's *Fioretta*, and if such a happening is foreordained your Broadway expert likes to be in at the death. Some of the most envied men on Forty-Second Street are those who once attended a dramatic premiere in which the star, a loved and respected lady whose many portrayals have added glory to the history of the American theatre, was intoxicated and stumbled through her role in shocking fashion. The New York newspaper critics maintained a decent reticence, although one gathered from their veiled allusions that something had gone awry, but along the Street the tale flew from mouth to mouth, gathering momentum with each telling. So it was that Abe Green feared the ridicule of the first night gathering in the theatre.

A bulb over the leader's stand flashed. It was the signal for the overture. The audience settled back with a murmur of contentment. The thumping minor chords which were so characteristic of Conroy swelled to a fury of syncopation. Out of this tumult of notes was born a melody—an eerie wail that shivered through the house. The brasses yelled brazenly—a muted cornet shot out its defiant boast—while the strings whispered m mute apology for this strange torturesome thing that was called music. The wild crescendo of notes came to an abrupt stop and the orchestra segued into a more conventional strain.

"Swell dance number," murmured someone.

Well trained ears recognized the cloying melody of the theme song. A hum of approbation stirred the air. This was fine, easy-going stuff. The dancers in the audience thought what a splendid soft shoe dance that would make. The band leaders realized how its tune could be adapted to that crooning style so popular now. Abe Green, chewing at his cigar, knew that two potential song hits were developing. So much for their fears about the score!

The overture came to an end with a shout of trumpets. So far all was well. There was scattered applause, enough to indicate that those out front were genuinely impressed. Then the blue curtain especially designed by one of the higher-priced studios parted semaphore-fashion, revealing the first scene. The effect was pleasing and received another ripple of applause. On the stage was massed the chorus in the expensive silks which parodied the conventional calicoes that are worn by village maidens in all respectable musical plays.. The girls advanced to the footlights and chanted the strains of the opening chorus. Then they were off in a tumult of kicking. The first nighters clapped rapturously. Abe Green stole a glance at Andy Lee standing a few paces off. Lee's hands were clenching and unclenching spasmodically. His body was taut with suspense. Only his eyes lived. They roamed swiftly for one end of the line of dancers to the other searching out errors in rhythm and movement. Green saw his jaw clench and knew that some luckless chorister was due for a bawling out.

The music shrilled, the dancers abandoned themselves to the spirit of the number and between stage. and auditorium ran that electric current of approval which signifies triumph. Breathless, laughing hysterically, the dancers tumbled into the wings. A storm of applause broke. Word flew backstage. The opening chorus had stopped the show! The opening chorus had stopped the show! Some girls wept from sheer excitement. Others, half fainting from the strenuous ordeal; leaned against the wall. The players strove to make their dialogue heard above the noise, but their efforts were unavailing. The audience was not to be denied.

Abe Green caught Andy Lee's eye. There was feverish excitement mirrored there; an exultation that was kept within bounds only by a stern effort of the will. Green knew that Andy wanted to chuck his hat in the air and yell for sheer joy. A good boy, Andy; he deserved the laurels. Andy was an East Sider; so was Abe. There was something about the stored up bitterness of those early years that made them great. Abe felt a wave of brotherly affection sweep over him. He began to beat his palms at the same time grinning genially in Andy's direction. But Andy was oblivious to everything save the riotous demonstration that filled the air. Wait till they heard about that in New York.

Quiet was restored. The play went on and now came those dull stretches of dialogue which every manager dreads. Abe Green cursed himself for a fool. Why hadn't he noticed how dreary and meaningless those lines were? They would be busy with the blue pencil tonight. Different players entered to varying receptions. Dorothy Brock was halted a full half minute, the loudest noise coming from a young woman in the front row who heartily detested her. That same young woman would fill the ears of eager listeners with stories of how many layers of make-up had failed to hide the wrinkles under Brock's chin.

Abe began to lose the thread of plot which bound the spectacular incidents together. He heard a snatch of dialogue between a lustrous show girl and Danny Moran as the country boy eager for his first encounter with the Broadway wise ladies. The show girl rejected Danny's proposal with a haughty, "You know I couldn't stand a little moron," and Danny's retort, "You could stand a lot more on." The audience laughed. That must be a good one. They'd keep that line in. But thank God the numbers were good, because the book was terrible. Words, words, words! Dorothy Brock and John Phillips were singing. An amber spotlight blended into their sentimental mood.

I found my rai-ai-nbow the day that I found you.

They loved that. No question but that the honors went to Conroy and Andy Lee. Encore after encore was demanded. Green marveled at Dorothy Brock. He saw a nimble-footed girl of eighteen smiling into the face of a man she detested, coquetting archly with him the while she muttered curses under her breath. She was just shy enough. As the lady in the front row remarked, "That jaded old trollop certainly can look dewy when she puts her mind to it." The role of shrinking violet suited Dorothy. Her light voice caught the proper note of romance and held it. She had "gotten over."

That opening night would live in Peggy's memory. The arrival at the theatre after passing the throngs who crowded the lobby at that early hour. The sound of movement out there beyond the asbestos curtain. Making up with hands which trembled so it required painful concentration to apply the mascara correctly. A room full of girls speculating on the evening's outcome—success or failure. Renewed groans when feet were squeezed into badly made shoes. A wardrobe mistress clucking at them like a worried hen. And then the swelling notes of the overture. They scrambled upstairs shouting out wishes for good luck to everyone. The thrice familiar tunes grew strange. This was a dream, and waking would bring Jerry Cole drumming at his piano once more.

The border lights beat down. The baby spots made pools of color upon the ground cloth. Behind the set the principals were busy buoying one another's spirits. A minor ingénue paused to scream a hearty "good luck" at Dorothy Brock's door. The two girls despised one another and yet that exchange of good will was sincere. Life holds no more philanthropic instant than the zero hour of an opening night. In a dim corner two chorus boys were hoofing to relieve the strain. Others scraped their patent leather shoes in the resin box. Two or three girls were crowded around a peek hole in the curtain, spying out well known personages. The stage manager was shouting:

"In your places, girls. They're finishing the overture. Now, then! On your toes, everyone, and give the best show you ever gave in your life. Come on! Lots of laughs! Talk it up! Look alive! Don't let 'em see you're nearly dead! All right! Here we go!"

The overture had ended. The burst of applause sounded faintly through the curtains. One girl clapped her hands gleefully.

"They like us!" she rejoiced.

The stage manager signaled the fly man. Slowly the great curtain parted and the show was on.

No, Peggy would never forget the breathless wonder of that night. It seemed that a part of her was numbed and unresponsive and the person who danced the energetic paces of Andy Lee's routines was some stranger. She had become a robot, incapable of thought or feeling. And always Terry was at her side goading her on. If she tripped he whispered encouragement.

"Smile, baby! They're looking at you! They say you're swell-lookin', sweetheart!"

She wanted to throw her arms around him then and there, but she mustn't think of that or she'd forget the steps. Flying figures knocked her left and right. She was borne downstairs on the crest of an irresistible wave. Someone snatched the costume from her shoulders and substituted another. They were all talking and laughing at once, paying no heed to the shrill admonitions of the wardrobe lady. From time to time there came reports.

"Brock and Phillips stopped the show."

"The Ryan Brothers weren't so hot."

"The boys' number flopped. It'll be out after tonight."

"Brock got a reception on her second entrance."

"The old girl's still going strong."

"Moran isn't as hot as they thought he'd be."

"Harvey Mason stinks. They won't laugh at him out there."

"Didja get a load of Phillips' wife in the box, with all the

Woolworth jewelry hung on her?"

"Sure. Everything but her gallstones!"

"Girls! Girls! Number's on; For God's sake, make it snappy!"

"Harry MacElroy—we'll never get this change. It's too hard!"

"Where's my hat? Where in *hell's* my hat? I bet that Oliver girl's got it on!"

Then stampeding up the staircase just in time for their second entrance. There were collisions and flare ups. Leading players resorted to tears. Stage hands rushed about coming within an ace of crushing out the life of anyone unlucky enough to cross their paths. The stage manager was frantic. Light cues were being muffed. The spotlight was entirely off. The orchestra leader's tempos were terrible. He, too, threatened to succumb to the overwhelming tide of misfortune.

Eventually the curtain fell. There was a concerted rush toward the exits. Lobby talk is always a feature of opening nights. Here the pseudo critics gather and impart wisdom through the smoke that curls from their cigarettes. In a bluish haze they consign productions to the counters of Mr. Tyson or Mr. Leblang. Abe Green wanted to linger and eavesdrop a bit, but his heart misgave him and he hurried backstage. Time enough to find out what was wrong when he read the notices the following morning. He squeezed through the tiny door connecting the auditorium with the stage and ran into the customary bedlam attendant upon intermission. He scampered out of this hectic atmosphere to the dressing room where Dorothy Brock sat screaming at her maid. He hesitated before knocking because the stream of oaths seemed unusually ferocious; but, after all, he was the boss. He rapped on the. panel.

"Who the hell is *that?*" snapped Dorothy. "It's me—Abe. Can I come in?"

"Jesus, Abe, not now. I'm not decent. Can't you let me alone till afterwards?"

"Sure, kid. You're doin' great! They love you out front."

"Thanks, Abe. I need encouragement with the bunch of yokels you picked to support me."

"Everything's going Well. Dialogue's slow—but we'll fix *that* up."

"*That's* your cheap comic, Moran. I've always told you that these burlesquers were no good."

"Oh, Danny's okay. He done fine in the drunk bit. Don't worry. Danny's *in!*"

"You sure wished some trick outfit on me, Abe. This masquerade mess—what is it? I'll bite!"

"Now, Dorothy, it's very smart. All the clothes is very smart."

"Smart—hell! I won't go on in it after tonight!"

"Why do you raise a row, Dorothy, when you're set so pretty?"

"I can't afford to look cheap, Abe. After all, I am the star!"

From some quarter there came an abysmal laugh and a shrill comment, "I hope the ceiling stays up after *that* crack."

"Second act! Second act!" called Harry MacElroy, speeding through the corridors.

"Do run along and leave me in peace," Dorothy begged. "I'm all nerves tonight."

"Well—jus' keep up the good work. That's all I gotta say," Abe beamed.

People ran about aimlessly. He saw Polly Blair, whose number had at the last moment been shoved into the final scene of the show, huddled on a stool in the entrance, with her mother fluttering ineffectually nearby. Polly had been there, fully made up, since seven-thirty, the first one on stage that evening. Abe gave her a friendly chuck under the chin and passed on.

"Dizzy kid," he chuckled, hastening back to his vantage point.

Now it was the second act. The audience settled back more comfortably. The verdict was still in abeyance. The time had passed when dancing and song "hits" could "make" a show. The crying need was for comedy and the laughs were not there. Danny Moran and Harvey Mason labored heroically but their material was threadbare. The first nighters shook their heads.

Peggy, on her way to the stage, stopped at the letter box near the stage door in the hope of finding a belated telegram.

There were several in the S box and presently her search was rewarded. She tore it open and read:

"Hope you will be the most famous belle in town. The other one is cracked, anyhow. Love, Pat."

She laughed appreciatively and tucked it into her bosom. Pat was a dear to remember. The orchestra was blasting forth, the entr'acte had ended. She hurried to her place in the line.

Once more the chorus was assembled. In the mêlée Terry squeezed closer to Peggy.

"You standin' it all right, kid?" he whispered.

"Fine! Oh, Terry, I love this! It's worth all the rest!"

"Yeah! Sure! It's swell! Didn't they tear loose for our first number? I bet ole Lee's higher 'n a kite about that!"

"To think the first chorus that I danced in stopped the show," Peggy exulted. She forgot burning soles and twisted ligaments. It is for moments like these that every performer lives. The grind is heart-rending but the reward dwarfs all pain into insignificance.
A thousand plans, a million hopes all pointed toward tonight. The dreams of many, the despair of a few, finding answer at the curtain's fall. Peggy listened to the hubbub of whispering. They were harking to the reception of every number now. It meant so much if people liked them. It meant a season free from the haunting spectre of poverty. It meant pocket money with which

to pursue favorite studies. The new chorus girl devotes a great part of her day to dancing and vocal lessons. When not employed in that fashion she garners a few extra dollars modeling clothes for dressmaking shops. Then there is "extra" work at the motion picture studios, posing for artists, and advertisements. But all these hang on the possibility of a New York engagement. It is vitally important that the show succeed.

Sometimes they wondered how an audience could be so heartless. Lines which had caused tears of merriment were coolly received. Once, when a nervous principal collided so forcibly with a door that the entire setting shook, Danny Moran cried, on the spur of the moment, "They don't build these houses the way they used to," and the biggest laugh of the evening was registered. So many personalities going to make up the machine. Billy Lawler striding disdainfully by, disliked by principals and chorus alike. Dorothy Brocks bellowing profanity at the defenseless stage manager. The adagio dancers warming up for their specialty. And the inevitable buck dancers at their work. Without laughter and applause for fuel, the machine would stop and these cogs would be separated and lost. What it takes a hundred brains three months to conceive, one audience can tear down in a night. Therein is the romance of show business, the eternal wish to tilt at windmills. No wonder Abe Green stood in the rear of the orchestra, tearing at his fingernails.

6

Harry Towne lay sprawled on the bed, dragging at a cigarette. A phonograph placed on the window seat was droning a jazz melody. From below came street noises—taxis halting before the hotel, street cars rumbling by, conversations drifting upward.

> She's got eyes of blue—I never cared for eyes of blue
> But she's got eyes of blue—so that's my weakness now.

Harry raised a hand and surveyed it critically. That shaking was pretty bad. He'd have to lay off the booze. Still, the dirty work was done—they'd opened and it looked like a hit.

He began to hum. The telephone rang. He reached out and grasped the receiver, pulling the phone over to him.

"H'lo! Oh, H'lo kid! Sure—the party's on. Terry's out gettin' the liquor now. Come on up! Yeah, bring her along; no, no—it's okay—we'll have a lotta laughs. Okay, baby. In ten minutes. Yeah—that's right—807. S'long!"

The clans were gathering. Directly after the premiere post-mortems are held by the members of the company, many of which begin as critiques on the evening's performance and end as drinking bouts.

Harry heard someone fumbling at the door.

"Hey, bozo, open up, will ya?" called Terry, kicking lustily at the panels.

"Aw, for God's sake," groaned Harry. He struggled upright and went over to admit his roommate.

"What's the matter? Forget your key?" he demanded. "How the hell can I reach it with my arms full o' bottles," snorted Terry. "Use your head!" He sidled over to the table and deposited his burden.

"Well, how much did they soak ya?" Harry asked.

"Plenty!" Terry assured him. "These wop bootleggers ain't what they used to be. They got wise to the racket by now." He sank into a convenient chair.

"I hope ya got good stuff," Harry ventured. "Jerry Cole's gonna drop by."

"Lissen," said Terry. "Cole'll drink this an' like it. Who the hell does he think he is? Nothin' but a lousy piano player! Where's the glasses?"

"We can phone down for 'em when the gang gets here," Harry suggested.

"Boy, you sure work yourself to death," grunted Terry sarcastically. "At the rate you're goin' you can't last more'n eighty or ninety years."

"Yeah?" Harry returned. "Who got the liquor th' last time?"

"When it was right next door, wise guy," said Terry; "Who's comin' up?"

"I dunno," Harry shrugged. "This joint's a madhouse. Anybody's liable to drop in."

"Oh yeah?" grumbled Terry. "An' we stand drinks for a gang o' muzzlers that're too cheap to buy their own? Jeez, you're sure a fall guy."

"Aw, what the hell?" Harry expostulated. "We'll be on plenty o' parties this week. What are ya crabbin' about? How much do I owe you?"

Terry lit a cigarette. "Four bucks," he said casually.

"*Four bucks?*"

"You heard me. I told ya the stuff ain't so cheap as it useter be."

"Give it to ya tomorrow. I loaned Matty Rogers ten an' it cleaned me out."

"If I don't shave till I get it I'll have a beard down to my knees," Terry gibed.

"Got ginger ale an' white rock?"

"I got the works," Terry replied. "Boy, I'm all set to get stinkin'."

"Me, too. What an openin' *that* was!"

"Marsh is a bohunk. What the hell does he know about *show* business? An' they oughtta give Brock a kick in the pants!"

"She sure is ritzy," Harry agreed. "An' that voice! They musta run it through a meat chopper. Still—the audience likes it."

"Who couldn't be popular when she gets the stuff handed to her on a silver platter? Boy, that society guy sure fell hard and she socked him for plenty dough. I'll be damned if any woman'll get me like that!"

"Says you," chuckled Harry derisively. "How about this Sawyer dame?"

"Now, lissen; cut out the kiddin' when she gets here," Terry admonished. "That kid's regular and I don't want none o' your wise talk."

"K.O., kid. I'm off the spindles myself for a while."

"Famous words of famous men," jeered Terry. "Why, a blonde looks at you an' you go so cold you could hire out for a Frigidaire."

"At least I don't go off my nut over a broad who says 'It's

I.' When they start handin' me *that* I jus' leave 'em to the intellectual guys."

"Why don't ya quit ridin' her?" Terry demanded. "She's gotta talk like that. Besides, I like 'em wit' class an' education."

"Class an' education!" sneered Harry. "Baby—if they know their stuff they can talk polack, s'far as I'm concerned."

"You're that way," said Terry. "Out for all you can get."

"What the hell *would* I be after? Their immortals souls or somethin'?"

"I want the love of a good woman," proclaimed Terry.

"Don't gimme that. Think o' my incision," Harry guffawed.

Terry moved restlessly. "I thought there was a party on."

"Sophie Gluck phoned before you come in," said Harry. "She's draggin' that wisecrackin' Morton dame with her."

"Why don't you lay off Gluck? She always pals around with Morton and as long as you're off the spindles why not give Soph the gate?" Terry suggested.

"Well, they say she's passin' it 'round so I might as well step up an' treat myself. I ain't no cripple," Harry philosophized.

This profound conversation was interrupted by a second knock. Terry sprang to his feet. "Bet that's Peggy," he murmured and hurried to admit the ne newcomers.

Two figures stood on the threshold—Peggy, wan and tired looking, and the pale slim Jack Winslow who drifted inside with a languid "Hello."

"Hi, Jack!" Harry grunted. "Glad ya dropped in."

Terry was none too pleased to see Winslow. "Nuts!" he growled.

"I met Jack downstairs—" Peggy began.

"So I says, 'Lissen, kid, they're throwing a brawl up to the joint so let's drag the hips up there,'" Jack Winslow finished.

"And here I am!" said Peggy.

"An' welcome as the flowers in spring!" Terry flattered her. "Put it there," he added, indicating an easy chair by the window.

"This is a nice room," said Peggy.

"Sure! I always like to be in swell joints. I can't stand the cheap ones," Terry replied. He gathered up the quantity of bottles and carried them into the bathroom.

"It's *gorgeous!*" Winslow agreed fervently. "The way I could drape my body around this place is *nobody's* business!"

Harry picked up the telephone. "Hello, operator," he called. "Will you send up a boy?"

"Lovely," screamed Winslow. "I'm glad I came. Please tell them to make it a blonde."

"I hope they cut out that *Manhattan Madness* number," Peggy sighed. "My knees are so stiff I can hardly walk."

Winslow shuddered. "My dear, another week of this and I'll go back to the Shuberts even if they put me on the Living Curtain," he vowed.

"The numbers are tough all right," Terry admitted. "They gotta be! Look at the show."

"Show? When that Brock belle let out a couple o' notes I thought I was back in the stockyards. She gave a swell imitation of a stuck pig. And that *fanny!* It looks like a blue print of the Rock o' Gibraltar."

"How that back of hers detours below the waistline," snickered Harry. "Boy, it sure has been the butt of many jokes. One time the Brock floozy was playin' a vaudeville tour with a pal o' mine, Johnny King. Johnny's a wise egg and lottsa guys hate his guts, but whether he knows where the body's buried or not he keeps on gettin' the breaks so I say give him credit. Anyhow, he an' Brock were co-featured on this certain bill, an' a pal o' Johnny's, comic name o' Jack Lenny, came over from Oakland to catch the show. It happened to be the openin' performance an' Brock missed it for some reason or other. Lenny comes back afterwards and asks Johnny why Dot wasn't on the bill, see, an' Johnny wisecracks, 'Well, I'll tell ya, she ships her fanny by freight an' got in this morning ahead of it an' couldn't open.' How's that?"

"Don't worry," Winslow maintained. "That one's coming across with *plenty* to hold this job down!"

"Can that, will ya?" 'Terry pleaded. "Peggy don't like that kinda talk."

"Dearie, the woman that don't like dirt, don't live!" stated Winslow. "I've kept *my* lips sealed long enough. I'm just a girl that has to dish!"

"Yeah?" Terry menaced him. "Well, ya won't do it here!"

"Gorgeous! Do you think he'll beat me up, Harry?" Winslow cried.

"Don't be silly, Terry!" Peggy insisted. "I'm over eighteen."

"I don't think a nice girl should have to lissen to that kind o' talk,' Terry sulked. "It's stuff like that gives show business a bad name."

"Aimee McPherson, get back to your kitchen!" railed Winslow.

"Aw, shut up! Where's that bell boy?"

"If I don't like him can he be exchanged?" inquired Winslow. "I brought my discount card."

"Any more of your nance comedy and you go out the door," Terry threatened him.

"Well—I'm just a great big gorgeous camp and I don't care who *knows* it," shrilled Winslow.

Shouts and alarums sounded from outside the door. Winslow sat bolt upright.

"That's Gluck and Morton," he said. "I knew those belles would be along the minute they smelled liquor."

Terry opened the door. Two young ladies with predatory eyes and coarse manners burst in with a frenzy of greeting.

"We'd of been here *hours* ago," Sophie Gluck declared, "but Mae ran into that trick sax player an' o' course she's fallen like a ton o' bricks. Boy, what a collegiate orchestra can do to a chorus troupe is nobody's business!"

"He's a sweet boy," said Mae Morton staunchly. "I don't care what you say about him, he knows his stuff."

"Yeah," Sophie deprecated. "But no money. An' you can't blow your way through life."

"Who *says* so?" Jack Winslow wanted to know.

Sophie glanced about her. "Do they give you a rate here, Harry?" she asked.

"Sure, eighteen a week, double," Towne replied. "Not bad."

"Anything extra for cockroaches?" Mae Morton inquired.

"Lissen, wisecracker, this is a swell dump," Harry snapped.

"Yeah, but I'll bet you still get your stationery in the Ritz lobby," shot back Mae.

Sophie went over to Peggy and sat on the arm of her chair. "Been holdin' off these gorillas, kid?" she asked. "They're a couple of yesmen that want yeswomen."

"Sophie only said 'no' once an' then she didn't understand what the man asked her," interrupted Jack Winslow.

"'No' is the first word in my vocabulary," Peggy assured them sweetly.

"Aw—Soph!" begged Terry. "Peggy might not realize you was kiddin'!"

The bell boy returned with an assortment of glasses. They were capacious if hardly ornamental. Terry kept an anxious eye on Peggy. These were his friends and he wanted to know how she would react to them. After tonight she had but to say the word and he would quit all this forever. He hated the thought. Peggy was swell, but there would be many lonesome nights when he'd want to sneak out for a talk with the gang.

But if Peggy were shocked she kept that fact to herself like a true lady.

They fell to dissecting the show, arguing the merits and defects of the cast. Admittedly the chorus numbers had scored. Resounding applause had greeted their every effort. But comedy, the bugaboo of every producer, was wanting.

Harry retired to the bathroom to mix the drinks. "Hey, you dames," he called. "Wanna help me fix up a coupla shots?"

Jack Winslow pounded Sophie. "Come on, Kate! He wants barmaids."

When they had gone and Mae had retired to a corner where she scanned the pages of a motion picture magazine, Terry went over to the perch which Sophie had vacated.

"Won't they need your services as expert barman?" asked Peggy.

"Not me. I always leave that to Harry. That's the only reason I room with him, really—he's so handy at fixing things up. Of course he ain't refined, exactly, but, what the hell he'd feel pretty bad if I was to take a run-out powder on him!"

"I can understand that," commented Peggy with a shade; of irony.

"You know, Peggy, until I met you I never saw a girl that I thought could really understand me. I played 'round lots—you sorta have to, you know—the women figure if you can dance an' ain't bad lookin' they gotta have you around. But I I'll say one thing for myself, no matter how much they chased me, I never let myself get spoilt!"

"Still the same modest home town boy," Peggy gibed.

"Don't kid me, Peggy. Gee, I'm nuts about you!" He wanted to put his arms about her but felt that a different technique was required. He loved her, but no one would give him credit for an honest affection. Even Peggy regarded his advances with skepticism.

Peggy began to speak very slowly. "You know you're a nice boy, Terry," she reflected. "I wonder why you're satisfied with all this; drinking—gossiping—gambling; that's how you fill your spare time, isn't it?"

"I ain't much different from all these wealthy folks that you read about," Terry protested.

"But don't you want to get anywhere? Haven't you any ideals?"

"Ideals? What's the good of 'em? Two years in show business knocked that bunk outta me," scoffed Terry.

She shook her head. "I think Marsh still has them," she said. "Fifteen years haven't destroyed his."

"Marsh!" sneered Terry. "Keepin' a young punk like Billy Lawler! I hope you don't think a guy's worthwhile because he's queer an' don't chase women!"

Peggy winced. "But don't you see," she endeavored to clarify her viewpoint, "Marsh has found something beyond the matter of fact world he lives in. He isn't satisfied to grumble through his job and then spend his nights getting tight. There must be thousands like him in show business. The successes of the world weren't made by loafers!"

"So you think I'm no good?" complained Terry. "You think I'm just a lousy hoofer that can't do nothin' but dance an' drink likker."

"You've wasted so many years of your life, Terry."

"Well, what else is there to do? I'm a good hoofer but I don't get the breaks. Why, I got the swellest Fred Stone imitation you ever seen, but they don't appreciate that over the Gus Sun time, so I gotta take my fifty bucks a week in the chorus and hope that someday I'll get a break like the rest o' these guys."

"I'm not trying to reform you," Peggy reassured him. "I hate the Reverend Davidsons of this world just as much as you do; but I will say this, show business gets a bad name from the no-accounts who clutter up the ranks of the chorus. What's the use in sticking with them? How about the others who use the chorus as a stepping stone? You'll see the names of lots of them in lights, Terry. They didn't forget their dreams and they hadn't lost the knack of plugging. The wasters in any profession are the ones who make the most noise. Look at Harry Towne; he'll be satisfied to go on this way until he's too old for the chorus, and then what future has he? Why don't you stop?"

Terry scowled gloomily. Here he was all set for a little petting party and all he got was a lecture. As a wife Peggy might prove a terrible nagger. The bright future faded. He didn't want a woman who was constantly prompting him to better his lot. Peggy was a sweet well meaning kid, but he couldn't be bothered with the banana oil she tried to stuff down his throat. Look at Andy Lee. He married a dame who wanted to be his little helpmate and now they were like cat and dog. The cynics must be right. This marriage game was applesauce. Harry's method was best, after all. And yet, if you could get to Broadway it would be worth all the. sacrifice.

"Aw, hell, I need a drink!" he decided.

Sophie appeared juggling three glasses filled to the brim with amber-colored liquid. "My God!" she gasped. "Haven't you two warmed up by now? I thought I'd find you in huddle that Red Grange couldn't break through!"

"Miss Sawyer is the cool collected type," drawled Mae, from over the top of her "fan" magazine.

"I heard that any girl who was cool collected plenty," said Peggy, turning a serene stare on the lady.

"Wisecrack! I'll spot you that one!" answered Mae cheerfully.

"I get it," said Sophie. "The chorus maiden. Made in New York and all points west."

Jack Winslow followed close on Sophie's heels, bearing additional glasses. "Gin high balls, or why girls go wrong," he gurgled. "My dear, that gin would make Mrs. Fiske do rolling splits."

Harry accepted a glass. "I got a toast," he announced, "To woman's greatest possession and man's greatest obsession- may it remain the same!"

They drank the concoction. "Ouch!" Mae yelped, shaken with a spasm of coughing. "Any of you boys see a loose tonsil around here?"

"One more drink and we'll give our *right* names," called Jack. "Mine's *Gertrude*!"

There was further pounding on the door. "Who's there?" shouted Harry above the din.

"The Ryan brothers," came the answer.

"My God, hoofers!" shrieked Mae. "Into your time step, everyone!"

"Come in!" Harry invited. Two dapper youths made their appearance. They bestowed a genial grin on the gathering.

"Ta-da—chord in 'G'!" sang Sophie—brandishing her glass. "Those two, boys are the best speakeasy sniffers in town," opined Mae.

"Well—we was invited—wasn't we, Freddy?" one Ryan exclaimed.

"Sure we was," the other substantiated him.

"You'll find plenty o' stuff in the bathroom," Harry directed.

"Thanks, kid," they acknowledged simultaneously and made a prompt exit.

"What'd Marsh want to see you about?" Harry yelled after them.

Fortified with drinks the Ryan brothers stood in their midst again. "Dorothy Brock kicked, so the tap black bottom goes out," Fred Ryan sighed.

"Sure—the biggest hand in the show," seconded Tony Ryan.

"The dance that *Variety* said should land us in production," Fred added.

"I hate these damn coffee an' cake managements," snarled Tony. "D'ye know what's the matter with this show?"

"Sure," asserted Sophie. "The Ryan Brothers aren't starred."

"Did ya get a load of the hand we got on them wings?" Fred demanded.

"That was the Mayor entering his box, you poor sap," jeered Terry.

"Aw—you guys don't know good taps when you hear 'em!"

"I s'pose if you boys ever get to heaven you'll ask to be billed, 'God and the Ryan Brothers'," conjectured Sophie.

"Nope," Mae corrected. "It'll be the Ryan Brothers and God."

"You think our stuff's easy," Tony argued. "Well—ask any guy in front of the Palace about the Ryan brothers. Just ask 'em."

"What I want to know is, where'd you get those trick tuxedos?" inquired Jack Winslow. "When I got a load of *those* outfits I thought I was back in *Florodora*." He swallowed the remainder of his drink and continued, "An' furthermore, when you get through with those straw hats you might just as well give 'em back to the horse!"

"Lissen, you," Tony advised. "First thing you know somebody's gonna hand you a pot o' lilies an' you won't be able to smell 'em!"

"The next time you do a split I hope you tear your New Year's resolution," hissed Winslow.

"Aw, don't quarrel with him, Tony; he can't fight back," said Harry.

"Who says I can't fight back?" shrilled Winslow. "I'll lay him to rest in forty shades of lavender."

The wrangling continued. Other guests arrived and were invited to partake. The room writhed with fantastic patterns of cigarette smoke. Eyes grew fixed and glassy; words dropped incoherently.

A horrible feeling of nausea overcame Peggy. It was more than the vile air and the burning liquor; it was some inner rebellion at the character of this gathering.

"Like hogs swilling up all they can hold," she thought.

Terry was fairly sober in deference to her wishes, but she knew that once her presence was removed he would make up for past abstinence. The majority of them had been existing in this fashion for four or five years. During periods of idleness they practiced stringent economy, but once the promise of a long engagement seemed certain they fell into old habits. This would be her life with Terry; he was not strong enough to resist its appeal. He might not surrender so completely as Harry Towne, but the atmosphere of tonight's party was necessary to Terry's happiness. She got up, hoping that her departure might pass unnoticed, but Terry saw her and volunteered to escort her to her room. She called a half-hearted good night which went by unheard in the confusion, and then gained the cool of the corridor.

"I s'pose you're disgusted," said Terry sullenly.

"I am," she admitted. "But please don't tell the others. They'd claim I was high-hat."

"You'd like the crowd if you'd only be yourself," he protested.

"I left because I was afraid I *would* be myself, and a scene."

"You know you'll never be popular in show business unless you act regular, Peggy."

"You'd better go back there, Terry. A party is rather stupid without its host. I shan't want your company. I'm going to bed."

He caught her arm. "Won't you give me break?" he pleaded.

"After tonight? Terry, I couldn't marry you, now, even if I loved you. I have too much self respect. Now let me go, please."

The liquor emboldened him. "Now lissen," he said. "I ain't ever been fresh with you. I treated you like the lady you was but you might as well get wise to this; they don't want Puritans in show business an' if you think we're a lot of bums just because we get tight once in a while you'd better scram: for New

England. I'll treat ya decent but I'll be damned if l can understand your attitude."

They were nearing Peggy's room. From various suites came loud laughter and sounds of revelry.

"There y'are," Terry pointed out. "Princ'pals an' chorus—they're all alike. After a show we gotta have our liquor an' all the pro'bition in the world won't change *that*. It's snobs like you that make trouble for people in show business. They see us take a coupla drinks an' then spread the word that we're no good. Well—we're jus' as good as any o' your damn New Englanders. An' the bigger the artist the bigger the drunkard."

They stopped before the door of Peggy's room. Terry turned on his heel and started back toward his own room.

"Good night, Terry," Peggy said, contritely.

He was instantly penitent. "You're a good kid," he mumbled, "I guess we weren't meant to mix, but I'm nuts about you jus' the same. I'm sorry for what I said comin' down the corridor. You know a guy takes a shot--"

"It's all right, Terry. I wish you'd promise me you won't drink any more tonight."

"I'll try. But you gotta keep up with the gang," he said.

"You'll feel terrible tomorrow," she reminded him.

"Who the hell cares about tomorrow?" he demanded irritably.

"You ought to," said Peggy. "This isn't going to be the end for you here. I want to see your name in lights, Terry."

"An' watch me turn into a louse like Brock?" he taunted.

"You can keep your head," Peggy answered shortly. "Good night!"

She gained the sanctuary of her room and threw herself wearily on the nearest chair. Presently she was asleep.

7

An incredible number of people seemed to have crowded into Dorothy's suite at the Ritz Lenox. It was one of those parties which act as a liaison between festivities just ended and others yet to be encountered. Show folk dropped in for a cocktail, exchanged a greeting and a bit of gossip and then drifted into the hallway in quest of the next stopping place.

In vain did the clerk at the desk telephone Dorothy and beg for quiet; there were moments of surcease from revelry and then they were at it again, more boisterously than ever. The clerk sighed. Theatrical people were certainly a trial. They demanded the finest accommodations at "professional rate," meaning a generous paring of the room's established price, and then, once installed, proceeded to make the night hideous with never-ending parties. No wonder some of the hotels had curtailed their hospitality to the Forty-Second Street crowd. It added nothing to the prestige of a hotel to have a continual round of brawls and drunken singing echoing from its windows. He cursed Dorothy Brock soundly and devoted his attention to other matters.

About the ever shifting guests in Dorothy's suite one little group stood firm as a rock planted midstream in a raging torrent. Here Dorothy held sway. In devoted attendance; could be found

John Phillips, Abe Green, Conroy, the composer of the show, Richard Endicott, and Mary Brock, a fragile, rather pretty child, who aped the manners of her more successful sister in the hope that some Broadway manager might find her suitable for a role in his new production. She traded heavily on the family name, and on the strength of billing herself as Dorothy Brock's sister obtained engagements in several second rate night clubs. But, despite the fact that she was on friendly terms with the most influential men on Forty-Second Street, the "Great Chance" still eluded her. Prettier than Dorothy, she lacked the charm and pseudo sweetness which Dorothy radiated over the footlights.

Dorothy was talking loudly. Too many cocktails had gone to her head and the little coterie was in a constant panic for fear that she might say or do something indiscreet.

Dorothy's gaze took in the horde of guests and she began to mutter, "Jeez' Chris', the way these bastards come in and lap up my gin is nobody's business. An' poor Dick risking his neck to get it off the boat for me. Aw, you're 'n old sweetheart, Dick, you're a love. I'm glad I decided to sleep with you for a change."

The scion of New York's oldest family gurgled incoherently and put a handkerchief to his flushed face. "Not so loud, honey, not so loud!" he spluttered with a furtive look into Conroy's smiling eyes.

"S'alright, Big Boy, s'alright. I'm not ashamed of it, an' you're not ashamed of it, so what the hell we care what the others think? Are y' gonna give me a teeny weeny kiss, Dick?"

"For God's sake, pull yourself together," snarled her protector.

"Oh, so that's the way it is. Well, nuts to you, Big Boy! I'm independent, I've got money in the bank. I don't need you and your lousy bonds!"

Mary Brock gave vent to several worried little noises and prodded Conroy. "Go play the piano!" she hissed. "Everyone's listening!"

Conroy nodded and forced his way through a group that swarmed about the gesticulating Dorothy. Someone recognized him and shouted:

"Attay boy, Russ! How 'bout a little number?"

He grinned. "Okay, folks. What'll it be?"

"Sing the Warner Brothers theme song, 'Rin Tin Tin, You Little Son of a Bitch, I love you'," suggested one besotted wag.

"Here's a new one. And mind you all shut up. My artistic temperament demands quiet!"

Mary pinched her sister's arm. "Ssh! Conroy's going to sing."

Dorothy shook herself free of the restraining hand. "T'hell with him. I have a few words to say to this Turtle Bay gentleman."

"Not now! Not now! Don't you spoil the party, dear!"

"Oh, alright, but you just wait, you rotten little bum!"

Conroy had tied a silk handkerchief about his head and was singing a comic ditty. They harkened attentively and rewarded his effort with cheers.

"More! More!" they yelled, pounding on the floor. Conroy grinned appreciatively. This was what he liked, having that bunch of hams recognize his God-given talent. What were they but a gang of mummers without a drop of originality in their veins? Why, if he didn't write decent tunes the whole kit and boodle of them would go plumb to hell! Dorothy Brock as well as the rest of them! He mentally catalogued numbers he had written for private occasions and offered his choicest tidbits for their approval. They shouted for still more. Russ Conroy was their favorite playboy of the hour and everything he wrote was met with rapturous acclaim.

A slight disturbance at the farther end of the room caused Dorothy to turn. Harvey Mason and three of the show girls staggered inside with loud whoops of merriment and made themselves at home with that equable assurance which fortifies the most timid soul after three or four drinks.

"Ev'rybody's here but Lawler," sang out Mason. "Dor'thy, you should be ashamed of yourself for not including our han'some juvenile."

"Who the hell wants that bitch?" muttered someone.

Conroy sprang to his feet. "Give the guy a break," he shouted. "Billy's all right. He did the same thing most any chap would have done in the same circumstances. How about it, Dorothy? Shall I ring him?"

"All right by me," shrugged the leading lady.

Conroy went over to the telephone. "Give me Mr. William Lawler's room, please," he called.

There was a moment's silence, and then the crisp voice of the operator answered, "Sorry, sir, but Mr. Lawler is very ill and Mr. Julian Marsh has given orders that no one is to disturb him."

Conroy glared and his face grew purplish. Then he gathered his wits together for a stinging reply. "Will you please tell Mr. Billy Lawler for me that the Ladies of Turkey declared their independence six years ago?" he said slowly and slammed the instrument down on its hook."

"So Miss Lawler won't be over?" snickered Dorothy Brock. "Well, I'll hand the kid this much. He knows which side his bread's buttered on. He's taking no chances."

"Oh," Mary contradicted, "Billy's a lad who'll risk a hazard—in short, he'll take a chance."

In another corner the jovial Harvey Mason was regaling his little clique with a somewhat Rabelaisian account of the misfortunes of an older actress. Between drinks his hearers laughed uproariously.

"Well—so the old bat went out in the show for a road to tour! It was *The Pekin Movement*, you know. She's ten years older than God as it is, so when I asked a pal of mine how come I said to him, 'Jim—how the hell does Julia Winters get through the part without collapsing? And where does she find wind to run up those stairs in the big scene of the third act?' So Jim says, 'Well, I tell you, Harvey, it's this way—we did a bit of re-staging and when it was time for old Winters to plough up the stairs we all gathered 'round her and the minute she was supposed to start somebody goosed her and the old girl flew up like a bat out of hell!'"

The din and confusion ran its course. Posturing drunkards were removed by more level-headed companions and gradually the room cleared.

Harvey Mason threaded a precarious route to Dorothy's side and whispered, "Didya hear that the depression in Turkey was so bad that the eunuchs 've agreed to take a second?" and toppled from the room.

"We're going on to Abe's place," called Mary Brock from the bedroom where she was selecting Dorothy's best-looking wrap for her own use.

"Be right with you," Dorothy screeched. A glass slipped from her hand and shivered to pieces on the floor. Endicott grasped her shoulders.

"You've had enough for tonight. You're going to bed," he instructed sternly. She struck his face with her clenched fist. He backed away startled—the blood trickling from a scratch on his cheek.

"You lousy little hell cat," he snarled.

"Who're you to keep ordering me around like this?" Dorothy berated him. "I'm my own boss—anyone 'd think you owned me—body and soul. Not for this little girl. I'm going on my own merry way to hell."

She raced into the bedroom—gave her sister a shove that sent her spinning into a corner, picked up the wrap that the astounded girl dropped from her grasp and bolted out of the suite before Endicott recovered his wits.

There was no one in the corridor. The entire building seemed shrouded in night quiet. She followed the twisted route to the elevator and rang a forceful summons.

"Come on! Come on!" she exhorted the unseen operator impatiently.

One thought was fixed in her mind. She needed Pat. She was sick of Endicott and his caviling. Endicott with his well bred sensuality and nerve-wracking jealousy! Pat was the stimulant necessary to bring her to herself.

The elevator reached her floor and she stormed inside, lashing the boy with a string of oaths. So concerned was she with her passionate denunciation of the Ritz Lenox system and its operatives that she failed to see the figure huddled in a corner of the cage. Mrs. Blair eyed the intoxicated star with a venom that she was hard put to control. Here was the instigator of all her woes. But for Dorothy Brock her Polly would have been the outstanding sensation of the show rather than the recipient of a mild pattering of applause. She'd get even with Brock all right! Probably the trollop was up to some mischief this very minute!

They reached the ground floor and Dorothy hastened across the lobby to the desk where the clerk was dozing. Mrs. Blair followed at a discreet distance. Dorothy pounded on the night bell and the startled clerk came out of his reverie with a convulsive start.

"I want to put a phone call through to New York," said Dorothy.

"Certainly, Miss Brock. But wouldn't it be more convenient to make the call from your room? There might be a delay at this hour."

"No, no, no, no! To hell with that. Too many people up there. This is a private call, understan'? I must have stric' privacy."

"Yes, Miss Brock. What is the number please?"

"Make this a party to party call. It doesn't mean anything if I can't get the person I want. Get me Mr. Patrick Denning, Bryant 8551."

A little band of actors huddled disconsolately before the stage door. Rain dripped from the eaves of neighboring buildings and fell with a monotonous patter about them. The overhead was no more leaden than their outlook on life. After repeated knockings the elderly gentleman nearest door shrugged.
"Guess Meehan was right," he said. "The play is shot."
They fell to murmuring, but no one suggested any likely move. Morgan had vanished, leaving behind a trail of worthless checks, among them the one which had been posted bond with the Actor's Equity Association. With the producer went the "high class drawing room drama" that promised long engagement to this group of performers. They were desperately in need of funds, all of them, but they faced this debacle with equanimity. Many had borrowed money with the assurance that once the play was in swing the debt would b promptly repaid. Others had faced long days of rigid dieting spurred by the thought of the prosperity that was sure to come. And now the grim September sky poured down its grief and the stone walls of the buildings loomed menacingly in the half light.
Pat lit a cigarette and extended the case to Geoffrey Waring.
"And here endeth the ninety-ninth lesson on why all good men and true should stay out of show business," he said.
"Take my lighter, Jeff, if the damn thing will work."
The two friends made an exit, with the good wishes of fellow actors ringing in their ears.
"God help the legits on a night like this," Jeff muttered.
"And now what to do?" Pat inquired.
"Agents, my boy. Who knows? They may have decided to inaugurate stock in Walla Walla."

"Where you supply your own wardrobe with a complete change every week?" scoffed Pat. "Rejected with thanks. Do you suppose one does vaudeville in September?"

"One does whatever one jolly well can," Waring reflected. "My immediate task will be to convince my landlady that money from home is expected any day."

" Good Lord, why speak of that?" Pat groaned. "And the first of the month is just near enough to let its chill breath of warning be felt."

"Pat, lad," Waring intoned solemnly, "we're in a bad way. How about the river?"

"I'm damn near drowned now," Pat objected. "Besides, I hate the thought of my waterlogged corpse being dragged to its final resting place. We might become sandwich men."

"Weak arches," Waring grieved. "That's out for me. It's a pity you gave la Brock the merry ozone."

"Mistaken nobility of character," Pat explained. "The possibilities of riches earned by my own talent rendered me unwise. Moral—never embrace decency until you're sure your manager has a hit."

"And not even two weeks' pay!" Waring regretted. "God damn Morgan and his lousy rubber checks. Pat, instruct me in the gentle art of harlotry, like a good fellow."

"Let's get tight," Pat suggested. "Then we'll find rainbows around our shoulders."

They repaired to Pat's apartment and divested themselves of clothes which were in a pathetic state. Then Waring wrapped himself in a huge woolen bathrobe and Pat removed a half dozen bottles from the cache. They fell to with a vengeance and in no time were beautifully tight—having achieved that state when it is impossible to do other than lie glassy eyed, watching the walls and ceilings move in chaotic patterns.

Hours later they emerged from this oblivion and faced the world in a mood of bitter disillusionment. Gone were the roseate fancies of the afternoon, vanished into limbo along with quantities of really excellent Bourbon. Bottles, the earthly shell of that divine essence, cluttered the hearthrug, but the soul had flown and only a wry taste remained as mute tribute to the glory that had passed beyond human ken. The sky was thick with darkness and there were no stars. Waring, with his wrinkled coat lending him an air of shrunkenness and dejection, bade Pat farewell and sallied forth. Pat picked up the bottles and carried them to the bathroom window where he dropped them into the courtyard. The splintering crash roused numerous occupants of the house to protest, but Pat heeded not. He was apathetically devising ways and means for enticing the steady flow of dollars in his direction once more.

The loud ringing of the telephone disconcerted him. He was tempted to ignore the summons, but suspected that it might be a friend who wanted to offer consolation and stimulant, the latter of which he particularly craved now that his own store was exhausted. He reentered the living room and took up the telephone receiver.

"Long distance—Philadelphia," cried a sing-song voice.

Wondering if Peggy had been moved to talk with him, he braced himself for a brief and cheering conversation.

"Pat?" shouted Dorothy Brock.

He backed away, alarmed. Those blurred tones meant that his former inamorata was drunk and hot on the trail of his affections once more.

"Yes—who is this?" he answered warily.

"You know damn well who it is. Lissen, I'm fed up with the whole crowd. I want you here, Pat, you're the only boy who can do me any good."

"But—" prudence cautioned him to remember the gentleman of gangland whose touch would be far less gentle the second time.

"We heard about your show," Dorothy rambled on. "Too bad, but, you know, an ill wind and all that sort of thing. How about it?"

"But, my darling, I'm stripped—flat broke!"

"I'll wire you the money. Be here tomorrow morning."

"Do you think it's wise? How about the noble mind that thinks of the star sapphire? Won't he be upset, to put it mildly?"

"To hell with him. Listen, are you coming or not?"

"Sweetheart—to put it bluntly, what's in it for me?"

"Have I ever let you down?"

"There's always a first time. I don't move from this flat unless there are four figures on your Western Union money order."

"My God, the man's a chiseler."

"Yes, dear. So what?"

"So, all right. Your Dorothy feels generous tonight. Pack up your tooth brush and roller skates and check in at the Ritz Lenox."

"Lafayette, we come."

A click warned him that they had been disconnected.

Mrs. Blair in the telephone booth adjoining the one where Dorothy was making her excited appeal to Pat felt that at last here was something tangible which might be used as a weapon against her enemy. From the fragments of conversation which were audible she pieced together the situation. Obviously Dorothy was seeking to renew an affair which for some unknown reason spelled danger to the show. Her heart seethed with righteous wrath. This Brock hussy was a menace whose influence for evil must be checked. She remained in the booth until long after Dorothy had made her agitated flight to the upper floor and then emerged with a casual demeanor which cloaked a mind almost beside itself at the realization of the power she could wield if she chose.

It was after two in the morning and the sleepy telephone operator looked startled when Mrs. Blair requested her to ring Mr. Marsh's room.

"I'm afraid I ought not to disturb him so late," the girl apologized.

"I'll take the responsibility," Mrs. Blair promised. "You gotta do this for me. It's a matter of life and death."

The operator looked incredulous. From oft-repeated experiences, she knew that people were capable of any device which might bring them into communication with the influential persons concerned with a new production.

"You needn't be afraid," Mrs. Blair coaxed. "My daughter is one of the leading principals in the show. He won't mind me callin' him at this hour."

The operator debated. This was ticklish business. Both parties concerned were guests of the establishment. True, Marsh occupied the largest suite of rooms in the hotel while Mrs. Blair and her daughter had been shoved into a narrow ill-ventilated little cubby hole in the cheaper section of the building, but Ritz Lenox training is thorough and painstaking and one of its chief tenets is that the guest is always right. The girl wavered and finally plugged the connection which rang Julian Marsh's telephone.

Mrs. Blair sought to word her revelations in a manner that would immediately arouse Marsh to action. She knew he had little use for her, but he guarded his production zealously and anyone who gave succor in the hour of danger should be in line for a sizable reward.

"Hello," called the operator, "Mr. Marsh?"

"Well, what the devil is *this?*" shouted an irascible voice.

"Sorry, sir, but there is a lady here who says she must speak to you on an urgent matter," apologized the girl.

"Tell him it's Mrs. Blair," whispered that lady. "The name is Mrs. Blair," said the operator.

"Oh, good God!" groaned Marsh. "Ask her to wait till morning."

"She says she can't do that, sir. She's most emphatic."

"More bloody trouble!" fumed Marsh. "Well, put her on."

"First booth, Mrs. Blair," instructed the operator.

"Thanks so much, dear," Mrs. Blair strode triumphantly to the booth and went inside. "Mr. Marsh " she asked.

"My dear lady this is most irregular. Of course I'm sorry about your little girl's dance, but all that will be remedied in time. Remember, this is just a tryout. Philadelphia means nothing. It's New York we're thinking of."

"But, Mr. Marsh, I'm not calling about Polly. It's something else or I wouldn't 'a' dreamed of disturbin' you so late."

"Oh?" puzzled Marsh.

"I s'pose you'll think I got my nerve buttin' in like this, Mr. Marsh, but I figured this is somethin' you ought to know about."

"Well—well—go on, my dear lady!" Marsh exhorted her.

"Dorothy Brock just called that boy friend o' hers long distance. He's comin' on here to be with her," stated Mrs. Blair.

Silence at the other end of the wire. For one chilling moment Mrs. Blair feared she had overstepped her bounds and Marsh had hung up.

"I don't know why that should concern you, Mrs. Blair," said Marsh finally. "I'm sure Miss Brock's affairs are none of ours."

"Certainly not, certainly not," Mrs. Blair agreed hastily. I just thought you might like to know-that's all."

"I see! Well—good night, Mrs. Blair."

"Good night, Mr. Marsh. The show was real lovely tonight."

"Thank you, good night."

Mrs. Blair retired for the night well pleased. She kissed the forehead of her sleeping daughter and then crawled into the other twin bed. By morning the forces which sought to keep the *Pretty Lady* production from jeopardy would be at work.

Billy Lawler opened the door connecting his bedroom with Julian Marsh's and stood there idly tying and untying the silken cord of his dressing gown. Half recumbent on the bed, Marsh was endeavoring to stem Mrs. Blair's flow of talk.

"What's up?" Lawler inquired.

Julian motioned him to be quiet and terminated the conversation with Polly's mother. When he had finished Billy sauntered to the side of the bed and sat down.

"Funny time of night for anyone to call," he remarked.

"It's some more trouble with our beloved star. Billy, that woman will ruin our chances. We've got to play *deus ex machina* once more."

"Brock's a trollop," yawned Billy. "Why don't you get some sleep, Julian. This can be straightened out in the morning."

"No, boy, we can't afford to run any risks. Do you remember Walt McDermott's private telephone number?"

"My God—are things that serious?"

"Indeed, yes. Let's see, it's Wickersham exchange, I believe."

"That's right. 8770."

Marsh picked up the telephone once more. "It seems strange to be allying ourselves with the public enemies," he said.

"They do it in the best of families," Lawler consoled him.

"Hello, operator. I'm calling New York, long distance, please. Wickersham 8770."

Tomorrow would bring their first press notices, The Philadelphia critics, smarting under the indignity of being used as "dog town" reviewers, would have some tart words at the expense of the show. Rough edges must be smoothed off, tedious interludes eliminated. The dramatic editors, accustomed to the uneven performances and slow pace of the average tryout, would heap invective on the luckless heads of Green and Friedman. They must disregard these whips and scorpions and sweep away the minor deficiencies so that the enterprise might be revealed in its full pristine splendor. Julian Marsh, alone, could do this. The others had given of their best, his now the task to weave the threads of many minds into one lustrous pattern. Again his likeness to a mighty god struck Marsh forcibly. The others could sing their songs, and dance their petty measures; he and only he could breathe life into the creature of his own making. From strange and devious sources he found the strength to accomplish that feat. The spider web of the production enmeshed men from totally different walks of life. But through it all he sat in the very hub of the web while such different beings as Billy Lawler and Walt McDermott were caught up and held fast in the net his mind was weaving. Above all—the show must be saved.

8

The room clerk at the Ritz Lenox was a forbearing chap, accustomed to viewing the adulteries of his clients with a tolerant eye. Though lust stalked ever so boldly through the chastely decorated corridors of the hotel, the gentleman at the desk never batted an eye. Truth to tell, he was bored with the long procession of business men, stenographers, actors and moneyed nonentities who sought gratification of the well known cosmic urge under the cloak of false registration. He accepted without comment Dorothy Brock's dictum that a certain incoming guest, Mr. Peter La Verne, be assigned to the suite adjoining hers "for business reasons." That Mr. La Verne was tall and well made, was no concern of his. That the gentleman was obviously a bit distressed at some mistake he had made in signing the register brought not a shadow of consternation to the clerk's unwrinkled brow. He called "front" in his well modulated voice, favored "Mr. La Verne" with a knowing smile and ordered the gentleman's bags transferred to his room.

Pat glanced uneasily about the lobby on his way to the elevator. Lurking behind one of the many newspapers might be some emissary of those forces who had so battered him physically and mentally a few weeks ago. He had no desire for another encounter. If he had not squandered her last contribution in a fit of drunken jubilation he would have ignored Dorothy's summons gladly, but now he must run the risk and hope to high heaven that no word of this escapade would reach the ears of the men who made it their business to frustrate the yearnings of Miss Brock.

The magnificence of the elevator impressed him. The brocaded walls with the pattern that somehow suggested the palace at Versailles were the last word in costliness and elegance. The operator was a good-looking youngster who bore his Roxyesque splendor with ease. This was the existence for which Pat had been destined—only the absence of funds deprived him of the surroundings which were his birthright. He heartily damned the social scheme which had flung him among struggling thespians and depressing failures.

The elevator halted at one of the higher floors and the bell hop courteously bowed him out. His feet sank gratefully into the thick carpet and he hesitated until the boy indicated the direction of his rooms. Not so bad, for a young man who two short days ago had been in the throes of despondency. Had the play gone on he might have resigned himself to his meager salary and the hope of a pleasant existence with Peggy. That source of income denied him, he must perforce rely again on the unfailing resourcefulness of his wits.

The suite of rooms was sun-filled and expensive. A tip of half a dollar endeared him to the bell hop. He stood in the center of his domain and surveyed it with an approving eye. What a background for the renewal of his liaison with the star of *Pretty Lady*. He was not allowed to ponder the situation for long. The telephone bell pealed insistently. He looked about the place, located the instrument on its stand and hurried over to answer.

"Hello, lover," cooed Dorothy at the other end of the wire.

"Hello, sweet. You see I'm prompt."

"The four figures?" Dorothy insinuated.

"Five. The four on the money order, and the one in the next room," he answered tactfully. "When am I going to see you?"

"I'm in my bath right now. Of course, it's hardly the proper moment—but if you were to try the door which connects our rooms you might find it open."

"Dare I?"

"You've never been called 'coward'—I hope."

"Gauntlet flung down by young woman eagerly snatched up by adoring young man. I shall be there presently."

"I warned you—of course, I didn't have the presence of mind to lock the bathroom door, either."

"Splendid! Just keep humming! I've a good bump of locality."

"I seem to recall that bump. It was well developed."

"Always at sight of you-my sweet. Bye."

"Don't be long. My bath is just the right temperature. I shall be furious if it grows too cool."

Peggy was half afraid to open the letter. A sort of premonition that things had gone awry assailed her. After all, there was nothing ominous in a communication from Pat. It should serve as added proof of his devotion. But there lay the very core of her distrust. For the mercurial Pat to wax suddenly constant gave the lie to all those characteristics which she had grown to know and tolerate. She went to her room with the letter still unopened.

Flo lay stretched full length on one of the twin beds. She wakened at Peggy's entrance and struggled to a sitting position.

"My God, am I late?" she demanded. "I heard the alarm and turned over on my other side. What time is it?"

"Eleven o'clock. You've got an hour yet."

"What's that?" asked Flo, indicating the letter.

"From Pat."

"My God, what frightened him?"

"I've been wondering the same thing myself. I'm half afraid to open it. You know—sudden death or sudden marriage—something like that."

"More likely sudden need of funds," Flo sniffed.

"How you love my little Patrick!" laughed Peggy.

"I hate all actors," Flo declared, slumping back on the pillows.

The remark went unheeded. Peggy slit open the envelope.

"Looks like good stationery," ventured Flo. "What lobby does he patronize? Good night, six months for talking to myself!" She rolled over on her left side and resumed the interrupted business of sleeping.

Peggy read.

Darling—

This is the rottenest thing I've ever done, Please don't think I have the consummate nerve to ask your forgiveness. I'll deserve hatred, cursing and whatever torture your little mind conceives for me once you know the truth. Perhaps, in your heart of hearts, you suspected long since. If not—hearken to a kept man's confession.

For that's what I am, sweet, just a lousy little gigolo dancing on the end of a lady's purse strings. Don't tell me that you haven't heard rumors. We're not pretty, we kept boys, but we do manage to get about in our quaint way and then people begin to talk.

There is no need to mention names. Why kiss and tell? This must suffice as explanation, my dear. I'm being terribly indiscreet, but you are a swell person and I know all this scribbling will find its way to the waste basket once you've finished. I hope you can chuck any emotion you've felt for me right along with It. Stripped of apologies and evasions the idea is this. A not too nice lady has rented my affections for a certain space of time and I can't afford to refuse. All those nice thoughts about the honorable state of marriage turn out to be just so much hooey when the bank balance shows a flock of zeros. My newest play went on the rocks. Rents have a way of coming due—and here am I, "reaching for the moon." So I've just said au revoir to sentiment and decency and taken up my life of sin again. It's not hard to do when you're this particular breed of cad, Not too particular, of course—cads can't afford to be. When you receive this I shall be en route to Philadelphia to join a lady who shall be nameless. I'm sorry things have happened this way, but a trip to Philadelphia was named in the bond. If you happen to guess the identity of said lady do me the very great favor of keeping that thought to yourself. We may run into one another, but that is unlikely as I am using a reasonable amount of discretion about my little liaison. I suppose the whole dirty business might have been accomplished without your being any the wiser, but I hate the idea of subjecting you to any misery—and if fortune failed me this would occur again. So best to say good-by now while there are no regrets.

Will you believe this, Peggy? It's empty as hell coming from me, but I should feel a small measure of comfort in knowing that you understand. For once in all my dishonorable years, I fell in love. I thought we two might make a go of it. But, so what? At the first puff of wind I was bowled over. I'm funny that way. You haven't lost a damned thing, sweetheart. You'll be a far happier girl—I shan't be present to inflict my presence upon you. But I do love you. I'll carry the dream of you in my heart forever and ever. Take that on faith, please, old girl. You're grand, you're noble, you're swell, and my worst punishment is that I couldn't come up to snuff.

So long, sweet, keep on being a good little girl and God, or whoever it is, will probably bless you. We'll meet one another, you and I, say 'How've you been' in our best party manner and then drift apart. Strangers, you see, complete strangers. I don't want to feel guilty of having aroused love in you. But for now good-by and the best of luck. I'll be cheering for you all the time except in those moments when I'm cockeyed drunk. Come to think of it, every hour of the day.

And that's *that*.

Love,

Pat.

She folded the letter into neat squares. Flo mustn't know! Ann mustn't know. This, then, was what you got. No matter what you had been taught to believe about love, this was the way things happened. What were all those dusty phrases about decency, and fair play, and integrity? The very sound of them was strained and laughable. People had no use for those qualities. They were labels for tiresome, out-of-date ideals that previous generation had seen fit to cram down present day throats. You were a fool and you built a gleaming structure. No, you couldn't have built this palace for there were no tools with which to work. Very well, then, perhaps it was a mirage or it was done with mirrors. The tragedy lay in the fact that you dared believe in this colossal fake. You were actually taken in—and when the trick was exposed in all its shabbiness you felt hurt. Why be hurt? Why care? What was precious about the thing you lost? She saw more dearly now. Pat, as an ideal, a hope, a person to be loved, was dead. Pat Denning from now on would be a name. Two words. Rather musical sound they had, a pleasant ring, but that was all.

And now what? Terry? How greatly Terry would fail her too. She remembered last night's party with a shudder. She had wakened at five in the morning to hear them stumbling through the hall, shouting at the top of their lungs, blind drunk on bootleg gin. Terry and his friends! *There* was a pretty future.

No, life must be lived without compromise. She must go onward, alone, without the necessity of a man's love to hinder her. Good-by Pat. Good-by Terry. Peggy Sawyer can take care of herself. A career—that's all that matters. When you have money and fame people respect you. They play the clown if, by doing so, they can attract your attention. Julian Marsh approved of her. He might give her some part to understudy. She was learning to be shrewd; there are politics in all professions. Billy Lawler was her friend—she'd coax Billy to put in a good word for her. One never knew when some principal would drop out. Temperament and outraged nerves sometimes boiled over and then there was room for a newcomer. That would be the beginning of the uphill climb.

She was tearing Pat's letter into shreds. Where was the waste basket? There—under the desk. The fragments of paper slipped out of her hands, one or two falling on the carpet. She retrieved them mechanically. Good-by, Pat. The best of luck to you. You'll need it!

She shook Flo roughly. The time was now eleven-fifteen and the company had been warned, with due impressiveness, that they must assemble on the stage of the theatre not later than eleven-thirty.

Flo, thus shocked out of her pleasant slumber, scampered madly about the room picking up a stocking here, a shoe there, until presently she was dressed. Peggy shoved a hat into her chum's hand and pulled her forcibly out of the room and toward the elevator.

"Wait and see—they won't start things moving for hours yet," Flo prophesied. "I've ruined more good pairs of stockings in mad dashes like this only to find out that I was the first dumbbell to arrive."

"Do you think there'll be many changes?" questioned Peggy as they rode to the ground floor.

"Plenty. Our troubles are only half over. From now on you can plan to be only two blocks ahead of a panic for a week at least. They'll switch everything around the war they think it'll go over an' then send Harry MacElroy tearing into the dressing room five minutes before overture to tell us to play the show the original way, after all. And try to remember what the original way was after Lee's been hollering and screaming all day! You'll find yourself out on the stage doing *The Dying Swan* in the middle of a hot buck number."

The hands of the clock on the tower of City Hall pointed to eleven forty-five as they sped down the side street leading to the stage door. They arrived at the theatre breathlessly and somewhat alarmed, to be casually welcomed by Harry MacElroy who was sunning himself in the alley.

"Plenty of time, kids," he assured them. "Brock hasn't shown up yet an' they're waiting to start on her numbers."

"What did I tell you?" Flo demanded. "So help me, tomorrow I get my beauty sleep if the Pope in person tells to get here at noon."

They ambled inside and sat down on one of the long benches where eight or ten girls were grumbling about chaotic state of affairs.

"Maybe we're in the wrong theatre," said Lorraine Fleming sarcastically. "Nobody here seems to recognize us!"

"I wish Brock would hop on her bicycle and come on over, grumbled Flo. "From parking around this joint for hours a time I'm getting callouses where no lady should."

"Get a load of mother and daughter," Ann nudged her.

Polly Blair and her mother had taken possession of the temporarily deserted stage. Polly, arrayed in dirty practice rompers, began to bend industriously while Mother's eagle eye studied every curve of her supple body.

"Polly the Pretzel making both ends meet," Flo commented.

"Old Brock better pray she never meets Ma in a dark alley after getting little Polly's solo cut out of the first act. Stage mothers and elephants never forget."

"Bend, Polly! Bend, Polly!" chanted Mrs. Blair. Secure in her belief that Polly's time would be occupied for some time to come, Mother strolled across stage to the bench where the circle of chorus girls was grouped.

"Funny they don't start somethin' around here," she remarked. "From what the papers say they's plenty to be done on the show."

"We're waiting for Dorothy Brock," chimed Lorraine Fleming.

Mrs. Blair's eyes narrowed. "Huh! Then we might as well go home right now," she declared. "Dorothy Brock ain't worryin' about us. She's got a show of her own to attend to."

"Why? What's up?" asked Flo, scenting gossip in the air.

"Nothin'! I s'pose I'm talkin' outta turn but a little bird whispered in my ear that Miss Brock ain't as concerned as she might be with puttin' this musical comedy over."

"Know any dirt?" inquired Ann bluntly.

"Well—don't say I told you—but the boy friend's supposed to be in town—and with him around we don't rate no attention."

"Endicott? He's been here all the time!" cried Lorraine.

"I don't mean Endicott," said Mrs. Blair. "Everything'd be okay if it was him. This is another guy who has the leading lady in an uproar."

"I don't believe it," stated Ann emphatically. "Brock's no fool. She's not dropped Endicott for any outside interest."

"Oh, ain't she? Well, you just don't happen to know, dear. Some feller arrived from New York this mornin'—and from what I hear it's a feller who's gonna wish he hadn't!"

"What do you mean?" questioned Peggy.

"Well—it ain't policy to go mixing up with the leading lady of a big show like this. Too many guys got dough invested and they'd do anything to stop the leading lady from makin' a fool of herself. From what I hear, this guy's apt to wake up in the hospital with a broken jaw or somethin'."

She eyed Peggy shrewdly. The episode at El Mirador was recalled vividly to her mind. Once again she saw the ornate lobby, heard the light-hearted conversation between Peggy and her escort, re-lived her own emotions as she recognized the man.

"Dearie," she said, bending over Peggy and endeavoring to keep the tremor of excitement from her voice. "It ain't none o' my business, but I hate to see any wise guy put it over a sweet kid like you so I might as well tell you the truth."

Peggy's heart was pounding madly. The letter from Pat this morning. The ill-concealed look of malice in the eyes of Mrs. Blair. She looked away, half afraid that she might faint.

Mrs. Blair's voice went on. The other girls had been attracted by the noise of an altercation between two chorus boys. She alone was listening to old Blair.

"That feller you was with up at the Mirador—remember? 'Bout a coupla weeks ago, on a real hot night? Well, *that's* the one. I seen him with Brock lottsa times. Him an' her has been raisin' hell together for a long time, now, an' that's what the management is sore about. You better forget that feller, dearie. He's a no good egg. A guy that'll play 'round with a dame like Brock ain't worth botherin' about." By this time Polly had finished her bending and glanced appealingly in her mother's direction. That good lady excused herself and trotted to her daughter's side, leaving Peggy to ponder the full import of her revelation.

Brock was the woman in the case. *Cherchez la femme!* All right, here she was. Dorothy Brock! And because he had dared to court Brock they might kill him. She found small room for doubting the truth of Mrs. Blair's statement. It fitted too neatly with the letter she had just read. For the moment she forgot her anger and was concerned only with sparing Pat the fury of Marsh's hired thugs. She wondered if her absence would be noted. The chorus girls were chatting unconcernedly. At the back of the theatre Green and Friedman were engaging Andy Lee in heated argument. In various corners the specialty dancers stretched and limbered. The tapping of the Ryan Brothers droned rhythmically above the low-pitched voices of the choristers. Jerry Cole was humped over the piano in the pit, playing aimlessly.

This state of inactivity promised to hold sway for another hour. The Ritz Lenox was not far; she could easily slip away for half an hour and none would be the wiser. She edged past the knot of chorus girls, made her way unobtrusively toward the stage door and gained the freedom of the street.

The sidewalks were thronged with crowds of perspiring shoppers. She pushed through them, winning many an indignant glance by her haste, and soon found herself on the main thoroughfare. The pavement was hot underfoot as the afternoon sun beat down. Philadelphia was still in her summer doldrums. Damp haggard women dragged along, clutching at the parcels they had bought in the downtown department stores, and hampered her progress. She was like the swimmer who struggles to breast an incoming tide. Anxiety urged her on, careless of the shrill complaints that were voiced by tired women with whom she collided.

The clerk at the Ritz Lenox was polite but noncommittal. No Mr. Denning was registered among the day's arrivals. On a sudden inspiration Peggy asked the number of Dorothy Brock's suite.

"Fifteen-o-six," the clerk informed her. "House phones on the right—over on the other side of the lobby."

She thanked him and, disregarding the hint to announce her visit, hurried into the waiting elevator. The operator noticed her extreme agitation and wondered if it were wise to take this woman upstairs. Her manner was that of an outraged wife stalking her prey. The starter signaled him, he shut the gate, turned to his sole passenger, and inquired the floor.

"Fifteen, please." Peggy's voice was a harsh whisper. He shook his head. Hysterical women boded ill for the dignity of the Ritz Lenox.

The fifteenth Boor seemed in the grip of a serene late summer afternoon. One or two maids walked quietly along the corridors, but no sounds of revelry issued from behind closed doors. She followed a winding course, guided by numerous signs, and presently read the numbers on the doors, "1502—1504."

She paused, half ashamed of her mission. Suppose Mrs. Blair had been talking idly and there was no immediate danger for Pat. That was the only excuse for her mission, otherwise she would never have approached him again. She waited in an agony of uncertainty, her ears straining to catch the murmur of voices.

"Here's mud in all their faces," sang out Dorothy Brock.

The cry came from the suite marked 1504. In a flash Peggy understood the situation. Dorothy. and Pat were occupying adjoining suites. She hesitated no longer but rapped on the door.

"Who's there?" called Pat.

She knocked again, hoping that he would answer her summons without demanding to know the identity of his caller.

"Who's there?" shouted Pat again.

"Maybe a bell hop," she heard Dorothy Brock remark. "We sent down for cracked ice about an hour ago."

Pat Bung open the door and stood aghast, facing Peggy.

"Peggy!"

"Listen, Pat. Don't think I'm a rotten sport—or a spy—or anything like that, but I must see you."

"Good Lord, sweet, not now—I—I—this is hellishly embarrassing. Let me call at your hotel later today."

"What's all the excitement?" shrilled Dorothy Brock. Peggy realized that she was quite drunk.

"Nothing, dear. Just a mistake in room numbers!"

"Really?" Dorothy's voice was sharp with indignation.

"Well, I'll tell the interfering fool a thing or two."

She thrust Pat aside and peered into the corridor. "Oh!"

Peggy was scarlet. The sight of Dorothy with her clouded eyes and disordered hair infuriated her. For this, Pat had been willing to deny himself a lifetime of happiness. She squared her shoulders and decided to risk her chances with *Pretty Lady* in an effort to make these two intoxicated idiots cognizant of their peril.

"Pat—you've got to get out of here," she said.

Dorothy Brock grasped her roughly by the shoulders. "Who the hell are you to come barging in like this?" she shrieked. "What is this? A frame up? Don't tell me we have an outraged wife on our hands, Pat."

Pat was speechless. He could only motion hopelessly to Peggy.

"I'm a friend of Pat's," Peggy explained briefly. "He's in danger. There are men in this city who'll do anything to break up your—your little arrangement."

Dorothy was stung to action. "I don't believe it," she declared. "You're a clever little tart all right, but I've been in the game too long. It's just a question of mixed dates, that's what it is. So you're still at your old tricks, Pat! I should have known! And a chorus girl in my own show! Why you cheap little chiseller! I'll get even with you—making me look like a goddam idiot."

Pat's restraining arm was of no avail. Dorothy was beside. herself with fury. Her eyes blazed hatred, her body shook with the force of her emotion.

"Well, girlie, here's your kept man for what he's worth. I give him back to you cheerfully. There are too many fish in the sea to worry about a lousy two-timing legitimate actor. *Legitimate!* He's never done a straight thing in his life! So, I'm financing a little spree for you two angels, am I? Not on your life! I've played the game too long. Now—*you*—get the hell back to your rehearsal while I settle with Mr. Denning here and now."

Peggy stepped inside the room and closed the door. "Pat—make her keep quiet. Those men—they may be on their way up here right now."

"What men? Who's telling me to keep quiet?" raged Dorothy. "Of all the lousy frame ups!" She snatched up her glass from the table. "You beat it, see? Beat it! One more crack and I'll see to it that you lose your job. The idea, interfering like this! At that, I'm glad you gave the show away or I might have gone on believing in this ham actor!"

But Pat was sufficiently roused to turn on Dorothy. "You shut up," he commanded. "I've taken one beating because of you and I'll be damned if I'll stand for another. Your sweet impresario doesn't mind going to any lengths so long as he can keep us apart. Well, I'm through being the fall guy. From now on find your own gigolos. You're not worth the risk of a broken jaw. Get out of my room."

Dorothy shrilled oaths. The vile words rained about his head, but Pat was immovable. He seized her arms and dragged her toward the door.

"They won't find you here," he declared. "I'm taking no more chances. Get out!" Pat was thoroughly frightened.

"I don't believe it—I don't believe it!" wailed Dorothy. "You're trying to put something over on me—you two! I'll see that you get yours—both of you!"

She found herself in the corridor—looking up at a tightly closed door. Fury rendered her almost demented.

"I'll have you put out! I'll shame you so you won't dare face anybody!" she screamed. "When I'm through with you they'll be laughing from one end of Broadway to the other."

Blind with rage she staggered toward the elevator. A petrified maid saw her lurching drunkenly along, half intelligible words spewing from her mouth. She was an appalling figure as, mad with jealousy, she stumbled, caught at a door knob and saved herself. As she neared the well of the staircase a treacherous gap in the carpet ensnared her foot. Plunging along, heedless of danger, she fell forward. The maid gave a frightened cry. And then Dorothy was tumbling down the stairs, the thick carpet muffling the sound of her fall. She covered her head with one arm to ward off the inevitable blow. A dreadful darkness engulfed her. The frightened shouts of the maid vanished in an all enveloping pall of blackness. One shoe described an arc in the air and spiraled to the landing far below. Her face hit the balustrade and her body twisted into a grotesque heap at the foot of the stairs.

9

The doctor closed the door to the sickroom. Abe Green's fingers wound tightly about the lapel of his coat and he said in a voice hoarse with the anguish of several hours' waiting, "Well, doctor, is she gonna pull through?"

The doctor nodded. "Nerves are shot. That makes it a bit more complicated. My God, what a pace she must have been hitting! You don't need to worry, though. All that's necessary is a few months of complete rest. There are no internal complications, fortunately, but concussion is a tricky thing to handle—and her back has been pretty badly strained."

Green made a despairing gesture. "A few months rest? Good Christ, doctor, don't you understand? She's gotta go on the stage tonight! She's gotta play a leading part! There's a hundred thousand dollar production depending on her. A few months!"

He talked on, as though the tumult of words might somehow marshal the frayed nerves of Dorothy Brock into their normal functioning.."Don't you see, doctor, we show people ain't like you folks? We can't be sick, we can't die, because there's always the show to consider. Dorothy's a real trouper; she won't let me down like this. She knows how much I done for her. Why, I give her the best parts she ever had in her life. Made a star out of her. And now, just because she gets in some goddam mess you say she can't go on. But it ain't so! It ain't so, I tell ya! She's gotta go on. Look at my cast. Look at my investment. You don't want to ruin me, do you, doctor? Help her get well so's she can play tonight. Tomorrow night, then—I can make a refund for tonight an' spend the night rehearsing. We need it, God knows! But, tomorrow night, sure! That ain't so much to ask. She ain't got any broken bones. Concussion—strain—what's a strain? I've seen guys go out on that stage half dead, but they pulled through. Jesus, doctor, one hundred thousand dollars in these days—and you'll let it get shot to hell for a strained back. All right! So it's a bad one! We'll cut out her dance in the second act. I'll have a nurse in the dressing room all through the show. Come on, doctor. That's your job—making people well. It can't be so awful tough. Nerves! What the hell are nerves? Show people can't afford to have nerves during a tryout!"

The little man brushed past him. "I have an appointment, Mr. Green," he said. "I'm sorry—but Miss Brock must be quiet. That's imperative and I shan't be responsible for the consequences if you disturb her in any manner whatsoever." He took his hat and left the suite.

Abe Green stood in the center of the carpet staring after him. "That guy's nuts," he muttered. "I'll get her out of bed. She ain't sick. He can't kid me. I know she ain't sick."

He wheeled abruptly and went into the bedroom. In the gloom he could distinguish the outlines of the bed, but from it there came no sound. Dorothy was sleeping. A wave of hopelessness swept over him. The inert shape lying quietly beneath the bed covers was so unlike the vibrant Dorothy Brock he knew. About her was the disturbing immobility of death. He withdrew from the room, stumbling in his haste to escape.

Let her sleep, let her sleep, poor kid. God knows she'd proved herself a hell cat many times but he loved her, loved her with all his heart and soul. If she got well—to hell with the hundred thousand dollars. Well, not exactly that. The showman in him playing tricks even at a time like this! Cheating at solitaire! Playing the eternal game of bull and blarney with himself!

He called the maid. "Don't let anybody come in," he warned. "Reporters especially. They have their orders downstairs, but some of these guys from the tabloids might sneak up. They'd murder their own mothers for an extra headline. The doctor says Miss Brock is very ill."

The girl nodded. "I'll take care of her," she promised. "The poor, poor lady. She is almos' like one dead."

Abe Green patted her shoulder. "You're a good kid, Therese," he said. "You've got the idea, all right. I can trust you."

He was satisfied. With Therese guarding the portals he feared no intruders. She was as effectual as an angel with a shining sword. He bade her good-by and went to consult with Julian Marsh.

He found Marsh lounging full length on a chaise longue, a book rather ostentatiously propped up beside him. On a nearby chair sat Billy Lawler. The scene gave the effect of a hastily devised stage setting. Green mumbled an apology. He sensed that he had interrupted some sort of tête-à-tête. Julian's eyes were clouded with an emotion that Abe preferred not to see. To him there was something sickening and unholy in this alliance.

As usual, Billy tossed him a cool and urbane greeting. Young Lawler was at all times the master of the situation. Abe wondered how much responsibility for unwarranted changes in the production lay on Billy's slight shoulders. That odd-looking blond chorus boy who had been so unceremoniously discharged, for instance. Looked like a bit of meddling on the part of Mr. Lawler. Green knew Billy's hatred for any person or circumstance that might lessen his hold on Julian Marsh. He concluded that the removal of Mr. Lawler from the cast might have its beneficent effect. But that could be accomplished through divine intervention only. On the question of his protégé Julian Marsh was a doddering, fatuous old man.

But this was no time for Marsh's private troubles. A hundred thousand dollar investment hung in abeyance. "Brock can't go on tonight," he blurted out.

Marsh sat bolt upright. "Accident or temperament?"

"No temperament, Julian. It's the real thing! I guess we done a little too much meddling for our own good. This is on the level all right. Concussion and a bad strain and the doctor said somethin' about her nerves, but that don't sound so important to me. Dorothy's out as far as this show's concerned. Do you get *that?* She's *out?*"

"And what about the chap? Wasn't his name Denning?"

"He checked out right after she took her fall. Notified the desk an' then paid his bill an' skipped. McDermott can locate him, I s'pose, but—what the hell—we ain't worryin' about *him* now! We got the show on our hands!"

"Meaning we must find a new leading lady," snapped Julian.

"A new leading lady is right! But, my God, *where?* The movies have got 'em all. Carroll an' Ziegfeld have the beautiful girls an' now the movies grab the principals. How the hell can I put on shows? I gotta retire!"

"Marilyn Eaton," suggested Marsh.

"Tied up with contracts for five years. I couldn't pay her, anyway. She wants five per cent of the weekly gross. Can you imagine that?"

"Mary Groody." Marsh was enumerating with his fingers.

"Impossible! She's in Europe. Couldn't get her back in time even if she'd take the job."

The four or five possibilities Julian named were soon exhausted. That left the theatrical agents.

"I better get busy sending wires," decided Abe Green. "Somebody's gotta go on tonight! My God, don't nobody realize we're givin' a show tonight? An' not even an understudy! We gotta full house comin' an' you know what it'll be like in Philadelphia once we have to start refundin' dough. They'll say the show stinks an' business will be shot for the rest of the run. My God, Julian, do *something* will ya? Why ain't there an understudy? Who can we get? That goddam second ingénue sings like a goat—they'd laugh her off the stage. There ain't a woman principal in the whole outfit can handle the job."

Julian Marsh held up a detaining hand. "Wait a minute! How about Mary Brock, dear Dorothy's sister and faithful imitator? She's played at being an ingénue for the past fifteen years. Do you suppose we could beat a little sense and showmanship into that stupid brain? She's your logical successor until a name player can be located."

"Mary's restin' up from an operation for appendicitis. If she went out there she'd tear somethin' she can't sew. And, God, is she *lousy!* Her *showmanship* hasn't advanced a day since *Rebecca of Sunnybrook Farm!*"

"You'd be better off with some kid from the chorus," declared Billy Lawler.

Abe Green eyed him with disfavor. "I suppose we're gonna get a little lesson in show business from the juvenile," he sneered.

"Quite possible," rejoined Billy imperturbably.

"Ah! You're still wet behind the ears! Chorus girl. What do you think this is? A Paramount Picture, bring the kiddies an' let 'em hear about Cinderella? This ain't a movie. Not one of those chiselin' gold diggers knows the first thing about showmanship."

"Very well. Forget it. It was only a suggestion," pouted Billy.

"Yeah. An' a lousy one!" grumbled Abe.

Billy retired to his corner with a disgruntled shrug. But out of the verbal tilt an idea was born. Abe Green was so damn sure of himself, so positive he knew each and every angle of show business. Well, obviously he didn't! No human being could be so omniscient.

"Have you two reached a truce?" drawled Julian. "All this bickering is a great help. Out of such encounters great ideas are born."

"Aw, that guy gives me a pain, sometimes," Abe growled.

"The guy in question could drop a few hints about management that might surprise you," retorted Billy. "What was wrong with my idea, Julian? Green doesn't like it—he hates me. If I were Gershwin he'd tell me I wrote bad music. But I say you can pick any kid from that chorus and groom her to do Brock's work. What's Brock? The musical comedy ingénue our mothers loved!"

"You'd like to pull down half the dough Brock's gettin'," shouted Abe. "Go ahead. Pan her! Razz the livin' daylights outta her. She's a greater artist than you are when she's asleep."

Julian ignored him. "You honestly think we have a girl capable of filling Brock's shoes?" he asked Lawler.

"I don't know about her shoes. Those suit cases would take a bit of filling. But I'll guarantee one thing. I've seen the logical choice for Brock's successor. She's under your 'very nose if you'll take the trouble to look."

"Abe, leave us for a half hour or so. I can't accomplish anything while you stand there moaning and wheezing," said Julian.

"I s'pose you're gonna lissen to your juvenile. Well, it's killin' me. Let him learn to do his own job right before starts givin' lessons to others."

"All right, Abe, all right!" Julian placated him. "But please do as I ask. We're in a bad way, you know, and quarrelling won't help."

"Oke! I'll get a bite of supper an' come hack. God knows I need air or somepin'." He stamped out of the room, favoring Billy with a hard look.

Billy stared at the closed door. "My pal!" he laughed.

Julian motioned him to sit down. "See here, boy, what's this great notion of yours? Is there such a girl in our chorus or were you merely pulling Abe's leg?"

Billy lit a cigarette and sprawled on the divan at Julian's side. "Certainly there's a girl, chief. You've been too busy or you'd have noticed her yourself. The Sawyer kid!"

"Sawyer? Sawyer? Oh, I remember, now. Little Miss Boston!"

"She's the one, chief!"

"Without a grain of showmanship. Pretty figure, nice voice, ingratiating smile. It won't go, Billy. We need more than that."

"Julian—her voice is lovely. You remarked as much yourself at the dress rehearsal. Above all, she's distinctive. She's easily the outstanding girl in the line. A little more poise, some intensive coaching and think what might happen. Julian Marsh would have discovered a new star."

"Abe was right. Your brain's gone Hollywood," laughed Julian.

Billy frowned and got up abruptly. "What do you think you'd be doing?" he snapped. "Establishing a precedent? It's happened before!"

"But, Billy, the girl's an amateur! Brock's such an easy performer she's fooled you. That sort of artlessness isn't developed overnight. It took years of training to perfect the coyness that dear Dorothy's public is so mad about."

"And which Peggy Sawyer possesses naturally," Billy maintained.

"It's impossible. Do you realize the number of sides she must learn?"

"All *right!* Cut the part down. Let your comedians have more to do. God knows we need laughs. Give me another number. I haven't a decent chance in the whole show."

"I'm beginning to see the light. This championing of the company's Cinderella isn't entirely unselfish."

Billy stormed over to the window. "Very well—if you *will* misunderstand me. I tell you, from the first time I met Sawyer, that day when some chorus boy was teaching her a time step, I've watched her. She's decent, she's civilized, she's no more a chorus girl at heart than I am. If you don't discover her, Someone else will. I've talked with her now and then in a 'How do you do, nice day, isn't it?' sort of way. She's the only girl in the show I'd bother with." He shuddered as he remembered the long weeks of snubbing and innuendoes he had endured. Peggy Sawyer alone had disregarded the hatred and contempt of the others and greeted him pleasantly. In his heart of hearts he was not convinced of her great ability but he felt that her treatment of him should be rewarded and here was the opportunity. Those other trollops would regret the fact that they hadn't shown him the proper respect.

"I wonder!" mused Julian. "You've an eye for details like this, Billy. Let's work the thing out together." He indicated the place on the chaise longue at his side. Billy hung back.

"I'm glad to see you appreciate my idea," he whined. "God knows I get little enough attention."

"Good Lord, boy; what's wrong? Aren't you the juvenile of a Broadway production? Haven't you been called in at consultation of the powers that be?"

"I'm in a lousy spot, Julian. Abe Green doesn't like me!"

"Abe Green has to like you," declared Julian grimly.

Billy went to him. "You're rotten to me, Julian," He complained. "I risk losing the respect of everyone m this damn game just to be with you, and what thanks do I get?"

"You're wrong, Billy," Marsh extended his hand. "You know my life means nothing to me if I can't make you happy."

Billy drew back. "For Christ's sake, stop acting like an old auntie," he snarled. "You talk like this when we're alone, but it's a different story if I try to get a better show."

"You're set to good advantage now," Marsh. protested.

"Set to good advantage—hell! Two lousy little numbers in the first act. At the end of the show they've forgotten I was ever among those present. Julian, if we put this deal through, I want the dance I do with the girls put in the second act. I deserve that much consideration, don't I?"

Marsh shook his head. "It can't be done."

"Why not?" Lawler demanded. "Brock's out, so there's nobody else to raise a stink. Julian—please, old feller, I need more building up. If you put Sawyer in you'll have to strengthen the show here and there. Do this for me, chief! Now I'm nothing but a glorified chorus boy."

"I'll see about it tomorrow," Julian conceded.

Billy placed an arm about the older man's shoulder. "Thanks, chief. You can be a swell guy, can't you?"

"I can be anything you want," said Julian. "You know it—damn your little soul!"

"You're telling me!" thought Billy sardonically.

A half hour later Abe Green pounded nervously on the door. Billy admitted him, a superior smile masking the dislike in his heart. Abe grunted a "hello" and crossed the room to the chaise longue where Julian still lounged at ease.

"Well?" he demanded. "What's the word?"

"Sit down, Abe. You're far too explosive. It's bad for the nerves, mine as well as yours."

Abe flopped into a chair and lit a cigarette with trembling fingers. "The story's all over town," he said. "They're sayin' we've got a flop on our hands an' Brock is just an alibi."

Julian smiled. "They'll change their tune before tomorrow night," he asserted. "Will you promise not to rave and tear your hair at my suggestions? They're a bit wild, I promise you, but—they're feasible!"

"What the hell is *feasible?* We're all goin' nuts an' you spring words like *that* on me! Anything, anything, Julian but we gotta give a show tonight!"

"My dear man," Marsh cut in, "you can't do that in any case."

"Well, spring it. I know it'll be, rotten—but spring it!"

"There's one girl in Andy Lee s chorus who might fit the part."

"Don't make me laugh! Not out of that gang o' leg lifters!"

"Oh, not for tonight. I grant you that. But how does this strike you? We refund all money paid for tonight's performance. The town must be flooded with publicity regarding our dear prima donna's accident. If necessary, we'll have Mary Brock ready to go on tomorrow, but I think this can be accomplished without getting another Brock into the mess. We'll take care of all emergencies. Wire every agent in New York to have some 'name' lead standing by in the event my plan won't work. But— we concentrate on a certain little lady from the chorus, groom her for the part—and accord ourselves the honor of introducing a new star to Broadway."

"Don't make me laugh. We gotta sell 'em names, nowadays. Half that audience was comin' to see Dorothy Brock tonight. What a razzing we'll get when another actress is shoved into her part—a chorus girl, at that. It won't go, Julian. The notices in the paper ain't strong enough to carry us without Brock's name. Jesus, she's got a *public*."

"Moran will carry it. Moran was a sensation last night."

"Who the hell knows Moran?"

"Change your ads in the paper tomorrow. Plug him as new sensation. Build him up the way Bert Lahr was built up."

"Sure—I'll let *Mary* Brock go on. I can't help myself; but lissen, the public ain't interested in understudies an' flop sisters. We gotta lightweight show an' I ain't takin' chances. But Mary can't dance—she's still taking treatments from some doctor, an' our leadin' lady 'll be about as much of a jazz baby as Lady Macbeth was."

"Abe, see here. The girl I'm thinking of is Sawyer. Know her? Probably not. She's hardly the sort to catch your eye. Nevertheless, Sawyer has appearance, a voice and a charm that is natural and unspoiled. Furthermore, she carries herself well, she's intelligent and she'll respond to coaching. The part must be cut down, of course. All those light comedy sequences will have to go; you can't depend upon a comparative amateur to handle that kind of stuff, but the girl will look beautiful in that straw spotlight, standing in the manly embrace of Mr. John Phillips. Don't take my word alone, Abe. Jerry Cole will vouch for her voice. It's sweet and true. She's naturally limber and Andy can re-routine Dorothy's specialty, making it a soft shoe high kicking number instead of a tap dance. The double dance with Jimmy Allen goes out. Give Allen back his solo, Lord knows he deserves the chance. I'll have Sawyer on in the part by tomorrow night. We'll keep Mary Brock standing by, but I don't think you'll need her."

"But who the hell knows Sawyer?" fumed Abe. "I don't even know her myself. I'm selling personalities. You've gotta do it these days. Maybe Brock ain't no daisy any longer bur they fall for her stuff. Then I shove in some trick understudy and, Hooey goes a hundred thousand dollars."

"I think Peggy Sawyer would fit," interjected Billy Lawler.

Abe glared at him. "So that was *your* idea! I might've known."

Billy returned the stare with innocent candor. He was daring Abe to growl at him. Billy felt secure in his domain. Marsh got to his feet. Unaccountably Abe's opposition made him confident of Peggy's success. Perhaps Billy was right, after all. Of such raw materials stars are made. His voice waxed silken, persuasive. "We've got to face facts about this show, Abe. It's no sensation. The settings are fine; the production is the sort of thing I always turn out, the music's not bad—but they're *not laughing*. That's fatal. You know your Broadway well enough to understand the point I m trying to drive home. For six years I staged revues that were the most beautifully conceived productions an audience ever looked on. I captured poetry and symmetry and translated them into the terms of an ordinary musical show, no critic has ever failed to comment on that, but one and all they harped on the leanness of my comedy. I paid out thousands of dollars for three or four chuckles from my audience. Every producer m New York has done the same thing. Sheer loveliness won't carry the day. We can't permit our show to be beautiful and dumb. Here's my proposition. Moran is excellent. They'll like him in New York and work themselves into a lather over their new find. But he needs backing up and Mason doesn't pass muster. He's a fine road show performer, totally lacking in inspiration. You're paying him four hundred dollar a week to deliver machine-made lines in a mechanical fashion. You pay Brock one thousand dollars to draw patrons to the box office. We can't have Brock and we need a name. Very well, then—give little Sawyer the Brock role. She'll be competent, I promise you. Then turn the Mason part over to Andrew Hughes. He and Moran will make a grand team of fun makers. Hughes earns four figures weekly. He really earns it, Abe. Take Brock's name off the three sheets and substitute Hughes'. Then send out a lot of blah from the press department about the thousands of young girls who have been hiding their light under a bushel. Cite Sawyer as an example. The dear public always falls for that particular line of bunk, as though every blonde phenomenon hadn't slept with the manager the night before."

Billy Lawler coughed indignantly and took his golden head from the room. Marsh was too intent on furthering Peggy's cause to notice his blunder.

Green listened attentively. After all, this was more attuned to his ears. He understood an argument concerning the relative value of male and female names at the box office.

"Mr. Ziegfeld does it," Julian said. "He paired off a Marilyn Miller with a Jack Donahue so that the disgustingly glum chap who refuses to fall for golden curls and toothy smiles may be snared through his weakness for just another laugh."

"D'ye think I can get Hughes?" asked Abe doubtfully.

"He just closed in June Night, so I think you'll be able to bring him to terms. And don't swoon when he mentions his salary because good laughs come high. I'll attend to Harvey Mason. It's a dirty job at best."

Abe was silent for several minutes. He had been swayed by Julian's logic, but not so completely as to forget the numerous obstacles which lay in his path. It was all very well to talk one comedian out of his berth with a few fine flashes of rhetoric, but how could one be certain that all these plots and plans would make for an easy and successful solution? He, himself, held a sneaking admiration for Harvey Mason's work. Julian was right, though. The Great American Public wouldn't laugh. Mason would be a swell comic for Shubert revivals and stock company presentations of Gilbert and Sullivan, but he was neither subtle nor modern enough to earn Broadway's acclaim. Too bad, but, what the hell, that's show business!

"Who's Hughes' agent?" he asked.

"Max Baum. You'd better send a wire immediately," Julian advised.

"Will you call Sawyer to rehearsal? And talk things over with Mary Brock?" pleaded Abe. "My God, I'm near dead already and the trouble ain't half over. Somebody must've put the curse on me. We'll prob'ly lose our shirts before it's over."

"Indeed we won't, Abe. I've never disappointed you yet. Run along and sell your papers. I'll have Peggy Sawyer up in the part by tomorrow night. Your immediate concern is disposing of tonight's audience. Give the papers the customary allotment of slop. That should help."

"My God, I hope we can do it, I get goose pimples when I think of a chorus girl in that part! Julian, so help me, this is my last show. I wouldn't go through this again to save my dyin' mother. Show business! Aaah! What do they mean, *business?* It ain't even a racket! It's just an off moment in somebody's brain. God give me back my cloaks and suits and those good old bargain sales when I was happy!"

10

There are times when the wheels move swiftly—moments when that cumbersome machine, the modern musical comedy, hums in a mad, almost frantic haste. One hour is sufficient to undo the labor of several days. In that short space of time troublesome elements have been disposed of, loose joints are tightened and the machine achieves its long hoped for stride. The evening papers carried front page stories of the tragic misfortune that had befallen Broadway's "well loved star." There were glowing accounts of Dorothy Brock's popularity with her fellow players—pictures of her Westchester home—her first three husbands—her sister, who was in devoted attendance at the sickbed—a list of the various musical shows in which the well loved star had glittered. In the column devoted to theatrical advertisements appeared a notice, in heavy black type, "Due to the illness of Miss Dorothy Brock no performance tonight— watch this paper for further announcements." In a surprisingly short space of time a long line curved from the box office half way around the block as patrons sought the refund promised on the tickets they had purchased. The performers in rival attractions were in a fever of speculation. Was this just a stall? Had the opening performance been so ragged that Green and

Friedman recognized the wisdom of not continuing without further rehearsal? The members of the *Pretty Lady* company clustered in little groups about the stage door. Wild rumors filled the air. There was an atmosphere of fearfulness and uncertainty. Everyone wondered what the next move would be. For hours, while Green and Friedman were closeted in secrecy, the tide of doubt surged ever higher.

Harry MacElroy, hurrying across stage in quest of Peggy Sawyer, stopped for a moment before the garden bench where Harvey Mason was stretched full length.

"Message for you, Mr. Mason," he said.

Mason straightened up and accepted the envelope. A swift misgiving shot through him. He dreaded to read the contents of the message; instinct warned him that some cold-blooded fate was about to trick him out of the glory he had hoped to attain. He glanced warily about. No one was watching him. Nervously he slit open the envelope and removed the enclosed slip.

For a moment it seemed as though his heart must have ceased beating. There were the unbelievable words neatly typed on the sheet of paper before him. Two brief sentences that terminated his Broadway career in as businesslike a manner as one could wish. No explanation—no apology—a mere statement to the effect that his services would no longer be required two weeks from date. He looked up suddenly. Incredibly enough no one guessed the truth. The buzz of conversation seethed about him—the piano continued to pound out the melody of *Manhattan Madness*—the tap dancers were at their buck and winging. It was over for him. The decade of service in vaudeville—the slow, sure progress toward that ultimate goal and now—nothing. A slip of paper, "This is to inform you..." Impossible! It might be some ghastly joke. That fool Moran was up to his practical joking again. A paragraph from one of the morning papers struck him with disquieting force. "Mason labored in an uninspired manner."

Hack! Small timer! Back to the three-a-day for you, little feller! Let the South Bends and the Sioux Citys have you. What the hell would you mean on Broadway? You were in vaudeville ten years? So what? This was the dream of your life? So what? You're through now, baby, washed up! They'll let you play your little part a few more times and every show there'll be some guy in the audience watching your every move, pitying you, thinking how he can improve on your performance, the boy that's going to take your place! He'll there on Broadway—the "dear public" will laugh with him—and to hell with Harvey Mason. Mechanically he worded a telegram to his agent. "Out of show. Wire me earliest date to open old act." He got up wearily—not because there was any place to go, but simply because he felt the need of movement. A chorus girl eyed his white face curiously. She whispered to her friend and pointed at the slip of paper which was clenched tightly in his hand. The whisper went from group to group. Mason stumbled into the alleyway unheeding. The whisper grew to a shout. In fifteen minutes the entire chorus knew that Harvey Mason had received his notice. Blackout for Mr. Mason! Finis! The king is dead—he was a lousy king, anyway! Long live the king!

Peggy picked her way along the sloping path that led from the stage to the rear of the orchestra. She was puzzled at Harry MacElroy's summons.

"The boss wants to see you in the office."

What could that mean? Surely not dismissal. Such details were attended to without this fuss and ceremony. An envelope with a slip inside—and the execution was performed. The bosses never intruded into such a matter. She walked cautiously through the darkened theatre and came to the small door under the stairs leading to the balcony. It stood ajar and glancing inside the room she saw Julian Marsh tilting back in the swivel chair before the desk. The green shaded light beat down upon his head throwing his tired face into relief. She thought with a throb of pity how this new obstacle must have wrenched his heart. She knocked timidly, afraid of disturbing his reverie.

Marsh started. "Yes? Who's there?"

"Peggy Sawyer. Harry said you wanted to talk to me."

"Oh, yes, Miss Sawyer. Come in!"

He rose and bowed as she entered. "Won't you sit over there?" With a nod he indicated the arm chair beside the desk.

"Thank you." She slid into the chair and lapsed into silence. Her fingers were kneading the handkerchief she carried into a hard lump.

"Miss Sawyer—this is your first show, I believe?"

"Yes, Mr. Marsh." What was coming? Perhaps out of the kindness of his heart he felt that the blow should not be dealt without some word of explanation. That was it. Julian Marsh was sorry for her. She slumped into the chair, her eyes haunted with misery.

Incredibly, he smiled. "Cinderella!" "I beg your pardon?"

"We've been pleased with your work, Miss Sawyer. You make your place in the line outstanding. I heard many favor able comments last night."

"Oh, thank you." Words of gratitude rushed to her lips. Unless—unless—this was kindly preparation for the sad news to follow.

"Miss Sawyer—have you played any parts?"

"Well—one or two amateur shows and four months in the local stock company. Of course, I realize that means less than nothing."

"Mm! I shouldn't say that. The point is—have you sufficient confidence to go before an audience and deliver lines without an attack of stage fright or something stupid like that?"

Her eyes lightened. A small part, perhaps. A reward for persistent endeavor. Her voice shook a trifle as she answered. "Oh, yes, indeed, Mr. Marsh. In fact, I wanted to talk to you about some understudy work—later on, when things got more settled. I—I know I'm capable."

"You've a lovely voice. It stands out clearly above the others. That's a bit of home town glee club I suppose. Technically you're a bad dancer, of course, but you handle yourself well. The main thing is people like to look at you. Don't think these are just idle compliments, Miss Sawyer. I'm merely thinking aloud. You see—there must be a successor to Dorothy Brock and—we've chosen you."

The blood thundered through her veins. There was a buzzing in her ears. All at once Julian Marsh's voice was faint and far away. A mist swam before her eyes.

"Oh—oh, be careful, Miss Sawyer. Too much emotion is a bad thing for a leading lady." The warning brought her back to earth.

"But, Mr. Marsh, I—I—" and she was crying.

He felt absurdly pleased with himself. There is no grander sensation than the abject gratitude of some lesser being.

"I'll do it, Mr. Marsh! I feel so ridiculous going on like this but—you've no idea. Why, if someone were to promise me heaven on a gold platter I couldn't be happier. I—I—oh, dear, there's so much to learn."

"Exactly—we must start at once. I have a copy of your 'sides' here. Mr. Lee will spend three hours with you on dance routines. You know the songs, I believe. Tomorrow morning we'll call Phillips and run through the harmony on those duets. You're going to be splendid, Miss Sawyer! Billy Lawler prophesied as much—and Billy has good judgment, you know! The best of luck!"

Somehow she found her way out of the office—the manuscript clutched in her hand.

In the New York office of Max Baum a secretary was calling the Lambs Club to ascertain the present address of Andrew Hughes. The first afternoon train westbound from Pennsylvania

Station numbered Hughes among its passengers. Accompanying him w as the astute Mr. Baum, himself. Such an important transaction could not be left to the judgment of an assistant. Mr. Baum in person would superintend the formalities.

While Dorothy Brock lay helpless the concentrated forces of *Pretty Lady* strove to eradicate all signs of her presence in the show. Men armed with brushes and buckets of paste were sent to remove her name from the billboards in front of the theatre. The publicity department invaded the sacrosanct corner, where a bewildered Peggy was going through the preliminary paces of Dorothy Brock's dance, to demand pictures and a life story in time for the morning editions.

Wires were sent to the New York dailies informing dramatic editors of drastic changes being made in the in production.

Green and Friedman both as a business firm and as private individuals tore their hair, bit their fingernails and wondered.

Soon the rumors of this state of affairs reached the ears of an ever alert chorus girl. She spread the report. In a few hours the entire company knew of Peggy's luck.

The girls were betting on the likelihood of her success. It is easy to belittle a more fortunate comrade. Even Ann Lowell experienced sharp misgivings.

"Well, if you ask me, it's beginner's luck," snapped Sophie Gluck. "A punk like that gettin' such a swell break."

"D'ye mean to tell me there ain't dirt there?" demanded Lorraine Fleming.

"Dirt—hell! That kid don't know how to handle the big guys yet," scoffed Ann. "Marsh liked her work and—zowie—she gets the part."

"Score one for the virgins," said Sophie.

"Well, I'm through. I'm washed up with show business," mourned Lorraine. "Here I been liftin' my legs in the merry-merry for five years now an' what do I get but strained ligaments and flat feet? Maybe mother was right when she told me to be a good girl."

"They coulda done worse," Ann declared. "The kid troupes like a thoroughbred. And did you get the way she's makin' Phillips step? I'm expecting him to lay her to filth any minute. You know, that egg ain't as young as he useter be and when the arteries start to harden the old kicks don't go up so forte."

"Well, we'll all be gettin' free feels from the new comic, I can promise you that—so things'll seem natural even though old Mason has taken the count," remarked Sophie. "When Hughes gets with any girl he thinks he's Columbus an' starts out to discover new land."

"Boy, how. those funny guys like to chase!" exclaimed Lorraine. "I hear old Lily Lowbottom, Andy Lee's girl friend, ran around with Hughes for a while."

"Yeah? When was this?"

"Oh, about five abortions ago."

"My God, what they're doin' to this opera is nobody's business," complained Ann Lowell. "Takin' out a swell number like *Hot off the Griddle* an' stickin' in that lousy reprise Phillips sings. That boy's falsetto note is all cluttered up with adenoids."

"Somebody told me he wears a toupee," ventured Sophie.

"That's the bunk. I yanked his hair the other day just to find out for my own satisfaction an' he yelled bloody murder. Nope—he an' the old wool aren't parting company yet awhile," volunteered Ann.

"I hear the agencies are coming all the way from New York to okay us," Lorraine Fleming put in.

"Baby, I hope so," sighed Ann. "It'll be my first break in three seasons. The minute word gets 'round I'm gonna break out in a new show Cain starts feeding his horses."

"Me, too," sympathized Lorraine. "I'm gonna look me up a nice quiet nook like salad girl on the *Leviathan* this season."

"They say our number with Lawler's gonna be stuck in the second act."

"Yeah—the little tin soldier gets anything he hollers for. Well, as far as I m concerned his mother went to that doctor three months too late."

In a sheltered nook Mrs. Blair and Polly were devoting their time to a hit of gloating over the unfortunate Dorothy.

"I knew she'd get what was comin' to her," exulted Mother Blair. "The trollop! Now you be very nice an' sweet to Marsh, dear, and I'm sure we'll get your high kicking dance put hack in the first act. He knows he owes me a debt gratitude for warning him about the way that hussy was carryin' on."

"Yes, Ma. I spoke to him already but he said he was busy an' for me not to bother him with details like that just now."

"Oh, yeah? Well, I'll make Mr. Julian Marsh talk turkey. I happen to know a thing or two about the goin's on in opera and we'll have that dance put back in or else—"

Danny Moran leaned against the grimy wall of the alley and explained the situation to his wife. A cigar protruded from his mouth at a jaunty angle. The new gray fedora hat was cocked at an alarming slant over one eye.

"Y'see, Daisy, they fin'lly got wise to themselves they gotta have comedy. All your Brocks an' pretty chorus numbers don't mean a damn thing. It's the comics who bring the dough into the box office. Now Harvey's a nice kid an' he'll prob'ly he okay for Broadway in a couple more seasons, but just now he ain't got finesse. That's why they're bringin' this Hughes guy on to support me. Hughes is good too, hut he's kinda had his day and they know he'd take it on the chin unless I was right back of him to help put a sock into the lines. Didya see the papers? Ev'ry one raved about me."

"It's swell, all right, Danny, only—"

"Only *what?* For God's sake—are you gonna start crabbin' again?"

"No, Danny. Bye. I'll see you at dinner tonight."

Danny shifted uneasily. "Well, hon, don't wait too long. You know how these things is apt to keep on far into the night. I may have to just run next door to that lunch room and grab me a sandwich. Maybe you hadn't better figure on eatin' with me tonight at all."

"Oh, Danny." Despite her efforts at self control, Daisy felt her eyes fill with tears. "I'm so damn lonely in this town. Nobody to talk to—nobody to eat with. I might jus' as well be in a convent."

"Sure, girlie, I know how it is," Danny assented, too eagerly. "Thass why I was thinkin'—mebbe you better run back to New York. You got all your girl friends there an' I'm so tied up with all these rehearsals I can't spend no time with yuh. Maybe you'd be happier back on the Main Drag, huh?"

Daisy eyed him distrustfully. Danny strove to look guileless.

"No—I think I'll stick around," she decided. "Y' might need me."

Danny shrugged. "Y'can do whatcha wanta about that " he said. "But remember—I ain't to blame if yuh have a 'bum time.'"

"I won't blame, you, Danny," murmured Daisy.

They stood there for several minutes in uncomfortable silence. Danny had suddenly discovered that he couldn't talk to Daisy. He was getting up in the world while Daisy's affections tied her to the small time existence she had always known. He gave her a perfunctory kiss and went inside the theatre. She lingered at the door just long enough to see him put an arm about the waist of Lorraine Fleming and drag her with him, laughing and protesting, until both were lost from sight. Her heart filled with an almost insupportable pain, Daisy stumbled blindly out of the alley into the hot afternoon sunlight.

But the machine could not pause to brood over the destinies of the human beings that were caught up in its motion. Machines are impersonal things not given to introspect and retrospect. All that driving force was pounding relentlessly toward one goal—a successful premiere on Forty-Second Street. The unwanted cogs, like Harvey Mason, were cast aside. The machine would not wait to consider the unhappiness of Daisy Moran, the thwarted ambitions of Dorothy Brock, the connivings of Billy Lawler. The machine which they had built with infinite care was now their master. From the lowliest chorus girl to the resplendent new star, Danny Moran, trifling intrigues and jealousies must be put aside—each cog had to function in its proper place.

Over all presided Julian Marsh—shouting, gesticulating, coercing. The chorus and principals were the groundlings whose vision was limited, but the mind of Julian Marsh could take wings and view from above, as a panorama, the musical comedy as a whole. The revisions and excisions went on ceaselessly throughout the day and night. By the following evening they would be ready to face their audience with renewed confidence in an improved and smoothly running production.

II

Once again Pat Denning resorted to the consoling powers of Bourbon. His drinking mate had long since departed on unsteady legs, leaving Pat to ponder darkly on a future bereft of the three feminine companions who had grace the days of his affluence. Now Peggy, Dorothy, and Amy were banished from his life. There remained only an alliance with a pouting Park Avenue dowager whose bunioned feet he had piloted over the dance floor at the Ambassador Hotel a few weeks previous. Since that afternoon he had remained a memorable spark in the ashes of her life and she was tireless in her solicitations for his continued "friendship." Until now he had ignored her pitiful entreaties, but faced with the loss of Dorothy's patronage once more, he made a motion toward the address book which housed the telephone numbers of the various ladies who had proven themselves angels of mercy on previous occasions. .

Fortunately the ring of the door bell saved him from the consummation of this dire destiny. He wondered which of his acquaintances was aware of his return from the fleshpots of Philadelphia. He pushed the buzzer and awaited events not without a few qualms, as the recollection of the hard-boiled gentlemen who had dogged his steps on two former occasions was unpleasantly keen. The apartment looked as though a cyclone had struck it, but he was beyond caring. Let Fate do its worst—he had resisted long enough, now he would accept all buffetings without complaint.

The visitor knocked, and something reminiscent in that summons stirred hope in Pat Denning's breast. He made haste to open the door and staggered back, dumbfounded, when he saw Amy Lee confronting him. She stood there, irresolute, as though uncertain of his greeting. He noted that she was admirably gowned in a new and expensive-looking outfit, doubtless the gift of her beleaguered husband.

"Hello, Amy," said Pat. He stood aside doubtfully, wondering whether she had come to kiss or kill him. Though her heart was filled with trepidation Amy successfully concealed the fact and Pat found it impossible to guess from her demeanor what her errand might be.

"You're all alone?" she asked, fixing her eye on the bathroom door.

"My last visitor has wrung himself out and left," responded Pat.

She gave a satisfied nod and crossed the threshold. The appalling litter met her eye and she shuddered. Pat must have been reduced to a pitiable state.

"I thought you'd never come back," said Pat, following her.

"You don't deserve to see me," she pouted. "You acted like a beast."

He granted the misdemeanor. "But I was terribly tight," he apologized. "And you've got such a damnable temper. I hope I didn't hurt you."

Amy giggled. "You certainly caught me right on my dignity," she confessed.

He motioned her to a chair and then dropped onto the sofa. He was watching her narrowly, wondering what her game could be. The old predatory instinct reasserted itself. Here was woman motivated by desire and, as such, fair prey for him.

But this time the terms must be exacting. Anyone who acted so abominably as Amy had done must be made to realize her dependence on the whims of the male.

"I've missed you, Amy," he began. "What a pity our little affair is ended."

"You're just pumping me," she retorted coolly. "You know you'll jump through the ring the minute I say 'allez oop.' Money talks!"

He shook his head. "Not this time, dear. I'm a little better fixed with worldly goods."

She was disconcerted. "They told me your show was closed," she snapped. "Besides, I heard rumors about shady carryings-on in Philadelphia. I don't suppose you know a thing about this Dorothy Brock mess."

"Dorothy Brock? I've not seen her in ages."

"I get it, Mr. La Verne," she baited him.

"La Verne?" he responded equably.

"Oh, drop it. Let's get to the point. I had very good reason to believe you were flat once more, what with the show—and all that."

"There were certain investments of mine," he murmured.

"Ridiculous. You couldn't play the stock market no more 'n a new born babe," she sneered. "Try another one!"

He did not deign to answer. The next move must be hers. Amy opened her vanity case and selected a cigarette. Pat made no attempt to offer her a light. She closed the case with a vindictive snap and demanded matches. He struggled to his feet and produced a battered lighter from the drawer of the desk.

"You're so very gallant," she remarked acidly.

"You give me no reason to be," Pat replied.

She gave a petulant shrug. "I don't see why you treat me this way. God knows I was good to you. That's my robe you're wearing now."

He bowed. "I was too drunk to notice what I'd put on," he explained. "With your kind permission I'll retire and take it off."

She lifted her hand. "Don't be silly, Pat. It's foolish to let one little quarrel come between us. We're going to hit it again, I know."

"You broke off yourself," he reminded her. "I'm not chasing any women. From now on they're poison to me."

She got up from her chair and squeezed onto the sofa beside him. "Darling, can't we let bygones be bygones? I'll admit I was a bad girl."

"Don't act like a child, Amy. There's nothing to forgive. I don't want to start the rumpus all over again so let's shake hands and part good friends."

She patted his head. "You can't get away that easy," she said.

"Can't I? I know every move in your game, Amy. You couldn't fool me—not even if the cards were stacked!"

"I've got an ace in the hole, big boy," she boasted.

He eyed her cynically. "After the degree of intimacy we achieved it isn't possible," he murmured.

She paused for a moment as though contemplating the surprise that she was about to spring. He waxed impatient. Amy looked badly in the daylight and he knew that whatever attraction she might have held for him was definitely finished. He lacked the resolution to tell her so, but if she persisted in these coy grimacings he'd be tempted to step out of character.

"How'd you like a trip to Paris?" she asked.

"Fine! How'd you like to marry Charles Farrell?" he rejoined.

"Don't be such a killjoy, Pat. I really mean it."

"No thanks. I don't fancy myself stripped to the waist, stoking coal."

She fished in her pocketbook and retrieved a crumpled envelope. "Look at those," she invited.

Pat wondered what sickening plan she had devised this time. He wished she wouldn't use that particular perfume. Its scent was revolting. Amy was tingling with impatience. Oh, well, he'd better get this over with. He slit open the envelope and inspected its contents. Instantly a startling conviction overtook him.

"For Paris?" he inquired. "You and Andy sailing?"

She shook her head. "Not Andy. I'm through with that bum."

"Well, I give up," he sighed. "Don't tell me it's an aged and decrepit mother."

She chuckled. "If the show's closed you won't be doing anything," she remarked. "How would you like to chaperon little Amy on her first European jaunt?"

It was his turn to grimace. "No thanks. The strain of shutting my eyes to your more flagrant sins would be too great. As chaperon I would suggest the entire vice squad."

"I'm not as bad as all that," Amy fussed. "And with you along I'd promise to come home every evening before midnight."

He snorted. "What's the game, Amy?" he demanded. "We're too wise for pretense."

"Just this," she replied. "I'm fed up with Andy. He was a pretty good scout but he's gone sour, and I'm not figuring on standing by while he carries on with every chorus girl on Broadway. I'm no dumbbell and I knew a time would come when the two of us would have to call it quits. Well, he's in Philly now, raising cain with some new jane and I've got plenty on him. Boy, how my detective's report would sell in Boston until the censors got hold of it. So little Amy is off for Paris and a divorce. I've got Andy so dazzled he won't know whether he's coming or going, and by the time I get through he'll be willing to pay any alimony I want. Besides, I gotta pile of dough speculating on the market. A few of my boy friends wised me up on a coupla good deals an' I'm right up in the money. Now I've cleaned up, the coin is rolling in an' it's high time I try to do something about my bright an' sparklin' future. I want a few laughs out of life. And that's where you come in. I don't know why, but I've got a weakness for you. God knows you aren't any prize package and I'll probably have to keep an eye on the charge account if I want you to stay faithful, but it can't be helped. I like you too much to say good-by without a struggle, so here's the proposition. We head for Paris on the same boat, but occupying different staterooms so it won't look too funny. Then I rush the divorce through and when the final decree is made I'm thinking very seriously of becoming the honorable Mrs. Patrick Denning."

Pat gasped. Shades of the Victorian ladies who pined away into pale spinsterhood if the men of their choice did not deign to woo them. The modern woman has her passion regulated with all the acumen of an efficiency expert, he reflected. It was difficult to believe that this brash young creature had disposed of one mate and gained another in a single bold stroke. Doubtless she had cornered the market with characteristic level-headedness and now regarded him as the spoils belonging to the victor.

Well, he'd be damned if he bowed to such a humiliating arrangement. Man was still the master and no auburn-haired devil could tempt him to forego the upper hand. He knew how completely at her mercy he would be once the union was consummated. Amy was a fierce and jealous mistress—he trembled at the thought of seeing her robed in the dignity of wifehood. Terrible to follow the call of her rasping voice, for that way madness lay.

She was leaning back against the cushions watching his reaction to her proposal. She was by no means certain of success. Pat had deft ways of dealing with feminine capriciousness. But this time. she would brook no half measures. He must be hers completely, her property, safe from the despoiling hand of treacherous women like Dorothy Brock. They faced one another like shrewd opponents in the game of barter. Neither would budge an inch until the other laid his every card on the table. Both were busy with their own thoughts.

Amy visioned a Paris where the atmosphere loaned a dream quality to sin. She was wholly reconciled to the Gallic viewpoint of morals. Once or twice Pat might slip the leash and she would be disposed to condone. But the best fruits of his amorous labor must be reserved for her. She was well aware that he was long past his spring blooming and that the ardors he offered would be the result of long practice rather than true passion, but she preferred that to the stammering emotion of the youngsters who desired her. The old adage that proclaimed one man supremely desirable to one woman held good in this particular case. Never had she been so stirred as in the embrace of Pat. If his love making lacked sincerity, it held a quality of rapture that she found unattainable elsewhere. For her it was Pat or the easy promiscuity that promised relief from boredom. As far as she was concerned, Andy was dead. Neither his tears nor his curses could move her. She realized that he had been nothing more than escape, escape from the bondage of the chorus, a means toward the accomplishing of those ends which her determined little mind had fixed upon early in life. And once the break was made Andy would be converted to a career of perpetual seduction. There are many, many show girls in the world who are eager to listen to the blandishments of those who wield power. Andy would mourn nothing but the inconvenience of alimony.

Pat considered her with the cold, shrewd intellect which he had brought to bear on all his affairs. He saw that Amy possessed the hard perfection of a flawless stone. There was brightness, and beauty, and monetary value. But always the blatant voice would intrude and the sensual mouth would command surrender to each trifling wish.

And Peggy? A sudden pain contracted his heart. That once he had loved sincerely. The bitter remembrance of her departure from his rooms in Philadelphia lay heavily upon him. He thought of the promises he had made in the early stages of their friendship. With what nobility he had thrust aside the shame of his youth. It was so easy to do when hopes beat high and the promise of financial freedom rode beside the pleasure of Peggy's companionship. Each dear moment together came before his eyes and he wondered if the sacrifice of that joy would be recompensed by the life Amy proffered. He believed that Peggy had loved him. This was neither arrogance nor self deception. He felt that her affection for him might have been strong and enduring. More the pity that it was wasted because his feet were so definitely clay. Her love necessitated courage and persistence, and he possessed neither.

The flagellating truth unnerved him. If he had been born wealthy—but why waste time with such useless conjectures. Paris—London—Berlin—the rainbow world which until now had been shrouded in the mists of poverty. If one were to mourn it was wiser to choose a background of Mediterranean skies rather than the mean walls of a Forty-Second Street rooming house. If he were tempted to philosophize, he might remark that his removal from the scene was a stroke of luck for Peggy. Any happiness that they might find together would be microscopic. They loved, but Pat was made of the stuff which demands far more than affection. Though he might love deeply, he would inflict hurt—better that Peggy forget him. He would go away without a word, perhaps a brief note, nothing more. The episode in Philadelphia would safely cauterize the wound caused by his desertion. He looked into Amy's eyes. They were bent upon him with an urgent desire.

He smiled slightly. At least Amy was forthright in her bargaining. She did not attempt to cloak her purpose with shrinking glances. He hoped that he was made of sterner clay than Andy, else she would destroy him.

Amy was becoming impatient. She knew he would accept, ultimately, unless some other woman had preceded her with a more tempting arrangement. This she doubted for she had acted at the instant news was wired to her of his return from Philadelphia. Private detectives were a valuable source of information, all right. It was a dubious manner of approach, but she had no notion to let him slip through her fingers because of false modesty. They were both children of Forty-Second Street and understood one another.

Despair smote Pat when he viewed the years of atrophy and decay that hovered like so many menacing forms over the future. By that time Amy might be well content to rid herself of him and he must ascertain that the faltering days of his life were well provided for. He would get her to make some allowance which even divorce was powerless to stop. Already he knew that he would accept. He marveled that she could face the prospect of those joyless years, but if that was her make-up he was content to string along. But what would Amy do when the parade of life passed her by, leaving her desolate among the shadows?

He took her in his arms. "But those tickets are for next Tuesday," he protested. "And I've heard it's a hellish job to get one's passport."

12

"It's all right, Don. Don't worry about me, I'll get along. A career is the main thing. A career—a career—." Peggy faltered.

"That's three careers the guy has had already," Flo commented. "Some baby!"

"Shut up, Flo. This is hard enough without any remarks from the gallery."

"Sure, babe, I know. An' don't think your old Aunt Jessie isn't proud of her little girl. Once more Old Flo, the pride of the Varicose Brigade, has a chance to say 'I knew her when!' Sure you won't go Hollywood on us, Peggy? Sure you won't drag the Boston accent outta mothballs and ritz the old gang?"

"Don't be silly! Read these cues for me like a darling. I'm the world's worst actress when it comes to remembering lines."

Flo accepted the battered script with a sigh of resignation. "Girlie, it'll take a shot of adrenaline to get you on that stage tonight. You're a nervous wreck. How the hell does Marsh think you're gonna waltz your form through this opera at such short notice? These guys ain't human. If you flop they'll raise hell an' say you ain't got a spark of genius in you. If you put it over they say, 'Not so bad, but it's too bad we haven't got our darling Dorothy Brock.'"

"Now! Now! Mother's little helper. Get over there and help me put over the big resignation scene at the end of the first act."

"Right! I can see the tears of your dear public flooding the aisles, while ushers paddle back and forth in gondolas bringing smelling salts to weak-minded women who have gone nutty over your emoting."

"One more remark like that, darling, and there won't be any little Flo to help her girl friend catch the bouquets and tin cans opening night," remarked Peggy.

"Come on then. 'Why, Marianne...'" Flo produced a bleating note that approximated the injured tones of John Phillips rather well.

The telephone blasted shrilly. Flo slapped the manuscript against the bureau with a snort of indignation. "Wouldn't someone call?" she demanded.

"Perhaps I'd better not answer," said Peggy. "It might be one of the kids and we haven't any time for a dishing party at this late date."

"Uh-uh," contradicted Flo. "Better see who it is. Maybe Mr. Godalmighty Marsh has a few more suggestions for his pet protégé."

Peggy nodded and went over to the telephone which rested on a small table between the twin beds. "Hello," she called.

"Hello, Barrymore!" answered a cheery voice. "Brother John and all the kiddies send their *very* best."

"Who's this?" demanded Peggy.

"I told you. Brother John. Just at present I'm making a personal appearance under the name of Lawler!"

"Why, Billy! I—I didn't recognize your voice."

"I'm giving it that well known microphone touch. How do you like these juveniles who croon in your ear? Well enough to step out for a cup of tea?"

"I couldn't, Billy, even though the microphone touch is swell!"

"Why not?"

"I'm up to my—"

"Uh uh! Mustn't say the naughty word!"

"Silly! I was just going to explain that I'm up to my ears in cues."

"Well, bring the darn part along. I'm a swell coach!"

"The boss would kill us both!"

"Not a chance. Come on. Be a good feller! I'm downstairs in your lousy lobby this very minute. Throw on a few ermines and join me."

"Oh—all right. But if I'm a miserable flop tonight I'll kill you!"

"You couldn't flop, gorgeous. You're the elect of the gods!"

"Be careful! This is a very old hotel. That last remark of yours probably cracked the ceiling!"

"How long will you be? And no wisecracks like 'Five foot four!'"

"There's not a wisecrack in my being today. Give me five minutes."

"My, what a lot of powder your nose needs!"

"There are other things that need attention, little boy!"

"Pardon I'm. Very well, I'll possess my soul in patience. But have a heart. My digestion is just raring to meet a hunk of French pastry."

"Right!" She replaced the instrument and danced over to the window where Flo had been avidly drinking in the conversation.

"Flo! It's Billy Lawler. He wants me to have tea with him."

"My God—these juveniles with their Oxford complexes!"

"Aren't you thrilled. Little Peggy's getting up in the world!"

"Yeah—well, it's no balloon ascension as far as I'm concerned. More like an undersea voyage!"

Peggy drew back offended. "Still harping on Billy's sins, aren't you?" she snapped. "After all, if it hadn't been for him I'd still be kicking my heels in the merry merry."

"Just like me! I get it!" Flo returned.

"Darling, darling, you know I didn't mean that! I just get so terribly annoyed at the attitude everyone in this company takes toward Billy Lawler. He's human like the rest of us, isn't he? He's flesh and blood—not a motion picture!"

"Sometimes I wonder!" vouchsafed Flo. "Anyhow, he's a mean baby. I hope you're not going to tell me that he didn't get poor Ray Hall fired—and didn't mess things up for Bobby Lynton. Your new friend is death on blondes—male blondes, at any rate. He'll stand for no competition—and if *that* isn't low down and lousy I don't know what *is!*"

"Well, you're going to do your darnedest to be nice to him for my sake," pleaded Peggy. "He's been such a good friend."

"Don't worry. I'll be nice for my own sake. Little Flo isn't dreaming of speaking out of turn and losing her job. She's a girl as knows on what side her bread gathers no moss!"

"Then help me get beautiful for my grand entrance, Peggy begged. "I look a fright. Loan me your new blue ensemble like a good scout?"

"Okay—but spill any tea on it and you'll be past tense from this day forth and even forevermore."

The two girls scurried about the room, opening drawers, spilling the contents on the floor, selecting a stocking here, a handkerchief there, until the outfit was complete. Peggy stepped up to the mirror and surveyed the effect. She smoothed her hair, tucked in a few loose strands at the back of her neck, and turned to Flo.

"Beautiful, Miss America! You get the tin cup!" said Flo.

Peggy found young Lawler sprawled in an easy chair near the elevator. He sprang to his feet as she approached, a grin of welcome on his face.

"Not bad for a novice. When you've been a principal a few months longer you'll learn how to keep expectant males waiting for at least an hour."

"I'll never do that," Peggy protested. "But you should have seen me. The wrath of God would be a mild burst of temper compared to what I looked like when you called. This memorizing of lines has me a nervous wreck!"

Billy escorted her from the hotel. "Shall we drop over to the Ritz Lenox?" he suggested. "It's fairly cool in the Palm Court and it's the only place in Philly where you can get a decent cup of tea!"

They walked along the street which was baking in the hot afternoon sun.

"Shouldn't I be highly honored?" teased Peggy.

"On the contrary. After tonight, our roles are reversed. You will have become the glamorous leading lady while I remain the also-ran juvenile."

"I don't believe it. Everyone thinks you're splendid in the part!"

"Behave yourself! The chorus down to the last hoofer thinks that I stink! I know—my ears have been wired for sound."

"That might be jealousy, you know."

"Perhaps. At any rate, I'm not worried about the opinion of a gang like that. Thank God, you're getting out of it. You never belonged in the chorus, Peggy. I could tell that the first time I spoke to you."

"Don't let the Boston accent fool you. I'm a pretty hopeless person at times. Why, if you hadn't dropped into my life I should be one of millions of colorless young ladies who hope to land a chorus job from season to season!"

"You'd never have stayed there. You were bound to rise."

"Thanks, Mr. Alger!"

They entered the lobby of the Ritz Lenox. Peggy was impressed at the self-conscious gentility which bore down upon her from every side. The appointments of the lounge fairly shrieked expensiveness. The well groomed women moved leisurely as they went their way to various rendezvous. The smartly tailored men talked in tones that fell gratefully on her ears after the weeks of association with the *Pretty Lady* ensemble. She gazed about her entranced. For the first time in her life she felt that she was definitely a part of these surroundings. Hitherto she had scuttled through the foyers of fashionable hotels, head down, face red with embarrassment because she was sure that the flocks of well-dressed men and women must immediately recognize her as an interloper. But now she was privileged to join the gay pageant. She might assume the role of woman of the world. It made her a little heady with excitement.

She clasped Billy's hand. "Oh, Billy! You're such a darling. Pray for me tonight, won't you? You do think I'll get over?"

Her appeal reached him. He was conscious of a definite liking for this young person who was so grateful for his intervention on her behalf, so appreciative of his talents. It is no easy thing to endure the scorn of an entire company, and. although Billy, aided by an unimpaired ego, had managed to weather the storm, it had not left him unscathed. He turned to Peggy as the one human being who seemed to respect him. None of the others dared defy him openly, but he could not help but notice their thinly veiled contempt. Peggy was worth cultivating. She might possess the requisite spark and then he would shine in the role of her discoverer. Shrewdness and gratitude for her sincere friendship combined to make Billy Lawler a staunch ally of the fledgling star. Henceforth Peggy would be safe from the caustic tongue of Andy Lee and other dissenters who considered her unfit for the part. Willfully or not, Peggy had gained an important friend. Flattery is the most potent weapon known to show business.

The head waiter favored them with a deferential bow and ushered them to a table near the fountain. The water fell softly into a marble basin and spread out in tiny ripples that lapped the sides of the pool.

"This is lovely!" breathed Peggy.

"It's the proper setting for you," Billy retorted. "Look here, Papa Lawler has a bit of advice to broadcast. You won't be offended?"

"Of course not. I'm the world's best listener!"

"This girl you're rooming with—what's her name?"

"Flo Perry. She's a grand scout. We have a million laughs."

"Yes, I know her. She's been in the merry merry for about six years. Never will get any further. You can't afford to be too friendly with people like that."

"Billy—you're not trying to make a snob out of me?"

"Far from it. I'm merely advising you to look out for number one."

"But Flo's been marvelous. I'd have been lost without her."

"Naturally. All this was new to you. But now you've gained a footing and it's time to strike out for yourself. You don't need the Flo Perrys of this world. From now on that little address of yours should contain only Wickersham phone numbers."

"Does yours?" she parried.

"Of course," he answered simply.

"You're by way of being a rather hardened young man, aren't you?" she said.

"If you're not tough, they'll lick you after a few seasons. There's no such thing as sentiment in our business. It's dollars and sex!"

"And the more sex the more dollars?" she asked.

"Right. Now, another thing. This chorus boy, you know, the one who taught you the time step—what about him?"

"Terry? Well, I've been thinking a lot about Terry. He's a nice boy, but I'd already decided that we weren't the sort who make bosom companions. I'm grateful to Terry and for a while I was—Well, I hate the word but it certainly expresses my condition, I was infatuated. He was so darned different, Billy.

You've no idea how fascinating a young roughneck like that can be to a sheltered young lady."

"I'm glad to hear he's definitely side-tracked. One other—that chap I've seen you with once or twice. Tall good-looking fellow who looks like the tailor's delight. Wasn't there something a bit phoney about that one?"

Peggy flushed. "Oh, Pat Denning!" she replied with forced lightness. "Just an acquaintance. I—went to dinner with him a few times and we played around. He's good fun, but I'd never dream of seriously considering him."

Billy eyed her keenly. "Um! Perhaps not! I hope not, anyhow. Tailor's dummies don't have much future."

Peggy remembered the many evenings in the British Tea Room, dining in secluded corners, watching the smoke curl from the tip of Pat's cigarette, listening to his half tender, half mocking love talk. That had been glamour and romance. No matter how falsely grounded were her hopes for a time she had been happy. It was not easy to forget Pat Denning.

Billy was speaking. "And that leads quite naturally to the subject of a new heart interest. How about me?"

"You?" Peggy gasped.

"Why not? A presentable Broadway juvenile with a flair for dancing. Don't I fill the bill? I promise to fulfill my obligations to the utmost. Your nights will be filled with the atmosphere of Sutton Place and the Mayfair!"

"What sort of proposal is this?" Peggy demanded.

"The usual kind. I'm staking my claim before the Park Avenue playboys get their chance. You're on the brink of fame, young lady. Snap out of it!"

Peggy considered. Obviously Billy felt that such a companionship would serve as a smoke screen for his relations with Julian Marsh. She knew that Lawler was incapable of genuine admiration for her. He could never be so completely selfless as to admire another before himself. But it served his purpose to be seen about town with a comely young woman who was a figure on the Broadway scene and he was not averse to taking that means of stopping gossip. Well, two could play that game. There were no Wickersham phone numbers in her address book, and Sutton Place meant no more to her than a block of apartment houses on the east side, but Billy would change all that. She would string along with him, and it would be to the mutual benefit of both.

Good-by Pat! Good-by Terry! Nice to have known you! Pardon me while I climb a few rungs on my ladder! Don't worry—I shan't tumble! My hands have a firm grip. I know what I'm doing and great heights won't frighten me! It flashed through her mind that these were the plottings of a selfish shallow mind. Her every action might be construed as a deliberate attempt to further her own career at the expense of fatuous admirers. But wasn't that the Forty-Second Street code? What matter if she summarily dismissed Terry from her mind? Another girl would come along and Terry's cup of joy would be overflowing once again. She seriously doubted the lasting qualities of Terry's love. Good hearted, well meaning, he was too much a son of the Broadway pavement to allow one love to hold his attention indefinitely. Most assuredly there would be others. For all his boorishness Terry was an attractive boy. Deep rooted in his none too clever mind there was a desire to emulate Casanova. That Peggy had held him decently in check could be accounted for only on the grounds that her unfamiliar manner overawed him. If Peggy had spoken Terry's language it would have been a question of here today and gone tomorrow. No, she was well rid of that entanglement. Terry might fancy himself the owner of a broken heart for a few weeks, but in the end he'd find consolation. Pat was definitely out of the picture. That once she had been hurt—she was willing to confess that. Pat was the sophisticated Prince Charming—the silver screen idol—the dream lover come true. There had been a touch of the school-girl-matinee-idol business in their affair. She had saved him from the consequences of his ill-advised liaison with Dorothy Brock and quite unexpectedly profited thereby. They were quits. No tears! No regrets! Pat had the right idea. He knew it all along. Good luck, Pat, but you've chosen a tough road. Remained Billy Lawler.

"When do we start the rounds?" she asked Billy.

"The minute we're back in God's country. I'm going to the opening dance at the Mayfair with friends and of course you'll come along."

"Should I find myself some broker with a penchant for supporting unprotected ingénues?" she asked.

"And have you live in 'Wicker-shame'? Heaven forbid!" he answered.

They left the Palm Court and strolled along Broad Street to the street where Peggy's hotel was situated. Peggy noticed a languid figure walking ahead of them, his hips swaying in a sort of rhythmic undulation. Two sidewalk hangers-on lounging in front of a cigar store, sighted this person in the same moment. One of them emitted a derisive laugh and the other called,

"Whoops, dearie, mind all the bad men or they'll change your name to Brown!"

The figure turned regally. Peggy gasped. It was Jack Winslow. He drew up haughtily and turned a withering glance on the hecklers.

"Lissen, girlie," he said with startling distinctiveness. "Don't think you're fooling anybody just because you've got hair on your chest. Every time you get a lump in your throat you start sewing baby clothes!" He sailed on, leaving two discomfited hoodlums in his wake.

Billy nodded in Winslow's direction. "That's what you want to get away from," he said. "Cheapness! Nastiness! Never mind what people do so long as it's accomplished with an air. But a boy like that—! And I'll wager my last dime that you've been on parties with him, had to laugh with him and treat him as an equal."

"Oh, Jack means well," said Peggy rather feebly.

"Means well! Means well!" stormed Billy. "What of it? People like that can't get you a thing. If you must know immoral folks get those who have graduated with honors, not dirty little failures who are bound straight for perdition!" Billy's counsel ended as they reached the steps of the hotel.

He had forgotten his irritation by then and turned to Peggy with a disarming smile.

"Thanks for the company, girl friend," he said. "As an inaugural party it was a great success. Many happy returns of the day."

"Billy, it's been grand. I loved every minute of it—and now as penance for being too happy I'll run upstairs and study that damned part."

"Don't let it faze you, child. No one expects the impossible tonight. Just stand out there, smile for all you're worth and nature will take its course. They're bound to love you—they won't be able to help themselves. I think you're a knockout and I'm a lousy bum. If you don't believe it, ask your roommate."

He waved good-by and hurried down the street. She stood looking after him for a long while, unconscious of the scrutiny of passersby. Billy was great! Let the rest of the world rail against him, she'd take him on good faith. She ran quickly up the steps and collided with Terry Neill.

"Hello, kid," he said. "Just called your room. Flo said you was out—havin' tea with Lawler or some bunk like that, What's that dame tryin' to do? Take me for a buggy ride?"

"No, Terry. We've been to the Ritz Lenox together, He's awfully nice."

"God, yes, he's just too ducky for words!" Terry grunted.

"Oh, well—" her eyes flashed displeasure. She shook herself free of Terry's grasp and went into the lobby. He followed her.

"Can I see you for a few minutes?" he inquired.

"Not now, Terry. I'm terribly busy. I've three whole scenes to study."

"Just as you say. You had time for Lawler though!"

"That's different!"

"Oh? Well, pardon my broken elbow. I'll be seeing you!" He started away.

"Terry," she called.

He turned, eagerly, and she knew it must be now. She braced herself.

"Terry, I don't think there'll be much chance for playing around after this. I've got so darned much to learn," she began.

He silenced her. "Save the actin' for upstairs," he advised.

"Don't worry, I get it. I guess I really caught the idea the night of the party. Well, good luck, baby, and don't think you can make me sore!"

He strode away, shoulders squared truculently. She wanted to feel sorry for him, but there was no room in her heart for unhappiness. Vale Terry! Vale Pat! Long live Billy! No—that was wrong—long live Peggy Sawyer!

13

Once again Abe Green stood at the rear of the orchestra. Once again the surcharged atmosphere of opening night on Broadway enveloped him.

In they came, this gay, glittering collection of amusement seekers, heedless of the shabby little man who crouched against the staircase leading to the first balcony. He swept them with his avid gaze.

The florid countenance of a leading financier and self-appointed patron of the arts. Close behind, Beatrice Lawrence, trailing her languid English self down the sloping aisle to a front row seat. Abe Green smiled grimly as he thought of the feud which had existed between Lawrence and Dorothy Brock.

Dorothy had occupied a chair in Row A at the premiere of Lawrence's first American musical comedy. There she sat, ruffling the pages of her program, an ermine wrap draped loosely about her shoulders. Whenever la Lawrence bounded upon the scene Dorothy's gaze dropped and she became intent upon her program. Lawrence was furious; Dorothy's discourtesy was so glaringly obvious. She made her exit cursing fiercely, and then was moved to comment bitterly, "Oh, well, she'll have to take the coat back in the morning, anyway."

Now it was Lawrence who occupied that choice location of the exhibitionist, the front row seat on the aisle, but Dorothy Brock would be missing. He wondered what Lawrence thought of this latest turn in the fortunes of her rival. Intense as their competition had been, Green knew that hatred soon vanishes when the foe is crushed. No doubt Beatrice Lawrence could find it in her heart to feel sorry for Dorothy Brock.

The overture had ended; the marvelous blue curtain, pet extravagance of Julian Marsh, parted and the thrice familiar setting greeted Abe's gaze. Cold, shuddering nausea gripped him. He and his partner had the temerity to launch a new star on Forty-Second Street. Here in the spot hallowed by the Millers, the Eatons and the Astaire's of the show world, he was robing a newcomer in the finery of stardom. The tabloid newspapers had made known Peggy's name to their hosts of readers, the heraldings of the press agent had stirred up a modicum of interest among the Broadway wise folk, but the attitude of the general public remained on the knees of the gods. In these days of motion picture presentation and the novelty of the talkies it was a brave firm that dared present an untested morsel to the Broadway palate. If they rejected Peggy it meant the end. One hundred thousand dollars gone to smash. Marsh must have been mad to suggest a simpering tyro as the leading lady for his production.

And the fifteen hundred that went every week to Andrew Hughes! Good comedians certainly came high. Hughes was known while Harvey Mason had been merely a competent journeyman. That cost the organization one thousand dollars more a week. He knew that Si Friedman would be fluttering about Peggy's dressing room, encouraging and cajoling. He, himself, hadn't the nerve for that sort of thing. The girl had come through like a thoroughbred in her Philadelphia showing. Night after night brought a sureness, a quality to her playing. She lost the novice's timidity without sacrificing that freshness and spontaneity which had first commended her to Julian Marsh. But this was an unheard of stunt! If they pulled it off, well and good. If not, how Forty-Second Street would howl.

The chattering of a belated group distracted him. He saw a theatrical agent, looking like a bloated vulture, escorting his latest blonde protégé to her seat. Someone had described Louis Hearn, rather aptly, as an abortion that lived. Hearn was the partner of Pete Dexter, but although he had played second fiddle to Dexter for years his natural astuteness had asserted itself and now his was the guiding hand in the office of Pete Dexter and Louis Hearn. He was a little man who wore exaggerated heels to lend height to his short, misshapen body. He fancied himself a Casanova and wooed one by one the younger ladies of the Broadway musicals. They accepted his dinner invitations because he was the Open, Sesame to many a closed door, but they did so with a quiet laugh at the expense of his vaulting ego. Hearn's face resembled nothing so much as a cartoon marvelously endowed with flesh and blood. His unfortunate nose was the subject of much sotto voce kidding. "Any time anything is lost they look in Louis Hearn's nose for it," one humorist had remarked. "And once they found a Belasco stage setting there."

Rival managers and their mistresses were coming in. Unemployed hoofers crowded to the orchestra rail, jealously guarding their allotments of standing room.

A crashing thunder of applause startled Abe Green. That opening chorus again. Four nights in succession had witnessed just such a demonstration. Even Philadelphia had recognized the number as a masterpiece of adroit footwork. Now Forty-Second Street had set the final seal of approval upon Andy Lee's footwork. Abe glanced at the indistinct figure lounging near the door. The man looked up, caught his gaze, and a smile passed between them.

"Great stuff, kid," whispered Green, and although Andy could not understand the words he knew that the boss was beaming.

"He'd better grin," thought Andy, aggressively. "Ziegfeld'll be calling me after tonight and then Green an' Friedman 've gotta dig up a new dance director. I'm through with them two tightwads."

He wished Amy might have been present. Funny how lonely a guy felt when someone he thought he hated walked out on him. It must be his pride, for he and Amy had been washed up for months. He knew there was another man, though no definite proof existed. Amy was a wise child, She'd eaten her cake and still intended to keep it. Andy Lee's money was welcome either as an allowance or alimony. It was all the same to her. She didn't give a damn. Andy wished he felt easier about the mess. Why couldn't he dismiss her with a casual good riddance? The way he figured, we're funny guys, we human beings; never satisfied, just natural hogs who gave happiness a swift kick in the ribs and then went around yelling because they'd lost the thing they kicked.

The moment of Peggy's entrance drew near. Green was in acute agony. For one dreadful second he prayed for some miracle by which Dorothy Brock might be substituted for this new uncertain quantity.

Listen to that reception for Danny Moran! They were determined to like him. Forty-Second Street so often makes fetishes of her low comedians. The crasser their manners and the more shocking their deportment in real life the better liked they are by a vast public. It was too bad about Danny and Daisy—but that was the way things happen. Abe had noticed her a quarter of an hour before, a forlorn figure in her gaudy evening clothes. Poor Daisy, utterly lacking in taste and finesse, left high and dry on the shoals of mediocrity while Danny sailed past her—into the realm of the favored of Broadway. There were rumors of separation and divorce, They were no longer living together. The hour of Danny's triumph must have seemed peculiarly empty to Daisy. Abe remembered that Danny was the latest recipient of Lorraine Fleming's smiles. Danny was caught in the maelstrom all right!

He was conscious of someone nearby pounding his palms together in a frenzy of acclaim. Harvey Mason! He wanted to slink guiltily away when he thought how terribly he had blasted Mason's hopes. Dear Christ, don't let that fellow turn around and see me now! I'd feel so cheap!

Billy Lawler bounced on in a veritable frenzy of youth. There was a smattering of applause from a few oversexed matrons and three or four Park Avenue homosexuals. "The belles stick together on a night like this," thought Abe.

A slight figure was moving in the yellow circle of the spotlight. Slim legs kicked far above the head with its mass of tossing curls. Abe chuckled. Polly in her glory. With the secession of Brock, the Blairs had come into their own. Every evening had witnessed a complete "show stop" for the little specialty dancer. Each night must have found Mrs. Blair down on her knees thanking God for the effect her treachery to Dorothy Brock had produced.

And more and more imminent was the entrance of Peggy Sawyer.

Oh, dear God, please make them like her, please make them like her!

In the wings Peggy shivered. So must the Christian martyrs have suffered as they waited outside the Roman arena. But those weren't lions out there beyond the footlights; they were human beings like herself, anxious to give a newcomer encouragement. She braced herself, patted the wave in her hair, placed her hands on her hips and stretched the muscles in her back; and then—the cue.

She heard a whisper, "Sock 'em, kid," and saw Terry, his face almost obscured in the sudden mist which swam before her eyes.

She emerged, mole-like, from the blackness of back stage, into the all-revealing glow of the spotlight. A dull murmur that swelled into tumult—a many-colored blur out there in the distance that swayed and murmured.

She stood uncertain for a moment and then began to speak. Her voice sounded strained and unnatural to her own ears. Oh God, don't let my voice go back on me; make them love me, love me, *love me!*

She was gaining confidence; objects which had been shadowy outlines were now clarified and became the well remembered set pieces of these past eight weeks. Why, this was easy! Exultation throbbed warmly through her being. This was like taking candy from a baby.

The quaver departed from her throat—she smiled confidently into the eyes of John Phillips.

"You're a knock out," he told her softly.

It was the hour for the fateful duet. She sat beside Phillips on the garden bench. The leader's baton poised nervously; he was staring up at her with an admiring grin. Out there, they were quiet. "Please, God, don't let me down now!"

She sang:

> Beyond the far horizon lies
> A lovely sort of paradise
> Which some men call the rainbow's end.

The notes poured forth sweetly and with assurance. She took new heart.

> It's where the winds are lulled to rest
> Not to the East—not to the West

Of fact and fancy it's a blend.

"You've even got Beatrice Lawrence jealous," whispered Phillips.

Of such a spot logicians are derisive
Deny that it exists, in tones incisive
But you and I are dreamers—and dreamers always go
To Lands of Milk and Honey that wise men never know.

"One—two—three—four—*chorus*," said John Phillips, laughing at her.
"Bless him for being a good sport," she thought.

There's not a cloud in the sky
And the days will drift by
In the Land Where My Dreams Come True.
I'll hear a song on the breeze
As it moves through the trees
In the Land Where My Dreams Come True.
I'll find the air as sweet as honey
Won't have to give a care for money
My laugh will ring long and loud
Far away from the crowd
In the Land Where My Dreams Come True.

She stopped. Yes, they applauded again; not riotously, but with appreciation. She turned toward John Phillips. Now they were no longer Peggy Sawyer and John Phillips, these two, they were lovers. She nestled close in his arms, while he poured out his heart in melody.

Some segment of her brain was noting the reaction of Beatrice Lawrence to all this. Lawrence, who hated all leading ladies on general principle, and American leading ladies in particular. Yes, Lawrence had forgotten her air of boredom; she was actually looking up.

And now the dance—fleetly their feet traversed the ground cloth, then down to the apron where the metal cleats on their shoes marked out a sharp rhythm. A burst of hand clapping interrupted the routine, from time to time, and that murmur of approval which any performer hopes to hear stole over the house.

In the wings she saw the beaming faces of the chorus—out there the slight smile on the mouth of Beatrice Lawrence. This was living—this was achievement—this was the star of Peggy Sawyer in the ascendant. She flung a smile to John Phillips and executed the complicated "break" that Andy Lee had taught her.

The music swelled as the end of the dance drew near. The saxophones blared, the tom wm of the drum thudded louder and louder. She whirled across the apron, landed safely in Phillips' arms, and it was over.

The beating of palms was like the roar of the sea. They took their bows. On, on, insistent as a tidal wave, not to be denied stormed the applause. They counted the bows—six of them—and Peggy knew that she had tasted triumph.

"Well, kid, you did the trick," shouted Harry MacElroy.

"Wasn't it wonderful!" she cried. "And, Harry, tell Phillips not to start the second verse so soon, will you? Who the hell does he think he *is?*"

The End.

Bradford Ropes was a prolific novelist and screenwriter. He toured the vaudeville circuits, danced professionally at night clubs, was a chorus boy on Broadway, and wrote several novels about the theatre, including *42nd Street, Go Into Your Dance*, and *Stage Mother*. He also wrote dozens of screenplays, including *The Time of Their Lives, Swing in the Saddle, Ice Capades Revue, Glamour Boy, Angels with Broken Wings, Hit Parade of 1941, Melody and Moonlight, Sing, Dance, Plenty Hot, Ladies in Distress, Meet the Boy Friend, The Hit Parade, Stage Mother*, and many others.

To read more about Bradford Ropes, see the 2024 biography, *Greasepaint Puritan: Boston to 42nd Street in the Queer Backstage Novels of Bradford Ropes*, by Maya Cantu

LITTLE NIFTIES INSIDE 42ND STREET
by Scott Miller

Little nifties from the Fifties,
Innocent and sweet;
Sexy ladies from the Eighties,
Who are indiscreet.
They're side by side,
They're glorified;
Where the underworld can meet the elite,
Forty-Second Street.
　　　　　"42nd Street," by Harry Warren and Al Dubin

It's a great irony that the title song written for the film *42nd Street* describes less the family-friendly 1933 movie it was written for, and more the *very* adult novel the movie is based on.

Bradford Ropes' scandalous original novel was *Valley of the Dolls* decades before *Valley of the Dolls*. Ropes wrote a wild, decadent, hilarious, adult potboiler about the needy, seedy, slangy side of Broadway, a twisted comic valentine to musical comedy and every one of the human vices. In this version, Billy Lawlor is *British* director Julian Marsh's boy toy. Leading lady Dorothy Brock is still sneaking around behind her millionaire boyfriend's back with Pat Denning, but this time, Pat is also romancing Peggy Sawyer, while also having an affair with the wife of Marsh's dance director Andy Lee, who has a succession of chorine mistresses of his own. And in this original version, Peggy doesn't cause Dorothy's accident; Dorothy falls down a flight of stairs in a drunken rage. Everybody is drinking, drugging, and screwing so much it's amazing they can get *Pretty Lady* ready for opening night! *Or can they?*

It's a trashy but terrific novel, fast-paced, funny, cynical, vulgar, nasty, incestuous, truthful, sad, wry, poignant, all underscored throughout with copious amounts of sex and booze. Like *The Wild Party*, it's a story about people who live outside mainstream cultural and moral norms, these creative (and often crazy and damaged) artists who have powerful drives and appetites, and even more powerful insecurities. The theatre has no glamour in the novel; it's what these people do for a living, and it's hard work. It's a grind.

At its core, *42nd Street* is about the nearly impossible work of making musical theatre, the slang, the industry lingo, auditions, rehearsals, the shaping and cutting of songs and scenes, rampant insecurity, flaring tempers, power plays, "showmances," the whole thing. It's a remarkably accurate portrait of the mechanics, the process, the long and winding road from conception to opening night; as well as the inevitable emotional and psychological potholes in the road when a whole bunch of artists work together.

Ropes lays out two alternating paths for his readers to follow, and we spend the whole novel jumping between them. On one track, we're following producer Julian Marsh and all the production and money people around him. On the other track, we're following chorus girl Peggy Sawyer, and the assorted artsies around her. Only a few characters inhabit both worlds, and it's only at the end, in crisis, that the two roads converge. Julian and Peggy have had virtually no interaction at all, but now they're thrust together, and each has to put complete faith in the other's work.

And if there's any doubt who our protagonist is, Julian Marsh disappears from the novel after he tells Peggy she's taking over the lead. It becomes just Peggy's story. The stories of Peggy Sawyer and Julian Marsh, representing the two sides of musical theatre creation, are heightened, exaggerated stories, but they're not fabrications. Ropes had been a chorus boy. He knew this world.

Strangely, in later years, writers of critical essays about the film (and there are a *lot* of them) seem to feel forever obligated to denigrate and dismiss Ropes' novel, to condemn the characters as cardboard and the plot as unbelievable. None of that is true. It's true of the characters *in the film*, because the screenplay leaves out about eighty percent of the novel. But the characters in the novel are complicated, conflicted, damaged, needy, and none of them are fully bad guys or fully good guys, fully strong or utterly weak. They're all deeply *human*. Even our hero Peggy – not nearly as innocent in the novel as her film avatar – has her dark, ambitious, needy side.

At the very end of the novel, in the middle of the opening night performance, Peggy in mid-triumph runs offstage after a big number and says to the stage manager, "Wasn't it wonderful! And, Harry, tell Phillips not to start the second verse so soon, will you? Who the hell does he think he *is?*"

That's the end of the book. Critics oversimplify the moment and bemoan the fact that innocent Peggy instantly becomes Super-Bitch Dorothy Brock. But that's not what happens here. That moment tells us that Peggy has become a Professional, understanding that as exciting and magical as it all can be, she has a *job* to do – a *hard* job. People paid money to see this show, and everyone's job rests on her success. She's not being bitchy; she's being practical. And she's also following the correct etiquette for such matters; it's better for the stage manager to tell the other actor about a problem than for Peggy to do it. *Ask any actor.*

Shuffle Off to Hollywood

The film rights were purchased by Warner Bros. for $6,000 even before the book was published. In February of 1933, when everybody in Hollywood was *sure* the backstage musical was dead, Warners released the first mature backstage movie musical, tougher and smarter than the others, and far superior both technically and artistically, the history-making *42nd Street*, with songs by Harry Warren and Al Dubin, including "You're Getting to Be a Habit with Me," "It Must Be June," "Shuffle Off to Buffalo," "Young and Healthy," and "42nd Street."

It was directed by Lloyd Bacon and choreographed by Busby Berkeley (and others), starring Ruby Keeler and Dick Powell. But despite the obvious talent, with each draft of the screenplay (and there were many), the story got sweeter and more innocent, and further from its source novel; and for some reason, Peggy's hometown changed a dozen times.

The greatest and darkest inside joke in the novel for theatre people – the character actor who literally drops dead during tech rehearsal – was cut. The kid specialty dancer and her toxic, Mama Rose stage mother were cut. The rich, colorful wisecracks that fill the pages of Ropes' novel were discarded one by one, for tamer, less biting wisecracks. Andy Lee was mysteriously demoted from dance director to state manager. And Dorothy was neither alcoholic nor over-sexed. And Julian now was broke and terminally ill...?

It was almost like nobody at Warners had read the book before buying the screen rights.

This was *42nd Street* for civilians. This wasn't Bradford Ropes' story anymore. Then again, most people seeing the movie hadn't read the novel, so what did the public care? It's almost as if the novel was a relic of the dark days of the Depression, and the movie was part of New Deal optimism.

This wasn't the *first* backstage movie – *Broadway Melody* had secured that honor in 1929 – but *42nd Street* was the first to do it well and relatively accurately. And it broke new ground not just in its subject matter but also in its form. Its big finale, the extended "42nd Street" dance drama, featuring the film's star Ruby Keeler, foreshadowed the more famous "Slaughter on Tenth Avenue" in *On Your Toes* (1936). *42nd Street*'s dark finale tells a tale of obsessive love, abuse, and drunken murder, all through the language of an elaborate tap dance number. It was a brave way to end a movie musical in 1933, one of the worst years of the Depression, but audiences loved it. Despite Keeler's enthusiastic but wooden acting and her awkward dancing in this, her first screen appearance, she exudes warmth and innocence, and audiences fell in love with her, catapulting her to movie stardom, just as her husband Al Jolson was tanking in the weird but fascinating flop movie musical, *Hallelujah, I'm a Bum*.

Though most of the *42nd Street* film never approached the musical or structural sophistication of *Love Me Tonight* or *Hallelujah, I'm a Bum!*, director and choreographer Busby Berkeley broke dozens of rules of the still young art form of movie musicals and it came out a huge hit. Warner Brothers hoped this optimistic film about an average girl becoming an overnight sensation – the movie that invented the American myth of the chorus girl shot to instant stardom – would coincide with a new public optimism in America. Warners touted the film as a "New Deal in Entertainment," hoping to tap into the presidential victory of Franklin Roosevelt, who would be inaugurated just one month after the film's release. *42nd Street* eventually took in $2,250,000 at the box office – in the middle of the Depression.

Critic Mordaunt Hall in the *New York Times* called the film "The liveliest and one of the most tuneful screen musical comedies that has come out of Hollywood." The *New York World-Telegram* called it "a sprightly entertainment, combining, as it did, a plausible enough story of back-stage life, some excellent musical numbers and dance routines and a cast of players that are considerably above the average found in screen musicals." And *Variety* said, "Every element is professional and convincing. It'll socko the screen musical fans with the same degree that Metro's pioneering screen musicals did."

The film was nominated for two Oscars, for Best Picture and Best Sound.

Busy Berkeley shattered the rules for filming dance in a movie musical. He did things no one else had done, and created staging that would never fit on any theatre stage. Berkeley understood that the secret to great filmmaking was to do what the stage could not. As Rocco Fumento writes in his introduction to the published screenplay:

> A few critics complained that, because Busby Berkeley's production numbers might be squeezed into Yankee Stadium but not within the tight confines of any Broadway stage, they were not realistic. Berkeley had years of stage experience before he ever went to Hollywood. Apparently these critics never stopped to think that Berkeley was the first to know that his numbers could not be performed on any "real" stage. It is their very liberation from the stage that makes them exciting. From the real, stage-bound world of the rehearsal hall, he plunges us into a fantasy world with no boundaries. His chorus boys and girls are performing for the mobile camera, not for the critic anchored in a

third row aisle seat. And the camera takes us where Berkeley wants it to take us, from a gigantic close-up of one gorgeous girl to a kaleidoscopic overhead shot of fifty gorgeous girls.

The soon-to-be legendary "dance director" Busby Berkeley had made his film debut in 1930 staging the dances for Eddie Cantor's *Whoopee*, after working on Broadway on a couple Rodgers and Hart shows. But Hollywood was where he would make his mark. Though many people don't know it, Berkeley did not dance. Other people choreographed the actual dance steps; Berkeley conceived the numbers, handled floor patterns, camera tricks, and general traffic control. There's actually very little *dance* in Berkeley's gigantic "dance" numbers. In fact, Ruby Keeler had to choreograph her own tap solo in the title song.

Berkeley's great achievement was to liberate the camera, allowing the movie musical for the first time to go where the stage musical could not go, allowing the camera to soar high up and capture his kaleidoscopic dance formations, to go under the feet of the dancers, to move around the dancers, to sneak inside a dance routine. He made the camera a performer just as important as the human performers. He understood that dance on film is movement *in relation to the movement of the camera*, quite unlike dance on stage. Berkeley even went so far as to cut holes in soundstage roofs and dig holes into floors to get the shots he wanted. For the first time, movie musicals could do what no stage musical could ever do, and the movie musical was now a distinct art form. Berkeley was the first to understand that a stage musical should not merely be filmed, but should be *adapted* for the screen, that film had different properties, abilities, and strengths. It was a new art form. He essentially invented music videos long before MTV debuted, pioneering the idea of taking a song and interpreting it in what were often abstract images.

Berkeley loved to tell people that he had never taken a dance lesson in his life and knew nothing about choreography when he started his career, almost as if he was proud of his lack of training, almost as if he wanted to make the point that what he was doing was not just dance, that it was more, that it was a new kind of performing genre, a kind of movement spectacle. He wouldn't just teach his dancers steps; he would show them formations on a blackboard, more like a football coach than a choreographer. He based many of his routines on military drills and marching formations that he had learned in the army in World War I while he was in France. And he learned his love of staircases and revolving platforms from the *Ziegfeld Follies*.

In his later films, like *Gold Diggers of 1933* (one of the few films to overtly reference the Depression), Berkeley's repeated successes allowed him to experiment, to get more sexual and more abstract, and it was precisely because so many of his images were so abstract that he could get away with the obvious sexual images and metaphors.

Before Berkeley, movie musicals were just records of stage musicals. After Berkeley, they were their own art form. And later, in the 1960s and 1970s, they would experience a major rediscovery as a new generation of movie goers recognized the genuinely psychedelic properties of Berkeley's kaleidoscopic images and surrealistic dream montages.

L.A. to New York

In 1980, a stage adaptation of the film opened on Broadway, nominally based on the novel but actually based on the movie, directed and choreographed by legendary MGM dancer and choreographer Gower Champion, with a book by Michael Stewart and Mark Bramble, using songs from the film, augmented with additional songs by Harry Warren and Al Dubin from other films.

The cast included Jerry Orbach, Tammy Grimes, Lee Roy Reams, and Wanda Ritchert. Champion knew the secret to classic musical comedy, and to this story in particular: *honesty*. No matter how broad the style, if the emotions are honest, the audience will connect and respond.

Tragically, Champion died the afternoon of opening night. The show was a huge hit, running eight and half years, and 3,486 performances. The original production (and some of the original cast) toured Japan in 1986 and the show was videotaped for Japanese television.

In the *New York Times*, Frank Rich wrote, "This brilliant showman's final musical is, if nothing else, a perfect monument to his glorious career. Indeed, *42nd Street* has more dancing – and for that matter, more dancers – than Mr. Champion has ever given us before. As it fortunately happens, this show not only features his best choreography, but it also serves as a strangely ironic tribute to all the other musicals he has staged over the past two decades."

John Beaufort wrote in the *Christian Science Monitor*, "The musical-comedy extravaganza at the Winter Garden Theater offers a fleeting, panoramic look at show-business history over the past 40 or 50 years. Its overview assembles a collage of creative influences and styles. It celebrates bygone cinematic glories. It speaks to theater history and even supplies footnotes on cultural and socioeconomic matters. Finally, when Jerry Orbach's Julian Marsh takes stage center alone, his defiant delivery of the minor-key serenade to 42nd Street's rhinestone glitter becomes a mordant reminder of what the ravages of time and decay have done to a once glamorous setting."

The show was nominated for eight Tonys and won three, for Best Musical and Best Choreography. It was honored with four Drama Desk nominations, and won for Best Choreography and Best Costume Design.

Experiencing this old-school musical in the beautiful old Majestic Theatre was like traveling back in time to the 1930s to see a quintessential musical comedy at the peak of the form, like being able to see opening night of *Anything Goes* or *No, No, Nanette*.

Gower Champion was our Way Back Machine, the link between Then and Now, and he did us all a great favor by showing us the real thing, the pure American art form created by George M. Cohan at the turn of the last century, perfected by George Abbott, and now today in this new century, being reinvented by a new crop of brilliant, adventurous writers as the neo musical comedy.

42nd Street was old-school, and it was certainly far tamer than its source novel, but it wasn't stupid or empty-headed. It wasn't trivial. Admittedly, *42nd Street* on stage wasn't complex in the way most contemporary musicals are; it was more like the 1930s shows it was imitating.

But it was also a fable about accepting the path in front of you and throwing yourself into it with all your might. It was a Hero Myth story, and that original cast took it seriously. Far from the stereotype of blissful (and phony) naiveté, a lot of those early shows were street smart, tough, and a little horny.

George M. Cohan's early musical comedies offended a lot of people because they were brash and aggressive and slangy, in a era when European operetta was still the dominant form. *42nd Street*'s style was the kind of enormous but truthful style we can see decades later in *Little Shop of Horrors*, *Bat Boy*, *Head Over Heels*, and *Urinetown*.

At that point in 1980, no one knew a new Golden Age of Musical Theatre was almost upon us, that the 1990s would bring us the neo musical comedy and the neo rock musical. Who could have foreseen *Bloody Bloody Andrew Jackson* or *Spelling Bee*?

42nd Street was perfect model for the neo musical comedies to come, in terms of style, tone, size, energy, pacing, and that delicate tightrope between emotional honesty and musical comedy's exaggerated, self-aware style. It was a remarkably authentic glimpse into the early art form, from the mind of someone who remembered.

In 2001, the show was remounted on Broadway, with Gower Champion's original choreography restaged by Randy Skinner, but without the heart and honesty of the original.

Ben Brantley wrote in the *New York Times*, "The production – in most respects, a faded fax of the last musical staged by the fabled Gower Champion – is a full-frontal assault by rat-a-tat tap, with everything else taking a distant back seat. . . [the 1980 production] seems positively electric compared to the current version of *42nd Street*, which has the thrice-watered-down feeling of a pastiche of a pastiche. . . By and large, however, the production's attitude toward its Broadway-as-fairy-tale plot is affectionately distant and stiff, like that of adults listening to someone else's two-year-old saying the darnedest things. As a consequence, excepting the droll Christine Ebersole, there doesn't seem to be one real character onstage, just a bunch of attractive dancing paper dolls."

Still, the revival was nominated for nine Tonys, and won two, including Best Revival. It was nominated for five Drama Desk Awards, and won for Outstanding Revival. It was also filmed for television.

In 2018, the Drury Lane Theatre in Oakbrook, Illinois, presented a totally re-orchestrated, jazz-funk version of the show.

Chris Jones wrote in the *Chicago Tribune*, "Here's the root of my enthusiasm: If you remove this show from its period and turn its corny comic ballads into torch songs and orchestrate some numbers like they were penned by a rapper, some like they belong in the 1970s, and allow the characters to float through the decades as it were, then the show's metaphor deepens. Instead of being about a Broadway of 1933, and thus having appeal mostly for nostalgists and purists, it becomes the story of every fragile artist from every fraught era. For, lest we forget, they all were fraught."

Scott Miller is a musical theatre composer, lyricist, bookwriter, historian, consultant, fanboy, and the founder and artistic director of New Line Theatre, an alternative musical theatre company in St. Louis. He holds a degree in music and musical theatre from Harvard. He has written eleven musicals, two plays, and more than a dozen books about musical theatre, and he writes the Bad Boy of Musical Theatre blog. He also hosts the theatre podcast Stage Grok, available on iTunes.

Made in the USA
Columbia, SC
11 October 2025